Andrea Carter grew up in Ballyfin, C
ated in law from Trinity College, Dubli
and moved to the Inishowen peninsula. Having practised law for twenty years, more recently as a barrister, she now writes full-time. She was shortlisted for the Irish Book Awards in 2019. Her Inishowen Mysteries series is in development for television. She lives in Dublin with her husband and dog.

Also by Andrea Carter

The Inishowen Mysteries
Death at Whitewater Church
Treacherous Strand
The Well of Ice
Murder at Greysbridge
The Body Falls
Death Writes

There Came A-Tapping

Andrea Carter

CONSTABLE

First published in Great Britain in 2025 by Constable

3 5 7 9 10 8 6 4

Copyright © Andrea Carter, 2025

The moral right of the author has been asserted.

All characters and events in this publication, other than those clearly in the public domain, are fictitious and any resemblance to real persons, living or dead, is purely coincidental.

All rights reserved.
No part of this publication may be reproduced, stored in a retrieval system, or transmitted, in any form, or by any means, without the prior permission in writing of the publisher, nor be otherwise circulated in any form of binding or cover other than that in which it is published and without a similar condition including this condition being imposed on the subsequent purchaser.

A CIP catalogue record for this book
is available from the British Library.

The Author received financial support from the
Arts Council of Ireland in the creation of this work

ISBN: 978-1-40872-403-3 (hardback)
ISBN: 978-1-40871-905-3 (trade paperback)

Typeset in Arno Pro by Initial Typesetting Services, Edinburgh
Printed and bound in Great Britain by Clays Ltd, Elcograf S.p.A.

Papers used by Constable are from well-managed forests
and other responsible sources.

Constable
An imprint of
Little, Brown Book
Group Carmelite House
50 Victoria Embankment
London EC4Y 0DZ

The authorised representative
in the EEA is
Hachette Ireland
8 Castlecourt Centre
Dublin 15, D15 YF6A, Ireland
(email: info@hbgi.ie)

An Hachette UK Company
www.hachette.co.uk

www.littlebrown.co.uk

To Geoff and Liath, my pack!

'But the fact is I was napping, and so gently you came rapping,
And so faintly you came tapping, tapping at my chamber door,
That I scarce was sure I heard you' – here I opened wide the door; –
Darkness there and nothing more.

Edgar Allen Poe, 'The Raven'

Raven Cottage, 1890

Mary Tiernan came often, fearful of death, pleading to be told her fate. Her father and brothers had died well before their time, but her mother lived till her eighth decade before the influenza got her, so it was her ~~advice~~ counsel that she sought. Watching Mary stomp back down the lane for the third time this week, Eliza could tell that the woman was robust like her mother, would see the village out, if fear did not choke her first.

A half-moon bathed Eliza's cottage in an eerie light as she tore up a heel of bread into tiny pieces and tossed it to the birds. The ravens flurried about, flapping their black velvet wings and flicking their diamond tails, her favourites pecking the crumbs directly from her palms. She knew they did not need feeding at this time of year, with grains and berries abounding, but she liked the ritual, this precious time to converse.

When she finished, she brushed her hands on her apron

and went inside, closing the half-door behind her. An oil lamp burned on the table, casting a yellowish glow over the book and the few shillings beside it. The sum was meagre enough, but times were hard, and there was a leg of mutton in the pantry from Mary that would go well with the potatoes she had saved and the mint from her garden. She had much to be thankful for.

She placed the coins carefully into the box she kept for that purpose, before checking on Gretta, sleeping peacefully. Nearly two now. Walking and talking, she'd made it so much further than her brother.

Pulling her shawl around her, Eliza picked up her pen. Dipping the nib into the inkwell, she scratched an entry into the book; firstly in the payments section, where she carefully wrote down the leg of mutton and the coins. Then she waited for the ink to dry, closed the cover, turned the book over and began to write again the other way, upside down – her account of what she had learned tonight.

Mary Tiernan was a ~~gossip~~ torture, driven mad by her imaginary ailments, but she often said something that might prove useful. Something to be squirrelled away for the future. People generally forgot what they said after they said it, but Eliza noted everything down, being one of the lucky ones who had learned how to read and write.

Tonight, Mary had told her of her younger brother James, a cooper by trade who had died the winter before, his tomb marked by a new stone in the graveyard down the lane. The poor man's falling sickness was well known; he had been prone to fits before he died. But Mary mentioned a birthmark, something she recalled from nursing him as a baby, a raised purple stain on his skin that he kept secret because he was ashamed of it. She had described it; fearful it was that which had marked him out for an early death. Fearful that she herself might have one, although as yet she'd been unable to find it. Maybe it was hidden under her hair? Could Eliza check? A notion that had just occurred to her; something new to worry about.

When Eliza had finished writing, she put the book in the box along with the coins, then sat by the fire awhile, poking at the peat burning in the grate. She was bone-tired. Three women had come to see her today. They asked so much of her, their lives harsh, their pleading faces desperate for comfort and guidance. Mary Tiernan could be dismissed as a fuss-budget, but there were others who had come to truly rely on Eliza, and she felt the burden of it.

They sought her advice, craving her connection to those who were all-seeing, who were wiser than they were because they had passed over, then shunned her. On the road. In the village. Even at the wake, although it was certain that they would seek her out soon after. She had come to expect the knock on the back door late at night. They kept their visits secret; each thought they were ~~alone~~ singular in consulting her. Which worked in Eliza's favour, since they felt free to talk about themselves and each other.

Eliza cared little what people thought, ~~she~~ cared little for human company, preferring her birds and her daughter. But she worried for Gretta, what future she might have in a place where her mother was a shameful secret.

Early draft of *Whatever Happened to Eliza Dunne?*
by Allison Garvey

PART I

CHAPTER ONE

Allie

You always remember that first flicker of unease. That tiny sense of foreboding. Mostly it's just your own dark thoughts run a bit askew, and mine certainly did that. I was a worrywart, an anxious Biddy. The type of person who'd message you to say *I'm here, table at the back!* at a quarter to one when we'd arranged to meet at one. But every once in a while, that distant rattle you hear isn't your imagination; it's a warning that the wheels are about to come off your life.

It began one Saturday night. I was alone in the apartment, waiting for Rory, scribbling in a notebook while Finn snored softly beside me, the deep and contented sigh of a greyhound who'd found his way onto the couch and not yet been turfed off.

Footsteps sounded in the corridor outside, and I closed the notebook, hastily shoving it beneath the upholstery, while the dog raised his head, ears pricked like the jackal-headed god Anubis. Rory reckoned that Finn's ears had about six different settings, but neither of us could decide if the movements were involuntary or if he was fully in control of them. He listened intently to the neighbouring apartment door open and close, before slumping back down in disappointment, chin resting on one of the supposedly out-of-bounds green velvet cushions.

'Where is he, eh?' I ran my hand along the top of the dog's silky head. 'Think he's stopped off in Galway to do a wine shop?'

I checked my phone, which was charging on the armrest. No messages. No missed calls. WhatsApp showed no change from the previous time I'd checked. *Last seen today at 09.04.* The exact time his last message was sent. *Leaving about three. X*

With an effort, I unfolded my legs, stiff from sitting in the same position for too long, and padded across to the kitchen to turn down the pot of soup I'd left simmering on the ring. I'd attempted mushroom and corn chowder for the first time, messaging Rory to say there'd be something warm when he got in, but he hadn't replied. I'd heated it up twice, expecting to hear his key in the lock at any minute.

Now the sweet, smoky smell of cumin made my stomach growl, so I opened a bottle of Malbec and poured myself a large glass.

Rain blasted the windows of the apartment, angry ribbons of water racing one another down the panes. Not for the first time, I wished we had a fire, even one of those fake stoves Rory wasn't so keen on; imagining the wine warming by the hearth instead of on the counter. Fairy lights on a yucca plant didn't quite do it.

My phone rang and I grabbed for it quickly, suppressing a dart of disappointment when I saw it was Olivia.

'Hey, sis. Time to chat?' She was driving and had me on speaker, shouting to be heard over the metronome to-and-fro of the windscreen wipers.

'Not much.' I sneaked a look at the phone's display. 'Rory's not back yet. I'll hang up if he comes in.'

'Aw, romantic reunion. How long's he been gone this time?'

'Three nights. He's filming that wildlife documentary on Inishbofin with Sam and Vince.' I paused. 'He's late.'

'Ah, I wouldn't worry. The weather's bloody awful. I got

drenched running from the car to the house. Had to change everything down to my bra and knickers. It's even worse now. And you know the west is going to be ten times as bad.'

I walked to the window; the houses across the river appeared smeared and insubstantial, as if you could just rub them out with your sleeve, the lamps on the bridge blurred like an oil painting. Half past eight and completely dark, the days so much shorter in October.

'I don't know,' I said doubtfully. 'They were due to finish at three.'

'Well, maybe they got delayed,' Olivia said briskly. 'No need to panic.'

Come on. Allow me this one, I thought, smarting a little. He *was* very late. If he had left when he'd said he would, that meant five and a half hours on the road for a journey that should take three at the most. Even if he had stopped to pick up a few bottles, he'd be well home by now.

'Allie? You still there?'

I made a begrudging noise of assent; not quite a word.

It was enough for Olivia. 'Good. I rang to see if you wanted to get afternoon tea in the Majestic? I have a voucher. They sent it to me when I complained about the toilets the last time.'

Despite being mildly pissed off with her, I laughed. No one could extract free stuff like my sister. 'When are you thinking?'

'Next Sunday. Tea, buns and prosecco. Cucumber sandwiches with the crusts cut off.' She paused, as if checking herself. 'I'm guessing about the cucumber sandwiches.'

'If there aren't any, you could complain and they might give you another voucher.'

'Ha! See? You made a joke. You up for it?'

'Sure.' I'd have to check with Rory to see if we were doing anything, but decided not to say that. Where *was* he?

'Great. You can buy the gin and tonics after. I'll text you when it's booked.'

We were interrupted by a squealing noise followed by a loud thump.

'Jesus,' I said. 'Did you hit something?'

Olivia sighed. 'Nope. That came from *inside* the car. One child trying to exterminate the other.' This was confirmed by an aggrieved howl. 'Anyway, I'd better go. I'm nearly home and I've a shit load of marking to do after I wrestle this pair into bed. See ya.'

She rang off before I could even say goodbye.

I took another sip of my wine. And another. I chewed at a hangnail on my thumb, drawing blood and feeling the familiar sting of pain as I tasted the metal tang mixed with red wine tannins. My innate conviction that something terrible was going to happen to the people I loved was a wound I constantly had to cauterise to stop it from getting infected. When Rory had called me the night before from outside a pub on the mainland, he was buzzing – they'd filmed curlews, lapwings and choughs, and the weather had worked in their favour so they'd got some great drone shots. A pod of dolphins had followed the ferry back in, and he was looking forward to going back out to the island this morning.

Olivia was right. They'd been delayed. That was all. They'd probably had another good filming day and stayed longer than planned. I forced myself to return to the couch, pulling out my notebook again and trying to get back to what I'd been doing. But I couldn't concentrate.

As if picking up on my agitation, Finn woke, gave an extravagant stretch, then dived off the couch and headed skittering for the door. I'd really hoped to leave his last walk to Rory; it usually happened around ten, in the middle of whatever we were watching on TV – recently one of those John Carpenter cult classics Rory had taken a shine to, the kind I had to bury my face in a cushion to watch. The dog would be apoplectic with excitement to see his master after three days apart. He had an unswerving, almost romantic love for Rory that made it impossible not to laugh when he circled like a roulette wheel before flopping down with his head on Rory's knee and his arse pointing towards me.

I patted the cushion in an attempt to entice him back up onto the couch, and he trotted over, raising my hopes. But then he slid into a downward dog, making his intentions clear. Followed by sphinx. He'd soon be in plank.

I sighed. 'Okay, okay, I get the message.' Grabbing rain jacket, leash and a couple of poo bags, I added, 'I warn you: it's not too pleasant out there.'

Downstairs, a chilly wind blew in from the courtyard, which was awash with water. Finn took one look outside and reversed a few steps, planting his paws and gazing mournfully up at me as if the lousy weather was somehow my fault.

'You're the one who wanted to go out,' I retorted, pulling up my hood and coaxing him through the door.

At the grassy area by the weir, I let him off the lead and waited as he sniffed about to find the right spot, all the while sneaking glances at the phone in my pocket, trying not to get it wet. At one point he darted suddenly towards the shrubbery, and I caught a flash of red, narrow shining eyes, a tail that had lost some of its lustre.

On our way back, a car drove in through the main gates, headlights dipped in the squally rain, purring as it waited for the gate to the underground car park to open. Finn looked up hopefully, but I could see it was a BMW, all shiny chrome and alloy wheels, while Rory drove a battered Nissan that he'd bought for eight hundred euros and that stubbornly kept passing its NCT. What if he'd broken down? I thought suddenly. Maybe he was stuck somewhere, unable to call. If that was the case, he might not be home tonight. I didn't like being alone; I'd only just made it through the past three nights.

I typed a message. *Everything okay? How far away are you?* Two grey ticks. Delivered but not seen.

Back inside, I towelled Finn dry, gave him a bacon twizzler from the treat cupboard, then checked to see if the ticks had turned blue. Still grey. I took off my waterproof jacket, hung it up and looked again. Still grey.

By half past ten, the only thing keeping me remotely together was the bottle of wine I'd nearly finished. Messaging produced no response. Calls went straight through to voicemail. I craved a cigarette, something I never did these days unless I'd had quite a lot to drink. And, I realised now as I swayed slightly, navigating my way back to the kitchen, I *was* drunk.

That sense of the ground not being solid beneath my feet sparked an unpleasant flashback to the night Rory left. I recalled a row, raised voices. Fragmented images from an old movie reel. I felt my heart rate quicken and forced myself to begin the breathing exercises I'd been taught to avert the onset of a panic attack. Box breathing. In for four, hold for four, out for four, hold for four. Eventually I succeeded in pushing the dizzy feeling back. *Keep the negative thoughts at bay*, I'd been told.

Easier said than done. If Rory had broken down, he'd have found some way to let me know. Unless he couldn't. Unless he'd had an accident. Unless he was hurt. Or worse. I felt myself spiral again. Why wasn't he getting my calls or messages?

His phone! I thought suddenly. Like his car, Rory refused to replace anything unless it fell apart completely, and while his phone did work, it was always giving him trouble, the battery failing to hold a charge. Often I'd text and get no reply, only for him to saunter in the door cursing, 'That shaggin' phone died on me again.'

I decided to ring Sam. I'd only met Vince, the cameraman, a couple of times, but we'd christened Sam, the director, Rory's work wife because they'd made so many documentaries together. If I called his home instead of his mobile, maybe I'd get Aoife, his actual wife? Maybe neither of them was home yet?

I felt a surge of hope as I pressed the call button, convincing myself this was true. I was such an idiot. I should have called Aoife ages ago. Saved myself this needless worrying.

Aoife answered with the same apprehensive tone I'd have used if someone had rung me at nearly eleven o'clock on a Saturday night. 'Hello?'

'Hi, Aoife. It's Allie.' I paused, certain that she would fill the gap with *Oh, I'm so sorry, I should have rung you*. She didn't. I swallowed hard. 'Do you know if the lads were delayed for some reason? I can't get any response from Rory.'

'No. I don't think so.' Aoife sounded confused. 'Sam's here. Hang on. I'll get him.'

Her words were like a punch to my gut. Sam was home. I heard a hurried whispered exchange before he got to the phone.

'Allie?' he said. 'Everything all right?'

'Sure. Great.' Faux casual. 'I was just wondering if you were delayed at all leaving Galway?'

'No,' he said slowly. 'We left pretty much on time, about three. Driving was grim, though. It pissed down the whole way. I got back about half six?' He checked with Aoife, who must have been hovering nearby, and I felt a wave of jealousy at their coupledom. 'Quarter to seven, Aoife says.'

'Right.' My voice quivered as resentment morphed into white-hot fear.

'Are you saying Rory's not back yet?'

'No. He's not. I haven't heard from him since this morning.' I gulped back tears.

Sam blew out a breath. 'Shit.'

'I'm going to ring the guards.'

'Right. Right, you do that. Call me back and let me know what they say.' He paused. 'Oh, and Allie?' He cleared his throat, as if reluctant to say what came next. 'I had some extra stuff to do with Vince, but he's home too – I spoke to him earlier. And Rory left before we did.'

CHAPTER TWO

A lone lorry trundled over the bridge as the city struggled to life. I reached for my phone. Nothing: no messages, no missed calls. My head ached with a dull throb and my mouth was dry, last night's wine sour on my tongue. It was six a.m. and WhatsApp showed the same information as the day before: Rory was last online yesterday morning at 9.04. Since then, I had sent – I counted – twenty-five messages, each one increasingly desperate in tone.

I usually wore ear plugs to bed, insomnia a side effect of my anxiety. I hadn't last night, afraid I would miss the sound of his key in the door, the thump of his bag landing in the hall, his footsteps as he made his way to the living room to greet Finn. But despite me straining hungrily, there wasn't one stray sound to raise my hopes, not a single partygoer stumbling home to one of the other apartments. The alcohol had muffled my fear, but there was no denying this morning's wretched reality. Rory had not come home. Everyone had been telling me not to worry, and here I was, proven right. Not that I could take much comfort from that.

After speaking to Sam and Aoife, I'd rung the guards, opting for the local station up the hill rather than calling 999. I'd wanted to shriek down the phone in panic, but the woman on the other end had been calm. It was clear that once there was no immediate threat to life, a grown man staying out late on a Saturday night wasn't top of their list of priorities. Somehow that had defused my fright, convincing me that at least in their view Rory was more likely to turn up than not. Although it didn't stop me from searching online for traffic accidents between Galway and Dublin. They took his registration number, contact details and description and told me to give them a call in the morning if he didn't come home.

But now it *was* morning and Rory wasn't here. Was six too early to call again? I wanted to claw at my skin in frustration, itchy with agitation and helplessness. Twelve minutes past now. Maybe I should wait till seven? I calculated the number of minutes till then and set the timer on my phone. Feeling that at least I was making progress as I watched the seconds tick by.

At eight minutes and forty-seven seconds in, my vision began to blur, the numbers dissolving before my eyes. I reached for the glass of water on the bedside table, my skull feeling too large for my scalp, as if the skin was stretched thin. I shouldn't have drunk so much, but it had taken the edge off my fear. And when I'd finally climbed into bed, I'd imagined drifting off to sleep in a boozy haze and waking to a chilly Rory slipping under the covers behind me, wrapping his arms around me to absorb my warmth. So why hadn't that happened? He'd had all night to come home. *All night.*

I gulped down some water, then picked up my phone again, scrolling through pictures Rory had sent me after our chat outside the pub. The first one showed Sam and Vince standing on a pier waiting to board a small ferry, rucksacks, cameras and a boom mike piled up alongside. The second was taken on the island itself. Three people I didn't recognise stood in a wet field surrounded by cattle. One carried a partially unfurled golfing umbrella as if it was about to start raining, black clouds stalking the horizon evidence of an impending downpour. The next showed the same three people strolling along a narrow track, Vince walking backwards filming them, a pewter sea partially visible in the background.

Rory appeared in only one. In it the group ate sandwiches and drank from flasks while he stood slightly apart, chatting to a woman by a ruined cottage outside which a quad bike was parked. As producer, he usually had more time to himself on actual filming days once the interviews and shots had been set up, so he'd have taken most of the photographs. But maybe Sam had taken this one? It had that curved arrow indicating it had been forwarded before it had been sent to me.

I turned onto my side, placing one hand under my head and letting the phone fall into the gap between the pillows. With my free hand I tapped the picture to zoom in, enlarging Rory's image. His hood was up, but it was so clearly him. I knew his shape, his stance – the way he stood with his feet planted widely and confidently. His smell. God, how I missed his smell.

I pulled his pillow towards me and buried my face in it, inhaling that familiar combination of soap and hair cream. I'd intended changing the sheets for his return but hadn't got around to it. Now I was glad I hadn't. I'd read of people holding onto loved ones' clothes after they died, and now I understood why. The thought gave me a start. Rory wasn't dead. He couldn't be. He was the most alive person I knew.

I checked the timer. Thirty-two minutes and three, four, five seconds. The numbers still spinning. A quarter to seven. Surely I could ring now? Heart fluttering, I dragged myself up into a sitting position and redialled last night's number.

The guard I'd spoken to wasn't there, but they had a record of my call. 'Someone will be around to see you this morning, Miss Garvey,' a woman said in a soft Cork accent. 'I can't tell you the exact time, I'm sorry. But just make sure you're in.'

I promised I would be and hung up. But a whine from the living room made a liar of me already. Finn needed to go out.

I hauled myself out of bed, dragging on a pair of tracksuit bottoms and a fleece over the Mick Jagger T-shirt I'd worn to bed. Catching sight of myself in the mirror, I pulled my hair into a ponytail. Not that it made much difference. Diluted by rain and tears, the mascara I'd put on for Rory's return had stained my cheeks, my hung-over skin sallow and tinged with grey. I looked like a ghoul.

The square was quiet, apart from a few delivery lorries outside the Spar. A woman standing near one of the cafés, vaping, gave me a look that left me under no illusion about my disordered appearance. Her standards were higher than mine; she was immaculately turned out, with a smart black coat and a sleek grey bob. Not a dog person, though; Finn went up to her wagging his tail and she jumped back as if she'd been burned.

Dawn was breaking as we headed into the Phoenix Park. The weather had cleared overnight, making way for a spectacular sunrise; streaks of burnt orange furrowed the sky while deer grazed wet grass in the mist. But everything felt wrong. Even Finn knew it, glancing back at me with a quizzical expression on his face. It was Rory who always took him out first thing. They would search for squirrels and Rory would wake me with pictures of their walk, my phone buzzing on the bedside table.

A crow goose-stepped across our path and Finn made a dive for it, almost pulling my arm out of its socket. So when a man with a mini Schnauzer appeared, I tightened his lead; his prey instinct kicked in whenever anything small and furry was in the vicinity. It didn't seem to matter if it was one of his own species.

The man was one of our neighbours. I met him on the stairs sometimes and we nodded although we'd never spoken. He looked surprised to see me. 'You on dog-walking duty this morning?'

I felt myself shrink under his gaze. 'Rory's away filming.' Saying his name aloud caused a painful lump to form in my throat as the cold wind stung my cheeks.

'Tell him there's a session in the Villager on Wednesday.' He paused, then added with a smile, 'You're invited too, of course, although I know it's not your thing.'

The truth was that I wouldn't have minded going. Rory had started playing the banjo; he'd had lessons while making a documentary about Bluegrass and joined a session in our local pub. But he claimed he wasn't very good yet, that it would make him self-conscious if I was there.

The neighbour was already on his way, walking past us down the hill as he called out, 'Great morning for it!' over his shoulder.

Leaving the park, I sent Rory a picture of two stags clacking horns. This time there was just one grey tick. I wasn't sure what that meant, but it was unlikely to be positive.

A squad car parked at the gates to the apartment complex gave me a jolt until I remembered that I was the one who'd called them. And when I reached our building, two uniformed guards, a man and a woman, were examining the line of doorbells.

'Apartment 16a?' I asked.

The female guard swivelled to face me. 'Are you Allie Garvey?'

I nodded and brought them inside, unclipping Finn's leash to allow him to bound up the stairs, finishing with a few zoomies at the top.

'Nice dog,' the male guard remarked. 'My dad kept greyhounds for racing.'

'Finn was rescued from the track,' I said, before turning to unlock the door, realising when I caught the eye-roll in my side vision that I'd said the wrong thing. I often said the wrong thing.

Finn trotted happily along the hall, leaping at the door to the living room.

'He thinks Rory will be here,' I said, and for one glorious moment I wondered if it could be true. I pushed the door open, and Finn rushed in ahead of me, whipping his head from side to side. But the room was empty, just as I'd left it.

The two guards hovered in the doorway, and I saw the apartment through their eyes: the empty wine bottle on the coffee table, the unwashed glass, the pan of soup congealing on the cooker. The fug of stale air. I imagined them judging me, then making allowances for the circumstances.

'Do you want tea?' I asked, reaching for the kettle. 'Or coffee?'

They shook their heads. 'Water would be great,' the female guard said.

I'd read somewhere that they did this to give you something to do. I was tempted to mention it, but after the greyhound comment, I didn't want to come across as a smart-arse. So I simply fetched a glass of water and indicated where we could sit.

They introduced themselves as Garda Dave Fitzpatrick and Garda Suzanne Phelan, arranging themselves on one side of the table while I sat on the other, as if I was attending some weird job interview. The man was huge, broad-shouldered and overweight, like a Disney hero gone to seed, and the woman was blonde and petite. Both were younger than me, with accents I couldn't place; I've never been good with accents outside of Dublin.

'I know you'll have been asked some of this last night, but just to confirm . . .' The female guard produced a notebook and took details of Rory's age, height, hair colour, what he'd been doing and where, and when I'd last had contact with him.

I answered her questions feeling weirdly disconnected, as if I was delivering lines in a play or sitting an exam. A flashback to my Leaving Cert Irish oral threatened to derail me; the realisation that it had happened less than two weeks before my parents died made me sway as if I had vertigo.

'Was he alone or working with someone?' asked Dave, the male guard.

'A director and cameraman. Sam and Vince. I can give you their numbers. They were with him in Galway, but they both came back last night.' My voice wavered at the injustice of it.

He nodded. 'Good. They'll be able to tell us what he was wearing, when he was last seen, that kind of thing. We'll also liaise with the guards over there.'

The words 'last seen' gave me a chill, reminding me of those missing person posts on Facebook: desperate pleas from friends and family where you knew the outcome wouldn't be good. Would Rory be one of those?

As if reading my mind, the female guard – I'd forgotten her name already – asked, 'Is he on social media? Twitter, Instagram?'

'A bit, I think. I don't really do any of that. But he has to publicise his documentaries.'

'Okay,' she said, taking a note. 'Have you a recent photograph?'

I showed her a couple on my phone, mostly with Finn, but I saw that the other guard was distracted, his gaze fixed on the bookshelf, where a framed picture sat propped up against an old thesaurus that Rory'd had since boarding school, something else he refused to throw out though it had long since lost its cover. He seemed to treasure his memories of that school despite some hilariously nightmarish stories about the food.

'Is that the two of you?' the guard asked.

I nodded and fetched it for him. It was a selfie taken the night we met. I'd gone to a club in town after work colleagues I'd been out with went home after the pub. Lightweights, I'd thought at the time. It didn't seem like a big deal – I'd wanted another drink and I liked to dance – although I couldn't imagine doing it now. Rory was coming from the Irish Film and TV Awards, where he'd won an award for a documentary on drug addiction, so he was rocking a tux and pretty stoked after his win. He claimed he fell for me watching me whirl around the dance floor on my own, and had no choice but to join me. In the photograph I was sticking my tongue out, Rolling Stones style, while Rory looked amused. I was twenty-eight and he was forty.

'It's five years ago, but he hasn't changed much.' He hadn't. Maybe a slight greying around the temples, but still *so* hot. 'You can have it if you think it will help.'

The guard examined it and nodded. It was difficult to read his expression as he extracted the photo and handed me back the empty frame. I ran my finger around the edges, feeling bereft, as if removing Rory's picture had taken a little more of him away from me, his energy diminished, enough for it to hurt.

'We'll use a digital one for social media sites,' the female guard said, giving her partner an odd look. 'And we'll upload everything to Pulse, where all stations can access it.' She shot a glance at my left hand. 'Sorry, Allie, just to clarify. You're his wife?'

I looked down. 'Partner.'

'Would this be out of character for him, not coming home when expected?' The male guard was still holding the photograph, his huge thumb planted on the image. I wanted to tell him to handle it more carefully and was relieved when he passed it over to his partner. 'Disappearing without letting you know where he is?'

I shook my head and looked away, like a child telling a half-truth, tugging at a cuticle on my thumb with my teeth and drawing blood.

'Any relationship difficulties?'

I sucked at it. 'No. None.' My voice wavered. 'I don't know what I'd do without him.'

'You didn't have an argument?'

Why was he pushing this? 'We didn't argue.' I got up again to fetch a tissue, relieved to be able to turn my back on them for a few seconds.

'Any reason to be concerned for his safety or welfare?' the female guard asked, her voice soft.

I turned quickly, tissue wrapped around my thumb like a bandage. 'What do you mean?'

'Did Rory have any mental health difficulties?'

And suddenly it dawned on me. She meant suicide. 'None.' I shook my head vigorously and came back to the table, eager that they shouldn't think this of him. Knowing he wouldn't want that.

'Sometimes people keep things from those who are closest to them.'

'I know.' If there was one thing I did know, it was that. 'But no, I'm sure. Rory's very successful at what he does. Filming was going well. He said so when I spoke to him last night...' I paused. Corrected myself. 'No, the night before, I mean. I spoke to him on Friday night.' Could it really have been two whole days?

She pressed on. 'Any medical condition, medication that he needs and doesn't have with him?'

I shook my head.

'People go missing for a variety of reasons,' the male guard interjected. 'Addiction issues, family difficulties. Some simply forget to make contact.'

It sounded like something he'd learned from a manual, what to say to a woman whose boyfriend hasn't come home. Ticking boxes. It made me wish them gone.

I clenched my hands, fists resting on the table. 'He wouldn't just forget to make contact.'

'I'm sure that's true,' the female guard said soothingly, shooting her partner another glance. 'It's just something we have to consider.'

She seemed kind, and I wanted to ask her name again; it felt careless to have forgotten it already. Then I remembered Rory's unreliable phone, his banger of a car. The things I'd meant to tell them. Things that might actually be relevant.

'We could make a request to see the last mast pinged by his mobile, but we probably won't get it,' she responded apologetically. 'Not if there's no threat to life.'

Should I have said there was? I scraped my nails through my hair, greasy and unwashed, screwed up into a messy bun because the ponytail kept falling out. A tear escaped and went rolling down my cheek.

I looked at the guards' faces, searching for answers, unable to escape the feeling there was something they were trying to tell me, something they hoped I'd pick up on. And suddenly I knew. It made sense. They'd seen the pictures: Rory's handsome face, a smile always creasing the corners of his mouth. And me standing in front of them now. Miserable, hung-over, pasty-faced, yesterday's make-up ground into my skin. Quite a contrast to the party girl in the picture. I knew what they were thinking. He's left her. He's one of those thousands of men who decide they want a different life but don't have the balls to tell anyone. So they just disappear. Walk out on their lives. Go out for a pack of cigarettes one day and never come back.

But Rory didn't smoke.

CHAPTER THREE

Suzanne

'He's left her. First opportunity he got, he's fucked off. Grabbed his chance.'

Suzanne watched Dave settle his soft bulk into the driver's seat of the squad car and slam the door shut after him. 'You think?'

'Clear as the nose on your face. Could you blame him?'

She clicked her seat belt into place, noticing Dave didn't bother. He probably reckoned it wasn't worth his while for the short drive up the hill to the station. Lazy arse.

'He's a lot older than her,' she commented. It was the first thing she'd noticed when she saw that picture of them together. At least ten years, she'd have thought, maybe fifteen. It was hard to tell. Although she had to admit he *was* good-looking, with that broad smile and the floppy hair. 'He managed to snag himself a much younger girlfriend. She might be a bit withdrawn, but she was gorgeous in that picture. Like a young Kate Moss. And she's still very pretty.'

Dave snorted. 'She's a lush. Did you not notice the booze off her breath? The empty wine bottle. Paddy said she was slurring her words when she called last night.'

Suzanne laughed. 'I've heard you slurring your words on a Saturday night plenty of times. Have a heart. Her boyfriend is missing. I think I'd have a couple to help me sleep if that happened to me.'

Dave winked. 'Ah, but the difference is, that wouldn't happen to you. Can't imagine anyone turning down the chance to spend a Saturday night in the scratcher with you.'

Suzanne rolled her eyes. Dave Fitzpatrick. God's gift. She watched him root in the pocket of his trousers for a packet of chewing gum, extract three pellets and stuff them into his mouth. His tiny ears looked as if they'd been superglued onto the sides of his enormous head, bobbing up and down as he chewed.

'Plus,' he turned the key in the ignition with more violence than was strictly necessary, 'she's a snooty bitch.' He mimicked her. '*He was rescued from the track*. South County Dublin. Sounds more Yank than Irish.'

Suzanne grinned. 'Careful, David.' She knew he hated being called David, especially in a Victoria Beckham accent. 'You're going to tip over if that chip on your shoulder gets any bigger.'

Dave sniffed. 'Anyway, I know him.' He started the engine and pulled out onto the main road.

Suzanne's eyes widened. 'You do?'

'Not *know him* know him. I've never actually met the guy. But as soon as I saw his picture, I realised. And the fact that she said he was off filming. He's fairly well known, produced a few things for RTÉ. Public-interest stuff, everything from inner-city deprivation to wildlife documentaries. Not quite Davey Attenborough, but still.'

'You're kidding. So that's why you were staring at that photograph. I thought you were perving over the girlfriend.'

Dave looked appalled. 'Me, perve?' He blared his horn at a souped-up white Audi that had veered suddenly left into a housing estate with no indicator, cursing loudly. '*Seriously?* Do people not notice when there's a squad car behind them any more?'

Another vigorous chew of his gum and he refocused. 'I don't think he's had anything on the telly for a while, but he'd have a bit of a profile.'

Suzanne took out her mobile and googled Rory O'Riordan. Dave was right. There were multiple mentions of him online: both Twitter and Instagram, plus reviews of programmes he'd produced. A picture of him at an awards dinner a few years ago, another at a documentary festival in Newcastle in the UK. None of the girlfriend, she noticed. Did partners not go to these things?

Mint wafted in her direction and she glanced over again at Dave. 'I wouldn't have had you down as a documentary fan.'

'Judgy,' he said indignantly. 'My interests are many and varied, I'll have you know.'

Suzanne continued to scroll through the search results, then stopped and let out a loud chuckle. 'Is this why you know him? He was a judge on *The Naked Lens*! *X Factor* for documentary makers?'

Dave grinned. 'It was axed after one season, but it was pretty good.'

'Hmm. I'm sure.' Suzanne had her doubts, judging from what she could see online. She pocketed her mobile. 'Well, we'd better get talking to his family and friends. If he did "fuck off", as you so delicately put it, maybe one of them knows about it. I have a mate in the station in Clifden, close to where he was filming, so I'll check in with him. We can have a look at number-plate recognition on the toll roads, see how far he got on his way back to Dublin.'

Dave nodded distractedly as he fiddled with the radio, and she knew that 'we' would very quickly morph into 'I'.

'Maybe you could talk to the hospitals?' she suggested. 'If he drives a dodgy car, he could have had an accident. Maybe no one knows who he is, and for some reason he hasn't been able to contact his girlfriend.'

Dave snorted again. 'I'm telling you – the guy's done a runner.'

CHAPTER FOUR

Allie

Our first date happened the day after we met. I'd have gone home with Rory after the club, no question, but he said he wanted to 'mind' me. This meant seeing me home in a taxi, taking my number and calling me the next day before I was even up. He then picked me up in the afternoon, a picnic basket covered in a red and white checked tablecloth nestled in the back seat of his car. I'd laughed, teasing him about channelling his inner Cary Grant. He seemed surprised – maybe he thought I was too young – until I told him I'd seen *To Catch a Thief* at the film club in college. He suggested I watch *An Affair to Remember* and *North by Northwest*. Which I did, along with *all* Cary's other films over the course of a 'Cary Grant season' he initiated one winter in the apartment. I went off Cary Grant after that.

But that was later. Back then, nothing like it had ever happened to me before; all my relationships had started with a drunken lunge. So a walk in the Dublin mountains followed by a champagne picnic? I loved it. He didn't even kiss me till we were walking hand-in-hand along a river, by which point I was gagging for it. I'd have shagged him there and then in that leafy glade if there hadn't been hordes of hearty-looking hikers marching past. He tortured me by leaving sex for a full month, another first for me. And when we finally did it, one lazy afternoon in a sunlight-filled room in a beautiful hotel, it was like a religious experience.

A heavily pregnant black and white cat stared unblinkingly at me from the ramp as I placed two empty wine bottles into the outdoor recycling bin that Monday morning. It was early, just after eight. I'd already been out with Finn. In less than an hour I'd have to log on to work and pretend everything was normal.

I'd considered taking the day off, but Sunday had been hellish and interminable and I knew I couldn't face another one like it. Plus, I could do my job with my eyes shut. I'd been working from home as a legal executive with a large Dublin law firm for two years, drafting debt-collection proceedings for banks. My law degree should have led on to a professional qualification, either the solicitors' exams or the bar, but things had fallen apart for me after college. *I* had fallen apart. I was still treading water career-wise, but the truth was that I was lucky to have a job, especially one that didn't require me to leave the apartment. I wasn't agoraphobic, nothing like that. I just liked being at home.

After a quick shower, my first in two days, I made a coffee and took it to my laptop. The morning passed quickly, but the apartment felt ominously quiet. I was used to hearing Rory on the phone, pushing to get projects green-lit, arranging shoots and interviews. Charming people and twisting arms, Rory's superpower. Though he found the new gender quotas frustrating. 'Maybe if I wear a fucking dress, I'll get something commissioned,' he'd ranted one morning, making me laugh; I'd stopped when he didn't join in. But I was confident that things would change. They always did for Rory. He'd find another wave to ride.

At one o'clock I logged off, checking my phone straight away. I'd kept it on while I worked, so it was a pointless exercise, but just in case. No texts. No calls. Other than Olivia, who'd left a couple of voicemails. I hadn't been able to bring myself to call her yesterday; telling my sister would have made everything too real. But I guessed I'd have to ring her back now. To fortify myself I made a sandwich, eyeing up the wine rack before forcing myself to make a pot of tea instead.

And then the doorbell rang. It rarely did unless Rory had forgotten his keys. I leaped to my feet, blood roaring in my ears, followed by Finn, who skittered eagerly across the floor behind me. I didn't bother with the intercom, just wrenched open the door of the apartment and raced out into the hall.

The floor tilted beneath my feet as my face fell in dismay. Olivia was peering through the glass of the inner door. I pulled it open, and two ginger-headed whirlwinds in mini Leinster rugby jerseys grabbed me by the legs, singing, 'Auntie Allie, Allie Auntie, Auntie Allie.' Max and Milo, Olivia's four-year-old twins.

'What are you doing here?' I asked. On a Monday afternoon she should have been in school; they should all have been in school.

'I had to take this pair to the dentist. And you're not answering your phone.' Her tone was accusatory.

'I was working.'

'Is Rory back?' she demanded.

'What?' I was confused. How did she know? 'No.'

Olivia's eyes widened. 'You're kidding. Aoife told me he hadn't come home on Saturday night, but I was sure he'd be back by now. I assumed that he'd just been delayed.'

Of course. My sister taught Sam and Aoife's kids; a coincidence not uncommon in middle-class South County Dublin, where like mixed with like.

'Jesus, Allie. When I talked to you on Saturday night, I thought it was just . . .' She trailed off.

'Me panicking as usual?' I said flatly.

She had the grace to look sheepish. 'I'm sorry.'

I turned to walk back into the apartment, sister, dog and nephews trailing in my wake. In the kitchen, I closed my laptop, lifted the kettle and pointed to the coffee. The boys had dived into Finn's bed with him. Lucky he was tolerant.

Olivia shook her head. 'I don't want anything. Just tell me what's going on.'

I told her what I knew, which wasn't very much.

'And you're just sitting working away as if nothing has happened? It's nearly two o'clock, Allie. He's over forty hours late.'

My jaw dropped. 'Don't you think I know that? Don't you think I've been counting every second? Forty hours is two thousand four hundred minutes, a hundred and forty-four thousand seconds...'

Olivia raised her hands. 'Okay, okay, I'm sorry.'

'I called the guards. They were here yesterday morning for an hour. I'm going to ring round his friends and family tonight.'

Her eyes widened. 'Tonight?'

I ignored the implied criticism. 'Yes. Tonight.' My eyes welled as I sank down into the kitchen chair in which I'd spent the morning, wincing as my back objected to a return to the same position so soon.

Olivia's face softened. 'I'm sorry. I just can't understand why you didn't tell me. And why you haven't told anyone else. I mean, what if someone knows something?'

'I kept thinking he'd walk back in the door and I wouldn't need to.' I looked down at my hands. My cuticles were bleeding again. When had I done that?

She sank down into one of the other chairs. 'Lord.'

'What do you expect me to do? Go looking for him?'

'Well, shouldn't you?' Her eyes widened in expectation.

Should I? Would that be the normal thing to do, the conventional response? 'I wouldn't know where to start.'

'How about the last place he was seen? The place he was filming that wildlife documentary. Where was it?' She clicked her fingers twice in quick succession, and I pictured her doing it at the front of a classroom, waiting for an answer from one of her students. 'Somewhere out west? Mayo or somewhere?'

'Galway. Cleggan. They were filming on Inishbofin but staying in Cleggan.'

'Well?' She spread her palms, as if the solution was obvious. 'Why don't you go?'

'Because he was on his way back. Sam said he left before him and Vince. He's not there any more.'

I flushed. I knew I was making excuses. In my place, Olivia would go and look for Rory. She'd take action, assume control of the situation and deal with it. But I wasn't like my sister. My anxiety held me back, making me freeze. We argued about it a lot, Rory and me. He teased me, but I knew he thought I could do more to help myself, to rein in my fears. And it was true, I could. I leaned towards the familiar, where I felt safe. There were times when my reluctance to try new things or go to new places drove him crazy.

Olivia reached out to Finn, who was mooching about uneasily, having relinquished his bed to the twins. She rubbed his head. 'Take Finn if you're nervous – he'll be company for you.'

'Maybe.' It was pointless arguing with Olivia, so I often didn't. But it didn't mean I agreed with her or that I was going to do what she said.

She wrinkled her nose suddenly and flapped her hand about. 'Jesus, Allie, it's a bit airless in here. Why don't we go for a walk?'

Finn pricked up his ears at one of the words he recognised, and Olivia smiled. 'Come on. He's dying to get out.' She waved at my laptop. 'Can you leave that for a bit?'

I nodded. 'I can take half an hour.'

'If Rory comes back, he'll be here when you get home,' she said gently.

My eyes welled again at the prospect, but I pushed the tears away. Hope was exhausting.

We made our way through the gate and into the park. A squirrel scuttled across in front of us and Finn strained at the leash, spinning like a top. Olivia waited until I got him back under control, then asked quietly, 'What are you going to do if he doesn't turn up?'

'Ever?' That panicky feeling returned. 'Do you think that's a possibility? He's only been gone two days.'

'I know, but don't they say that the first twenty-four hours are crucial when someone goes missing? I mean, what if . . .' Her gaze moved to her feet.

I stared at her disbelievingly. My *own* sister thought the same as the guards. 'You think he's left me, don't you?'

She shook her head. 'Of course not. But Allie . . .' She hesitated, digging her hands further down into the pockets of her coat. 'He does have form.'

I felt my insides shrivel. How could she bring this up now? When it was her support I needed, not a reminder of the worst time we'd had as a couple. I walked on silently, refusing to engage.

But she wasn't letting it go. 'Have you thought about contacting her?' When I didn't answer, she said, 'What was her name again? Claire? Caroline?'

'Clara.'

Not a name I was likely to forget. The woman I'd thought was a bloke called Charlie until Rory had fessed up, returning from a week away during which I thought he was climbing in the Highlands with his mate. He told me that he'd left me, something of which I had been blissfully unaware, but that he'd made a mistake. He regretted it. It was me that he loved. Somehow, not knowing that he had left, not ever actually *feeling* left, had made it easier for me to take him back, as if it wasn't even my decision. He'd deleted the post before making it public, changed his mind about the chess move before lifting his finger from the piece.

'Shit.' Olivia said suddenly, whirling around in panic. 'Where are the boys?' Her expression softened when we both spotted them at the same time. One of them had heaved the other up by his legs to peer into one of the park bins. 'Boys, get out of the bloody bin!' Olivia called, as the pair of them tumbled to the ground amid peals of laughter.

'What's that all about?' I asked.

She grinned. 'They're obsessed with rubbish. Figuring out what's compostable and what's not. Examining everyone's bins and telling them off for using the wrong ones for their recyclables. I'm raising a pair of refuse fascists.'

I smiled. It felt good, briefly. Briefly normal. But then a wave of guilt washed that away, reminding me that things weren't okay, weren't normal.

'Do you have contact details for this Clara person?' Olivia asked.

'I could probably track down her email,' I admitted grudgingly. 'You don't think . . . ?'

She shrugged. 'It's just about covering all bases, isn't it? Did you tell the guards about her?'

I shook my head. Clara had never seemed real to me. I didn't know what she looked like, what she did for a living or where she lived. Rory said there was no need for me to know, that she wasn't important. But I'd come across her email address on his laptop about six months later and, unsure as to why I was doing it, hastily scribbled it down.

'Okay,' I said reluctantly. 'I'll email her. But he's not in contact with her. He'd have told me if he was.' I'd wondered at the time if he had left the laptop open on purpose so I could see that the last contact was months before. So I'd trust him again. It was the kind of thing he'd do.

'I'm sure you're right.' Olivia paused, stopped walking and touched me on the arm. 'Look, why don't I stay with you for a bit?'

'No.' I snatched my arm back, shaking my head.

She looked at me in surprise. 'Why not? What's wrong?'

I lowered my gaze, embarrassed, nails digging into my palms. 'Sorry. I'm just a bit jumpy. Not much sleep. But honestly, there's no need. You have work and the boys.'

'I'm worried about you, Allie.'

'I'm fine,' I insisted, setting off again up the hill with Finn. 'Rory will be back.'

Olivia trotted after me to catch up. 'That's what I mean. Just for a few days, until he comes back or . . .' she hesitated, 'you have some news. I can get to school easily enough from here. And Pete can mind the boys.' She smiled. 'It'll be good for him.'

Before I could protest any further, my phone rang. I recognised the garda station number.

CHAPTER FIVE

'What did they say?' Olivia asked when I got off the phone.

I'd thrust Finn's leash into her hand and rushed off to take the call, sitting hunched up on one of the park benches while the autumn leaves swirled around me. When I returned, the boys were bashing a tree with sticks, trying to get some conkers to fall, though the grass was littered with them, prickly outer cases bursting open to reveal shiny brown innards.

I tried to remember everything that Garda Suzanne Phelan had just told me. 'The B&B in Cleggan says that Rory left on Saturday afternoon. Toll-station cameras at Ballinasloe show his car passing about four o'clock. There's no sign of it broken down or crashed, so he must have left the motorway at some point, but they can't tell where or when.'

'So he's just disappeared in a puff of smoke?' Olivia was incredulous as she handed Finn's leash back to me. 'And no one knows anything?'

I shook my head miserably. 'No. They spoke to his brother, Andrew, so at least I don't need to ring him. He'll contact the rest of the family.'

This was the one positive I'd taken from Garda Phelan's call. I'd dreaded speaking to Rory's family, fearing that somehow they'd find a way to blame me for his disappearance. There were dark moments in the middle of the night when I agreed with them.

'Okay,' Olivia said slowly, the furrows in her brow deepening. 'Don't you think you should ring him anyway?'

No, I didn't. I avoided her gaze, pressing my hand to my forehead, which was burning up despite the chill of the day. 'The guard said Andrew mentioned setting up a Facebook page appealing for information, so he'll probably call me.' A Facebook page, the very thing I'd dreaded. I closed my eyes, but I was too late; a tear escaped and snaked down my cheek.

Olivia pulled me in for a quick hug, then took out her mobile. 'Okay. No arguments. I'm going to ring Pete. He can bring over a bag for me and collect the kids at the same time.'

This time I didn't have the energy to fight her.

Two emails came in the following morning after Olivia had left for work.

The first was from 'this Clara person' in response to the one Olivia had helped me draft. No, she hadn't been in touch with Rory for some time. Was there anything she could do? Predictably concerned, overly invested, clearly knowing nothing. It made me feel better about not mentioning her to the guards, but childishly resentful of Olivia for what had turned out to be a waste of energy. I deleted the email immediately, disliking it fouling up my inbox.

The second was from Con O'Neill, solicitor, addressed to Rory and copying me in. My stomach dropped when I read the heading and I sank back into my chair, mouth suddenly dry. *Raven Cottage.* I'd forgotten all about Raven Cottage.

It had been Rory's idea for us to move out of the city for a while. He wasn't alone; since COVID, all anyone talked about was achieving a better work–life balance. Half the population of

Dublin had aspirations to move, meaning that property prices in rural Ireland had sky-rocketed. But Rory had a stroke of luck. While filming in the Midlands, the Slieve Bloom mountains in County Laois, he'd come across a cottage owned by an American couple who'd returned to the States after the pandemic. They'd needed to sell, so the price was good.

I hadn't been keen, my cautious nature fearful of change, but Rory's enthusiasm swept me along like a rag doll fallen into a river. The reasons he came up with were endless. We could both work from anywhere. We could keep animals, grow vegetables, do all the things we'd talked about. He made me watch *The Good Life*, another specimen from the dark ages of television – he had a thing for Felicity Kendall. Finn would love it, he said. The garden was huge; there were fruit trees, apples and a plum, even a henhouse. And we would own it together while the apartment – which he would hold on to – was Rory's alone; he'd bought it years before I'd met him. It would be a real commitment for us.

He'd taken me to see it, and although it was a bit run-down, it was a proper cottage with a blue half-door, small square windows and an open fire. We had to act fast, Rory said; the sellers would put it on the open market if it didn't sell quickly, catapulting it out of our price range. So we got a loan from the Credit Union and signed a contract.

I read through the email. One word stood out. *Closing.* Heart thumping, I checked the calendar. Nothing. I flipped it over to next month, heart sinking when I saw that next Friday, the first Friday in November, was marked RAVEN COTTAGE IS OURS! in capital letters. Rory was a capital letters kind of person.

Bracing myself, I rang the solicitors' office.

O'Neill was upbeat. As far as he was concerned, he was delivering good news. 'It's all in place. Unless something shows up on the searches, you'll have the keys next week.'

In a halting voice I explained what had happened: that Rory had been missing since the weekend, that I couldn't do this without him, that I needed more time. It was clear that O'Neill didn't know how to react. I imagined a disappearing client wasn't something that cropped up very often.

'I'm sorry but it's all in place,' he said, not without sympathy. 'You're tied in, I've transferred the money to the vendors' solicitor. Once the searches are in, she can release it. The cottage will be yours next Friday.'

I chewed my lip, biting down on a ragged piece of loose skin, tugging at it with my teeth. If I thought hard, I vaguely remembered Rory telling me that the money was coming out of a joint account we'd set up, into which we'd put the Credit Union loan. He took charge of electricity bills, property tax, Wi-Fi, all our financial stuff. I was ashamed to admit that I barely even registered most of it.

O'Neill's voice cut through my thoughts. I'd missed what he said, so I asked him to repeat it, but the doorbell rang before he could. 'I have to get that. I'll call you back.'

An uncertain-looking young couple in jeans and puffer jackets waited for me downstairs in the foyer, eyes flitting nervously about.

'Hi,' the man said, looking up, hand outstretched for me to shake it. 'Pavel and Maria Oshenko. We're the people who are moving in.' His black hair was cut very short, almost shaved, giving him a threatening look that was at odds with his expression.

I frowned. 'Sorry?'

He dropped his hand when I didn't take it. 'In two weeks?'

The woman nudged him. 'The week after.' She was pale and thin, and looked anxious to please, peering timidly out from behind a curtain of blonde hair. 'It's Monday two weeks,' she said to me apologetically.

The man repeated her words, 'Monday two weeks,' looking relieved, as if this should solve the problem. 'We wondered if we could have a quick look? We've only seen pictures so it would give us an idea of what we can bring with us. Maybe even take some measurements?'

I felt as if I'd stumbled into a Kafka novel. I shook my head, feeling the need to dislodge whatever blockage was preventing my thoughts from flowing freely. 'You've lost me. Moving in where?'

They glanced doubtfully at one another. 'Your apartment. You're 16a, aren't you?'

Uh-oh. 'Yes.'

'We're renting the apartment for six months. From the fourteenth of November?'

A pins-and-needles sensation worked its way up my neck and into my face, like an allergic reaction. My throat tightened and I couldn't breathe; it took everything I had to think and speak normally. 'Wait a second, please.'

I still had my phone in my hand. I stepped outside into the courtyard and rang O'Neill's number again, gulping in big mouthfuls of fresh air.

The solicitor cleared his throat when I explained what had happened. 'That's what I was about to say when you hung up. I assumed you knew. Rory has leased the Dublin apartment for six months. You'll need to be out before the fourteenth. Ten days after you close on the cottage.'

I forced myself to stay calm, but my legs felt as if they were about to give way. Had Rory told me this? The apartment belonged to him and we weren't married. I had no legal right to it, but I wouldn't have forgotten something like that, surely?

'Rory told me you'd be moving down to the cottage for a while. Try out the country life.' The solicitor tried to inject a note of jollity into his voice and failed, clearly realising the impact this news was having on me; that it was, in fact, *news*.

'I suppose there's nothing I can do about it?' I said, weakly.

'I'm sorry. It's a fully furnished rental so there's no need to move any furniture at least. But if you don't vacate the apartment, they can—'

I sighed. 'It's okay.' I knew the legal remedies. I'd had to draft one myself the day before. *Shit*, work. I checked my watch. It was half past nine. I should have logged on by now.

I ended the call and went back in to face the now very concerned-looking young couple. Attempting a conciliatory smile, I brought them upstairs, where they spent less than two minutes looking around the apartment, clearly regretting their bravery in calling in at all. Maybe even their decision to rent it, since the place was a mess and I was clearly a nutcase.

After they left, I poured myself a glass of water and drained it, my mouth bone dry. I was certain Rory hadn't told me he'd leased the apartment. Had he been afraid I would drag my heels in moving to the cottage, so had forced me into a position where I had no choice? It wouldn't be the first time he'd done something like that. What the hell was I going to do? My first panicked thought was that Rory would know, but that was like breaking up with someone and wanting them to be the one to comfort you. It was Rory's absence that was the problem. Maybe Olivia was right. Maybe I should go and look for him.

I rang her at work, catching her between lessons, blurting it all out in a rush. 'Will you drive me? It would just be one night. I can get one of the neighbours to walk Finn.'

'Of course. I've a training day on Thursday that I can easily skip, and the Hallowe'en break starts on Friday so I've no classes.' She paused. 'And Allie, I think you're doing the right thing. It's time you took back control of your life.'

CHAPTER SIX

Suzanne

'Would you believe it? He had a bloody affair,' Suzanne said, slamming the phone down onto her desk.

'Who did?' Dave looked up from his egg and onion sandwich. He spoke with his mouth full, splattering tiny globules of chewed white bread onto the report he was finishing.

'Rory O'Riordan. His brother just told me. He clearly didn't want to, was keen to paint Rory as some kind of saint, but he must have finally decided that we might actually need to know that kind of thing.' She glared at the phone as if it were to blame. 'What is *wrong* with people?'

'I keep telling you. He's fucked off.' Dave brushed the wet crumbs off his desk with his sleeve. 'When?'

'The affair? Year and a half ago. Short-lived, apparently. A woman called Clara Biggs. Someone he worked with. Didn't come to anything. Brother said he was very unhappy, yada yada yada.' She paused to wave away the stench of sulphur wafting in her direction. 'Do you *have* to eat that egg in here? It stinks.'

'I like eggs.'

She shook her head in exasperation. 'Anyway, you'd think *she'd* have told us. Allie. I'm pretty sure we asked her if there were any problems between them.'

Dave nodded. 'We did.'

'The brother says she knew, that Rory confessed and she forgave him. Brother sounds as if he'd have preferred if she hadn't; he doesn't seem that keen on her. But apparently they carried on as if nothing had happened.'

Dave nodded sagely. 'Women are funny about that sort of thing. Great at putting on an act, giving the impression that everything's rosy in the garden.'

Suzanne watched him take a slug of his cherry Coke, whack himself on the chest and burp loudly. 'You'd wonder why we feel the need when you're all so damn perfect,' she muttered.

Dave flashed her a grin, a tiny sliver of slimy green watercress peeking out from between his front teeth. He didn't even care that he was a slob, she thought wearily. He was proud of it.

She took a note of the call from Andrew O'Riordan, then looked up. 'And you know how we asked her to ring round his friends and family to see if anyone knew anything?'

Dave nodded.

'Well, she didn't. The first the brother heard about Rory being missing was when I called him on Monday to check in. Not bloody happy, I can tell you.'

'I'll bet.' Dave narrowed his eyes and sat back with his arms crossed. 'Why are you so bothered about this anyway? The man's an adult.'

Suzanne shrugged. 'Just doing my job. Trying my best for his girlfriend, who must be going through hell at the moment. And his family.' She sighed. 'Anyway, it's four days in. No luck on the mobile phone company, so I'm going to send a request to his bank. See if he's accessed his accounts. If he has run off with someone, he'll need money.'

Dave's phone rang and he answered it, communicating with the caller in a series of grunts. When he hung up, he said, 'Three fellas beating the crap out of another outside the doctor's on St Lawrence's Road. We've drawn the short straw.'

Suzanne grabbed her jacket and stood up.

Dave's eyes widened as he chucked the sandwich packaging into the bin before picking up his own coat. 'Hey! Maybe she did him in.'

'I thought he'd done a runner,' Suzanne retorted. 'Make up your mind, for God's sake.'

He shook his head. 'I'd say she's well capable. There's something about those cold eyes...'

CHAPTER SEVEN

Allie

For a long time, I didn't have much in my life. So Rory very quickly became my everything. The attraction between us was immediate, and his conviction that we would be together for ever was enough to convince me. As I've said, his superpower. I moved into his apartment after six months. And as often happens with couples without kids, we became each other's family; the love doesn't get diluted. At least that was what Rory said. He was the seam running through everything I did and everything I felt. Without him I was missing a limb. Two limbs. I was like one of those dogs who'd had their hind legs amputated and needed wheels.

So when Olivia mentioned my taking back control, of course I was upset. I said nothing at the time since I needed her to drive. But when she started the car on Thursday morning with 'It's good we're doing this. It's been too long since you made a decision without Rory', it was the final straw.

'You're the one telling me what to do, not Rory.'

'What do you mean?'

'You made me email Clara...'

'I did not *make* you. I simply suggested that you consider the possibility that—'

'And now I'm going to Galway, *also* what you told me to do. If I'm anyone's puppet, it's yours.'

Hurt radiated off her like steam from a wet coat, but I ignored it, rubbing condensation from the window with my sleeve as we drove along the M4 in silence. I knew I sounded petulant, but Olivia made me feel like one of her twin boys strapped into his child seat.

Finally she glanced across at me. 'I'm sorry. I know I have a tendency to take charge. It's the teacher in me.'

I rolled my eyes. I was the older sister, but that was never the dynamic between us. Olivia had always been the bossy one.

But she also forgave easily, and she gifted me a smile before indicating to overtake a truck. 'I was reading about how people respond to someone they love going missing.'

She moved confidently into the outside lane and I sucked in a breath, reaching my hand out to grip the dashboard. As she accelerated, her gaze flickered briefly in my direction, and I had to stop myself from shouting at her to keep her eyes on the road, heart hammering in my chest. It seemed like an eternity before we returned to our lane.

She flicked off the indicator, frowning. 'Are you still ... I mean, I know you don't drive, but I thought you had—'

'I did. I'm fine.' I shut her down, and turned to gaze at the hard shoulder, wondering if I might see Rory's battered red Nissan, hazards flashing while he changed a tyre or flapped at smoke billowing from the engine. 'Finish what you were saying. People's response to someone going missing?'

She shot me one last concerned glance. 'Apparently it's the uncertainty that's the worst. They call it ambiguous loss.'

This was typical Olivia. Do the research. Read the book. I said nothing, afraid that whatever I did say would be wrong. Because the truth was that uncertainty *was* better than the alternative for me. At least then, in one possible outcome, Rory came back and the world returned to the way it had been.

'This might help,' she said. 'This trip. Talking to the people he saw last. We might get some clue as to what he was thinking. Where he might have gone.'

'Gone?' I turned to look at her. 'You still think he's just gone off somewhere?'

'I didn't say that,' she said, choosing her words carefully. 'But wouldn't it be better than the alternative? Maybe he's had some sort of breakdown. Gone away to clear his head.'

I wrapped my arms protectively around my middle. 'The guards have suggested suicide. Not in so many words, but ... They say he hasn't touched his bank account. His passport is still with mine in the trunk in our bedroom. The fact that he was working by the sea.'

'But then why hasn't his car turned up? On a beach or somewhere?'

I shook my head. 'He hasn't taken his own life. I know he hasn't. He's just not the type. Plus, he'd never leave Finn.'

Olivia nodded. 'I'd probably agree with that. He is rather a big presence. But then you never know what people are hiding.'

I noticed that she hadn't responded with *And he'd never leave you.*

My phone rang on my knee and I picked it up. It was Sam. 'Hey, Allie. Are you on the road?'

I'd called him to get the address of the place where he, Rory and Vince had stayed.

'Yes. My sister's driving.'

'Okay. Well, my shoot in Clare this afternoon is cancelled, so I could take a run up and meet you if you like. Introduce you to some of the people we met. People Rory met.'

I glanced at Olivia, who mouthed, 'Yes, say yes.'

'I can ring and set up a trip to the island too,' he added. 'Some of the scientists we were filming with are out there again today and it might be good for you to speak to them.'

'Okay,' I said. 'Thanks. We'll be there in about two hours.'

'Great. I'll meet you at the pier.' A pause. 'Hang in there, Allie.'

'So this is where they stayed?' Olivia pulled into the last remaining space in the yard of a small whitewashed farmhouse not far from the pier that appeared in Rory's photographs.

I nodded. 'They spent Saturday morning on the island but called in here to collect their bags before heading off. Sam says that Rory left straight away but he and Vince hung on a bit longer.'

'Very John Hinde,' Olivia remarked, then added, after a pause, 'My twins could be on a John Hinde. Although they'd have been horrified by the bins back then.'

I grinned, picturing those nostalgic Irish postcards depicting red-haired children with donkeys. Until I remembered why we were here.

'You're allowed to smile, you know,' Olivia said, tugging on the handbrake.

'I know.' My voice wavered, and she reached out reassuringly and squeezed my hand. But she said nothing, and I was grateful for that.

We were greeted at the B&B by a stout woman in a housecoat, looking as if she belonged in the 1950s. 'Aye, he stayed with me. He's gone missing, I hear.' She clasped heavily veined red hands to her cheeks. 'Hard to believe something like that could happen. The guards from Clifden were here asking about him.'

The idea of guards asking complete strangers questions about Rory gave me an odd feeling of disquiet. Had they told this woman something they hadn't told me?

'I don't suppose he said anything to you about where he might have gone?' Olivia asked.

The woman seemed to consider this, then shook her head. 'I'm sorry. He didn't. I've been racking my brain ever since. I asked him where he was headed next and he just said he was driving back to Dublin.'

There was a long pause during which I felt I was expected to say something, but I couldn't seem to get my brain working.

The woman seemed to sense my discomfort. 'Anyway, I'll show you both to your room.'

She ushered us upstairs to a large comfortable bedroom with two single beds, looking out over the water, left keys on the dressing table, then lingered in the doorway. Her bulk seemed to fill it entirely, giving me such a sense of claustrophobia that I had to suppress the urge to push past her and run back down the stairs. Had this been Rory's room?

'Ciarán is ready to take you to Bofin whenever you want to go,' she said.

'Thank you.' Olivia wisely opted to do the talking. 'We're just waiting for Sam – do you remember him? Sam and . . . Vince?' She looked at me for confirmation and I managed a nod.

'I do. Quiet fella.' The woman gave me an almost mischievous smile. 'Not like your man. Quite the charmer, he was. Brought me flowers to thank me for the great breakfast. I said to him, you're paying me for the great breakfast.'

Olivia shot a quick glance in my direction before picking up one of the keys. 'Let's take a walk, shall we? Maybe we can get something to eat.'

The woman recommended a café on the main street and we left the house.

Looking at the faces we encountered as we walked around the little town, I couldn't help wonder which of them might have met

Rory or spoken to him. Should we be showing a picture? Before I could say as much to Olivia, Sam rang and we shelved the plan for food.

On the pier, he gave me a hug. It was the first time I'd seen him in a year, although Rory worked with him a lot. His hair was longer than I remembered, tied in a ponytail at the base of his neck, and he looked grey and worried. I wondered if I appeared the same to him.

Ciarán was a ruddy-looking individual in yellow waterproofs, who I realised was doing us a favour when he sympathised with me as if Rory was dead. Confirmed when I saw that we were the only passengers.

The journey took about forty minutes, during which none of us spoke very much – I felt queasy as the waves rose and fell, spray peppering the windows of the empty ferry as it ploughed a route through the restless water. Until Sam suggested that we make our way on deck, where the three of us stood at the rail, breathing in the salty air and watching the island appear as a grey-green smudge on the horizon before the rocky outcrop of pirate queen Gráinne Mhaol's castle came into view. Everything seemed eerily familiar from the pictures Rory had sent.

Gulls swooped and called overhead as Ciarán threw a coiled rope onto the pier, secured it and lifted the barrier to allow us to disembark along the gangplank.

Leaving behind the cluster of buildings at the harbour, we walked for about fifteen minutes to a less inhabited part of the island. Empty and abandoned houses punctuated rectangular fields populated by cattle and small lakes, the sea an ever-constant presence in the distance. I'd lived in the city for so long that this place felt strange and other-worldly, especially when it hit me that if Rory had wanted to die by suicide, this would have been the place to do it, with the wild Atlantic Ocean on all sides.

Following Sam, we trudged up a narrow lane edged with crude stone walls, arriving at the gateway to a field of wild grass. A few figures hunched over in the far corner looked up when Sam called, and came towards us. Over the gate he introduced us to a woman and two men, ornithologists I recognised from the pictures that Rory had sent. Olivia hung back pointedly and I knew she'd taken my earlier mutiny on board. They were friendly and sympathetic, but they'd seen Rory even less recently than Sam, having stayed on the island when the crew left on Saturday lunchtime.

Then I remembered the woman Rory had been speaking to in the one photograph in which he appeared. She wasn't here today. As the scientists returned to their work, I took out my phone to show Sam. When I found the photo, I enlarged the background to zoom in on the two of them. While Rory was partly blocking her in the picture, I could see that she had something in her dangling right hand, something small. A cigarette? I froze. Was she vaping? Her face was over-pixelated, so her features weren't clear, but with that long coat, she could easily be the woman I'd seen outside the café on the way to the park. The one who'd jumped back when Finn approached.

I swallowed and told myself to get a grip. Lots of people vaped these days. I was losing my mind, tilting at windmills.

I handed the phone to Sam. 'Do you know that woman? Is she another scientist?'

He took it, gave the screen a quick look and then shook his head. 'There were quite a few people here that day. Day trippers, birdwatchers. Also some contributors Rory organised who we ended up not having time to include.' He handed back the phone. 'That often happens with a documentary. She might have been one of those.'

I knew about this. Rory had told me that sometimes people got annoyed when they gave up their time and weren't used.

But Sam seemed evasive and I couldn't shake the feeling that he wasn't telling me everything. The scientists had nothing to tell us, so the visit to the island seemed pointless. Was there another reason he'd wanted to meet us here?

On the way back, while Olivia texted her husband inside, I took the opportunity to corner him on deck, shouting to be heard over the noise of the engine. 'Is there something you're not telling me, Sam?'

He gripped the handrail, the wind whipping his long hair about his face, considering his response. 'We had a row, me and Rory. Before he left.'

My stomach dropped. Was Olivia right? Had Rory been having an affair? With that woman in the picture? Sam was a devoted family man, so I felt sure he wouldn't approve. Was that what they'd argued about?

He looked down at his shoes, old hiking boots with frayed laces. 'I've been torturing myself about it.'

'What was it about?' I asked, terrified of the answer, salt stinging my dry lips.

'Oh, work stuff. Technical details of filming.' He tried to smile, made inverted commas with his fingers. 'Creative differences. But it got pretty heated, and Rory drove off upset.' His smile faded. 'I keep thinking, what if he had an accident because of it?'

'Was that why he left before you and Vince?'

Sam nodded. 'We needed to talk through some edits and we'd intended going to the pub to do it, myself and Rory. But he stormed off and Vince and I ended up doing it ourselves.'

I gazed into the vast expanse of the sea, picturing Rory speeding out of town, angry and reckless. The spray of water on my face was a cooling relief. 'But they'd have found his car if he had an accident. Wouldn't they?'

'Maybe.' Sam didn't look convinced. He didn't seem willing to say anything more either, so I didn't press him. I knew how guilt could eat away at you.

The shadows lengthened as we motored towards the pier, and I had the strangest sense that Rory was just ahead of us, barely out of reach. It was like trying to grab his shadow. Or his ghost.

We thanked Ciarán for his kindness. Sam left to drive back to Clare while Olivia and I returned to the B&B.

'What do you want to do now?' Olivia asked, flopping down onto one of the beds. 'Sam said they went to the pub each night, so maybe we could try there. We haven't eaten since breakfast.'

I nodded gratefully. My stomach roiled from lack of food.

The barman, a slim, pale-faced young man, leaning on the Guinness tap with his sleeves rolled up, revealing the sinewy arms of a seasoned GAA player, remembered Rory. He nodded. 'The telly fella. He was in on Friday night. Said he was a big banjo player, so he borrowed a guitar from Tom and joined in the session.' He nodded towards the corner table, empty now, where I presumed the session took place. I imagined we were too early, since it was still only six o'clock.

'That sounds like Rory all right,' Olivia said, looking up from the menu. She didn't quite roll her eyes, but something about her tone jarred.

'He seemed to be having the craic,' the barman said. 'His mate didn't like it, though.'

'His mate?' I said.

'Bloke with long hair. I saw them having words outside. Didn't hear what they said, but it looked intense.'

I frowned. Sam. Disagreements were inevitable when they worked so closely together, but it must have been serious if it continued into Saturday.

We ordered lasagne and chips, and little pub bottles of wine. Olivia stuck with one, mixed with fizzy water, but I was very quickly on my third, eventually pushing my food away half eaten, what I'd managed already curdling in my stomach. 'God, I wish he was here.'

Olivia didn't respond, just kept sipping her watery drink.

Oh, I know I shouldn't have. I knew that my sister had given up her time to support me, that my thinking was neither straight nor sober and that I was opening up a whole can of worms it wasn't in my interests to release. But those pursed lips, that lowered gaze, the *silence*. I couldn't stand it.

'I know you don't like him.'

She sighed, making circles with her glass on the table, clinking the ice cubes. 'I don't like the influence he has on you.'

'What's that supposed to mean?'

'He seems to be able to persuade you to do almost anything.'

I glared at her. 'Isn't that a good thing? Without him I'd just sit in the flat, rotting. I'm such a coward.'

Olivia looked up, appalled. 'Did *he* say that?'

'Of course not.'

'Is that what you think?'

I shrugged. 'Remember my birthday last year, when he arranged that hang-gliding thing? If he'd told me in advance, I'd never have done it. You know I wouldn't.'

'But Allie, you hated it. You were terrified. You rang me beforehand, remember? I was tempted to drive there, pick you up and bring you home.'

I shook my head. 'I was glad afterwards.'

'Those kinds of daredevil stunts were never your thing,' she persisted. 'Hardly surprising, given what happened.'

Tears gathering, I stared into my glass.

Her voice softened. 'What about your writing? That writers' group you were in. That was something for *you*. Have you given it up completely?'

I laughed bitterly. 'I wasn't any good.'

'Of course you were. You had that short story published.'

'That was years ago.' The tears finally spilled over, and I swiped at them with my sleeve. 'I need him, Liv. I need him back. I don't feel safe without him.'

CHAPTER EIGHT

As soon as our landlady left the room the next morning, having delivered two full Irish breakfasts, Olivia slid a box of Nurofen across the table. I took them gratefully, pushing two tablets from the blister pack and swallowing them down with my orange juice.

She watched me, peering over her teacup. All she was missing were the bifocals. 'It's not going to help, you know, drinking so much. You need to decide what you're going to do if Rory doesn't come back.' She put the cup down. 'Why don't you come and stay with us when the apartment is leased?'

I didn't reply. I couldn't think that way yet. I wasn't ready.

Olivia chattered endlessly on the journey back, something she always did when she was worried, while I was monosyllabic. My head was pounding and my mouth dry, but I couldn't even bring myself to ask her to stop for a drink.

The trip had been a failure. Other than Sam's argument with Rory, we'd found out nothing. I'd known they squabbled about work, but Rory maintained that their differences made them a great team. He talked to people and established relationships while Sam was the quieter, more creative one. It had clearly been a serious row, but I imagined the reason Sam felt so bad about it was because he hadn't had the chance to make it up. I knew how that felt.

In the underground car park of the apartment complex, Olivia turned off the engine, regarding me with that same mournful, conciliatory expression she used with the twins. 'Look, I'm sorry we argued. I should be supporting you, not criticising Rory.'

'You should. We were happy. *Are* happy. He's a good man.'

She dropped her head. 'Okay.'

'You liked him at first too. I know you did,' I urged. 'Remember the first time you met? You were pregnant with the twins.'

Olivia and I had been sitting outside a café in the Italian Quarter when Rory happened upon us on his way to a meeting. She'd had a dizzy spell, and while I'd just panicked, he'd immediately fetched her a glass of water and produced a banana from his bag. We'd made him late for his meeting.

'And he's great with the twins,' I added, pictured him tossing one into the air while the other screamed for it to be his go.

'I know.' She bit her lip. 'But I also know that things haven't been easy for you.'

'If you mean Clara, I told you, we're over that.'

'No, I mean since Mum and Dad. Everything that's happened since.'

And there it was. The thing we rarely talked about because it was too painful: the death of our parents in a car crash when we were teenagers.

'You lost them too,' I said quietly, grateful that she didn't mention the elephant in the room, the massive and obvious reason why she'd coped better with their deaths than I had. In fairness, she never did. The one unwritten rule of our sibling relationship was that it was up to me to bring it up. 'Anyway, that has nothing to do with this.'

'Are you sure?'

I shook my head, knowing the path she wanted to take, determined that I was not heading down there with her.

'Did you mean what you said about not feeling safe without him?' she asked.

'No, of course not,' I said dismissively. 'I'd had too much wine. I just miss him, that's all. And I'm worried. Let's go upstairs. Finn will need to go out.'

Every cell in my body wept with exhaustion as we walked up the stairs to the apartment, the second wave of hangover hitting with a vengeance. Finn gave a weak tail thump when I suggested a walk, and we left Olivia alone to call Pete and the kids.

My head was thick with tiredness as we made our way into the park, my stomach still bilious from last night's wine. And now, thanks to Olivia dredging up the past, I was even more rattled than I had been before.

She didn't get it. She didn't understand how Rory had saved me. That before I met him, I was only pretending to be a person. Pretending to be okay. I actually thought I was good at it, convinced that if I refused to stay still long enough, people wouldn't see me clearly, wouldn't spot the hollow where something important should be.

But Rory saw what most people missed. I could talk to him because he had survivor's guilt too. As a child, he'd seen his best friend killed by a drunk driver on their way home from school. He blamed himself, though rationally he knew he wasn't responsible. I pictured his grief as he told me about it, broad shoulders hunched, floppy hair falling over his face, still devastated more than thirty years later.

Broad shoulders hunched, floppy hair falling over his face.

Suddenly, there he was. Rory! Standing by the bench just inside the gate to the park, looking down at his phone.

I felt dizzy with excitement as I rushed over, wondering why

Finn wasn't reacting as I was. Until I was a few metres away, and the spell broke. The man turned slightly as he sensed my approach, and I saw immediately that it wasn't Rory. Of course it wasn't. I swayed, feeling as if I was about to faint.

'Are you okay?' he asked.

I nodded and stumbled away.

Still shaken when I came back in, I fed Finn and went to our bedroom to unpack. Olivia was still on the phone. I could hear her voice in the spare room.

I felt utterly lost. All Rory's things were still here, in this room we had shared for four and a half years. The book by his bed, a hefty tome on architecture for a documentary he was planning to make that didn't get commissioned. A pair of his jeans, hanging over the back of the chair, looking as if his legs were still in them. His wardrobe door, which never closed because it was so stuffed with shoes, which he piled up at the bottom. Rory loved shoes. They were his one extravagance, but he still refused to throw out the old ones, so there were probably runners at the bottom of that heap that hadn't seen the light of day since he met me.

I sank down onto the chair, feeling a wave of despair, a need to see him that was almost physical, like a hunger pang. Olivia's voice sounded clearly from next door. The wall between the two bedrooms was thin; I'm sure she didn't realise how thin, how the noise travelled, or maybe she hadn't heard me coming back from the park. But I caught every word.

'I'm worried about her. He's made her feel that she can't be safe without him. Made her reliant on him.' There was a pause. 'I know. I thought the writing was helping too. But she's stopped. Probably because *he* can't do it with her. It's not *his* thing.' Her tone was derisive. 'Christ, she seems to have no friends any more. I'm fucking furious with him.'

I stormed out of my bedroom and into hers. 'I want you to leave.'

Olivia blanched. She was sitting on the spare bed in her socks, knees up to her chest. 'Allie, please, there's something I want to—'

'This is Rory's flat. I don't think you should stay here if that's how you feel about him. I'm going to the shop and I want you gone when I get back.'

I slammed the door behind me as I left.

She *was* gone when I got back. I was a little surprised, to tell the truth. But while I was out, I'd reached a decision. There was no way I could move in with Olivia now; I'd go to the cottage instead, like Rory wanted.

I opened my laptop to look at what the solicitor had sent, what I needed to do and when I needed to move. It seemed straightforward enough. Plans made. And without Rory. Imagine that. Although my defiance concealed a fear I didn't want to acknowledge even to myself. I wasn't good with change; I suspect that was what had triggered things going wrong for me after college. So, before turning off the laptop, I distracted myself by scrolling through some celebrity and news websites I sometimes visited. *Irish actor tipped for Oscar success! Diplomatic row between Ireland and UK escalates.*

But I found it difficult to concentrate. A link to a Facebook page popped up and I clicked on it. Massive mistake. I still don't know why I did it. It wasn't as if I ever posted anything – I was a lurker.

A picture of Rory that I'd never seen before beamed out at me from some family gathering I had no memory of attending, with the word *MISSING!* underneath. Andrew had posted it, pleading for information about his brother's whereabouts. The post had been shared multiple times. Rory was officially a missing person.

My hand shook as I scrolled through the comments below.

Didn't he make that documentary on the badger?

Didn't see it but I worked with him a bit in RTÉ. Lovely guy. I wonder what happened to him? He hasn't done a lot lately. Do you remember that awful X Factor type thing?

God yeah. The Naked Lens. Utter shite. He was a judge on it.

And then...

This post is from his brother. Isn't Rory married? What's the story with his wife?

Pretty enough but spoiled. Snooty Southside cow. You know the type. A laughing-face emoji had been added and the comment had been liked by four people.

I was at a do in the conference centre, I think it was the music awards, and she made him go home. Had some kind of a meltdown because he was talking to some other woman for too long.

Why do men like that always end up with such sour-faced bitches?

Don't be so mean. She might be reading this.

He's probably left her. Found some way to escape.

Cheeks burning, I slammed the laptop shut, blinking as if I were under a spotlight. But immediately my phone started to buzz with texts from people who'd seen the post.

I felt hunted.

CHAPTER NINE

Suzanne

Suzanne leaned forward and tried to catch her breath, hands resting on her thighs. Another lap? she asked herself. She checked her watch. Maybe not. If she didn't get a move on, Tony would be back before her and into the shower, dropping his wet towels and spreading water all over the bathroom floor, which she hated.

She straightened up and began to stretch her quads, holding onto a nearby telephone pole for balance. Her eyes landed on a poster taped to it, with a photograph of a smiling man, a telephone number, and the words *Have you seen this man? Rory O'Riordan. Missing since 22 October.* Oh, for feck's sake. Her one day off this week, and she couldn't get that damn missing persons case out of her head.

One more lap, she decided, setting off again at a smooth jog. The legs might not need it, but her head certainly did.

She ended up doing two more circuits of the football pitches behind her estate in the hope that exhausting herself physically would silence her chattering brain. It worked, while she was running at least. But as soon as she stopped to cool down, walking the short distance back to the house, it all started to crowd in again. Dave was a slob, but she knew he was right. Her interest in Rory O'Riordan's disappearance was a little odd. They had far more serious cases on hand. Plus, people went missing all the time, so it was hardly unusual. Sometimes they didn't want to be found and sometimes they didn't want to live. Neither was a crime.

Which was why she hadn't succeeded in getting any information from O'Riordan's mobile phone company. It would have been helpful to know the last mast his phone had pinged, but as she'd expected, the request hadn't met the threshold, since no actual crime had been committed. *Yet.* Why did that word keep getting tagged onto the end of that sentence in her head?

She'd done everything else that was required: a missing persons file had been set up, O'Riordan's details uploaded onto the garda Pulse system, where anyone in any station could access it. Suzanne herself had contacted his friends and family, the colleagues who had seen him last, along with the hospitals, the bank, the toll station and her mate in the garda station in Clifden. There was nothing more she could do. Chances were it would end up being one of those open-ended cases that were never resolved. The ones she hated.

So why couldn't she get it out of her head?

She pushed open the little gate and walked up the path to her house, rooting in the pocket of her leggings for her key. When she stepped inside, pulling the door after her, she was immediately hit with the scent of freshly applied aftershave. Damn it. Tony was back from the gym. The bathroom would be swimming.

A voice called out from the kitchen above the stabbing guitar sounds of Fontaines DC on Spotify. 'Do you want eggs?'

Suppressing an image of Dave with watercress between his teeth, and conceding that there were compensations for sharing a house with your boyfriend, she called, 'Yes please. Just give me ten to have a shower,' before running upstairs.

Unlacing her runners and peeling off her sweaty running gear before shoving it into the laundry basket, she resolved to stop thinking about Rory O'Riordan for a while, sealing the deal by clamping the basket lid firmly down.

But when she stepped into the shower, her brain refused to follow orders. One of the things that bothered her was the contrast between the girlfriend's approach and the family's. The family were clearly determined to get Rory's disappearance into the public eye as soon as possible – she'd seen their Facebook post and felt sure the posters were their idea too. But Allie seemed shyer, keen to avoid the spotlight. Almost as if she were embarrassed by what had happened.

As the hot water sluiced down her body, she thought about Dave's suggestion: *maybe she did him in*. Suzanne was more inclined to think that the woman was vulnerable; she'd seen and read the comments underneath the Facebook post and hoped that Allie hadn't. The brother had recently made it publicly shareable, so inevitable contributions of the 'I'll step in and give her one if he's not around' variety had started. Suzanne vaguely remembered Allie saying that she didn't do social media and hoped that that was true.

Replaying her conversation with Andrew O'Riordan in her head, it was obvious that the family didn't like Allie; the brother had said as much, seemed almost to blame her for Rory's disappearance, although it was hard to put your finger on why. But again, how unusual was that? Suzanne suspected Tony's mother wasn't too keen on *her*, and she was a catch, a fact of which she reminded him regularly.

She squeezed shampoo into her hand and lathered it vigorously into her hair. Maybe she should ring Allie on Monday, to check in? Keep the lines of communication open. Something in her gut was telling her that was important. And Suzanne always listened to her gut.

CHAPTER TEN

Allie

Raven Cottage was smaller than I remembered when I stood in front of it some two weeks later. Low to the ground, roughly rendered and whitewashed. Built to withstand time. I imagined it was once probably thatched, though it now had heavy black slates, and ivy dangled like matted hair from the gable ends. With its half-door and square windows, it looked like a house that a child would draw; the only thing missing was a wisp of smoke from the chimney.

A shed sat to one side like a smaller sibling. I hadn't spoken to *my* smaller sibling since she'd left the flat, despite repeated calls and texts from her offering to help me move. I suppose I was lucky she didn't just turn up like she had on the Monday after Rory disappeared, but even Olivia knew when to back off sometimes.

'Do you want to carry this one yourself? It's marked fragile,' Sam called out from the van he'd borrowed to help me move down. When he and Aoife had offered, I hadn't hesitated. I knew he still felt guilty about his row with Rory. He'd also helped put the rest of our belongings from the apartment into storage.

'Will do.' I'd been lost in thought, gazing at the house that would be my home for the next six months, with Finn by my side.

The cottage was at the end of a long lane, little more than a shared track. The only other inhabited building was a bungalow that sat a few fields away, alongside slatted sheds and a barn and the original farmhouse, which was now abandoned, ruined and used as a cowhouse. Agricultural land lay all around, but behind the cottage rose the purple and brown Slieve Bloom mountains. Rory, who saw himself as a climber, had referred to them as hills, although they looked like perfectly respectable mountains to me.

I reached out for Finn's head. 'What do you think, boy? Space for you to run?'

He yawned as he always did when he was unsure about something; the dog was a master of deflection. I could learn from him. It was a combination of fight and flight that had made me go ahead with this move – the flurry of calls from concerned people who'd seen the Facebook post only increasing the urge to leave – but now all I felt was afraid. What the hell was I doing, moving without Rory to a house that *he'd* wanted, to a place this isolated, where my only company was a dog who loved him more than me?

On the other hand, what choice did I have? The apartment was leased from Monday. I couldn't afford to rent anywhere else in Dublin, and I couldn't stay with Olivia after what she'd said. And anyway, I wasn't functioning there. I couldn't eat. I couldn't sleep. I saw Rory on every corner. I spent my time scrolling through social media, torturing myself with what people were saying. There was even a thread about his disappearance on Reddit. You can only read so much online vomit before you begin doubting your understanding of yourself.

I didn't say goodbye to anyone before I left. I'm sure some of my neighbours knew what was happening, but no one mentioned it, and neither did I. I did call my boss, who made me take some time off. And Rory's brother. At first Andrew's response was negative, outraged that I would desert Rory, but when I explained that the cottage had been his idea and that he hadn't left me with much choice, I sensed his relief that I'd be out of the way. There was talk of a leafleting campaign and a public appeal, which I suspected they'd find easier to manage without my presence. I'd never been what they imagined Rory's partner should be. Maybe if I wasn't there, they could conjure up an image better fitting their vision.

The night before, I'd slept in an apartment empty of all our possessions, the paraphernalia of five years of coupledom dissipated in a couple of weeks. And now here I was. Everything stripped away. Alone. My old life dismantled.

I took a last look at the cottage, glancing up to see a line of crows observing us from a telegraph wire, before turning towards the van. Sam and Aoife were unloading the contents onto the cobbles in front of the house so I could decide where everything should go.

'How are you going to cope without a car down here?' Aoife asked, looking worried.

I shrugged with a half-smile. 'The village is within walking distance.'

I caught them exchanging a glance as I took my box to the door and placed it with the others. I turned the key, then, undoing the latch below, pushed open the two halves.

On the threshold I stopped dead. The interior was so dim that I couldn't see what I was walking into. Sam and Aoife were just behind me and there was a cartoon-like domino effect when we collided. 'Oh, sorry!'

I stepped carefully into the cottage and they followed me. I felt around for a light switch, but it seemed there was no central lighting at all, just lamps. Eventually I found one with pink glass that looked as if it had been converted from an oil lamp, and switched it on.

I blew out a breath. The house was way worse than I remembered. The front door opened directly onto a living room dominated by a deep stone-arched fireplace, its walls and ceilings darkened by centuries of woodsmoke, its square curtained windows almost too grubby to see out of. The floor was made of stone flags, partially covered by two stained mats that bunched up as if something lurked underneath.

There were two armchairs, a table and two chairs, and an old-fashioned dresser with plates and cups. The sellers hadn't wanted the trouble of disposing of their furniture, so Rory and I – Rory really, I hadn't cared – had agreed to take the basics, deciding we could buy our own when we could afford it and had time to choose what we wanted. At the time, there'd been throws on all the furniture, but now I saw that everything was badly worn, so much so that I wondered if the couple from whom we'd bought the cottage had themselves taken the contents from the previous occupants. The house looked as if it hadn't been updated for decades. Dust lay everywhere and there was a smell of damp and smoke.

Neither Aoife nor Sam said anything. With the three of us inside, the room felt cramped and airless. Sam seemed to sense this and stepped into the room next door, a sort of side room off the living room, too small to be a proper bedroom. I remembered Rory saying during one of his persuasive conversations that I could use it as my office.

'Jesus, it's freezing in here,' Sam called back. 'I hope you have heating.'

There was no heating, I remembered suddenly. That could be a problem; we were now in November, on the cusp of winter.

Before I could reply, Aoife's voice sounded from the back. 'There's a shed full of turf out here.' I hadn't noticed her leave. She reappeared rubbing her hands on her jeans. 'That's a nice bonus.

You'll need it.' She shivered. 'You should get yourself an electric heater too.'

Sam came back in with an odd expression on his face. 'Seriously, it's much colder in there than here. Try it. I can't figure out where the draught is coming from.'

Stepping into the small room, I found that it was about half the size of the living room. It felt claustrophobic; there was a tightness in my throat that made it hard to breathe, but maybe that was just the dust. Sam was right, it was freezing in here, at least a couple of degrees colder than the rest of the house. An ugly armchair and sideboard were pushed against the back wall, below a cheap print of Van Gogh's *Wheatfield* curling in its frame: crows flying in a turbulent sky and a path that seemed to follow them. I shivered. I'd seen a documentary about the artist's life and knew that a few months after he'd painted it, not far from that very field, he had stepped behind a barn and put a bullet in his chest.

Finn appeared in the doorway, stopped dead, then turned on his heel and walked back out.

'Good call,' I muttered, following him and pulling the door shut behind me. Whatever was causing it, I needed to keep the chill from invading the rest of the house.

I walked through the cottage, refreshing my memory. I'd only been here once before, a quick viewing narrated by a highly animated Rory, who'd predicted what we would do with the garden, where we'd put our furniture, how we would decorate. It had been hard to think independently that day, to feel anything other than swept up by his enthusiasm.

Finn trailed after me, sniffing into each corner and around the edges of every door. The original dwelling was made up of three rooms with vaulted ceilings – the small room, living room, and bedroom – while the kitchen and bathroom were part of a cheap lean-to extension with mildewed walls and a crude out-pipe for a gas cylinder attached to the cooker. Green fungus grew on the walls of the bathroom. In the bedroom, a brass-framed bed was shoved against the wall, along with an ancient dressing table and a huge old wardrobe.

When I was finished, I joined Sam and Aoife outside and we stood there with Finn looking mournfully at what was – there was no denying it – a rather dingy cottage.

'Cosy,' Sam said, breaking the tension; we all laughed.

'Seriously,' Aoife said, looking genuinely worried, 'I know the apartment is leased, but you don't have to stay here. Come to us for a bit. We've a spare room.'

I smiled tightly. 'I'll be fine.' A lie if ever I uttered one.

She shook her head. 'You've lost a lot of weight. Maybe we could feed you up and then you can move in? I don't like to think of you on your own down here. You don't even know anyone.'

I didn't know many people in Dublin any more either, I thought but didn't say. 'It's what Rory wanted. It will make me feel closer to him if I do this. At least for a while.'

'Okay.' Aoife put her arm around me and gave me a squeeze. 'Let's have a look at the garden,' she said brightly.

The garden was the real bonus as far as Rory was concerned. Over an acre of land, with apple and plum trees, the old henhouse and that big shed. But it was unkempt and overgrown, filled with briars and weeds, making it impossible to tell where the boundary was.

'You'll need some help with that,' Sam said wryly.

'You volunteering?' I asked with a half-smile.

He raised his palms in surrender. I was grateful to him. Despite the guilt he felt, they owed me nothing. He had taken on another producer for the documentary and looked uncomfortable when he told me about it. But Rory had been gone nearly three weeks. What else could he do?

A call from above made all three of us look up. The birds had risen from the telegraph wire and were circling, lifting their wings against the wind.

'You might have to watch out for them nesting in your chimney,' Aoife said. 'I remember jackdaws in our bedrooms when we were kids.'

'I think they're ravens,' Sam said, shielding his eyes with his hand. 'See the long beak?'

Aoife nudged him with a smile. 'One wildlife documentary and he's an expert.'

Their easy intimacy gave me a pang. 'They must be the ravens the cottage was named after.'

The birds took off in a cloud across the fields, reminding me uneasily of the painting inside.

Once everything had been transferred from van to cottage and Finn's bed placed by the unlit fire – he refused to get into it, preferring to pace restlessly – Sam and Aoife were ready to leave.

Aoife looked as if she didn't want to go. 'Are you absolutely sure about this?' She'd seen my cautious, fearful nature over the years, so this must seem like a crazy thing for me to do.

'Yes,' I lied.

I stood at the half-door to wave them off.

'You'll have to get yourself a pipe,' she joked through the passenger window, but I could see the concern still etched in her face.

I watched the van disappear down the lane. Turning to face the house, I saw that the sun was already beginning to slip behind the mountains, blood-red seams streaking across the sky. And I realised that I was alone. Properly alone.

CHAPTER ELEVEN

The chill hit me anew when I went back inside; a cold wind sneaking in through the gaps in the windows and doors. I told myself that the walls were made of stone so it was only natural there would be some draughts, and that once I'd got myself a heater, I would be fine.

I'd brought a rug from the apartment, so I unrolled it now onto the stone flags, taking up the stained old mats and dumping them in the shed. While I was there, I fetched some turf to make a fire. It was one of the few things I was better at than Rory. Whenever we stayed in a house with a fireplace, it was my job to light it, while Rory did his Gordon Ramsay bit in the kitchen, singing while he opened the wine and peeled the garlic. The memory made me feel his absence anew, that yawning chasm in my gut that I couldn't seem to fill. Aoife was right. I had lost weight. I felt nauseous every time I tried to eat, as if it was something I shouldn't be doing, continuing to live normally while he wasn't here.

The fire sputtered and smoked but I thought it would take. While waiting, I went to make up the bed. Finn followed me, watching as I stood by the old brass bedstead, wondering if I could really sleep there. On inspecting the mattress, I was surprised to find that it appeared brand new, possibly the only thing in the house that was, which made things a little easier. When I'd finished with the bedclothes, I unpacked my toiletries, arranging them on the old dressing table. I couldn't get the mirror to stay fixed; it kept tilting to give a view of the ceiling. Feeling a wave of irritation born of tiredness, I decided to do the rest of the unpacking in the morning.

Returning to the living room to find it choked with smoke, I opened the half-door and watched it billow out. When it cleared, I made some tea and toast and sat by the fire, Finn beside me in his bed. As the flames licked the turf, it hit me that for the first time since Rory had disappeared, I didn't feel like a drink to dull my feelings.

So I let the tears come; everything I'd been holding in while Sam and Aoife had been here. That awful lack, so real in this silent place. Finn put his head on my knee, and when I pulled myself together, I felt marginally better.

While I ate I tried to watch something on my laptop. But of course, there was no Wi-Fi. I had internet on my phone but it kept buffering so I gave up. I wondered if the walls were too thick; the windowsill was at least two feet deep. I'd need to sort that out before I went back to work in a few weeks.

Instead, I dug into the bottom of my bag and took out my notebook. Something else Olivia had been wrong about. It was Rory who had given me the courage to write, who had encouraged me to enter competitions, to submit to journals. But apart from that one success, all I'd had was rejection. He said he knew how that felt. For him it was work, so he had no choice but to keep submitting. But for me it was just a hobby. And if something was hurting you, it was better to just stop. I'd given him some pieces to read, and while he said they were good, I could tell he was only being kind. So now I did it in secret, hiding my writing from him because I knew he would only worry.

By ten o'clock, I couldn't stay awake any longer. I let Finn briefly out into the garden, before putting him back in his bed by the dying fire. He looked up at me doubtfully, and I rubbed his head. 'I know just how you feel, boy.'

I washed in cold water in the bathroom. There was an electric shower, but I couldn't face it tonight, if it even worked.

In the bedroom, I closed the little curtains, shutting out the world. Then I opened my bag and took out a small bottle of Rory's Safari aftershave, one of his few belongings I hadn't put into storage. I sprayed a tiny bit on the pillow, then climbed into bed and turned out the light. As I snuggled down, inhaling his scent, I imagined myself curling up behind him, feeling his heat as we spooned; the ripple of muscle on his shoulder, the mole on his neck just below his hairline and the way he held a pillow to protect his back. Every time we fell asleep together, I thought about how devastated I was when he was distant and cold before the affair, how worthless I'd felt at the time. And how grateful I was that he was back. Now I pleaded for that to happen again.

It was so quiet here; no traffic, no noise of any kind. On the threshold of drifting off, it occurred to me that the house was holding its breath until I fell asleep.

Ouch. I woke with a start. My head lolled forward onto my chest and I lifted it with difficulty; I had a painful crick in my neck and my left arm was completely dead. As I came to, I realised it wasn't just my arm, but my shoulders, legs, feet; everything was numb. I was freezing. My first thought was that the duvet must have slipped down. But when I reached for it, it wasn't there. Had I kicked it off the bed?

I peeled open my eyelids, rubbing them with a hand that was so cold I could barely feel it. A dim grey beam seeped in through the window, a small square of light falling on the stone flags. Too silvery to be sunshine. Moonlight. It was still night-time.

For one panicky moment I couldn't work out where I was. Images filtered through the fog of my brain, and I remembered I was in the cottage. But why hadn't I closed the curtains in my bedroom? And then it hit me – I wasn't in bed. I was sitting upright in a chair. As my eyes adjusted to the gloom, I figured out where I was – it was the small room off the living room, the really chilly one, and I was wearing thin pyjamas with bare feet, just as I had been when I fell asleep. I rubbed my arms to get some feeling back into them.

How had I got here? Had I been sleepwalking? There was a time, after Rory's affair, when I'd find myself on the balcony of our apartment in the middle of the night with no idea how I'd got there. It was frightening and unnerving, but Rory had been kind, regretful of the hurt he'd caused. Was it possible I was doing it again?

A scratching at the door followed by a whine made me freeze, every cell on high alert. Something or someone was trying to get in. But then the whine was followed by a piteous whimper, and I breathed out in relief. Of course. Finn was in the living room. As he clawed anxiously at the door, I stood up, my limbs stiff from sleeping in the chair. How long had I been here? I wondered.

When I turned the knob and tried to open the door, I discovered it was stuck. I felt a flash of panic, my heart beating so fast I could hardly breathe. Confined spaces terrified me. It was why I never used lifts. I told myself to stay calm, and tried again, managing to open it with one sharp tug. Finn stood on the threshold, rigid as a statue, eyes alarmed, ears flattened against his head. He let out a low throaty growl but stayed on the other side just as he had the day before.

When I stepped into the living room, he leaped up, planting

his paws on my shoulders, before circling and rubbing his chin against my pyjama legs, his whole body shivering. I hugged him tight. It reminded me of the first time he'd seen Rory swim in the sea, following him in then turning back, panicking completely when he submerged his head. When Rory reappeared, it was as if he had returned from the dead.

I closed the door behind me, tempted to lock it, but when I searched for a key, there was none. The living room, while not exactly toasty, had at least retained some heat from last night's fire, but I decided to drag Finn's bed into the bedroom. He followed me and slumped down into it with a sigh.

My own was cold when I climbed back in, the duvet icy against my skin, making me think that I must have been gone for some time. I made a mental note to put an electric blanket or hot-water bottle on my shopping list.

As I tried to sleep, I noticed again the absolute silence, a thing that didn't exist in Dublin. There was always some distant traffic or noise emanating from other apartments. I hadn't realised how comforting the sounds of life could be. The quiet suddenly seemed ominous, although I'd liked it a few hours before. How could something appear benign one minute and malignant the next?

CHAPTER TWELVE

When I woke in the morning, I was relieved to be in the same room in which I'd fallen asleep, grateful for the sound of Finn snoring softly beside me. Light bled through the curtains, and I got up to open them, surprised at how little difference it made until I realised that it was raining; daylight barely penetrated through, condensation on the windows making the world outside appear smeared and insubstantial.

I climbed back into bed and pulled the duvet over my shoulders, feeling heavy and tired as I watched dust motes float in the dim light, amazed that I'd slept at all after that strange interlude in the middle of the night. Listening to the rain hammering on the roof, the moaning rise and fall of the wind and the birds making a racket in the eaves, I imagined how Rory would feel waking up here, his dream become reality, and wished again that he were beside me. Refusing to allow self-pity to take hold, I forced myself to make plans, the first of which was to give the place a good clean.

A tractor roaring by on the lane confirmed that the silence of the night before was truly over. So when Finn stretched and yawned in his bed, I hauled myself out of mine, briefly rubbing his head before pulling on a dressing gown and woolly socks. The bed was warm, but there was a chill in the air; nothing compared to the icy stillness of the room in which I'd woken in the night, but still cold. Sam and Aoife were right – the house needed more heating than the fire would provide, especially as winter approached.

The bathroom smelled of mould, cold and damp exhaling through the cracks like breath, but it seemed clean enough. Blearily I turned on the hot tap, then pulled my hand back, yelping. The water was scalding. How had that happened? Was there an immersion I wasn't aware of? When I went looking, I found a water heater. With a hand that was pink and throbbing, I turned it off, wondering who on earth had switched it on.

In the kitchen, I made some tea, craving a coffee but discovering that I didn't have any, having brought only the minimum of provisions. Feeling suddenly overwhelmed, I sank onto a chair. What on earth had made me think I could do this? I'd never lived on my own, never even lived out of the city.

But then Finn nudged my knee and trotted towards the door, sniffing urgently at the gap underneath. I needed to take him out. I gulped down my tea, ran to the bedroom to get dressed, then grabbed a rucksack belonging to Rory from the pile of bags on the floor.

Intending to walk to the village and buy some groceries, I opened the door. Finn shot out of it like a bullet from a gun and I stepped out after him, feeling as if I was emerging from a cave. It had stopped raining, and the air had that after-rain freshness, sweeter than the city and a relief after the claustrophobic smokiness of the cottage.

A feeling of being watched drew my gaze upwards to a row of ravens perched silently on the wire, just like the day before. It made me think of the Hitchcock film *The Birds*. Very little scared Rory, and clearly he filmed birds, but that movie had freaked him out completely. Andrew had made him watch it when he was small, forcing him to keep his eyes open when he'd wanted to hide behind the couch. A loud cawing followed by a rustling of wings heralded a mass exodus, and I watched fascinated as they flew off, becoming nothing more than a scattering of black specks across the sky.

Google Maps on my phone gave directions to the village of Rath, confirming what I vaguely remembered from the journey down. End of the lane, turn right, then about half a kilometre more. Although the cottage felt much more remote than that.

I pulled the two half-doors after me, attached Finn's lead and started down the lane, which was still mucky from the earlier rain, striding determinedly along in what I soon realised was very unsuitable footwear – my blue Converse runners. The rutted track twisted and turned, allowing a brief tantalising view of the mountains before curving away again just as quickly. Rough scrub grass marked the centre, and there was just enough width for a car to pass. Or tractor, I thought, remembering the rumbling outside my window this morning.

Brambles on either side held the end of the blackberry season, the fruit shrivelled and dying on the hedges. They were punctuated by broken stone walls topped with a combination of barbed wire and electric fencing that buzzed like an approaching bee in summer, and the scent of moss and bracken filled the air. Finn was having a ball, sniffing a myriad of new smells and cocking his leg with aplomb; I couldn't help but notice he was considerably happier outside the cottage than in. I stepped to one side to avoid a cowpat, and a horse loomed abruptly over the hedge, making me yelp in fright. I imagined Rory laughing as he called me a city girl.

Past the bungalow and the abandoned farmhouse, our only neighbours, we came across the ruin of an old chapel, with a graveyard alongside. It was derelict and crumbling; in places little more than rubble, with lichen-covered sunken gravestones.

Birds – ravens too, I thought, since they looked similar to the ones at the cottage – were startled by our presence and rose up in a cloud, wings flapping, as we passed.

Other than the birds, the horse and a few distant cattle in a field, we didn't meet a single soul. It was a profound rural quiet that I'd never experienced before. Sixty miles from Dublin didn't seem much, but if you didn't drive, it was a lot. I had the sense of having passed through a major crossroads in my life, the route I was on chosen by someone else.

Eventually we reached the main road, greasy after the recent rain, with no footpath and quite a bit of traffic. So I was glad when eventually a sign appeared saying *Welcome to Rath. Please drive slowly through our village.*

We attracted some curious glances, Finn and I, as we walked along the narrow main street. 'Strangers in town,' Rory would have said with a Western twang. I kept hearing his voice in my head, narrating everything I did.

The street was no more than five hundred yards long, with a supermarket, pub and café, the end of the village marked by a petrol station behind which the mountains appeared closer than they did from the cottage. A church with a modern graveyard made me wonder if it had replaced the ruined one down my lane. Though I had no religious belief, I was tempted to step briefly into its cool quiet; I'd always found churches to be calming. But Finn pulled on the lead, anxious to move ahead, before coming to a sudden halt on discovering an interesting scent at a bin.

While I waited for him to investigate, a voice called out to us from across the road.

'Handsome dog.' A tall woman with curly hair threaded with grey, tied up in an orange and black scarf, stood in the doorway of the café, gripping a glazed blue pottery mug.

I smiled. 'Thanks. It's a bit like taking a nose for a walk sometimes.'

The woman laughed, causing her nose stud to glint. Then she waved her mug towards a battered wooden door behind the bin. 'There a cat lives in that house. That's probably what's sparking his interest. Though I wouldn't advise taking on that moggy. She's a tyrant!'

'Noted.' My eyes moved to the café. It was pretty, with a red door and a carved wooden bench outside surrounded by flowerpots. Finn finally raised his head, and I took the opportunity to lead him across the road. 'Is this your place? It's lovely.'

The woman nodded. I saw that she was wearing an apron that said *Feck it. Sure it's grand!* 'Thanks. Though it's hanging on by a thread after the few years we've had. I don't know how much longer I'll be open.'

'Can I come in and have a coffee? Or I can stay out here, if you want, with the dog.'

'Ah, I wouldn't leave you outside today. It's freezing.'

The café was cheerfully furnished with tables of roughly hewn wood and unmatched bookcases, and there was a small counter with pastries and sandwiches. Leafy green walls were dotted with paintings of mountains that I assumed to be the Slieve Blooms, and jam jars filled with wild flowers were distributed about the room. Despite the obvious care, it was completely empty. Not a single customer.

The woman rolled her eyes. 'I know. Hopping.' She put her empty mug on the counter. 'What'll you have?'

'Just a coffee, please. White.'

'Fancy a scone with it?' She gestured to a plate under a plastic cover. 'I have blackberry or cheese and basil?'

A rumbling in my stomach reminded me that I hadn't had any breakfast, and that dinner the night before had consisted of tea and toast. 'Blackberry, please.'

'Great. It's on the house. I baked too many and I don't want to have to throw them out. Have a seat. If you can find somewhere.' She grinned. 'And I'll get some water for Finn.'

'How do you know his name?' I asked, surprised.

She winked. 'It's on his collar. I'm Maggie, by the way.'

'Allie.'

Maggie bowed. 'Good to meet you, Allie and Finn.'

While Maggie busied herself with the coffee machine, I chose a seat at the window. Finn stretched out by my feet, providing the perfect obstacle for anyone wishing to get in or out. The long-bodied greyhound would have made a great draught excluder, but more often than not he was an accident waiting to happen.

There was a small paperback on my table, and I began to leaf through it; it was a selection of walks in the Slieve Blooms.

Maggie called out to me over the hiss of the milk frother. 'I think the blackberries in your scone came from up your lane. I freeze them. You've just bought Raven Cottage, haven't you?'

I looked up, astounded. 'How did you know that?'

She tapped her nose. 'Small village. You were clocked arriving last night.' She paused to stir the hot milk, brushing a stray hair from her eyes; it was more than the scarf could manage to contain the curls. 'My great-great-grandmother lived in that house.'

'Really?'

I wanted to know more, but before I could ask, she said, 'You know, I've just thought of something. Bran was one of Fionn mac Cumhaill's hounds. Bran means raven, and you're at Raven Cottage with this lovely hound called Finn.' She grinned and made a ta-da gesture with her hands.

I laughed. Fionn mac Cumhaill was a legendary Irish hero and leader of a band of warriors called the Fianna. 'You know your history.'

'Ah well, it's mythology really. And Fionn mac Cumhaill did come from Laois: Ballyfin. Or so we claim.' She emerged from behind the counter with my coffee and scone. 'I met your partner when he was down, by the way. Making some kind of a documentary, wasn't he?'

That ever-present undertow of grief must have shown on my face, because Maggie's hand flew to her mouth. 'Oh no. I've said the wrong thing. Don't tell me you've split up?'

I shook my head, swallowing back tears.

Her eyes widened. 'Oh Lord. He's not . . . is he?'

I sort of shrugged, thinking how strange it must appear that I didn't know. Then I tried to explain, making it worse, stumbling over my words.

Maggie's face crumpled. 'That's awful. I never heard.'

'You mustn't be on Facebook or Twitter. It's all over social media.'

'Not my thing. All that baring your soul to the world. Feels like offering yourself up to be slaughtered.' She sank down on the other chair at my table. 'You poor thing. You're a brave one moving down here by yourself. It's a lonely enough spot, Raven Cottage.'

I told her what had happened with the apartment, and she listened, shaking her head in sympathy. A skin formed on my untouched coffee while I talked, and she spotted it, offering to get me another. When she returned, she had a couple of cold sausages for Finn, which he took with relish.

'You'll have a friend for life now.' I smiled, my voice wavering as I added, 'He misses Rory.'

'I can't imagine how hard it must be not knowing what's happened to him.' When Maggie reached out for my hand, I saw that there was a tattoo on her wrist that was partially covered by her sleeve. 'All you can do is take care of yourself and your sanity.'

If going to sleep in one room and waking up in another was a measure of sanity, that ship might have sailed, I thought.

The door opened and a man with a tanned face came in, wearing jeans and a fleece. Maggie withdrew her hand and stood up quickly, brushing invisible crumbs from her apron. 'Morning, Pieter.'

He gave her a friendly smile. 'Black coffee to take away, please, Maggie.'

'Right you are.'

He came over to pet Finn. 'Morning, fella. You're making short work of those sausages.' He had an accent I couldn't place – Dutch or Belgian, maybe? – and ice-blue eyes. 'He's an old-timer, I'd say, is he?'

'We think he's about eight.' *We.* When was I going to stop saying that? Would I need to?

Maggie called the man over for his coffee, and they chatted at the counter while I went back to flicking through the book. A coffee-stained leaflet for a local walking club from a couple of years ago was being used as a bookmark.

When we were alone again, I waved it at Maggie. 'Do these still happen?'

She crossed her arms. 'In a smaller way than they used to. There's a few of us who still walk on a Sunday. Pieter is one. As a matter of fact, we're going tomorrow, up to Glenbarrow. Do you fancy it? You could bring Finn.'

My first response to any invitation without Rory tended to be 'no' – I'm sure Olivia would say that was Rory's fault – but it hit me that if I cut myself off in a place like this, I might speak to no one for the next six months. So instead, I said, 'That would be great. Thank you.'

'I'm guessing you don't have a car.' Maggie nodded towards the rucksack, which Finn was now using as a pillow. I shook my head. 'It's going to be awkward living here without one. It's not like the city, where you can get a bus or a DART wherever you want to go.'

'I thought there was a bus service?'

'There's one goes into Portlaoise, but that's only twice a day.' She frowned. 'Don't you drive?'

I flushed, not wanting to admit that I didn't. 'Rory had our car with him.' Lowering my gaze at the half-lie.

Maggie's eyes creased in sympathy. 'Don't worry. We'll help you sort something out. In the meantime, I'll call for you at the end of your lane at eleven. Bring a snack and some water. We'll be out for a few hours.'

Taken aback by this unexpected kindness from someone I'd only just met, I bought three more scones to take away, before leaving to go to the supermarket. As I unhooked Finn's lead from the chair, Maggie told me to ask for the farm eggs they kept under the counter.

'Why under the counter?'

She sucked air through her teeth and see-sawed her hand. 'It's not strictly legal to sell them. Which is why they won't tell you about them – you have to ask.'

In the little supermarket, I gathered essentials: coffee, bread, pasta, tins of tomatoes. Milk. A bottle of Chilean white. And, remembering my resolve, cleaning products.

At the counter, which was spread with Saturday and local newspapers, I plucked up the courage to ask for the eggs. The shopkeeper, a surly-looking man in his sixties, handed them to me without a second glance, giving me the confidence to attempt some small talk.

'I might think about getting some hens of my own. There's a henhouse where I am, just waiting for occupants.'

He grunted, without interest. 'Eighteen euros fifty-eight

cents.' Though he hadn't said a word while I mooched around the shelves with Finn, he looked down at him now with disdain. 'No dogs allowed.'

I reddened. 'Oh, sorry, I'll know next time.'

I had another go at conversation as I tapped my card and packed the groceries into the rucksack. 'I've moved into Raven Cottage.' There was no response. Rory was always telling me to speak louder, so I added, 'The one up the lane?'

The shopkeeper didn't look up from the till. 'I know where it is.'

I dropped my head, embarrassed, only for my gaze to land on a headline in the *Mirror*: *A family's appeal. TV producer missing for three weeks.*

CHAPTER THIRTEEN

Suzanne

'Do you want to grab some food?' Suzanne asked Dave on Saturday afternoon, as they drove past Cherry Orchard Hospital on their way up the Ballyfermot Road. They were on their way back from a shoplifting call at Penneys in the Liffey Valley Shopping Centre, so lunch was late. 'We could take it back to the station.'

'Chipper?' he suggested, with disappointing predictability.

Suzanne groaned. 'We've been there three times this week already. What about Koffee + Kale – it's coming up just here on your left.'

The traffic slowed almost to a halt; the lights were red and weekend shopping was at its zenith.

Dave lowered the driver's window. 'How's himself?' he bellowed to a grey-bearded man on the footpath pushing a pram occupied by an ancient-looking terrier.

The man turned to give him a rather toothless grin. 'Ah, sure, he's the right side of the maggots! Like meself.'

Once they'd exchanged affectionate insults, Dave pulled his head back in and made a face at Suzanne. 'Kale? Isn't that cattle food?'

'It's green,' Suzanne said. 'You like green. You eat watercress, I've seen it between your teeth often enough.'

'That's because I like eggs. They seem to come together. And I can't be arsed to pull the little feckers out.'

Suzanne rolled her eyes. 'They've got other things besides kale.' Adding, in a stage whisper, 'They do eggs.'

Dave cursed loudly at a white van that cut across in front of him. 'Yeah, all right.' They reached a black railing that ran along the top of a low wall, fronting a couple of retail outlets. 'This it here?'

She nodded, eyes widening in surprise at how quickly she'd won this battle.

Dave pulled in and parked in the last remaining spot. 'Jaysus, Sue. You didn't tell me it was beside the undertaker's.'

She grinned.

'Fine.' He sighed. 'You go in, though. Choose something for me. I wouldn't know what to order.'

She unclipped her seat belt, afraid to hang about in case he changed his mind.

In her haste, she'd left her phone behind on the passenger seat, and when she came back out ten minutes later laden down with bags of food, Dave was on it. On *her* phone.

She glared furiously at him as she got back in, and he mouthed, 'Calm down. It's the station.'

She waggled her hand at him to pass it over, but he just said goodbye and hung up. And when she reached for it, he held it above her head, taunting her with it like some playground bully.

'Oh, for fuck's sake,' she muttered.

'Grouchy,' he said, handing it to her. 'Time of the month again?'

'Christ, Dave, if you're going to be misogynistic, at least think of something more original to say.' She handed him his takeaway bag containing coffee and a breakfast baguette, and examined her phone. 'What did they want?'

'I'm not going to tell you if you're going to be mean to me.' Dave adopted a Shirley Temple lisp that really was exceptionally creepy.

Suzanne glared at him, and he relented. 'All right.' He opened the bag and sniffed it. Seeming satisfied, he said, 'It was Paddy. Our missing telly producer's little girlfriend has moved to the sticks. The brother just rang to tell tales on her.'

'What? Where?'

'Somewhere in the Midlands. Laois, I think.' He shook his head. 'It's an old cottage that she and Davey Attenborough were buying together as a holiday house.'

'Stop calling him that,' Suzanne said automatically. 'When?'

'Yesterday, apparently.' He pulled out onto the main road for the drive back to the station. 'Who the hell moves to Laois?'

'Says the man from Longford.' Suzanne struggled to absorb what Dave had just told her. She'd tried to call Allie a couple of times in the past ten days, leaving messages of support, but never heard anything back. 'Whatever about that, who moves house when their partner has gone missing? Isn't that a little odd?'

'She *is* odd. I keep telling you. If it wasn't an apartment they lived in, I'd say she had him buried in the garden.'

Suzanne ignored this. 'But he's been gone what? Three weeks?' She scratched her head. 'Don't people usually stay put when someone close to them goes missing? Parents refuse to move for decades when their child disappears, afraid they won't be able to find them if they move house. They put their lives on hold, hoping the kid will come back.'

'Yep.' Dave rummaged one-handed in the bag of food on his knee and pulled out a piece of bacon, which he rammed into his mouth.

'I know this isn't a missing child, but still . . .' Suzanne gazed out the window, unseeing. 'What on earth has happened to him?

He hasn't touched his bank account since he disappeared. No Twitter or Facebook, and he was a regular poster before that.'

Dave kept chewing.

'I think he's going to turn up dead,' she said flatly. 'It's the only thing that makes sense.'

'So you agree with me then? She's done him in?'

'No, of course I don't,' she snapped. 'I think it must be suicide. But what? She can't stay around for long enough to find out?' Suzanne tried to imagine herself doing the same thing, moving away out of the city with Tony missing only a few weeks, and couldn't.

'I keep telling you—' Dave said.

'I know. I know. She's odd.'

'The whole thing is odd.' He raised his eyebrows and gave her a side-glance. 'Including the fact that you're so interested in it.'

Suzanne was beginning to agree with the first part of that statement. She found to her surprise that she now couldn't decide if Allie Garvey needed protecting or watching. If it was the latter, then it was going to be considerably more difficult with her living in a cottage in the middle of nowhere. Was it possible that was why she'd moved?

Suzanne resolved to call her again after the weekend.

CHAPTER FOURTEEN

Allie

The straps of the rucksack were chafing painfully against my shoulders by the time I reached the end of the lane, weighed down with the shopping. The sky had darkened to a leaden grey and I'd forgotten to turn off the lights, so the cottage looked almost cosy in the gloom, with its three yellow squares for windows. Finn didn't agree. About ten feet from the door, he planted his paws and refused to move, gazing up at me with those liquid brown eyes, as if to say, 'Do we really live here now?'

I wasn't surprised he hadn't yet relaxed into this new place, refusing even to explore the garden, which Rory had thought would be such a draw to him. Finn disliked change even more than I did. After his failed racing career, he'd been dumped in the Dublin mountains before Dogs Trust had taken him in, and was constantly convinced that it was going to happen again. When Rory went away to film, Finn trailed around the apartment after him while he packed, terrified of being left behind. It was no wonder he was struggling now. But a tug on his lead and he relented, following me to the front door, tail drooping.

I peeled the rucksack off my back to root for the keys, unlocked the door and pushed it open. I was immediately hit with that same damp smoky smell I'd got the day before, strengthening my resolve to clean and air the place properly. If I was going to spend six months here, I might as well make it comfortable. Plus, I needed to finish unpacking; that little island of bags and boxes on the living room floor had become a roundabout for Finn.

I turned off the lights, then set about unloading the shopping. Whoever had cleared out the house for the sale had taken a very loose view of what that meant. Old newspapers lined the drawers, countertops had sticky surfaces and there was a generally stale, grubby atmosphere about the place. Half a bottle of washing-up liquid lurked under the sink, along with a packet of Brillo pads and a can of Pledge. In the cabinet above the sink a jar of coffee hid down the back, the grains completely solidified into a chocolatey-looking lump. I resolved to start my cleaning frenzy in here. I couldn't eat from somewhere that wasn't clean.

I began by scrubbing everything down, cleaning out the cupboards and washing the countertops and floors. It took less time than I'd thought. The room was only marginally bigger than the galley kitchen in the apartment – not even wide enough for a table and chairs.

When I was done, I fetched the cardboard box with the kitchen things I'd brought from the apartment. I found black scissors in one of the drawers, which I used to slice through the tape to open the flap. Then a movement in the corner of the room caught my eye. A vague form, a disturbance of light, followed by a scrabbling noise. I made my way over, cautiously peering around the fridge, fully expecting to see a mouse.

It was a small crow. Or if Sam was correct, a raven, with a strange white marking on its shoulder. It twitched, eyes fixed on me, totally calm. Why wasn't it battering its wings against the window, I wondered, desperate to get out? No sooner had the thought crossed my mind than it flew at me. Finn came running into the kitchen as I threw up my hands to shield my head, ducking the flapping blackness. The bird threw itself against the window frame over the sink in panic, a mass of shit and feathers.

Heart pounding, I reached for the catch and pushed the window fully open, allowing the bird to escape. As I closed it again, breathing heavily, I glanced around me, confused. How had he got in? I'd left the lights on, but I was sure I hadn't left a window or door open. How long had he been there? I hadn't noticed him when putting away the shopping or cleaning. Unable to answer either question, I cleaned up the mess, then dragged Finn's bed from the bedroom to the living room. While he settled himself into it with a sigh, I picked up my cases and took them back into the bedroom to unpack my clothes, hanging things in the old wardrobe and filling the drawers of the dressing table. I thought about Maggie, the woman in the café, and how easy I'd found her to chat to. How it had given me the confidence to try the same with the shopkeeper and how dismally I'd failed. Rory said I had no idea how to read a room, that I tended to say the wrong thing to the wrong person. Maybe he was right.

I was folding jeans and putting them in a drawer when my phone buzzed with a text from Olivia. *Have you seen this?* A photograph of the headline I'd seen in the supermarket was attached. Olivia didn't read the *Mirror*, so I assumed that someone had sent it to her. I put the phone down without replying. We'd make up eventually, we always did, but I wasn't ready yet.

Back in the living room, I realised that in order to clean it properly, I'd need to move some of the furniture into the small room. Reluctantly after my experience the night before, I stepped inside it, taking care this time to wedge the door open with a folded piece of cardboard.

I stood in the still grey light, filled with strangely conflicting feelings. The damp chill should have driven me out, but I also had the strongest urge to stay; it was as if grief and sadness were pulling me in and repelling me at the same time. I knew that must be all in my head, but I wasn't imagining the cold; the room was way colder than the rest of the house.

I carried Finn's bed in there first. He refused to go with it, choosing instead to flop down onto the stone flags in the spot in the living room where his bed had been. I couldn't blame him. Not only was the air in the room frigid, but there was a strangely bitter smell in there, like hand-rolled cigarettes, which disappeared when I chased it. I wondered if it came from the floor, since this was the only room that was carpeted. If I removed the carpet, would the smell go?

When as much of the furniture as I could fit was in, I closed the door and set to work washing the stone flags, having found a surprisingly clean mop in the kitchen. Then I scrubbed the area around the fireplace and cleaned the windows. Sitting back to admire my work, I saw that the walls needed some attention too; there were unpleasant brown stains on the wallpaper and the paint was blistered in places. Maybe I should strip them. I had a few weeks left before going back to work, and staying busy helped my head. The loneliness and isolation I'd felt in Dublin had lost some of its sharpness here.

By the time I'd put all the furniture back, dusk had deepened and I decided to light the fire. Walking back from the shed in the sinking daylight, with a basket of turf in my arms, I wondered if I could also do something with the garden. It was in a terrible state: thistles and brambles choked the fruit trees, and a clothes line was barely visible in high tufted grass. Perhaps I could get someone to clear it so that Finn could at least run around.

I used empty cardboard boxes to light the fire, and then, feeling grubby after all the cleaning, I decided to have a bath. After my near scalding this morning, I at least knew there was hot water.

When I emerged half an hour later, pink and tingling, the cottage windows had grown dark. I cooked some pasta and opened the bottle of wine, sitting by the dim lamp on the living room table to eat. A sudden draught from the small room made me shudder so I fetched one of the old mats from the shed and bunched it up underneath the door.

When I'd finished eating, I took a second glass of wine to the fire, where Finn lay curled up in his bed, whimpering in his dreams, paws twitching. I wondered if he dreamed of Rory like I did. There was a creak in the eaves as I sat in the armchair, as if the old house was settling down for the night too.

An abrupt whirring noise gave me the strangest sense of having company, until I realised it must be the fridge. But as the turf crackled in the grate and the flames cast flickering shadows on the walls, I was suddenly conscious of all the generations who had lived and died here in this cottage, years and decades and centuries of people, their spirits absorbed into its fabric. Maggie's great-great-grandmother, for instance. All old houses must be like this, I thought, with their creaks and sighs, their atmosphere of past lives. This didn't feel like the happiest of places; the furniture was old and dark, the windows too small to let in much light. But somehow that didn't bother me. It was being alone that frightened me. And maybe I wouldn't feel quite so alone here.

Comforted by that thought, I took out my notebook and started to write. I'd been tinkering with a piece of flash fiction and I worked on it a little now. After a while, I looked up and noticed a small door to the right, high above the fireplace, which I presumed must be a cupboard, or a hot press. With its proximity to the fire, it would be a good place to keep linens warm and dry in times past.

At ten o'clock, I let Finn out for the last time, standing on the back step as I watched him sniff about. How completely dark it was here, I thought, nothing but a few stars. I remembered going to the Gaeltacht in Kerry to learn Irish as a teenager and experiencing true pitch black for the first time in my life. I was brave then, before my parents died. Didn't it get dark in Dublin? the rural kids had asked. I'd explained that we had street lamps; that there was always some sliver of man-made light bleeding in through the curtains.

A rustling overhead made me step out into the garden, and I saw that the ravens were back; a row of them perched on the roof of the house. I felt goosebumps, the fine hair on my arms standing up straight, only partially from the cold. Was my little visitor there? I wondered.

As I watched, they fell silent, as if they had all fallen into a deep sleep. I bowed my head and went back inside, calling for Finn to follow.

CHAPTER FIFTEEN

Tap-tap-tap. From far away a sound penetrated. I resisted its call, sliding back into unconsciousness, sleep reaching up from the dark to pull me down. It came again. *Tap-tap-tap.* I batted my eyelids open and saw that it was raining outside, wind rattling the windows just like the morning before. Was that what I'd heard? The room was cold. I pulled the duvet over my shoulders, heart sinking at the thought of the walk I'd agreed to go on today. Finn was still asleep in his bed on the floor, undisturbed.

Tap-tap-tap. The noise came again, and I strained to identify it. The back door? It didn't sound like it, but then I already knew the house had odd acoustics. During the night, I'd heard sounds that I couldn't place, rustles in the eaves that I assumed must be the ravens on the roof.

This time Finn awoke, got out of his bed and went to the door, coat bristling, nose moving along the frame. I climbed out of bed too, pulled on slippers and a dressing gown and made my way to the back door with the dog in my wake. Opening it, I saw a figure walking away, a man hunched against the rain. I called after him, but he didn't hear me, and I wasn't about to go chasing after some stranger in my night clothes.

I closed the door, confused when I heard the noise again.

Finn dived into the living room, and I followed him as he padded straight to the small room, growling when he reached the door, body rigid, head cocked, listening.

I held my breath. He was right. The sound was coming from inside that room. Heart beating uncomfortably fast, I twisted the knob and opened the door. A bird flew out. Finn backed away as it circled the room, wings brushing the walls and windows. I stepped quickly towards the front door and flung the top half open. As the raven flew out, I noticed a strange white marking on its shoulder. How weird was that? The same bird as yesterday. How on earth had it got in? Again I knew I hadn't left anything open. Was there a hole in the wall somewhere that I hadn't noticed?

Closing the door, I stepped backwards and nearly fell over Finn. I put my hand out to reassure him and he leaned against me, just as he used to with Rory. The memory brought a burst of loneliness that almost knocked me off my feet a second time.

The day before had been manageable; I'd stayed busy and made myself so physically tired that I'd slept well. But this morning, time seemed to stretch endlessly ahead with no resolution. No Rory. How had my world tilted so much in such a short time? A month ago, I'd been living in Dublin with my boyfriend. Now I was alone, outside a tiny village in the Slieve Bloom mountains, in this strange limbo. What if this new life wasn't temporary?

And what if it was all my fault? Every time I thought about the night Rory left, I was filled with dread. Anxiety lied to me, fragmenting, splicing and altering my perception of reality. As much as I tried, I couldn't piece together the memories of that last row. All I remembered was Rory finally driving away, angry, leaving me alone in the underground car park. He'd called and texted me after that, though, so he must have forgiven me. Mustn't he?

Finn nudged my side, and as I dropped a kiss on his head, it hit me that the house was really cold. While the fire provided enough warmth in the evening, the place was freezing during the day, and I couldn't always keep warm by cleaning. I'd soon be working again, sitting still at a laptop. And the weather was only going to get worse.

The flags drained the warmth from my slippers as I made my way back into the kitchen, so I pulled on some boots before letting Finn out the back, relieved to see the rain had cleared.

While he mooched about, I made coffee, following him into the garden with my mug, exploring it properly for the first time. I imagined it was probably an acre, though terribly overgrown; fruit trees gnarled and pollarded, and what might have been a herb patch badly overrun with weeds. It was amazing how Rory had been able to make me see it all so differently.

Still, I liked the notion of restoring a garden that had once been loved.

Finn and I left the house to meet Maggie, watched by the ravens from their perches above. A tractor trundled by us on the lane with a red-faced man at the wheel. He gave me a desultory wave, and I wondered if he was my neighbour who lived in the bungalow, if it was he who owned the farming land on either side of the cottage. And if it was he who had been at my back door early this morning. If so, why didn't he stop to speak to me now?

It occurred to me that Rory would already have introduced himself. It was the kind of thing he relished, calling to someone's door to announce his arrival, offering immediate friendship, assuming immediate friendship. I was the opposite. More often than not I preferred people not to know I was there.

At the junction with the main road, a battered brown Audi pulled up, and Maggie stuck her head out, elbow resting on the window frame. 'You can put Finn in the back. He'll be comfy enough there.'

I pulled open a door with loudly creaking hinges and Finn leaped in happily, settling himself down on an old red blanket laid out on the back seat, while I climbed into the passenger seat.

Maggie drove off, seemingly unconcerned either by the loud rattling noise emanating from the engine, or by my unsuccessful yanking at the seat belt before giving up. 'So, how are you settling in?'

'Okay.' I sat with my hands in my lap, swaying from side to side, feeling unmoored without the steadying effect of the belt, suppressing the fear I always felt in any kind of moving vehicle. 'I need to do something about the heating, though.'

Maggie's eyebrows rose. 'Oh, of course. That house must be freezing. It only has the fire.' She paused to think. 'I have an ancient electric yoke I can drop around to you if you like. It's pretty awkward and it's no beauty, but it throws out great heat.'

Realising that I hadn't actually thawed out since throwing off the duvet that morning, I breathed out in relief. 'Thank you.'

We drove for a couple of miles, taking a lesser road past Coillte plantations before turning down a lane signposted Glenbarrow. It led to a small car park, where a few other cars were already parked. A group of people in walking gear stood about chatting under a tree.

Finn trotted over to make friends while I held back, feeling a quiver of social anxiety without Rory by my side. When we were together, people's eyes generally passed over me to rest on him. If I was introduced to someone, they said how nice it was to meet me, asked politely what I did, then turned away; on meeting me a second time, they said how nice it was to meet me before turning away again. I was a file that was automatically deleted. I didn't have a problem with that; I was content to dip beneath the radar.

So I was glad I'd come with Maggie and didn't have to face this on my own. Pieter gave me a friendly smile, but a couple called

Jim and Cathy, wearing expensive-looking jackets and hiking boots and carrying walking poles, caused me to glance worriedly down at my runners.

We set off along a path leading to a densely wooded river valley. Rushing water echoed through trees that still dripped from the earlier rain as we followed a needle- and cone-strewn track meandering through forestry. Though wet underfoot, the carpet of mulch permitted my runners to do the job reasonably enough. Finn trotted eagerly ahead, tail up, stopping every so often to burrow his nose in a ditch or chase some imaginary prey. It was good to have him off the lead, and I thought how different his mood was outside the cottage.

Everything appeared damp and shiny, the cold air flavoured with mint. Drops of rain remained on the leaves, and everything felt cleansed and fresh. Though it was November, there was still a lot of green around: grass, ferns and lichen, and moss that was emerald and spongy underfoot. Even the brambles that trailed along the route displayed only the odd splash of ruby red.

I watched a single leaf fall spinning to the ground, and I realised it was exactly how I'd felt in the past few weeks: plummeting to the earth with no one to catch me, and nothing to grab onto on the way down. Today as I breathed in fresh air, to the rushing sound of the river and in the company of people I barely knew, I felt a little better. The ground more solid beneath my feet.

CHAPTER SIXTEEN

I stayed close to Maggie at first, but discovered there was competition for her company; the others stopped her continuously to ask questions, deferring to her on plants and fungi. Red toadstools with white spots, straight out of a fairy tale, were fly agaric, I learned.

In the gloom of the woods, I found myself falling into step with Pieter. For a little while neither of us spoke. It seemed I'd met someone who was as quiet as I was.

'Glad you came?' he asked eventually, flicking aside a branch on the ground with his stick.

'On the walk or moving here?'

'I meant on the walk. But I suppose moving here too. Although I imagine you haven't been here long enough to know the answer to that yet.' He looked down, stepping over a knot of exposed tree roots. The route required vigilance, particularly for someone like me, accustomed to city parks with smooth paths. 'Maggie told me about your husband.'

'Partner,' I said, swallowing. 'We aren't married.' I wasn't sure why I felt it necessary to clarify that, and I flushed.

But Pieter just nodded in acknowledgement. 'I'm very sorry. I can't imagine how terrible it must be waiting for news. How long has it been?'

'Three weeks. A bit more.' I took a deep breath. 'It feels wrong to be just carrying on while he's missing, but I don't know what else to do.'

'What choice do you have?' Pieter's face was kind. 'Panic ebbs eventually from pure exhaustion.'

I looked at him gratefully. That was it exactly. I was tired of feeling the way I did.

'You have to just keep going,' he said. 'Put one foot in front of the other every day.'

I looked down at our feet, his large boots and my now very mucky runners. 'His family have set up a Facebook page,' I said, wondering if this was too much information. 'They're all in Dublin. Maybe something will come of that. And the guards are involved.'

'Maybe so.' He nodded. There was a pause, and he pointed over my head. 'Your cottage is just over there. What's the expression? As the bird flies?'

I smiled, relieved at the change of subject. 'Crow. As the crow flies. I'm seeing a lot of crows, actually. Or ravens.' I told him about the bird that had got into the cottage that morning and the day before. I didn't say I thought it was the same one; that sounded a little crazy.

The man who'd been introduced to me as Jim, a sturdy middle-aged man with a square face and salt-and-pepper hair, moved closer, falling into step on the other side of Pieter. He leaned in to listen. 'Foretells a death you know, a bird in the house.'

Pieter frowned. I imagined Jim didn't know about Rory; there was no reason why he should. 'Maybe two means something different. Like with magpies: one for sorrow, two for joy...'

Jim shook his head. 'Nah. They're vermin. You need to sort them out. They're a menace. Get yourself a shotgun. That neighbour of yours, Harkin, he'll lend you one if you need it.

He'll be drilling his winter wheat now, and he won't want them stealing it.'

Maggie was listening now too, pausing in her chat with Jim's wife, Cathy. 'That's rubbish, Jim. Crows are intelligent social birds. And you're right, Allie, those are ravens at the cottage. You could try making friends with them.'

Ignoring Jim's snort, I asked, 'How do I do that?'

Maggie's eyes creased in amusement. 'A combination of feeding them and ignoring them. I'll give you some tips on what they like.'

But Jim was persistent, bullish. 'You live in Raven Cottage, don't you? Bought it from that American couple? They didn't last long.'

'I know. They went home after the pandemic.'

Jim smirked. 'Is that what you were told? Nah. That place was empty for ten years before they bought it. No local would touch it. Not even yer man Harkin, and his farm surrounds it; if he knocked it down and cleared the garden, it would be an extra couple of acres for him.'

I tripped over a tree root. Pieter caught me before I hit the ground and steadied me.

'They thought it was a laugh, of course. The Yanks,' Jim continued, unaware of the effect he was having. 'Thought the locals were a bunch of backward gobshites. They'd big plans, keeping hens, growing vegetables. Didn't do any of it. Lasted six months. The wife kept thinking there was someone in the house.' He grinned. 'She didn't mention the crows getting in, though. That's a new one.'

'Ravens,' Maggie corrected him, sharply. 'And there's nothing wrong with that house that a bit of tender loving care won't fix. I for one am very glad to see it lived in again.'

Her authoritative tone succeeded in shutting Jim up, and

when he spoke again a few minutes later, it was to grouse about a broken bootlace. But Maggie's intervention came too late for me. My mind was racing. Did Rory know about the house's reputation? That *no local would touch it*? Had he lied to me about why it was so cheap?

We walked for three hours, following the course of the river, passing a pretty waterfall and returning along the other bank, by which time it was drizzling heavily. Damp clung to my clothes and socks as we headed back to the car park, and I began to seriously regret my choice of footwear. If I was going to keep doing these walks, I'd need some proper boots.

By the time we'd said goodbye to the others, dried Finn off with an old towel Maggie found in the boot and climbed into her car, I was bone tired.

I thanked her as she pulled out of the car park.

'You're welcome. I'm glad you enjoyed it.' She paused. 'Don't mind Jim, by the way. People love a good spooky story.'

'Is it true, though? Does the cottage have a reputation?'

'I suppose it does,' she conceded. 'But that doesn't mean anything. It's old and it was empty for a while. People are superstitious. Put it out of your mind.'

Not something I was capable of doing, had ever been capable of doing. Anxiety produces a chattering mind, and mine was demanding answers. 'But what's the history of the place? *Why* does it have a reputation?'

Maggie swung the old car back onto the main road before replying. 'The woman who lived there was a sort of medium, a spiritualist.'

'Was that the great-great-grandmother you mentioned?'

She nodded. 'Houses with anything like that in their history always end up with a reputation. But that was well over a century ago. And it's called Raven Cottage, of course. That doesn't help.

Ravens are supposed to bring messages between the living and the dead.'

I gave an involuntary shiver, and she smiled. 'I imagine it's just a coincidence that there are so many ravens around the cottage. There must be a food source somewhere.'

'What happened to her? The medium?' I couldn't help myself.

Maggie sighed as if reluctant to tell me. And when she did, I understood why. 'She disappeared. One day she was there and the next she wasn't. Vanished without a trace.'

I swallowed. *Like Rory.* 'Did she live on her own?'

Maggie nodded.

'And no one knows...?' I trailed off.

'No one knows. But she was missed. All the local people went to her.' She corrected herself. 'The local women. Anyway, that's why people like Jim are convinced the cottage is haunted. But pay no attention to him. That American couple left for family reasons, but it doesn't make for such a good tale.'

I looked away, rubbing the condensation from the window with my sleeve. I so badly wanted to believe her; wanted to believe that I had not moved alone to a haunted cottage at the beginning of winter.

It was already dusk; the Audi's beams illuminated the hedges as we passed, reminding me of Rory's habit of turning off the headlights if we were driving in an unlit area at night. He did it, he said, to see how it felt. To challenge himself, live on the edge. Even though it terrified me.

Maggie braked suddenly to avoid a cat running across the road, and I reached for the dashboard, heart in my mouth. It was all I could do not to cry out.

'Are you okay?' Her concerned voice pulled me back.

I gave an embarrassed laugh, and removed my hands. 'Fine.' I checked on Finn in the back seat, ensuring that he hadn't been catapulted onto the floor, and she propelled the car forward again.

'Why did you move here?' she asked gently, and I knew she thought I was a frightened mouse. 'I know you said your apartment was leased, but...'

'It was too strange without Rory.' As I said it, I realised it was true. 'All the parts that made up our life were still there, but he wasn't. It was like a jigsaw with a missing piece.'

'Better to just paint a new picture?'

Was that what I was doing? I wondered. Painting a new picture without Rory? It wasn't what I wanted.

It was raining properly by the time Maggie pulled into the lane, so she drove right to the end and dropped me outside the cottage.

Inside, I peeled off my wet clothes and had a shower, then heated up some tinned tomato soup, which I ate off my knee by the fire. As the wind rattled the windows and gusted down the chimney, I was sharply aware that unlike the apartment, which had shelter on all sides, the cottage stood alone and unprotected.

The mat was still bunched up under the door to the small room, keeping out the draught, and I wondered suddenly if that was where the medium used to see people. If she summoned spirits there. I was surprised to discover that while I was curious, the thought didn't frighten me, and I remembered Maggie's comment about painting a new picture. Maybe here, in this quiet place, I could be someone new, someone braver than I had been before.

The fire sent out a spark that hopped over the grate, and I leaped to my feet to stamp it out, leaving the rug smouldering. Maybe I could even get used to being alone. Eliza had lived here on her own a hundred years ago. Why couldn't I?

I started. I was pretty sure Maggie hadn't told me, so how did I know her name was Eliza?

CHAPTER SEVENTEEN

Suzanne

At nine o'clock on Monday morning, Suzanne was sitting in the station, glued to her desktop, busy doing something she shouldn't be. She knew that there was a recommended policy for missing persons, a perfectly sensible system of review and supervision, and that there was no reason to consider Rory O'Riordan a high-risk case. Also that she had plenty of *actual* work to do. But she couldn't shake that disturbing sense of waiting for the other shoe to drop. That something was happening that hadn't shown itself yet, like a burglar lurking behind the curtain, Reebok Classics partially visible. She was mixing her footwear metaphors.

Since Andrew O'Riordan's phone call to the station on Saturday to let them know about Allie's house move, Suzanne hadn't been able to get the woman out of her head. And so she was fishing. She'd found out all she could about Rory, but other than the online stuff about his TV work, there was very little. She'd had a look on YouTube at *The Naked Lens*, the *X Factor*-style show that Dave had mentioned, on which Rory had been a judge, and it really was awful. Not only did the format not work (a TV show about making TV shows; whose big idea was that?), but the quality was dire, the contestants looking as if all they wanted was to be allowed to return to their darkened basements to continue tinkering with their laptops. The problem was that Rory had expressed as much on Twitter, when he'd agreed with someone who criticised the show. A mortal sin in telly land. Biting the hand that feeds.

But other than what appeared to be an oversupply of good taste, the man was squeaky clean. He had no previous convictions, not a speeding ticket, a mobile phone offence, nothing. So Suzanne had decided to take a closer look at Allie. Not because she thought there was anything in Dave's theory that she had done Rory in, but because it didn't hurt to check. There was no denying the woman was a little peculiar.

She looked up briefly as Dave himself passed on the way to his own desk in the corner, thankfully not bothering to lean over her shoulder to see what she was doing, as he often did. Nosy bastard.

A quick massage of her temples, an even quicker slug of her coffee, and she was back in. She reckoned she had about another five minutes before they had to go check out a dispute between neighbours in Palmerstown. One that had turned if not exactly violent, then certainly unpleasant. Fishing maggots through a letter box. The thought made her stomach churn.

One more screen, she told herself. She'd been trawling through garda records, searching under Allie's name, reversing back through the years. She was almost ready to give up, having taken the woman back to her early twenties. Allie was unlikely to have committed any offences when she was a child. She wasn't the type – private-school-educated, one of those South County Dublin blondes that Dave so disliked. The polar opposite of the undernourished city kids who ended up as young offenders in the cells of the children's court in Smithfield.

And then, bingo! Mention of an Allison Garvey.

Suzanne squinted at the screen. It was a road traffic accident that had occurred back in 2008. South Dublin. So possibly the same Allison Garvey. She did a quick calculation. Allie would have been young then, seventeen or eighteen at most, barely old enough to drive.

She read down through the incident report. *Shit.* The collision had been fatal. Only one vehicle involved. Two fatalities. One survivor. The driver had been Allison Garvey herself. The fatalities were her parents.

Suzanne sat back, reeling, rereading, taking it all in. She was right, Allie had been only eighteen. The car had collided with a disused railway bridge that spanned the road on the way back to Dublin from Bray. Both passengers were killed outright, while the driver was relatively unhurt. *Jesus.* How would that affect you, if you accidentally killed your parents when you were eighteen?

Because it did seem to be an accident. The garda statements indicated that it was late at night, about one o'clock in the morning. Temperatures were below zero and the roads had been treacherous, with patches of dangerous black ice. Allie was an inexperienced driver who'd only just passed her test, with no idea of how to handle a skid. She'd braked on a bend, which was entirely the wrong thing to do, something a more experienced driver would have known, losing control of the car and crashing into the bridge's base. What were the parents thinking, Suzanne wondered, allowing her to drive on a night like that?

The toxicology reports answered her question. There was no alcohol or drugs in Allie's system, but both parents had been drinking, and fairly heavily. Suzanne checked the date; it was New Year's Eve. Had they been on their way back from a party?

'What are you up to?'

She jumped. Dave was behind her. *Dammit.* He'd seen what

she was looking at. She moved a little to the left to allow him to read what was on her screen. No point in trying to hide it now.

'Is that Lady Attenborough?'

Suzanne nodded.

His eyes moved over the screen, left to right, left to right, like one of those memes of kittens watching tennis. 'Jaysus. Might explain a few things.'

Suzanne was surprised and pleased. 'That's what I thought. Imagine something like that happening when you're eighteen. How would you ever get over it? She and her sister were orphaned.' She rubbed her cheek thoughtfully. 'And now her partner goes missing? No wonder she's a little odd. It gives me a reason to check in with her, I think. Make sure she's okay.'

Dave shook his head. 'No, I meant what if she drove into that bridge on purpose? Lizzie Borden style? Maybe that was her first killing. She gets a taste for it. And then fifteen years later she does the boyfriend in too.' He grinned.

Suzanne rolled her eyes. Dave's parents were both dead and he was often unsympathetic when it came to what he saw as excessive grieving. It was also the reason he hadn't appreciated Allie's remark about his dad's greyhound racing. In contrast, Suzanne's own father was alive and very much kicking – a retired garda inspector. She tried to imagine what it would feel like to lose him at eighteen, and couldn't. And by her own hand. What would that do to you?

Dave sniffed and straightened himself with a groan. 'Are you ready to go visit Tweedledum and Tweedledee?'

She nodded, still staring at the screen, unable to tear her eyes away.

'I'll go down and get the car.'

'Grand. I'll meet you in the car park. I just need to use the facilities. Too much coffee this morning.'

Dave made the face he always did when Suzanne mentioned any bodily function other than sex, and headed out.

Reluctantly she logged off. It seemed unfair that so much tragedy could happen to one person, while others just sailed through life with nothing bad ever happening to them. She herself was one of the latter. More than ever, she wanted to help Allie.

Dave could wait five minutes. Time to make that call.

CHAPTER EIGHTEEN

Allie

My phone rang before I was even out of bed. Grey light bled through the window, so I knew it was late – it didn't get bright till half eight now. I'd had a wakeful patch in the middle of the night when the wind had woken me whistling around the cottage, but I must have gone back to sleep for longer than I'd expected. Since that first night, when it had seemed eerily quiet, the cottage seemed to come alive after dark. I presumed it was the ancient plumbing, air moving through old pipes. Or the ravens, which seemed ever present.

My phone was on the floor, charging at the other wall, electricity sockets few and far between in the cottage, so I pushed aside the duvet and climbed out of bed, padding over to get it. Finn stirred and looked up, and I touched his head as I passed.

The phone stopped before I reached it. It must have been ringing for a while. Noting the time, I unplugged it and took it back to bed. Nine o'clock. Late. I felt almost drugged. My head was heavy with fatigue and my limbs ached. Was I really so unfit that a two-hour walk in the mountains had knocked me out?

I checked to see who had called. My first thought was that it was Olivia, still trying to fix things between us. But no, it was a Dublin landline, a number I recognised but couldn't place. My stomach flipped when I played the voice message from Garda Phelan, but it kept breaking up. These bloody thick walls. She'd left a couple of messages before I left Dublin but there had been nothing for over a week.

I pressed callback, hands shaking, tensing myself against the panic. Had they found something? *Someone?* Had they found Rory? Breathe, I told myself, just breathe. The call was answered, but reception was so bad I couldn't hear what was being said.

Frustrated, I hung up and went into the kitchen to try there. The extension, with its thinner walls, had better connectivity. Finn mooched in after me, yawning widely, sitting on his haunches to watch as I leaned back against the cooker, hugging my middle, shivering. My thin pyjamas didn't offer much protection in this icy room.

'Hi, this is Allie Garvey. I missed a call from Garda Phelan. I presume it's about my partner, Rory O'Riordan.' My voice shook, and it wasn't from the cold.

Within a couple of seconds, Suzanne Phelan came on the phone. 'Morning. I'm sorry for bothering you so early. There was no need to call back.'

Why wouldn't I need to call back?

'I just wanted to check in with you at your new address. Let you know we haven't stopped looking.'

'Oh.' My shoulders slumped in disappointment. 'So you've no news?'

'I'm sorry. I did say that in the message.' A pause. 'How are you doing? Settling in?'

How did she know I'd moved? I wondered. I'd been meaning to call, but hadn't.

'I'm okay,' I said. That was a lie. I was rocking now, feeling suddenly light-headed. I reached my free hand to the back of my neck and found that it was wet. Blood? No, perspiration. I was burning up. But the room was still freezing.

'And your lovely dog, I bet he's loving the space.' Another pause. 'Allie? Are you still there?'

A gurgling, creaking noise emanated from my stomach, but I managed a weak 'yes'.

'I'm so sorry. I know it can't be easy, but I promise you we're doing our best to find Rory. We're continuing to post on social media. All his details are up on Pulse, his picture, his registration number. We're keeping an eye on...'

Her voice faded and I swayed, feeling as if I was about to pass out. Bile rose in my throat. I wasn't going to pass out, I was going to be sick.

'Sorry, I have to go. I'll ring you back.' I pressed the end-call button, dropped the phone on the draining board and ran to the bathroom, making it there just in time.

I kneeled on the freezing floor and retched. I retched and retched again, throwing up everything I'd eaten in the past day, the blood-orange remains of the tomato soup from the night before splashing into the toilet bowl. When I finally finished, I rinsed out my mouth, brushed my teeth and wiped the sweat from my forehead and neck, returning to the kitchen to pour myself a glass of water from the tap.

When I began to feel better, I let Finn out into the garden, standing for a minute in the doorway to inhale the damp air, fresh and clean after the night's rain. I glanced at my phone, still lying where I'd dropped it by the sink. I knew I should call the guard back, but I couldn't face it. I knew too that she'd meant well, but her call had sent me spinning back to how I'd felt when Rory had first gone missing. Yesterday had been a relief; a day off from feeling sick and frightened. But now I could feel myself being drawn right back into that whirlwind of misery.

As if needing to punish myself further, I reached for my phone and opened the 'Missing Person Rory O'Riordan' Facebook page that his family had set up following the success of Andrew's post, steeling myself for what I would find. I was the woman in the horror movie descending the steps to the cellar while everyone shouts at the screen for her to stop.

The *Mirror* article was now the page's banner: *A family's appeal. TV producer missing for three weeks.* New posts indicated that his family were organising a vigil, a leafleting campaign. The posts were public, so the comments below each one had multiplied like maggots, the keyboard warriors out in force.

Is he still missing???

Yeah, I was talking to an old school mate the other day, the family are really worried. The girlfriend has done a flit.

What?? Do they think she had something to do with it?

You mean she did him in?

Fuck. I've just googled her. You know she killed her parents?

Wha 😨😨😨 *?*

They *say* it was an accident.

Why do men like Rory always go for such bitches? Look at Brad Pitt and Johnny Depp.

Ah Jaysus. Rory O'Riordan was no Brad Pitt.

You're kidding, aren't you? He was gorgeous!!

He certainly thought he was 😂 😵.

Tears pricked my eyes, and I felt my legs give way, sliding down the wall and onto the floor, where I sat with my knees folded, arms clasped around them, burying my head. It was as if a huge searchlight was blinding me, leaving me nowhere to hide. *Done a flit?* Was that what people thought? That I didn't care? A wet nose nudged me, and I lifted my head. Rubbing Finn's ears, I dragged myself up to standing, and went for a shower.

There was a missed call from Olivia when I came out, and I

felt my eyes well again. It was time, I thought. I needed my sister. So I rang her from the garden, watched by the ravens; a row of ebony soldiers shifting and shuffling on the eaves.

She answered straight away, as if she'd had the phone in her hand. There were voices in the background, too many and too old to be the twins, so I assumed she was in school. I pictured her striding along a busy corridor, on the move as usual.

'Allie. I'm so glad you rang. I'm so sorry that I—'

I cut her off. 'It's fine. You're just worried about me. I get it.'

'I am,' she said, sounding genuinely surprised to be forgiven so easily. 'How are you doing there? Is it okay?' She paused, lowered her voice. 'I presume there's no news.'

'No. Nothing.'

I heard a door open and close, and the voices faded into silence. She must have stepped into her classroom. 'I see his family are pulling out all the stops.'

Olivia was an active Facebook user, so I was sure she'd have seen everything I had. Including the comments.

'Do you mind if we talk about something else?' I asked.

'Of course.' There was a scraping noise as she sat down at her desk, pulling the chair in to meet it. 'So, how's the rural idyll?'

I watched Finn high-step over tufted grass in the jungle of a garden, and noticed for the first time an old gnarled hawthorn bush, alone and isolated like some strange outcast. 'I think it's going to take some work to turn it into any kind of idyll.'

'Ah, right. A cute little fixer-upper then.'

'Something like that.' I went over to touch the tree, thin and stark, a tangled mass of quivering thorny branches laden with glistening orange berries. My foot hit something and I yelped. 'Ouch.'

'Are you okay?' Olivia asked.

'Yep. Just stubbed my toe.' I looked down. I'd hit a stone.

There was a circle of them around the base of the tree, as if they had been placed there on purpose, in some kind of ritual. They looked almost as old as the house, covered in lichen and moss.

'I found out that the cottage has a bit of a dark history,' I said, bending down to run my hand along the stone that I'd kicked, as if in apology. The lichen was soft and damp, like a deep-pile carpet onto which someone had spilled a glass of water.

'You're kidding. Haunted?'

'Maybe.' Looking back at the house, I had the strangest sense that it was observing me too, hunkered down against the gloomy day.

'Tell me everything,' she said eagerly.

Olivia was a history teacher and loved anything connected with the past. So I told her what Maggie had told me, thinking as I did so about the layers of history laid down since the cottage was built, imagining what might have happened here, what Raven Cottage might have witnessed.

'Ooh,' she said. 'A medium who disappeared. When was this?'

'Late eighteen hundreds, I think. Maggie said it was well over a hundred years ago.'

I could almost hear Olivia's mind whirring. 'Spiritualism was very popular in the mid nineteenth century in London, Paris and New York. I suspect it took longer to get here. A group called the Spiritists started in France. They believed that when we die, the body decomposes and the soul is released but still wrapped in its perispirit.'

'What on earth's a perispirit?' I gave a half-laugh.

'A sort of envelope for the soul. The spirit was supposed to be a combination of soul and perispirit; a human being liberated from its body by death.' Olivia chuckled. 'Like the destitute of the spirit world.'

'How on earth do you know all this?'

'I had to look it up recently for a kid doing a project.' I heard her footsteps crossing the floor of her classroom and then a rustle as if she was straightening something. 'I'm looking at it now, as a matter of fact. He wouldn't win any awards for his drawing, but it's not bad. It's all complete bollocks, of course. Mediums claimed to be middlemen for spirits, sharing their messages with the living at seances and suchlike.' She paused. 'Was that what your lady was doing?'

I glanced now at the back wall of that unsettling room. It looked completely blank; the only window faced the front. 'I don't know,' I admitted.

'Most were right charlatans,' Olivia said. 'They took advantage of vulnerable people who'd lost loved ones and were desperate to communicate with them. People consumed by grief.'

I wondered if I'd feel that way if Rory was dead, and realised that I already did. If I was given the chance to communicate with him, I'd jump at it. But, as I reminded myself, Rory *wasn't* dead. I'd sense it if he was. I'd know. Wouldn't I?

'They practised hypnotism and telepathy, went into trances,' Olivia continued. 'Claimed all sorts of crazy stuff; one said he could lift a table with his forefinger. Others that they could levitate. They did automatic writing or table tapping. That was started by the Fox sisters—'

I stopped her. 'Table tapping?' I'd heard tapping, but I'd convinced myself it was someone at the door, or the ravens in the roof.

'It's where the spirits rap yes or no in response to a question, or indicate a letter of the alphabet. I think it's still done.'

Had the medium who lived in this cottage practised table tapping? Was it possible that what I'd heard was an echo of what had happened over a century before?

But Olivia was laughing. 'People were much more gullible back then. No internet.'

I was inclined to think that the internet made people more gullible, not less, but I didn't say.

'You said all of this was happening in London and Paris and New York,' I said, imagining opulent houses and city salons while I gazed at my own mildewed cottage. 'What about here in Ireland?'

'It was more underground here, I think. People were afraid of angering the Catholic Church.'

I rolled my eyes. 'Of course they were.'

'There was a law called ... hang on, I'm just going to look at that project again ... the Witchcraft Act of 1735. People were afraid of falling foul of it, so Irish spiritualists opted for more clandestine meetings.' Olivia snorted. 'You know how secretive Irish people can be – this would have been just another thing they didn't want anyone to know.'

'Hmm.'

'Although they believed quite openly in fairies back then. There are some real horror stories: people convinced their loved one had been stolen by the fairies and replaced with a changeling. There were drownings and burnings to get rid of the interloper.' She sucked air through her teeth. 'I read one awful account of a man setting his wife on fire, convinced it wasn't her, and their little boy seeing him do it through the window of their cottage.'

'Jesus.' I breathed out. 'That's grim.'

'I know. Anyway, you should try and find out a bit more about this woman.'

'Maybe.'

Olivia mistook my reluctance for fear. 'All old buildings have history, Allie. And most cultures have rituals for communicating with the dead. It's just about reassurance. But the whole thing was and is just one big con.'

CHAPTER NINETEEN

Suzanne

Suzanne eyed the phone on her desk and willed it to ring. It stayed stubbornly silent. She checked her watch. Ten whole minutes since Allie Garvey had hung up on her. Dave would be waiting impatiently downstairs, trying not to rev the engine. She drummed her fingers on the desk. What had happened to make Allie break off the call so suddenly? Was she all right? Should Suzanne be worried?

Dave was right about one thing. Allie Garvey was a strange one. An enigma. Her reactions just weren't what you'd expect from the partner of someone who had gone missing. Suzanne knew there wasn't a one-size-fits-all in any situation; if she'd learned anything from her five years as a guard, it was that. And this woman had lost her parents when she was a teenager in the most traumatic circumstances you could imagine, so she must be a bit damaged from that. But still.

She bit her finger. Allie clearly wasn't going to ring back. Maybe Suzanne should text? That would mean giving Allie her mobile number. She knew she shouldn't. But what harm could it do? It wasn't as if the woman was going to be making a pest of herself. Suzanne didn't think she'd rung once since her initial calls to the station when Rory first went missing.

Most people railed against it when someone they loved disappeared, refusing to accept the reality of it, determined to find answers. Rory's family were like that. The station *was* getting phone calls almost every day from them. But Allie just seemed to submit to it. That was it, Suzanne thought. *That* was what was so curious about her, so atypical of the partner of someone who had gone missing. She was completely resigned to it, almost passively so. Almost as if she'd expected it.

What did that mean? And what the hell had happened to Rory O'Riordan, this relatively successful TV producer who seemed to have very few problems and everything going for him? A home, a partner, a successful career, a family who cared about him. And what else could Suzanne be doing to find him, other than what she was doing?

She was about to text Allie when her phone buzzed with an incoming one. Dave. *Where the fuck are you? Have you got the squits or something?*

CHAPTER TWENTY

Allie

I'd always wished I had Olivia's certainty about things. She was so sure that spiritualism was one big con that there was no room for an alternative view, the possibility that there might be something genuine amid all the trickery. I'd often wondered if her absolute conviction that she was right came from being a teacher, but she'd been like that even as a child. Olivia made a call and stuck with it. For me, things had always been more fluid. I was generally open to persuasion. Although maybe that was just weakness. The elder daughter syndrome. The good girl wanting to please.

Still, she'd given me some good advice about researching the history of the cottage.

'First stop, public library,' she'd said confidently. 'There'll be a librarian there with responsibility for local history. Talk to him or her. If you have a date and location, have a look at the local newspapers from the time. That would be . . .' I'd heard her rapping on her phone. 'Oh, the *Leinster Express* in Laois. Excellent. They're one of the oldest regional newspapers. They'll definitely have microfiches of the old editions in the local library.'

I'd found a pen and paper and scribbled a note. 'Great. Thanks, Liv.'

'No problem. Good luck. Let me know what you find out.' And then, because of course she hadn't been able to resist pushing her own agenda a little bit, 'Maybe you could write about it?'

I could hear the smile in her voice. She knew what she was doing. So I'd resisted resisting, for which I was quite proud of myself, saying that I'd let her know how I got on and hanging up.

But now I was cold. Despite the heavy jumper and jeans that I'd put on after my shower, I felt a chill down my back that made me shiver. Time to light the fire.

Arriving at the shed with the empty basket, I noticed a large space behind the fuel that I hadn't realised was there. Dropping the basket and stepping around the pile of turf to investigate, my heart sank. If the previous owners had taken a loose approach to clearing out the house, it was nothing compared to the shed: boxes of duvets and sheets, chipped mugs and kitchen equipment were shoved in willy nilly, just dumped. I felt a blast of irritation. How was I expected to get rid of all of this without a car?

But then something in the corner drew my attention: an open box with paintbrushes and a scraper, a stripping knife and a couple of tins of white paint, new and unopened. There was even a little stepladder propped up against the wall. DIY plans never carried out? I wondered. Maybe I could make use of the stuff. I'd painted the apartment once when Rory was away, and although he was annoyed not to have a say in the colour – it was my first reminder that the apartment was his and not ours – he did concede that I'd done a good job.

Walking back to the house with the turf, I was already making plans, resolving to get rid of the awful wallpaper and paint the rooms white. A little raven watched me expectantly from the windowsill as I pushed open the back door, and I smiled when I saw the white marking on its wing. The same bird!

I dropped the basket by the fireplace. If I was going to start the paint job today, there was no point in lighting the fire. The work would keep me warm.

Instead, I went back into the kitchen to make myself a coffee. The smell made me nauseous. Odd. I loved coffee. I'd had a couple of cups the day before. But when I tasted it, I immediately felt as if I was going to be sick again. What was wrong with it? I sniffed the milk carton and it was fine. And then it hit me. I'd thrown up already this morning. With a sinking feeling, I remembered feeling queasy on the ferry to the island a couple of weeks ago, and a similar nausea the next day that I'd blamed on stress and wine.

Suddenly all of this felt horribly familiar: feeling dizzy and sick as if I was no longer in control of my own body; that terrible tiredness. I'd been pregnant once before. Last year. A failed pregnancy that had ended with an induced miscarriage at nine weeks. I'd been devastated. Rory too, although it hadn't been planned and he always said that the loss of his childhood friend had meant that he didn't want children. He'd been devastated for me.

I reached out for the wall to steady myself. The room felt claustrophobic, the air thick and oppressive. I opened a window as I frantically tried to remember dates, cast my mind back to when Rory and I last had sex. I hadn't had a period for a while, I knew that. I could well have missed one, with everything that had happened.

I shook my head. No. I couldn't even consider it. I couldn't. Olivia used to call me an ostrich, but this would be too unfair. Not now. Not when I was on my own. My future had changed to something unrecognisable now that Rory was no longer in it.

I threw the coffee into the sink and retreated to the bedroom, where I discarded the heavy jumper, replacing it with a warm checked shirt. Denial it might well be, but I had work to do.

Returning to the living room, I stood with my hands on my hips and took a deep breath, ready to meet the worst that the cottage had to throw at me. I decided to tackle the living room and small room together. I couldn't keep closing the door. The cottage only had five rooms and I couldn't afford to lose one. Maybe if I ripped out the carpet and repainted, I'd get rid of that odd smell, that lingering rank odour like old cigarettes. And if I replaced it with some warm rugs and got some proper insulation, then surely it would be warmer. I might even be able to put a single bed in there, have someone to stay, though I couldn't imagine who would come other than Olivia. I pushed away the prospect of someone else sleeping there, someone small.

Back out in the shed, I pulled some sheets from one of the boxes – if the American couple couldn't be bothered to take them, I'd make use of them too. Inside I draped them over the furniture, which I shoved and dragged into the centre of the room. I was surprised to find the radio app on my phone worked once I left it in the kitchen with the door open.

I filled a bucket with water and started to wet the wallpaper in the living room with a sponge, working my way around the room. Once it had soaked for fifteen minutes, I began to scrape it off with a putty knife. Progress was slow; it would take at least today and tomorrow to do both rooms, at which point I could start painting. But I felt a wave of satisfaction seeing the piles of shredded paper build up on the floor. A sickly pink paint was revealed underneath, but I was relieved it wasn't darker; two coats of white with primer would cover it easily enough. The house had been built more than three centuries ago, each generation adding their own stamp. The thought gave me a strange comfort, making me feel less alone, and I sang along to the radio, feeling my mood lift as I worked.

I had never lived in an old house. Olivia and I had grown up in a 1970s semi-detached in the suburbs, our aunt and uncle moving in to care for us after our parents died. We'd attended school in a modern flat-roofed building with prefabs, while university was the ugly sprawl of University College Dublin. What followed for me was a succession of shared apartments in modern blocks, together with a protracted stay in a defiantly light-filled institution designed to counter the darkness of its residents.

By lunchtime, my arms ached, but my mind felt clear. I made a sandwich and fed Finn, resolving to take him for a walk once we'd both finished eating. He'd been surprisingly patient, sitting with his chin on his paws, watching me while I worked.

I ate in the living room, perched on a sheet-covered armchair, admiring my work. The place looked raw and exposed, almost skinned, with the pink emerging underneath. My eyes were drawn to that small high door to the right of the chimney breast that I'd noticed before, and I wondered again what was behind it. Curiosity getting the better of me, I put down my sandwich, fetched the ladder and climbed up. The door was painted a sickly yellow, chipped and blistered, with a knob and a keyhole. I gripped the knob and tugged with no success. Maybe it was locked? If so, where was the key?

I tried once more, and this time it jerked open, causing me to stagger back off the ladder, landing on my feet and regaining my balance just in time. I looked up as the door swung open, revealing a yawning darkness within. Was it a cupboard? The ceiling space above my bedroom would be just behind; it hit me that there could be a tiny attic room there.

I climbed back up the ladder. Peering into the pitch-black space, I realised I needed a torch. But a torch was the one thing I didn't have. Disappointed, I closed the door and climbed back down. I should probably buy one, I thought, in case the electricity went. Maybe some candles too. And then I remembered the torch app on my phone. I could use that.

But first I needed to take Finn for a walk. Dammit, where was he? Alarmed, I spun around. He was here a second ago. I went into the kitchen. The back door was open. I was sure I hadn't left it like that. I dived out into the garden, calling his name and whistling, but there was no response.

Panicked, I went back inside, grabbed his leash and my phone and headed out, running breathlessly up the lane. I got as far as the old graveyard without any sign of him. There was a stile accessing it, lichen-covered, rinsed after the rain. Finn had strained at the leash on our previous walks, clearly wanting to go in, but I'd hesitated, wondering if it was private property, although there was nothing to indicate that it was. Could he be in there?

I clambered over the stile, hands wetting on the soaked limestone. Brushing them off on my jeans, I glanced around me, eyes darting towards the remains of the old chapel and the scrubby grass surrounding it. And then I heard a whimper. I raced towards the sound, almost tripping up in my eagerness to follow it.

Finn was lying on his side in the grass. Was he hurt? Heart in my mouth, I kneeled down beside him. He looked at me as if confused, and then awkwardly got to his feet. I stood up too and nearly cried in relief when he did a full body shake. He was unhurt.

'What happened to you, boy? Did you go chasing after a rabbit?'

He leaned his skinny body against mine, and I attached the leash to his collar, waiting for my breath to return to normal, so grateful to have found him. I couldn't lose Finn too. The prospect did not bear thinking about.

As the fright gradually dissipated, I began to take in my surroundings, glancing curiously at the chapel and the graveyard, deciding to examine them more closely now that I was here. I wondered if they dated from a similar time to the cottage. Wandering over to the ruins of the building with Finn, I saw that while the roof was long gone, it was still possible to make out a nave where the altar would have been. I walked around, touching the walls, getting the same feeling as I had in the cottage earlier, that sense of past generations still present, the dead existing alongside the living.

After a few minutes, Finn bit on his lead to get my attention. He'd exhausted any smells worth investigating around the chapel and wanted to move further afield, so we made our way to the little graveyard.

It seemed a sad sort of place; graves clustered together as if jostling for space in a piece of land no bigger than the garden of that semi-detached in which I'd grown up. Barbed wire surrounded grass-covered mounds, stumps of limestone and the odd fallen cross, the land outside it clearly farmed, whoever owned the field having fenced off this paltry parcel to preserve the rest for tillage.

It felt mean-spirited somehow, ungenerously squashing the graves into the smallest area possible, leaving not enough room for the dead to breathe. I knew how strange that sounded. These souls were long gone. So long that the inscriptions on the headstones had been erased by the passage of time and weather. A raven, glossy black feathers, strong wings, landed on one of the stones, and perched there preening himself. I shivered, feeling a damp chill as I realised a mist was descending; I hadn't noticed it coming in.

CHAPTER TWENTY-ONE

When Finn barked, I turned in surprise. It was something he hardly ever did. For the first six months he'd lived with us, he hadn't made a sound, too traumatised by the cruel racing industry from which he'd come. But now he was growling, hackles up, staring wildly at a man who was blocking the entrance to the graveyard, foot planted on the bottom step of the stile. A tractor was parked behind him, barring the way out, taking up the full width of the lane. Finn didn't like large vehicles; they made him cower in fright. But he wasn't cowering now.

I recognised the man as the one who'd given me a cursory wave soon after I arrived, although he didn't look particularly friendly now, glaring at me red-faced and surly, eyes hooded. Was this Harkin, the farmer Jim had mentioned? Was it him I'd seen walking away from my back door?

'What are you doing in here?' he barked.

'I was just having a look. Is it private?' Had I been trespassing on his land? 'I'm sorry, I didn't realise. There's no sign.'

He pulled his cap down on his head so that I couldn't see his eyes any more. 'It's not private, but there's no reason to go in there.' He waved one gnarled hand in the direction of the graves. 'I'm assuming you've no people in this ground.'

I shook my head. He was stating the obvious, must be well aware that I was a new arrival, but he nodded as if satisfied that he'd won the point.

'Bar the graveyard, this is my land.' He transferred his gaze to Finn, giving him such a look of contempt that I put my hand protectively on his head. 'So you'd need to keep that dog on a lead. There's sheep around here.'

'He *is* on a lead.' I indicated Finn's very obvious leash with the red handset. Choosing not to mention the fact that up until five minutes ago I hadn't a rashers where he was.

A loud cawing made us both turn to see about a dozen ravens alight on the safety frame of the tractor, conveying unmistakable aggression. A couple of them flashed the whites of their eyes; I didn't even know birds had whites.

Without uttering another word, Harkin climbed down from the stile and got into his cab. The ravens rose in unison as he started the engine and roared off. I decided it was time we left too, waiting until he was safely out of sight before returning to the stile.

Finn trotted happily along the lane, nose down like a bloodhound, seemingly unaffected by the unpleasant exchange. The weather was now strangely clear, despite the mist in the graveyard, a few patches of watery blue visible through the cloud. My phone buzzed with a text: *Hope everything is okay. Call me any time. Suzanne.* Garda Phelan. I'd forgotten to ring her back. I sent a one-word reply: *Thanks.*

It was only when we were nearly at the cottage that I noticed a couple of ravens flying above us, stopping every so often to land on a branch and allow us to catch up, almost as if they were escorting us home. I imagined Rory's laugh if I said that aloud. But I remembered Maggie's suggestion that I make friends with them. So once I'd unclipped Finn's leash and given him a treat, I grabbed some bread, shredded it and scattered it on the windowsill. The birds kept their distance, so I took Maggie's additional advice to ignore them, and went back to scraping the walls.

I worked all afternoon, and was just about to finish for the evening when I heard a car pulling up at the front of the cottage. I opened the door to see Maggie herself, dressed in a bulky yellow waterproof jacket over yoga pants with lace-up boots, lugging something large and heavy from her boot.

She looked up. Her hair was wrapped in a sort of orange turban. 'Oh, hiya. Sorry I didn't get a chance to come up earlier. The beginning of the week is mental with deliveries. Anyway, I'm here now, with this old contraption.' She set down an ancient-looking radiator, about three feet tall, with patches of rust and a short flex. 'It's no beauty, but I swear it could heat the Sistine Chapel.'

'Thank you,' I said, meaning it. 'I'll be very glad of it.'

Between us we managed to drag it into the living room and shove it against a wall.

Maggie straightened herself with a groan and looked around her, hands on hips, taking in her surroundings. 'So you're renovating.'

'Well, painting, anyway. I found some unopened tins in the shed and thought I might as well keep myself busy. They must have been left there by the last people.'

'Good on you. The place could do with a bit of freshening up.'

I laughed. Understatement of the year. 'Would you like a coffee or something? I only have instant, nothing like yours, I'm afraid.'

Maggie looked amused. 'Coffee would be a bit of a busman's holiday for me. But I did think we could christen the place.' She gave a mischievous smile and produced a bottle of red wine from the voluminous pocket of her jacket.

Following me into the kitchen to hunt for some glasses, she

smiled when she saw the bread on the windowsill. 'So you took my advice with the ravens. I didn't think you would.'

'Not that they're eating it,' I said, opening and shutting a few cupboards and coming up empty-handed. 'Mugs do?'

Maggie nodded. 'If you really want to win their favour, they like nuts: peanuts, walnuts, almonds. They're also quite fond of dried dog food, but Finn might not appreciate that.'

'Noted.' I grinned, glancing worriedly at the bottle. It was red, so probably had a cork. 'I might not have a corkscrew.'

Maggie waggled it. 'Screw top.'

I quickly lit the fire while she plugged in the heater and pulled the sheets off two armchairs. We clinked mugs and watched the fire come to life.

'I know it's a hard time for you, but I hope you manage to find some peace here,' she said, her voice soft around the edges.

Maggie had been so kind to me, though I'd known her only a few days. I'd never been good at making friends and was even worse at keeping them, though I did try. But it occurred to me that while she knew my situation, I knew very little about her – whether she had a husband or children or even where she lived. I hadn't bothered to ask. Maybe that was why people didn't stay in my life for very long.

'Nope, all on my own, just the way I like it,' she said when I asked, giving a slightly wistful smile. 'No one to let me down or disappoint me.'

'Where do you live?'

'Above the café. Always have.' She glanced around her now, eyes narrowing, and I remembered her connection to the cottage. 'So what else are you planning to do?''

'Ah, not much. I can't really afford to, plus I don't want to make too many decisions in case . . .' I trailed off, staring into the deep red liquid in my mug.

'In case Rory comes back?'

I nodded, and then remembered the coffee this morning. My suspicion that I might be pregnant. All of a sudden, the wine didn't have the same appeal, and I put the mug back down on the stone flags.

Maggie regarded me curiously for a second, then said, 'Well, I hope he does. In the meantime, is there anything else that would make the place more comfortable?'

'I'd love to tackle the garden, but it's so overgrown I wonder if it needs some kind of machinery.'

'I'm sure Pieter would clear it for you.'

I bit my lip. 'I don't have much money to pay him.'

Maggie waved her hand dismissively, silver rings catching the firelight. 'He won't charge you much. I know he doesn't look it, but Pieter's wealthy, sold a big tech business in Brussels. Moved here for a quiet life, but he likes to take on jobs to keep him busy.' She took a deep sip of her wine. 'I'll mention it to him if you like. He comes into the café most mornings.'

I thanked her. The thought crossed my mind that I wouldn't mind seeing the man with the kind eyes again, before I immediately felt a flash of guilt.

To cover up my embarrassment, I said, 'Also, that small room is freezing. I wonder if there's anything I can do about it? Damp-coursing or something.' I rolled my eyes. 'I don't know why I said that. I don't even know what damp-coursing means.'

Maggie stifled a laugh. 'I'm not sure you should damp-course a stone cottage, but I'm sure Pieter could help somehow.'

'That would be great.' I reached for my mug again, before pulling my hand back as if it was scalding.

Maggie looked at me suspiciously now. 'You don't like red? I'm sorry. I should have checked.'

'No, I do,' I said hurriedly, face flushing as I searched for a way to change the subject. 'Did you know the couple who sold the house to us?'

She shrugged. 'Not well. But then I suppose they weren't here long enough. Don't tell me you're worrying about what Jim said again?'

'No. It's just that I'm using their paintbrushes and paint, so I get the feeling they left in a hurry. They left lots of things behind.'

Maggie nodded. 'I think one of their parents was ill so they had to go back to the States. They got stuck here during the pandemic and left as soon as they got the chance. Look, don't pay any attention to Jim. He likes taking the seed of a story and turning it into a loaf of bread.' She drained her mug. 'Right, that's me. Place feels a bit less arctic at least.'

I stood up. 'You've saved me from a dose of pneumonia this winter, so thank you again.'

At the door, Maggie stopped to pull on her big yellow jacket. 'Are you walking on Sunday? We're doing the Clear Lake. Jim will tell you it's bottomless. But it's a beautiful walk. Sometimes we even swim. I can pick you up if you like.'

'I'd love to. Thanks. It'll be great to let Finn off the lead again.'

Outside, I paused. The wine had forced me to come to a decision. 'How do I get into town without a car? Did you mention a bus?'

A vehicle sounded on the lane, and the tractor I'd encountered earlier pulled in at a field about twenty yards away. Harkin climbed down to open the gate, glancing over at us and then away. I wasn't surprised he didn't greet me, but surely he and Maggie knew each other?

She didn't even look in his direction, turning instead to open her driver's door with a loud creak. 'Portlaoise, you mean? There's a bus passes the end of the lane around ten every morning. Comes back at lunchtime. But I've to go in myself in a few days if you want a lift.' She paused with her hand on the roof of the car and threw me a knowing glance. 'There's a big chemist there if you need it.'

CHAPTER TWENTY-TWO

How had Maggie guessed I might be pregnant? I wondered while waiting at the end of the lane a few days later. Was it the wine, my sudden reluctance to take a sip? If so, it was quite the leap; I'd forgotten about it myself until I'd drunk a quarter of what I'd poured.

But then reaching for the mug that second time, it was the weirdest thing. Suddenly I was sure that I wanted to *be* pregnant, wanted the baby if I was, and couldn't possibly do anything to jeopardise it. Throughout the following couple of days spent scraping the remains of the wallpaper from the walls, I nursed that feeling in my heart. Even before Rory went missing, I'd felt blurred around the edges, unsure of my purpose, but now I was clearly defined. Solid. Strong. I wasn't sure I'd ever felt strong before.

Which was why I'd decided to take the day off before starting to paint, allowing the walls to dry, and make this trip into town. If I *was* pregnant, I needed to know as soon as possible.

A low rumbling heralded the arrival of the bus. Maggie's offer of a lift had been kind, but somehow I wanted to be alone for this errand. It turned out to be a large coach of the kind you got on bus tours, and I hoped they'd allow Finn on board. After his break for freedom a few days before and our encounter with Harkin, I hadn't wanted to leave him.

The door swung open to reveal a youngish driver with flaming red hair and a stubbly beard.

'Morning,' he said brightly. 'You bringing himself?'

'If I can,' I said. 'He's well behaved, I promise.'

'No bother. Have one myself at home. Well, a lurcher. That's a greyhound, by the looks of him? They're great old souls.' He winked. 'Just don't tell anyone. Health and safety will be down on us like a shower of bastards.'

We climbed on board and I paid for my ticket. The bus was almost empty: a sixty-seater with no more than eight or nine of them occupied. I was surprised to hear my name called from the back, followed by an enthusiastically waving hand embellished with orange nail varnish and gold rings.

As I approached, weaving my way down the aisle with Finn behind me, I saw that it was Jim's wife, Cathy, looking very different to how she had on the walk, in full make-up and blow-dry. I'd hardly spoken to her then, but now she smiled broadly and indicated the seat beside her. Finn's presence allowed me to get away with sitting across the aisle with him at my feet, but she didn't seem to take that as discouragement, chattering away to me at high speed, as if accustomed to competing for airtime. 'Jim has the car, so I thought I'd take the bus. I'm meeting a friend for a boozy lunch.' Her brow furrowed inquisitively. 'Don't you drive? I saw Maggie gave you a lift on Sunday.'

'No.' The bus sailed around a sharp bend, and I reached out for the back of the seat in front, feeling that sudden falling sensation like vertigo, the need to steady myself.

'Oh, you should if you're living on your own.' She flushed, as if she'd mentioned something taboo. 'I heard about your husband. Sorry now, but I looked it up on Facebook.' She stopped as if waiting for me to say something in response. When I didn't, she asked, 'How's the house?'

'Good.' I almost felt sorry for her. She wanted so much more from me than I was giving.

'Sorry about Jim. He loves a good scary story.' She raised her eyes to heaven. 'Thinks he saw a woman in the graveyard putting flowers on the graves – you know, the old one down your lane?'

The journey took about fifteen minutes, but it felt like an hour. Cathy played the tour guide, pointing out local landmarks – the old fairy fort or rath after which the village was named; *Havenwood*, the six-star hotel with the golf course and river that was once a boarding school; the stables where she kept her horses. But then her focus switched, and I felt like a butterfly pinned to a display while she tried to fix my wings, suggesting I take up riding to 'pass the time'. I assumed she meant until Rory came back.

Portlaoise was a larger town than I expected, with lots of new housing estates reaching their tentacles out into the countryside, but the centre was attractive enough, with an old war memorial, cafés and shops. I'd only ever bypassed it, on the motorway to Limerick or Cork.

Cathy walked me to the bottom of the main street, where I spotted a large chemist, saying that she'd see me on the bus home, unless her lunch ran over, in which case she'd call Jim to collect her. Then she made a beeline for the chemist. *Dammit.*

I was about to go searching for another one when I noticed the library on a corner site just opposite. It occurred to me that I could kill some time doing as Olivia had suggested. But what about Finn? I doubted the librarians would be as accommodating as the bus driver. Luckily, a kindly security guard spotted us hesitating in the doorway and offered to keep an eye on him, explaining that he regularly minded dogs for library users and proving it with a pocketful of treats.

The librarian, sombre and balding, glasses halfway down his nose, looked up when I approached the counter. 'Hello. Yes?'

'Hi. I was hoping to do some research on local history.'

'Hilary!' He called out to a grey-haired woman who was rooting through cards in a drawer.

She stuck up a couple of fingers. 'Two minutes.' A jewelled clip shone in her pearl-grey hair.

I stood back to allow a boy in school uniform to get to the desk.

'Sorry about that.' Hilary came to the counter. 'If I hadn't finished that section, I'd have had to start again from scratch.' She shook her head as if to clear whatever she had been doing from her mind. 'Right. What can I do for you?'

'I've just moved into an old cottage outside Rath and I'd like to find out something about the history of the place.'

'The village or the cottage?'

'Well, both, I suppose. But particularly the house, if that's possible.'

She tapped her forefinger on her chin. 'What era are we thinking about? How far back do you want to go?'

I thought about what Maggie had said – *well over a century ago* – and took a shot in the dark. 'The end of the eighteen hundreds? Beginning of nineteenth?'

She nodded. 'Follow me.'

We made our way up a staircase that led to a sort of mezzanine level, from where I could see the main street, including the pharmacy opposite. There was a row of computers and a couple of machines that looked like a cross between a desktop and an old television set.

'These are microfiche readers, which you can use to read old editions of the *Leinster Express* newspaper,' Hilary said.

So Olivia had been right. Not that I'd doubted her.

'Have you ever used one before? No? Well, microfiche is transparent film used to store printed information in miniaturised form. I'd suggest you look up the parish notes for Rath, and if anything of note happened, you'll find it in the main paper. The problem is, unless you have a date, it's going to take you a while.' The librarian smiled. 'Using a microfiche isn't like using a search engine. You'll have to trawl through all the editions. The *Leinster Express* came out every week. Still does.'

I wondered when the security guard's dog treats would run out.

She clapped her hands together. 'So, what years would you like – shall I get you the last ten years of the nineteenth century to be going on with?'

'That would be great. Thank you.'

When she came back, carrying flimsy sheets of plastic film, she showed me how to place one under the lens of the reader machine, magnifying the densely typed text and allowing me to navigate its contents.

I thanked her and got started. Scanning through edition after edition, scrolling past ads for Zebra Grate Polish and Shaw's Millinery, Drapery and Outfitters and headlines about the arrest of union officials, made me appreciate Google. I found the parish notes for each week, and searched out Rath, squinting around the age spots blurring the tiny print that covered everything from marriages, births and deaths to summer fetes and special church services. There was nothing of note.

After a while, I got up to stretch my legs, making my way to the top of the stairs. The library was bright and modern, with high ceilings. The floor beneath was the children's section, with a turreted blue and grey castle and chairs in bright primary colours. Looking down gave me a strange feeling in the pit of my stomach. Was it possible that I might be bringing my own baby here?

The rush of emotions that accompanied that thought was too much, and I retreated to my desk. And then suddenly, there it was. On 7 January 1891, Rath was mentioned. The headline gave me a start. Because it *was* a headline, not a parish note.

Rath woman vanishes without a trace on New Year's Day. Child found abandoned.

I began to read.

> Elizabeth Dunne, spinster of the parish of Rath, has disappeared from her cottage, a mile outside the village. The surrounding fields and ditches have been searched but no trace was found. Miss Dunne also abandoned her child, a two-year-old girl, who was found alone in the cottage kitchen and taken in by neighbours. Local woman Bridget Kennedy, who spoke to this paper, claimed it was said that Miss Dunne was stolen away by the fairies.

I breathed out. Elizabeth. Eliza was short for Elizabeth. I'd been right about her name. How on earth could I have known? And a child? Maggie hadn't mentioned a child. Though now that I thought about it, given that Eliza was Maggie's great-great-grandmother, there must have been one.

Hilary, the librarian, appeared at my shoulder, leaning over me to see what I was reading. 'Is that the cottage you've moved into?'

When I nodded, she frowned. 'I've heard of that case. I think it got a mention in ... Hang on.'

She turned to walk back down the steps. While she was gone, I scrolled on to have a look in the parish notes, but there was nothing. And nothing in the following week's edition at all.

Hilary reappeared carrying a large red and black hardback clasped to her chest. 'I'd a feeling that woman's disappearance got a mention in this. It's a collection of old photographs.'

She opened the book to a black and white photograph of Raven Cottage. The house had been thatched then, but was immediately recognisable. A woman and toddler stood in front of the half-door, while a bird pecked on the ground at their feet. Although her features were unclear, I imagined the woman looked a little like Maggie. Would I have seen a resemblance if I hadn't known the connection? I wasn't sure. She wore a dress and apron to her ankles, and held a rolled-up cigarette between her fingers.

The caption below the picture read: *Eliza Dunne, before her disappearance. Circa autumn 1890.* And there was a footnote: *Eliza Dunne, noted Irish spiritualist, with her daughter Gretta outside her cottage, near the village of Rath in the Slieve Bloom mountains in County Laois, or Queen's County as it was known then. (Plate 5, p.265.)*

I turned the page. There was more. I was desperate to read on, but I quickly checked my watch and saw I'd been here over an hour already. Too long.

'Would it be possible to borrow this?' I asked.

'Of course.' Hilary beamed. 'That's what we're here for. We're a library!'

'But I'm not a member.'

'That's easily solved. Go downstairs to Paul; he'll sign you up and you can take that book with you today.' Her eyes widened as something occurred to her. 'As a matter of fact, he's from Rath himself, though he lives in town now. He might be able to tell you something about that case.'

'And the . . .?' I waved towards the microfiche machine, which I'd left switched on, the stack of film alongside.

'Don't worry. I'll put those away. Come back if you want to have another look.'

I thanked her and went downstairs. The bald librarian was

still at the counter. He gave me a short form to fill in, had a look at some identification and checked the book out.

'Hilary said you were from Rath,' I said. 'It's Raven Cottage that I'm researching.'

'Oh, right,' he said with interest. 'Why's that then?'

'I live there. I've just moved in.'

'I see,' he said slowly, narrowing his eyes. 'Well, the person you need to speak to is the woman who runs the café. She knows all about that cottage. The little girl who was left behind – I presume you know about that? That was her great-grandmother.' He bit his lip. 'I think I have that right. Generations always confuse me.' He counted on his fingers.

Of course, I thought. That child would be Maggie's ancestor too. Gretta. I wondered what had happened to her after she was taken in by those neighbours.

Before I could ask, the librarian pushed the book towards me. 'You have it for three weeks. If you want to extend the loan, you can call or go online. Here's your library card.'

'Thanks.' I shoved the book in my bag and pocketed the card.

He frowned and crossed his arms. 'I think that little girl was taken in by a local farmer's wife and brought up as one of their own. Lucky child. Back then she could have ended up in the workhouse, or worse.' He tapped his forefinger on his nose. 'And Maggie Dunne. Cut from the same cloth as Eliza, she is.'

CHAPTER TWENTY-THREE

I collected Finn, distractedly thanking the security guard for his help, absorbed in what I'd discovered. Craving another look at the book I'd borrowed, I found a café and sat outside it. It was cold, but I didn't care; I took the book from my bag and opened it at the couple of pages of print following the picture. A teenager in leggings, apron, and a pink crop top that despite the chill hovered above an enviably flat brown stomach took my order for tea and a baked potato, and I settled in to read.

> Claiming to be the seventh daughter of a seventh daughter, Eliza Dunne was born on a small farm a few miles from Tullamore. When she was fourteen, she was employed in the local post office, but it soon transpired that she had a gift, something that would allow her to make considerably more money than her work as a post office assistant ever could.
> When her parents died, she moved. By the time she was twenty, she was renting her own cottage a mile from the village of Rath, in County Laois, at the foot of the Slieve Bloom mountains, and conducting her clandestine business as a medium. Eliza never married but she had a baby, a little girl. Rumours that the child wasn't the first, that she'd had another

baby who died, were accompanied by hints that she was taken advantage of by local men. No doubt a woman living on her own would have been unusual at that time, and vulnerable because of it.

But Eliza preferred to live alone. She kept ravens as pets – birds that were rumoured to carry messages between the living and the dead. She grew vegetables and herbs, and kept hens, becoming essentially self-sufficient, cultivating solitude, which must have suited her secret trade. The one exception was her eggs. Every three or four mornings, Eliza walked into Rath to sell them at the village shop. On New Year's Day 1891, the village shopkeeper, Mrs Sadie Fitzpatrick, noticed that there had been no sign of her for nearly a week. She persuaded Eliza's neighbour, Tom Harkin, who had called into the shop, to look in on her and make sure she was all right.

What he found shocked him. The door to the cottage was ajar and there was no sign of Eliza. The table and chair had been knocked over, and Eliza's little girl, Gretta, was playing alone in the kitchen. A search was mounted in the surrounding area, but Eliza Dunne was never found. Tom Harkin's wife took in the little girl and brought her up with her own eight children.

Harkin, I thought, sitting back in my chair. My irate farmer neighbour. Had his ancestors taken Gretta in? I recalled the old farmhouse, now used as a cowshed. Was that where Maggie's great-grandmother had been brought up? If so, why hadn't he and Maggie greeted one another; surely they were almost related? And why hadn't he bought the cottage if, as Jim said, his land surrounded it? I reached for Finn's head – he was flat out under the table – and continued reading.

Eliza Dunne was an integral though publicly unacknowledged part of the Slieve Blooms community. Her practice as a medium may have been disapproved of by the Church, but local women believed what she had to say; they trusted her to communicate with their dead and made decisions based on what she told them. Women who had no money for frivolities still found ways to pay Eliza.

But after she disappeared, that changed. No one wanted to admit to any connection with her. People claimed that she drank porter, that she didn't go to Mass. That she was a slatternly mother who had abandoned her child for drink or a man. Even that she was a changeling who had been taken back by the fairies.

The arrival of my food jolted me back to the present and the bustling main street. As I started to eat, my gaze moved again to the photo, and I saw now that while there may have been a resemblance between the two women, Eliza's hair was very different to Maggie's in that it was cut short, almost shorn. I imagined it must have been unusual then for a woman to wear her hair like that. But that wasn't what bothered me about the picture. It was the cigarette. Something in the recesses of my mind irked me about it, but I couldn't get a handle on why. Was it the proximity to the child? Maternal instincts kicking in already? And then I had it, remembering with a start that strange smell in the room off the living room. The pungent smell of rolled cigarettes. Feeling suddenly nauseous, I pushed my plate away. A smell didn't last a century.

I took a sip of my tea, hand reaching involuntarily for my stomach. Why was I wasting time on something that had happened so long ago, when what I really needed to do was to buy that pregnancy test? I paid the waitress for my uneaten lunch, concocting a story about a forgotten appointment in which she had zero interest, and left.

Outside the chemist, a man emerging from an office building alongside, wearing a charcoal-grey suit and brown brogues, stopped me with a look. 'Allison Garvey, isn't it?'

With a start, I recognised O'Neill, the solicitor; I'd forgotten his office was in this town. A brass plate affixed to the door he'd just come out of confirmed it, along with gold lettering splayed across the windows.

'How are you doing? Any news on Rory?'

I was surprised he remembered me. We'd met only once, in Dublin to sign the contracts; he'd been in the city for a case and Rory had set it up. We'd had a coffee together, the three of us, but it was brief, although Rory had ordered champagne after he left. The memory made my eyes fill with tears and O'Neill quickly suggested that I come inside for a chat. I guessed it wasn't a good look for a solicitor to be seen with a weeping woman on the street.

I followed him into a reception area that was overly warm, with heavy dark furniture, deep-pile carpets and up-to-date newspapers, quite a contrast to the draughty cottage where I now spent my days. I declined tea and he brought me into his office, a large high-ceilinged room that looked out over the main street. No one seemed to object when Finn mooched in after me, so I sat in one of the leather-backed chairs while he slumped at my feet.

'All the documents have been lodged, and the deed has gone for stamping. Luckily, you both signed everything early on.' O'Neill smiled, then trailed off with a grimace. 'Sorry.' Realising, I imagined, that the fact he hadn't been inconvenienced with his paperwork wouldn't have been of much comfort to me. 'Is there anything I can do? Is the cottage okay for you?'

I paused. There *was* one thing. 'You know the American

couple we bought it from? I can't remember their names. They've left a lot of stuff. The shed wasn't cleared out at all.'

'Oh, that's not great.' O'Neill stood and made his way over to a filing cabinet, from which he retrieved a brown folder. He opened the cover and flicked through the contents. 'We definitely asked for the house to be cleared apart from the items you specified. The few bits of furniture, white goods, et cetera. I'll get on to their solicitors.'

'I guess there's not much they can do about it now that they're back in America,' I said hurriedly, thinking about the paint and brushes of which I'd already made use.

O'Neill frowned. 'Oh, they're not in the States, I don't think.'

'I thought one of their parents got ill and they had to go home?'

He looked confused. 'No, I'm not sure where you heard that. They just moved to Tullamore. We're acting for the people they bought their new house from.' He bit his lip. 'I probably shouldn't have said that. But I don't think it's a secret.'

Rory. It was Rory who had told me. And it had been confirmed by Maggie. *They got stuck here during the pandemic and left as soon as they got the chance.* Was Jim the only one who had told me the truth?

'So why did they sell?' I asked, a slight quiver entering my voice. 'If only to move half an hour away?'

The solicitor shifted uncomfortably in his chair. 'I'm afraid I don't know the answer to that.'

There was a bus waiting when I came out of O'Neill's, so I climbed on, feeling the need to get out of town as quickly as possible. It was full. I squeezed past a man wearing huge headphones and found a space for Finn and me at the very back.

I gazed moodily at my own reflection in the glass, watching the fields and hedges zip past, a blur of green and brown. A once-in-a-lifetime chance, Rory had said, when in reality Raven Cottage was cheap because nobody else wanted it and the sellers had been frightened living there. I felt like the only kid in the schoolyard who didn't get the joke. What else had he hidden from me? The bus dropped me off at the end of the lane and I walked slowly up it with Finn, reluctant to reach the cottage and annoyed at my own reluctance.

When I got there, I turned the key and pushed open the door. I could feel something on the other side, dragging along the floor. Filled with foreboding, I stepped around it and looked down. Something black lay on the mat. Finn sniffed at it with interest, and I had to pull him back by his collar to get a proper look. My stomach turned when I realised that it was a dead animal of some kind.

And then I saw feathers. Black velvet, with a polished sheen, and a long black beak. It was one of the ravens. What had happened to it?

I remembered Jim mentioning Harkin's shotgun, but there was no evidence of the bird having been shot. No blood. Poisoned? If so, who had done it? And who had left the bird here? My first thought again was Harkin. But why would he do that? To scare me? And how had he got it inside the house? There was a tiny letter box in the door, but this raven was too big to fit inside it.

Though I knew my little friend was considerably smaller than this bird, I searched for a white marking on the shoulder, hoping not to find it. The raven was on its side, so I gently turned it over using a poker, so relieved to find no mark that I started to cry. And then I remembered: I'd forgotten to get that pregnancy test, my sole reason for going into town the first place. What was wrong with me?

Pulling myself together, I found two plastic bags in a drawer. Covering my hands with them, I put the body carefully into a shoebox I'd shoved into the wardrobe when unpacking. Then I carried the box into the garden and, using the shovel from the fire to dig a small hole, buried it. I stood there for a few minutes gazing at the little pile of earth, while Finn sat on his haunches beside me, like a tiny gathering in a graveyard.

A rustling noise caused me to look up. There were ravens everywhere. A row had gathered on the eaves of the house. Another on the telephone wire. More than I'd ever seen.

Mourning their dead.

CHAPTER TWENTY-FOUR

Suzanne

'There's someone waiting for you downstairs!' Paddy shouted at her across the room on his way to the coffee maker. The machine on this floor was the only one that worked, so he snuck up from the front desk about a dozen times a day.

Suzanne looked up from the report she was trying to finish. 'Who is it?'

Paddy wrinkled his nose, as if trying to remember the name. 'The brother of that guy who's gone missing. The TV fella. Eamonn, I think his name is?'

'Andrew.' Suzanne stood up immediately.

She strode quickly across the floor and made her way downstairs to reception, where a bearded man in a heavy coat and scarf was sitting on one of the phenomenally uncomfortable white plastic chairs. She'd never met Rory O'Riordan's brother, although she'd spoken to him on the phone several times. Far more than she'd spoken to Allie.

He stood up as she approached, and she could see that his beard was one of those carefully curated specimens, not the lazy can't-be-arsed-shaving kind that her boyfriend grew occasionally. Dave would describe him as a hipster, if he was being kind. A word beginning with 'w' and rhyming with anchor if he wasn't.

She offered him her hand, suddenly conscious of her badly bitten nails. His was cool and dry, with carefully manicured fingers. Not a manual labourer, then. 'Good to meet you in person, Mr O'Riordan.'

Once the formalities were over, Andrew shoved his hands back into the pockets of his coat and began rocking back and forth on his toes, as if about to make a pitch. 'We've had an idea. The family.'

Suzanne noted the specific. *The family.* As distinct from the girlfriend. *The family of origin.* She knew that they'd conducted searches, held vigils and put out regular appeals, none of which had involved Allie, even speaking to the *Mirror* newspaper, who she suspected only took the story because it had the tiniest whiff of celebrity.

'Go on.' She indicated the chair from which Andrew had just risen, and sat alongside him in the one next to it. He smelled expensive.

'What about a segment on *Crime Files*?' he said eagerly. 'About Rory's disappearance. A TV appeal.'

'Maybe,' Suzanne said slowly, wondering if her boss would go for it. RTÉ's garda programme that asked the public for assistance in solving crimes was definitely something she'd considered. But she knew how difficult it was to get anything included, and she wasn't sure if Rory's disappearance would even qualify, since there hadn't actually been a crime.

Plus, she wondered what they could show. Reconstructions were a big part of *Crime Files*, and a clip of Rory driving through the toll bridge wouldn't make for riveting TV. Although she guessed they could use something from his documentaries. *The Naked Lens*, maybe?

'Don't you think it's a perfect case for *Crime Files*?' Andrew said intently. 'He's a TV producer. He's done some work for RTÉ.'

He leaned forward, eyes blazing. 'I can't believe we didn't think of it before now. Someone must have seen something.'

And Allie? Suzanne wondered. What about her? She broached the question. 'I'll need to contact his partner.'

But Andrew shook his head, stony-faced. 'I'd rather you didn't.'

'Any particular reason? I don't think I have much choice.'

He took a deep breath, his reluctance to speak written all over his face. 'Rory had a hard time with Allison.' Suzanne noticed the use of her full name. 'We're hoping he won't go back to her when we find him.'

She frowned. 'Hard time how?'

'She could be difficult.' He paused, rubbing his jaw uneasily. 'Do you know about her parents?' When Suzanne nodded, he said, 'I think she's damaged. And yes, I feel sorry for her because of that, of course I do. But she has a temper, and my brother got the brunt of it. He said she drank too much. I believe they had some terrible rows.'

We didn't argue, Suzanne remembered Allie saying when they called to the apartment. Another accidental omission? Or a deliberate lie?

She nodded slowly. 'Well, judging from my experience of her, she probably won't want to take part, but as a courtesy, I will have to inform her.'

'Okay,' Andrew said quietly. 'I understand.'

CHAPTER TWENTY-FIVE

Allie

Eliza's story seriously piqued my interest. The next morning, once I'd ordered a pregnancy test online, I found that I was happier thinking about her and imagining her living in Raven Cottage with her daughter than attempting to unpick the lies Rory had told me. Or wondering about that dead raven, and how its corpse had ended up on my mat. I even wondered if Olivia was right, if it was possible that I could write about Eliza. Although I'd always preferred fiction, probably because of the circumstances in which I'd started writing.

As suicide attempts go, it was pretty inept: driving my uncle's car twenty feet and ramming it against the wall of next door's garage. I'm not even entirely sure it *was* a suicide attempt. But the doctors didn't believe it was an accident, deciding that it was a delayed reaction to killing my parents, and so they convinced me. I was twenty-three. It was the first time I'd got behind the wheel since the crash five years before, and I did succeed in putting a hefty dent in my forehead, which required stitches, to say nothing of the dent in my uncle's prized Merc. An extended stay in St John of God's Hospital followed. I could almost see my university from the window.

The therapists there encouraged me to keep a journal, desperate to find some outlet for my feelings of 'emotional trauma'. The journal quickly morphed into short stories; I discovered that I preferred wearing the mask of fiction.

But Eliza's story was compelling. While I continued with the decorating, painting the entire living room in a morning – one advantage of living in a small cottage – I couldn't stop thinking about her. It was a job keeping Finn out of the room and I knew he'd brush his coat against the wet walls if I didn't, so when I'd finished, I decided to head into the village, surmising I could also talk to Maggie about Eliza. Two birds with one stone, I thought, and then winced. Strange, the expression had never bothered me before, but now it seemed cruel.

Maggie was wiping down a table, and she straightened up when I came in, crossing her arms with the cloth clasped in her silver-ringed hand. 'How's the heater working out?'

'Good, thanks.' There were two other people in the café: a youngish woman with a baby having coffee and cake in the corner, and a man in paint-splattered jeans eating a pastry.

'I told you. Sistine Chapel.' She gave Finn a rub. 'I have something I think you'll like, sweet fella.' She transferred her gaze to me. 'Coffee? Almond slice? Just out of the oven.'

'Thanks. Tea, though, please.'

I took a seat at the table Maggie had just cleaned and drew the library book from my bag, opening it at the picture of the cottage. I saw her glance at it without comment. When she returned with my tea, she gave some cold bacon to Finn, who wolfed it down in one. 'Where did you get that?'

'The library in town,' I said. 'I caught the bus in yesterday.'

'I told you I'd give you a lift.' Her expression was hard to read, as if a shutter had come down on her face.

It made me hesitate. 'I thought I might do some research on the cottage.' Was I making a mistake bringing this up? 'I found out that Eliza left her little girl behind – your great-grandmother?'

Maggie stiffened. Everything about her suggested that the subject was unwelcome; I wondered for a second if she was going to turn away and leave me sitting there. But she didn't. She joined me, sitting down heavily on the other chair.

'Her name was Gretta.' Her fingers traced the grain of the wood on the table, and I saw again that tattoo on her wrist, clearly this time – it was three ravens in a circle. 'I'm not sure how much good will come of digging it all up again.'

'Even if there's an unsolved mystery?' I asked. 'I presume they never found her.'

'Especially if there's an unsolved mystery. Mysteries usually stay that way for a reason. Often because more than one person is keeping it like that.'

'But what if there's an injustice?' I thought about the things that were said about Eliza after she disappeared. Things I couldn't help think were untrue, though I had no basis for this.

'An injustice to whom? Eliza? She's long dead, whatever happened to her. That's not going to change. Same with my great-grandmother.' Her eyes closed wearily. 'My mother wanted it forgotten about and I'm inclined to agree with her.'

But I was living in the cottage, I thought. Surely that gave me a right to take an interest, if nothing else? 'Do you mind if I continue to read up on it?'

She gave a tight nod of her head. 'Of course. Let me know if you find anything interesting. But maybe don't go around asking other people about it. You might not get the same response.'

I wondered if I heard a warning note in her voice. Wondered if she meant Harkin.

After the café, I called in at the supermarket to buy some groceries, together with a couple of bags of nuts and a torch. On the street outside, I ran into Pieter, barely recognisable in work gear so covered in building dust it was almost white. His face and hair hadn't fared much better, although his eyes were bright and you could see that his skin was weather-beaten beneath the grime. I tried to imagine him as the owner of a large tech company and failed.

He stooped to pat Finn. 'How are you settling in? Maggie mentioned that you might want someone to have a go at clearing the garden?'

'Oh yes, thank you.'

He nodded silently, rubbing Finn's ears, and I wondered if he was going to say that he couldn't do it. To fill the gap, I said. 'It's a bit of a jungle.'

He looked up. 'When would you like me to come?'

'Any time really. I don't start work for a couple of weeks. Actually,' I remembered suddenly, 'I'm going to need internet. I don't know if there's anything you can do about that?'

He smiled. 'Maybe you can do me a list. I have a few hours free in the morning.'

Tap-tap-tap. I awoke in a sweat to my own heart pounding, and that knocking sound again. I held my breath, checking my phone on the chair by my bed: 04.35. Who would be calling round at half four in the morning? Was it Harkin again?

A shard of moonlight speared through the curtain and the knock came once more. This time Finn lifted his head and growled, hackles up. I forced myself to get out of bed, pulling on my dressing gown. As I tied the belt around my waist, I sensed a hand on my shoulder and spun around, but of course there was no one there.

Still feeling spooked, I flicked on the light and, digging my nails into my palms, made my way into the kitchen. Finn followed, nails clipping, skidding giddily along the stone flags.

I unlocked and opened the back door, but there was no one

there, nothing but silvery moonlight casting flickering lines across the garden, and silence. Absolute and profound silence. Somehow just as I'd expected. Had I imagined the knocking? Was it a dream? I breathed in the cool night air and forced myself to calm down.

So when the knock sounded again, my heart almost stopped. This time I knew it wasn't coming from the back door; I was holding that very door ajar by the latch. I held my breath and listened; it was coming from the little room again. Finn figured it out at the same time as I did, and shot through to the living room like a bullet, eerie-looking with its sheet-covered furniture. He stood at the closed door to the small room, ears pricked, every hair in his coat bristling, emitting a low growl from the back of his throat. Tail erect and body tense as if he was about to spring.

Gingerly I opened the door and stepped inside, filled with trepidation. An avalanche of feelings swept over me. Sadness, grief, regret, fear. A dark shadow flitted past the window, the moon disappearing briefly from sight as though something or someone was walking past. My imagination was running away with me. But I couldn't deny that pungent smell of cigarettes, which was here again, reminding me of the rollies my grandfather used to smoke.

Suddenly the door slammed shut. My heart nearly stopped. I couldn't believe it had happened again, but I told myself to breathe, that it must just have been a draught. Finn whined on the other side, having refused to come into the room as usual. I switched on the lamp. The bulb flickered, hissed, popped and then went out.

I tried the door, turning the knob. It spun but didn't catch, as if the mechanism was broken, had come away somehow. I was locked in. I tried again, panic rising, grabbing the handle with both hands and shaking it. This time it caught, connected and turned. When I pulled the door open, Finn leaped on me, his entire body trembling when I hugged him. I felt my own eyes well at his distress.

Before returning to the bedroom, I threw a last backward glance at the door. Had I pulled too hard in my anxiety to get out? Or was the mechanism just old and unreliable, temperamental? Either way I needed to have it looked at. I couldn't afford to get locked in there; the windows were too small to climb out of, even if I could break them. With no phone coverage, I could die in there and no one would know, with poor Finn on the other side unable to help. I decided to add it to the list for Pieter in the morning.

In bed, my heart rate finally slowed to a normal rhythm, mind still racing. I lay there with my eyes open, imagining Eliza sleeping in this room with her child, a hardier woman than me; no electric heater or duvet for her. I wondered again if that small room was where she had seen people. Contacted their dead. I pictured them calling to her back door late at night so they wouldn't be seen, denying any connection to her after she disappeared. Maybe even that woman Bridget Kennedy, who'd been quoted in the newspaper article.

My laptop was lying in the bottom of the wardrobe along with a printer that I needed for work. I knew I wouldn't be able to sleep, so I took it out and brought it back to bed with me. I opened it and began to type, summoning a scene in my head so real it felt like fact.

> Bridget Kennedy came late at night, appearing at the back door long after Eliza had gone to bed. Gretta woke briefly, but Eliza was able to settle her.
>
> The clock chimed one as she made tea and brought it into the small room. The fire still smouldered in the living room

~~the main room~~, but she liked to keep her work separate. She did not want sadness seeping into the walls where she fed her daughter or where she and Gretta slept.

The young woman's tears had stopped but the bruises were bad this time. Eliza had seen her in the village with a black eye, but tonight her cheek and mouth were cut too, her eye blooming purple in the light of the lamp.

Eliza handed her some tea.

'He says I'm not his wife. That I've been left by the fairies. That no wife of his would fail him the way I do.'

Bridget Kennedy's childlessness was well known, bringing shame to her husband and herself. But Eliza knew the danger of being called a changeling, the fairy fort after which the village was named only fuelling the stories. She knew too the remedies used to outwit 'the good people': the herbal concoctions, the beatings, the drownings and burnings. Knew that Bridget was in danger, in peril of her young life. Her husband a brute, a man too free with his fists and his whiskey.

'You must leave him,' she said.

Bridget shook her head. 'Father Brophy says I must stay. That my place is with my husband. That I've made my bed and must lie in it. He gave me five rosaries for even thinking about leaving.' Her long fingers were clasped in her lap, clutching a bloody handkerchief. 'He says that Edward is the man of the house. That I respected my father and now that he has gone, I must do as my husband says.'

'Even if he beats you?'

'I make him angry because I am barren. He thinks he got a bad bargain.' She looked up, meeting Eliza's gaze. 'He is a different man to my father.'

And with that Eliza knew why she had come. Bridget would not ask directly, but she had mentioned her father now for a second time. The young woman could not overcome the authority of the fairies or the priest. But she would accept guidance from the dead.

CHAPTER TWENTY-SIX

I didn't wake until after eight, when Finn began stirring in his bed. Lifting the covers and putting my feet down onto the cold floor, I felt a sudden wave of nausea, with the need to reach out and steady myself against the wall. It waned after a few seconds, so I pulled on a dressing gown and slippers and trudged to the kitchen to let Finn out. After his escapade at the beginning of the week, I waited until he was safely inside again eating his breakfast before going to have a look at the door that had caused me such grief in the middle of the night. Of course, it seemed to be working perfectly this morning.

Blearily I went back into the kitchen to make tea. While I drank it and ate a banana, I tried to process everything that had been happening. Maybe all the weird stuff was connected with the pregnancy, some kind of hormone imbalance. Noises at night, waking up in the other room. Although I wasn't convinced about that. At times it felt as if the cottage was trying to speak to me, to warn me or ask something of me. That little room appeared to be the focus. I rarely went in there of my own accord, but last night it was as if I'd been summoned there, and the room had tried to keep me there once I was in.

Despite the hot tea, I felt suddenly cold, a shiver sliding down the back of my neck. I didn't believe in ghosts, but I understood now why the house had the reputation it did. This didn't scare me in the way I'd have expected it to. I rather liked the idea of telling Eliza's story, even if it was my own version of it. Later, I'd print out a copy so I could read what I'd written from the page rather than the screen.

A raven landed on the sill outside the kitchen window; it was my little friend with the white marking. He stared at me through the glass, head swivelling to the left and right, black eyes fixed on mine. In the past I'd have banged on the window and shooed him away. Now I emptied the rucksack, taking out the bag of nuts I'd bought in the village.

As I was scattering them on the sill of the shed, I heard a whistling at the front of the house. Pieter. Damn, I'd forgotten he was coming. Mortified, I ran back into the bedroom, where I quickly pulled on some jeans and a jumper over my pyjamas, hoping he wouldn't notice, scraping my hair back into a ponytail. I took a quick look in the mirror and went to the front door to let him in.

He was standing on the threshold dressed in jacket and jeans and a scarlet woolly hat with tiny wood chippings caught up in the yarn. 'Morning. Am I too early?'

'No, it's fine.' Breezy.

Finn appeared, and he produced a chewy chicken stick from his pocket. 'I always have treats for the dogs in the houses where I work.' He smiled. 'Helps to make friends.'

There was a pause, and I realised we were still standing on the doorstep. 'Sorry,' I said, flustered. 'Do you want to come inside or see the garden?'

'Maybe we could go around the back. I'll see if I can work without disturbing you some mornings.' Pieter grinned and I knew I was busted.

Suppressing my embarrassment, I took him round the side of

the house into the garden. 'It's a bit of a mess. I don't think anyone has tackled it for a long time.'

'So I see.' He began to walk towards the far hedge. I went to follow him, but he waved me back. 'No, it's fine. Don't worry, you wait there.'

I looked down and saw that I was still in my slippers. Pieter high-stepped through the long grass and walked around the perimeter, pushing brambles out of his way. After a few minutes he came back, brushing leaves from his hat.

'Yes, I can clear it for you, no problem. There are some fine fruit trees that just need a little room to breathe. I know plants.' He smiled. 'Not so much the wild ones, like Maggie does, but I know the cultivated ones. I think there may have been a vegetable and herb garden here at one time. I could replant that for you if you wanted.'

'That would be amazing, thank you.' A couple of cherry tomato plants and some mint and lavender on the balcony was about as far as I'd been able to manage in Dublin. Now I saw myself growing all sorts of wonderful things and felt my eyes widen in pleasure.

I pointed to the hawthorn tree, stark in the middle of the garden. It wasn't the prettiest, with its twisted, fissured boughs, its greyish-brown bark teeming with insects. 'I'm not sure what to do with that. Should we dig it up, do you think?'

Pieter shook his head, appalled. 'Oh no. You can't do that. That's a fairy tree.'

'A what?' I looked at him with a slight smile. He didn't seem the superstitious sort.

'A fairy tree. Or a holy tree. I've come across them when I've been doing work in old houses. You can't touch them. It's considered really bad luck to cut them down or even remove branches.'

'Okay,' I said slowly.

'Also, a hawthorn tree used to be planted to mark where a baby who'd died in childbirth was buried. They couldn't be buried in consecrated ground.'

Involuntarily I touched my stomach, then snatched my hand away hoping he hadn't noticed.

He smiled, misinterpreting my frown. 'You think what a strange thing it is for a Belgian man to know this. I've been here a long time, and people tell me things. It helps me not to make mistakes.' He shrugged. 'People have superstitions you have to respect.'

'Do you think that might be the case here? That a baby might be buried there.' It gave me a very odd feeling, remembering suddenly what I'd read about Eliza having had another child, before her daughter.

'Very possibly.' Pieter nodded. 'The tree is out there on its own. And you see those stones clustered around the base? That's to prevent animals from digging it up. And the bones, I suppose.' He gazed thoughtfully at it for a few seconds, then took a breath. 'Is there anything you want done inside?'

'Oh, yes.' I brought him in the back door, through the kitchen and into the living room, which was a mess, paint and brushes still strewn about. 'Sorry. I'm in the middle of painting.'

'So I see. Looks good.'

I showed him the door and told him what had happened. As he went down on his hunkers to examine the lock, I found myself gazing at his strong shoulders and broad back. When he stepped into the room to look at the door from the other side, I followed him in. Immediately the temperature dropped and the room felt claustrophobic, as if the very air was preventing me from taking a breath. So much so that I had to step out again. I was about to ask Pieter if he felt the same, but he seemed unaffected, just continued fiddling with the door handle.

He looked up. 'It seems to be working fine, but I can easily replace it. You don't want to take chances with locks when you're living on your own. And I'll sort out internet for you too. When do you need it?'

'In about a week?' I smiled. 'Thank you. I'm very grateful. Coffee?'

Over hot drinks in the kitchen, I found myself becoming more relaxed with him, realising that what I had interpreted as taciturnity was a calm self-assurance. He was the polar opposite of Rory, who was always on, always performing. I sometimes wondered if all the noise Rory created was what had attracted me to him in the first place, because it allowed me to take a back seat.

But now I began to consider the possibility that I might actually be able to do this without him. Live here, have the baby. Even if I was on my own. Eliza Dunne did it all those years ago, in much more difficult circumstances. So why couldn't I?

CHAPTER TWENTY-SEVEN

Suzanne

Suzanne stood up from her desk and stretched her back. All that pounding of pavements wasn't doing her joints any good, but it was necessary to clear her head. She could have done with a run this morning, but she was in the station. On a Sunday.

It looked as if Rory O'Riordan's family were going to get their way. Suzanne couldn't remember things ever having moved so quickly before, but the segment about his disappearance was scheduled for *Crime Files* this week. She wondered if they'd used some of Rory's contacts to pull a few strings. That was how things worked in Dublin, she knew; it wasn't how deserving your case was, it was who you knew.

In any event, she'd done her bit, passing on all the information the producers had requested. She'd just emailed everything off, including some CCTV of Rory's car driving through Cleggan that she'd managed to track down. She composed the voiceover in her head. *If anyone has seen this man, please call the number at the bottom of the screen. Concern is growing for his welfare amongst his family, friends and colleagues. Last seen leaving . . .* She knew the drill.

Although you'd have to assume by now that the man was dead. It seemed impossible that he could stay under the radar for so long without accessing bank accounts or his phone. Suicide being the most likely outcome. Even Dave had conceded that, shelving his theory that Rory O'Riordan had done a runner on his girlfriend, or that the same girlfriend had done him in. And while Rory's family seemed convinced that Allie had driven him away – Andrew's claims that Allie had a temper had certainly wrong-footed Suzanne – even they would have to admit it seemed unlikely she'd had anything to do with his actual physical disappearance.

But it *was* baffling. If he had taken his own life, why hadn't his body been found? It had been nearly a month. Maybe this extra bit of publicity would stir something up.

Suzanne pulled on her coat. She'd come in especially to sort the stuff for *Crime Files*, but now she was out of here, looking forward to a couple of days off. Dinner, the cinema, pints in the local. She really didn't care. Tony was nagging her about spending too much time at work, and for once she had to admit he was right. Her head was full of the crap she'd been dealing with all week, and it would be good not to have to look at Dave's ugly mug for a day or two.

Her mobile rang, vibrating in her coat pocket. She extracted it reluctantly, cursing to herself. It was Frank, a friend from Templemore, now in the garda sub-aqua squad based in the west. There'd been a vague plan for a gang of them to meet up in Dublin before Christmas, but nothing had yet been arranged. She assumed that was why he was calling. Living outside the city, he'd have to organise a bed, and Suzanne expected it would be the one in her spare room.

She was desperate not to answer, to let the call go to voicemail and start her few days off right now. But of course, she did. No matter how tempted she might be otherwise, Suzanne Phelan always did the right thing.

'Frankie,' she said brightly. 'What's the craic? Are you returning to civilisation for a few days?'

Frank was shouting over what sounded like fairly lousy weather. 'Not yet, I'm afraid. I'll come back to you on that. That wasn't why I was ringing you.'

'Oh?' Suzanne took her keys from the drawer of her desk, shoved them into her coat pocket and started to walk towards the exit.

'Did I hear that you're involved in that case about the missing TV producer?' There was a pause, and it sounded as if he had switched the phone to his other ear. 'What's his name? Rory something?'

Suzanne stopped with her hand on the door, having pulled it open a few inches. 'Rory O'Riordan. Why?'

'What was it he was driving? I can't read Pulse on my phone. It's fucking pissing down out here.'

'An old Nissan. An Almera. Red. Why?'

'We've just found one.'

Suzanne turned on her heel, letting the exit door swing closed, and began walking back towards her desk. 'Where? Is it the same reg? Do you want me to get it for you?'

'No point. We can't tell yet.'

She held her breath. 'Why not?'

'Because it's submerged off a pier in Mayo. We have to wait till we get it up. Weather's too rough to do it yet.'

'Okay,' she said slowly.

'I've been down for a quick look. But we'll have to free it from the mud and silt on the seabed. Drag it up. Looks as if it's been there a while. Might take a bit of time.'

Suzanne paused, swallowing before asking, 'Is there a body in it?'

The wind took away Frank's voice, but not before he had a chance to reply. 'Looks like it.'

CHAPTER TWENTY-EIGHT

Allie

On the doorstep, I attached Finn's leash to his collar, ready to meet Maggie for our Sunday walk. I could smell a change in the weather. It was the third week in November. I'd be glad of her heater as the weather turned colder.

Pulling the door behind me, I turned to look at the cottage. My cottage, as I now thought of it. We seemed to have settled down with one another, Raven Cottage and me. In less than ten days it was beginning to feel like home. Despite the strange things that had happened – doors getting stuck, odd noises, the dead raven – the place was mine in a way the apartment never had been. Of course, I'd rather have Rory. But somehow I didn't feel as lonely as I had in Dublin. I had Finn. And Maggie and Pieter. Even the ravens felt like friends; not just the little one with the white marking, but other individuals too: the bird with the slightly wonky foot, the one with the eye that swivelled. And now, if I was right, a baby. I was glad I wasn't surrounded by concrete and traffic, my pregnancy connecting me to nature, to the earth and the trees.

There wasn't much heat in the sun, but I smiled as I turned my face towards the sky and watched Finn do his little hop of excitement, echoing my mood.

We'd just set off at a slow stroll, allowing fifteen minutes for Finn to sniff and pee, when a car sounded on the lane. If it was Maggie she was very early, and it didn't sound like her growling, tractor-like car. Could it be Harkin? I wondered.

And then it came into sight, a white Honda Civic with a yellow stripe down the side and the word GARDA splashed across the front. I felt my legs threaten to give way as the ground tilted beneath my feet. A familiar figure sat in the passenger seat. Garda Suzanne Phelan.

They must have news, I thought. Why else would they have driven all the way down from Dublin? The car came to a halt in front of the cottage and two guards got out, the driver a different man to the one who'd come to the apartment. Was he local? Panic spread through my stomach like a stain.

Suzanne approached, her expression grim. 'Good morning, Allie.'

'Have you found him?' My heart was beating so fast I could hardly breathe. I didn't have time for pleasantries, wasn't prepared to wait for them to put the news into a more palatable package.

She reached out to touch my arm. 'Let's go inside,' she said gently.

I shook my head and a wave of nausea washed over me, bile rising foully in my throat. I felt as if I could throw up right here in front of them. 'No,' I insisted. 'Tell me now. Have you found him?' Firmly, removing the shrill tone, anything that might be perceived as hysteria.

Suzanne dipped her head. 'We think we've found his car.'

'Where? How? Was he in it?' Myriad questions came into my head, words and thoughts tumbling over one another in their rush to get out.

'It's the same make and model. It was found submerged at the end of a pier, as if it had been driven off it. A boat collided with it and the sub-aqua crew went down to have a look. They're raising it later today.'

I swayed, picturing the pier in Cleggan, and remembering that sense I had of chasing Rory's shadow the whole time we were there. Was it possible he'd been there all this time? That I'd been that close to him? I felt a sudden urge to go back.

'Is he in it? Is he in the car?' I felt light-headed, and my head was pounding, blood roaring in my ears.

Suzanne Phelan nodded. 'There's a body in it. It's male.'

A scream. Falling. Air rushing into my lungs. Arms clutching my sides.

Suzanne Phelan and I sat in the living room. I'd nearly fainted, and the two guards had helped me inside. They'd given me a glass of water and then the other guard had gone to make tea. Finn followed him into the kitchen, as if craving male company.

'Where exactly was it found?' I asked again. I hadn't taken it in properly the first time. I'd felt as if I was floating above my body watching my own reactions. It was all I could do to stay focused now. 'Which pier?'

'Roonagh, in Mayo.'

'But he was in Galway.' I shook my head as if this meant it couldn't possibly be him. 'And he was seen at the toll station on the way back to Dublin.'

'Yes. We know.'

I felt confused, as if the guard was speaking in a language I didn't understand or used only occasionally. 'And you're sure it's his car?'

'It's the same make and colour,' she said calmly. 'And we're pretty sure it's the same reg. Although we won't be a hundred per cent sure until we raise it.' Her voice was soft. 'And we know the body is male. I'm so sorry.' Sitting in the armchair opposite, she kept her body angled towards me and her eyes fixed on mine.

I gazed down at my hand, picking at my cuticles, scratching at my thumb with the nail of my forefinger. 'So what do you think happened?'

Suzanne shook her head. 'We don't know. We have divers searching the sea around the pier. None of his things seem to be in the car, no bank cards, wallet, bag. Although we may find something when we raise it. The driver's door was open. As you know there's been no bank activity since he disappeared.' She paused. 'It does look like suicide.'

I shook my head, insistent. 'Suicide just isn't Rory.'

'I know,' she said. 'His family said the same.'

I looked up suddenly. 'You've spoken to them already?'

She looked apologetic. 'We had to. There was a *Crime Files* segment organised for next week. I tried to ring you about it. We've cancelled it, of course.'

I felt another wave of dizziness. *Crime Files*. Television. That blinding spotlight again.

She leaned forward, elbows resting on her thighs, her voice earnest. 'Does the location trigger anything? Have you any idea why he might have been there?'

I shook my head. 'I've never heard of that pier.' I had a sudden horrible image of Rory lying in the driver's seat of his car, submerged in seawater. 'Do you need me to identify him?' I asked, my voice shaking.

'That won't be necessary. There will be a post-mortem, of course, and we'll do DNA testing for identification.' For the first time Garda Phelan avoided my gaze. 'The car has been underwater for some time.'

Before she got back into the squad car, she said, 'You have my mobile number, Allie. Ring me any time. I mean it.'

They'd asked if there was anyone they should call to be with me. I'd said no. But as I watched them drive away, standing alone in the doorway with Finn, I felt frightened.

I realised that I hadn't truly thought that this would happen, that Rory would be found dead. The delay had given me a weird sense of postponement, which was a kind of comfort. Like that feeling in a waiting room before the dagger thrust of bad news. I should ring people to let them know, I thought distractedly. Soon. In a little while.

In a daze, I went back into the cottage to clear away the tea things. I felt a cramp at the fridge as I put the milk back in, but it passed quickly. Shock, I presumed.

Then I rang Olivia, standing at the front door, where I'd discovered there was also decent reception. She answered brightly. 'Hiya – how's the research going?'

For a minute I didn't know what she meant. And then a massive second cramp almost knocked me over, stopping all coherent thought. I was doubled up in pain when another car sounded on the lane. Louder than the squad car. Maggie's. I'd forgotten all about Maggie.

I barely heard her when she lowered the driver's window and called out, 'Is everything all right? I've been waiting ages, and now I've just seen a garda car coming out of the lane.' Her smile faded. 'Allie?'

'Allie?' Olivia said as I dropped the phone.

Maggie leaped out of the car and rushed over. And then everything went dark.

PART II

CHAPTER TWENTY-NINE

Allie

I stood alone at the back of Raven Cottage, watching Finn mooch about sniffing at the hedgerows and the grass. Autumn had long disappeared into winter, the changing seasons marked by chilling rain and low mist, although today was dry but grey.

Pieter had cleared the brambles and weeds, managing to save quite a few choked shrubs and fruit trees. He came every couple of days to do a few hours, the erratic nature of his visits making me feel better about not being able to pay him very much. His presence was gentle and unobtrusive, which was all I could handle now when everything seemed to hurt, a profound hollow ache permeating everything I did. I bent forward to pick a blade of grass, rubbing it between my thumb and forefinger, watching the green juice stain my skin. Holding something solid helped to ground me when I felt as if I was about to float away. I'd begun feeling blurred around the edges again, insomnia having tightened its grip. The nights were grim, and a seething darkness lurked at the edge of my days.

Finn leaped back comically, startled by something in the hedge, an overly exaggerated movement like an actor in a silent movie. I wanted to laugh, but it felt all wrong, like exercising a muscle I'd damaged. There was space for him to run around now and he barrelled about happily, using up steam, which allowed him to snooze for most of the day, something I'd find useful when I started work again on Monday. Pieter had sorted my internet too. I needed the money from my job, but more importantly, I needed distraction, somewhere else to put my thoughts.

Olivia emerged from the house to hand me a coffee, and I clasped my two hands around the mug, cradling it for warmth; after the miscarriage, I was no longer disgusted by the taste.

When I'd dropped the phone after starting to bleed, Maggie had picked it up, explained to Olivia what was happening and taken me to the hospital, while Olivia had driven down from Dublin. A small procedure followed and I was home the next day. All very straightforward, physically at least. If I hadn't also lost Rory.

I was surprised and touched that Garda Phelan – or Suzanne, as she'd asked me to call her now – had visited me in hospital, dressed in jeans and a fleece so as not to give me a scare, I suspected. *Another* scare. I imagined she felt guilty, although they said it would have happened anyway, that the loss of my pregnancy had nothing to do with the shock I'd received. It had simply been 'not viable'. Just like the last time.

For the couple of days that followed, Pieter took Finn for walks while Maggie looked after me, calling in twice a day and bringing food from the café, which she insisted was leftovers. And then Olivia appeared with the announcement that she'd taken some personal days from work.

I found her presence oppressive. She was sleeping on the floor of the small room, using cushions from the armchairs and a sleeping bag. She must have been uncomfortable, although she clearly didn't feel the atmosphere in the room as I did, or she wouldn't have been able to stay there. But it wasn't concern for her comfort that made me want her gone. With her shiny hair and perfect nails, my sister didn't fit the cottage. She was out of place and jarring here. The cottage was mine, and I wanted it to myself.

'You've a lot of crows,' she remarked.

The birds were making quite a din, landing and swooping in a frenetic noisy display. Scattering from tree to hedge to roof to telephone wire, skimming the ground. Swirling ebony squadrons of them, cawing and calling out to one another.

'They're ravens,' I said. 'I assume that's where the cottage got its name.'

She stepped forward to shoo them away, and I grabbed her flapping arm, surprised at my own strength. She shot me a startled look. But she stopped.

Two birds landed on the hawthorn tree, which Pieter had left untouched, mowing the grass only as far as the cluster of stones underneath would allow. They perched on a branch together, silently watching.

'Some people plant a tree when they lose a baby.' Olivia took a sip from her mug.

'I know.' I wondered again if the bones of Eliza's first baby were there. I'd thought about it every time I saw the tree since I came home from hospital.

'Maybe we could do it together,' she said. She gave me a half-smile. 'That handsome Belgian bloke could help.'

I shrugged. In truth, it was the last thing I wanted to do. I wanted to forget. It hurt too much to remember.

'Anything more from the guards?'

I shook my head. In the hospital, Suzanne had told me that Rory's wallet had been found on the seabed when his car was raised. This reduced the urgency on the DNA results, which would now take a couple of weeks, since it was assumed that the body was his. My sister liked her i's dotted and her t's crossed, but her constant enquiries weren't helping.

I braced myself. 'Olivia, seriously, I'm fine. There's no need for you to stay any longer.'

She regarded me doubtfully. 'Are you sure?'

'Yes. You can't keep sleeping on that floor. You'll get sick.'

'But—'

'I'm going back to work on Monday anyway. Have the weekend with your family. Go home.'

She dropped her chin. 'Fine. I'll go and pack. I'll leave after lunch.' She tossed the remains of her coffee onto the grass and went back inside.

She seemed a little hurt, but I was too exhausted to care.

I continued watching the ravens on the hawthorn. The smaller of the two flew off, then returned minutes later, landing a couple of feet away from me in the grass with a twig in its beak. It was my little friend; I could see his white marking. He approached me with his strutting walk and dropped the twig at my feet. When I picked it up, I was surprised to see that there was a rubber band wrapped around it. He'd crafted me a gift. I bowed and thanked him, smiling as he flew away again.

'Are you sure you're going to be okay?' Olivia stopped scraping plates into the bin for long enough to give me one of her concerned looks.

I knew she meant well, but I hated Olivia's concerned looks. Especially now.

'Certain.' If I said it with enough conviction, I could make it true, I thought, turning on the hot tap and determinedly squirting washing-up liquid into the sink.

'I'm worried about leaving you here on your own.'

'I'm not on my own. I have Maggie and Pieter if I need anything. And Finn.'

'I suppose.' Stacking the plates carefully on the counter, she picked up a tea towel. 'I admit you've coped far better than I expected, moving down here. Redecorating the cottage. Making friends. I'm proud of you.'

Setting aside a mild sense of irritation at her patronising tone, I said, 'It was hardly redecorating. I did a bit of painting, that's all.' The truth was that I hadn't even finished that; the small room hadn't been touched.

I loaded dishes into the soapy water and started to wash up, willing the subject closed. But Olivia had more to say. Olivia *always* had more to say.

'Don't take this the wrong way, Allie, please. But do you think that might have been because Rory wasn't here? The man who was pulling you down was gone? Like removing a magnet, giving you the ability to move freely.'

Olivia had prepared these lines, I could tell. How long had she waited to use the magnet metaphor?

I counted to ten, wearily closed my eyes and took a deep breath. 'I don't want to fight with you, Liv. But I've just lost my baby and the father of my baby in one week.'

She nodded, staring at the mug she was drying, hand inside it like a puppet as she carefully wiped the crevices, while I often put wet things straight back into the cupboard. 'I know that. I just want you to—'

There was only so much deep breathing I could do. 'What, Olivia?' I cried. 'What do you want me to do?'

She put the mug down. 'I just want you to talk to me.'

'What do you think I'm doing? You do nothing except talk; I have no choice *but* to talk to you.'

'That's not what I mean. You're not talking about what happened. This is a lot for anyone to process.'

'You mean even a normal person? Someone who isn't unhinged like me?'

To her credit, she ignored that. Sisters are well capable of navigating around each other's landmines if they choose to.

'It's not good for you to keep it all bottled up. If not me, then talk to *someone*.' A pause before she lowered her expensive boot onto the detonator. 'Remember what happened the last time.'

I withdrew the credit. 'That was different.'

'It seems similar. I hear you up in the middle of the night, the nightmares. You're talking in your sleep, but during the day you're hardly speaking. Or eating.'

I'd seen her look with disapproval at my relatively untouched plate. 'I'm fine.'

She shook her head. 'You're not, Allie. You seem disassociated, just like before. It took a long time to get you back last time. I don't want that to happen again.' Her eyes teared up. 'I missed you.'

'I was a teenager, Liv. I'd killed our parents. How did you expect me to react?'

She looked staggered. 'Do you still think that? Seriously?'

'I volunteered to collect them, all cocky having just passed my test. And then I drove us all into a fucking bridge and they *died*. What other way of seeing it is there?' I took my hands from the sudsy water and shook them dry. 'Tell you what. Why don't you finish the washing-up if you're so keen to help.'

I stormed out of the kitchen and into my bedroom, almost closing the door on poor Finn, who'd trailed in after me. I was tidying away a load of laundry that Olivia had done when she reappeared in the doorway.

'I'm sorry,' she said quietly. 'I know it's not something we talk about.'

I lifted a shirt, which she had folded so precisely it looked as if it should be in a cellophane wrapper in Marks and Spencer's. 'I don't know why you think bringing it up is going to help.'

She dipped her head. 'Maybe not.'

'Look, I get it. I didn't deal with it at the time and it came back and bit me on the arse years later. This is different. I *am* dealing with it. And I'm an adult now.'

'That's the problem. I think that what happened back then and your relationship with Rory are connected. I have done for a while.'

'How?'

'Well, for a start, he was so much older than you.'

I rolled my eyes. 'Please tell me you're not going to give me some father-figure bullshit. I killed my own father so I went looking for another.'

She looked appalled, but shook her head. 'No, I'm not. I know it's not something you want to admit, but Rory wasn't good for you. Before you moved down here you were convinced you couldn't survive without him. I think that came from him. If you keep someone socially isolated and tell them negative things about themselves, they believe them. I think that's what happened to you.'

'He didn't keep me isolated. That was my choice.'

Her internal struggle flickered in her eyes. Then she took a deep breath. 'There's something I haven't told you.'

I looked up, a cold feeling settling in the pit of my stomach. Did I really want to know whatever this was? Surely I had enough to deal with?

'I saw him, in Dublin airport. With a woman. They were having a drink. They looked very close.' Her arms were crossed and she said it quickly as if afraid she would change her mind.

I rolled up a pair of jeans.

'What was he doing in the airport?' I asked quietly. I felt pathetic, but I couldn't help myself. As far as I knew, Rory hadn't travelled abroad since he'd gone to Paris last year to film a segment for a documentary.

'I don't know,' Olivia said. 'I was taking the kids to Geneva on that school tour. Remember? I rang you that evening from the hotel and you said he was in an editing suite in town. It was clear you didn't know he was at the airport.'

I worked back in my head, remembering Olivia laughing as she told me about catching a couple of fifth years with a bottle of vodka, and the teachers polishing off the confiscated booze themselves. 'So, a couple of weeks before he went to Galway?'

I'd been pregnant then but hadn't known it. Rory hadn't known either.

Olivia nodded. 'I was shepherding the kids towards the flight. I suppose I didn't want him to know I'd seen him. I kept thinking I'd ring him and ask him about it.'

'But you didn't?'

She shook her head. 'I guess I knew it was pointless. That he'd talk his way out of it like he always did.'

I opened a drawer and shoved the jeans in.

Olivia pinched the bridge of her nose in exasperation. 'Aren't you going to say anything?'

I closed the drawer. I needed sleep, that was all.

CHAPTER THIRTY

Suzanne

'Can you believe it?' Suzanne fumed. 'Bastard locked her in the bathroom. All night. Accident, my arse. He took the key and locked it from the outside; that doesn't happen by accident.'

Dave shook his head despondently. 'I know. I agree with you. But what can we do? She's backing him up. The kid's evidence just isn't enough.'

They were walking from the car to the station, on their way back from a call-out to a domestic, a terrified eight-year-old boy who'd rung to say his father and mother had had a fight and that he had locked her in the bathroom. His dad said it was a game. But he hadn't let her out, the boy said; she'd had to sleep in the bath, and he was worried she would be cold. Also, he'd whispered, he wanted to pee but his dad told him to do it in the sink.

Dave had been surprisingly good with the kid, showing a sensitivity that Suzanne hadn't known he possessed, distracting him with chat about some video game they both played. But her partner was right – there was little they could do in terms of prosecuting without the wife's co-operation.

'I'll call Tusla,' Dave said, taking his phone out. 'See what they think. Just make sure the young fella isn't at risk.'

Suzanne raised her eyebrows in surprise. Dave volunteering to follow up on something instead of leaving it to her?

She pushed open the door of the garda station, and he came in after her, already on the phone to social services. Her own phone buzzed with a text as the door swung back. She took it out, read it and cursed loudly.

'What's getting on your tits now?' Dave asked, hand over his phone, apparently on hold.

Not a complete personality change, then.

'Still no bloody DNA results.' Suzanne didn't need to tell him whose. 'Could be another two weeks. Two weeks! Not urgent, they say. Try telling that to a family who are trying to organise a funeral.'

'No pal in the forensics lab then?' Dave said with a grin. 'Thought you had a sailor in every port?'

Suzanne didn't dignify that with an answer. Although Frank *had* been very helpful, keeping her informed about the raising of the car, the preservation of the scene and the post-mortem. But it didn't solve her present problem, the need to have something concrete to tell Allie, who hadn't been ringing, and Rory's brother, who had. Twice a day, every morning and afternoon, at nine and five. If his wallet hadn't been found, she might have something by now, but the overwhelming presumption that the body was Rory's, being a male of approximately the right age, with the car reg and wallet also a match, had pushed it off the priority list.

As they walked up the stairs to their floor, Dave breathing heavily in her wake, Suzanne admired his tenacity on the phone; despite being transferred from Billy to Jack and back to Billy again, he wasn't giving up.

She needed to call Allie and Andrew, she thought. Let them know about the delay. What worried her was that Allie Garvey was clearly more fragile than Suzanne or anyone else had given her credit for. A different creature certainly to the poor cowed woman they'd just met, whose gaze slid constantly to her husband, petrified of saying the wrong thing, Allie was composed enough for Dave to think her a cold bitch, her move to the Midlands creating the impression that she was able to carry on without Rory. But what if they'd been wrong?

Suzanne pictured that pale, stricken face on the pillow in the hospital. It had made her wonder if she should have kept the discovery to herself until the body had been properly identified. But she knew she couldn't have. The delay itself had shown that. They had an obligation to let the next of kin know, and in person if possible. Not least because they needed to gauge their response. Although Suzanne wished that she'd known Allie was pregnant. There might have been some way to manage things differently.

Dave hung up the phone. 'I have to ring them back in ten.' He pushed open the door to their floor. 'That poor kid. I'm going to keep an eye on him and his mother on the sly. That pathetic specimen of a father won't know what hit him if he tries anything like that again.'

Suzanne couldn't disagree with that.

Dave made a beeline for the coffee machine. 'Want one?' he offered over his shoulder.

Suzanne nodded, and sat at her desk, ready to make her own calls, searching for the numbers she needed.

'Hey, is it weird that Allie Garvey's parents died in a car crash and now her partner has died the same way?' Dave called over, interrupting her thoughts.

Oh God, don't start that up again, Suzanne thought. 'But she wasn't with Rory, she wasn't driving. It's different.'

Allie had been desperate to leave the hospital when Suzanne had visited, appearing almost panicked in the sterile room. Her sister, Olivia, whom Suzanne had met on the way in, had let it slip – or wanted her to know – that Allie had had a bad breakdown after college, which resulted in a prolonged stay in St John of God's. Olivia was clearly concerned for her sister, but then Andrew O'Riordan had been concerned for his brother too, claiming that Allie had a temper and that Rory had got the brunt of it. Who was telling the truth? Was it possible they both were?

Dave shrugged, on his way over with two mugs, taking a slurp out of one. 'Still, it's a bit of a coincidence. Did you know some of his documentaries are up on YouTube? I might have a gander.'

Suzanne looked up. 'Really?'

He nodded, plonking her coffee down and sloshing some out on her desk. 'Someone's put them up since he disappeared. They've had tons of views. He's more successful dead than alive.' His phone rang and he reached for it. 'Yes, excellent. Thank you for ringing back.'

As he made his way back to his desk, phone clamped to his ear, Suzanne took a sip of her coffee. It was annoying, but Dave sometimes hit the nail on the head. And her antennae were starting to twitch.

CHAPTER THIRTY-ONE

Allie

Tap-tap-tap. A face stared at me through the bedroom window, a long finger rapping on the glass. A dark shape lurked in the corner of the room, and the figure was inside, whispering to me, touching my face. I tried to move away, but couldn't. Not a muscle. Tried with all my strength to move my little finger. Nothing. I screamed, but no noise came out. Sleep paralysis: an affliction I'd had since my parents' death, which returned when I was unhappy or under stress.

Tap-tap-tap. The noise came again. This time I woke with a jolt, head pounding. A merciful release until that devastating loss hit me like a juggernaut, as it always did once those few blissful seconds of forgetting were over, my eyes dry and itchy from the tears I'd cried before going to sleep.

The wardrobe door swung open, making me jump. I watched it move slowly to and fro, creaking like a hangman's noose in an old cowboy film. When it came to a stop, I hauled myself out of bed and wedged it shut with a chair. How had it opened by itself? I wondered. I remembered closing it when I'd put away the clothes that Olivia had washed. I checked the time on my phone: 03.32.

Back in bed, I closed my eyes. I'd just begun to doze off again when Finn barked. My eyes opened to see him standing upright in his bed, ears pricked. He walked to the bedroom door, clearly wanting to go out.

'Ah, Finn, it's the middle of the night,' I groaned, climbing out of bed again and padding into the kitchen with the dog in my wake.

As soon as I opened the back door, he bolted out of it like a horse from a gate, sprinting about the garden as if searching for something while I stood there bleary-eyed, head thick with sleep. It reminded me of when Rory would whistle for him and hide. Finn would bound about, nose in the air, desperate to obey the summons and be a good dog. I'd always thought it a little mean.

A half-moon cast a dim shadowy light on the garden, and I watched for a while as the dog circled the hawthorn tree. But it was cold, fog blanketing the grass, and I shivered. I called for him to come in, but he'd disappeared, probably behind one of the fruit trees that Pieter had uncovered.

I was about to go out after him, concerned he might take off again, when I felt a sudden rush of air, like someone sweeping past me, leaving the house. I stood with my hand on the latch, heart pounding. And then in the mist I saw a figure; a woman silhouetted in the moonlight, standing at the hawthorn tree. I looked at her so hard, it was almost as if I willed her to disappear. One second she was there, and the next she wasn't.

I reached for the kitchen light, groping around in the dark to try to find the switch. And then something brushed against my thigh and my heart almost stopped, until I saw it was Finn, his black coat making him easy to miss. Relieved, I touched his head and turned the light on, briefly moving around the room checking things, still half asleep, before locking up and going back to bed.

In the morning, I woke in a state of acute unease, afraid I was starting to imagine things again: that face at the window, the woman in the mist. Though I'd denied it, Olivia was right when she said this was similar to what had happened before. Darkness crowding in, dread swirling like a violent wind before a storm. My field of vision narrowing, wanting to shut down so I didn't have to face any of it.

Since Rory's car had been found, I'd tried hard to remember that last row, what he'd said, what I'd said, what I'd done. But all I had was the beginning of the evening, my drinking too much, and then nothing but black spots. It wasn't the first time it had happened. More than once I'd woken with a crippling hangover, only for Rory to fill me in on what I'd done the night before. He would be distant for a few days, but always forgave me eventually.

Rationally I knew it was unlikely, but I was terrified that something I'd done or said had caused him to take his own life, just as I'd driven my parents into that bridge. Just as it was my fault that I'd lost our baby. I'd drunk wine and coffee and climbed ladders. *My fault.*

Guilt had been part of my life for as long as I could remember. In the aftermath of my parents' deaths, I became disconnected, as if I wasn't part of the world. I'd functioned at some sort of normal level for a few years, scraping through my degree, but after I left college, it all fell apart. A Pandora's box of fragmented, guilt-laden memories that I'd tried my best to pack away returned, landing me in hospital.

I'd recovered eventually. But then years later, when the guilt came back, as it always did, I'd used drugs and alcohol to dull things. Which was when Rory met me. Outwardly fun, inwardly rotten. Olivia was wrong about Rory. He hadn't isolated me. He'd protected me, rescuing me from myself. I knew I was difficult to be with, difficult to live with, difficult to love. But he had managed all three. I thought about Olivia's magnet metaphor, that

Rory was pulling me down. Whereas it was more likely to be the other way around.

What if he'd been struggling to get away from *me*? Maybe that was what he'd been doing at the airport. If you don't chatter nineteen to the dozen, people think you have nothing to say, that you're a little stupid. But I wasn't stupid. And I wasn't blind. I knew Rory had an effortless easy charm, that only one side of his character was on display. But I had a dark side too. With a flush of shame, I remembered him telling me about times when I'd lashed out at him. He'd show me bruises the next day that I had no memory of inflicting. So I hurt people too. I *killed* people.

I felt the room start to spin. I ran my hands through my hair and a clump came out. Staring at the tangle of strands in my palm, I knew that I needed to pull myself together. I couldn't allow myself to turn inwards as I had done in the past. This time, I needed to fight it.

And then something cold touched my arm; Finn was nudging me with his nose, his head poking in beneath the duvet.

There was post on the mat, the first I'd had since I'd moved here. A small package that I opened without thinking. It was the pregnancy test I'd ordered. I threw it against the wall, and then binned it.

While Finn ate his breakfast in the kitchen, I stood at the sink and looked out at the hawthorn tree, remembering again that figure in the mist. I knew I couldn't afford to get spooked; I'd enough inner turmoil going on without seeing ghosts as well. But I found myself fantasising that the figure could have been Eliza, whose baby, like mine, had died. Whispers from the realms of the dead; the idea was strangely comforting.

Condensation bubbled on the window, making a liquid

pattern of trickling peaks and troughs, showing the dip in temperature outside. And suddenly it seemed to me that the most solid thing in my life right now was the cottage. My cottage. If I was feeling unmoored, the house would anchor me. I had two full days before I needed to be back at work. Maybe I should paint the little room.

But when I stepped inside it, I was immediately aware of that same tension I always felt in there, like a change in pressure. It was as if I was being watched, the atmosphere alive and brimming as though something terrible had happened in there, seeping into the very walls. And I knew instantly that I couldn't paint them.

Back in the living room, I caught sight of that small door to the right of the chimney breast. I had a torch now; I'd bought one in the village. Maybe I should take another look inside. If the house was trying to speak to me, perhaps I needed to listen.

I found the torch, slipped two batteries in, fetched and opened out the stepladder and climbed up. This time I tugged gingerly at the knob until the door unstuck and opened. I switched on the torch and scanned the space. It was sizeable enough, about a metre and a half square, a bit deeper than it was wide, containing nothing but cobwebs and dust. I was about to climb back down again when the torch's beam caught something at the back. I couldn't see what it was; it was too dim. I'd have to get up into the space to investigate, the very thing I'd dreaded since I'd got locked in the little room.

Finn looked up at me, his brown eyes anxious. And I had an idea. I climbed down, fetched the library book and used it to block the door so it couldn't shut. This time I wasn't taking any chances.

The space was large enough that I could almost stand up in it, although I wouldn't have wanted to – the claustrophobia if my head hit the roof would have been too much for me. Thankfully the floor felt solid beneath my feet. I supposed it must be made of stone, being above the door into the bedroom, in the middle of a supporting wall.

I shuffled across on my knees to see what had caught my eye. The space was filthy with the dust of generations, but the torch was powerful and I was glad I'd picked the more expensive one in the shop. What I found was another small door; a sort of cupboard within a cupboard. I imagined that when the main space was full of whatever was stowed in here, linens or suchlike, this little door wouldn't be visible. It would be a good place to hide something you didn't want found in a cottage where hiding places were scarce.

There was no knob on this door, just a nail hammered in and twisted to form a hook. It was this that had caught the beam of the torch. I pulled it, surprised to find that the door opened easily, onto a much smaller space. This one wasn't empty. It contained a wooden box the size of a large jewellery box. I reached for it, drew it out of its hiding place, closed both doors and took it back down the ladder.

Finn's joyful relief at my reappearance made me smile, his tail wagging to a blur. I placed the box on the table and cleaned the dust off. It was carved, wooden, about the size of a petty cash box. The carving was so old it had faded almost to blue, making it impossible to see what it depicted. It had a keyhole and a little clasp, which I rattled, but it was definitely locked. Was it possible that it had belonged to Eliza Dunne? Or was that just wishful thinking on my part? There must be many generations who had made Raven Cottage their home.

Finn whined and stretched, dropping a gigantic hint. Reluctantly I put the box in the bedroom with the library book and grabbed his leash.

CHAPTER THIRTY-TWO

Though I hadn't intended to, I found myself walking the whole way to the village, for the first time since my visit from the guards to tell me that Rory's car had been found.

In the café, Maggie looked up from arranging cakes at the counter. 'Ah, Allie, it's good to see you out and about.'

'Thanks for being so kind to me the past week.' I swallowed, suppressing the self-pitying urge to wallow in her sympathy, and asked, 'How are you?'

She leaned on the counter, tea towel tossed over her shoulder. 'Not too bad. I have some decisions to make.' She looked tired, dark shadows beneath her eyes, and I wondered if she too hadn't been sleeping.

'Really? Like what?'

'Ah, I'll tell you when they're made.' She paused. 'No news, I suppose?'

I shook my head. Somehow, I didn't mind Maggie asking so much. She hadn't known Rory, hadn't disliked him in the way Olivia did.

'I suppose these things take time.'

'They tell me it could be a couple more weeks.'

'Lord. That's tortuous. You've been through a lot, you poor

thing.' She waved at one of the tables. Again the café was empty, despite it being a Saturday morning. 'Sit down and I'll bring you something to eat. You look as if you could do with feeding up. Your sister gone?'

I nodded. 'Yesterday afternoon.'

Remembering that I still had the twig with the elastic band in my coat pocket, I showed it to Maggie, and told her about the little raven bringing me a gift, thinking she would appreciate it.

She turned it over in her hand, smiling. 'You must have been kind to them. They remember, you know. They remember cruelty too.' She raised a finger. 'Actually, I have something for you as well.'

She disappeared out the back of the café and reappeared seconds later with a pair of hiking boots that looked brand new. 'Any interest? I bought the wrong size online. They're way too small for me and now I've left it too long to return them.'

I turned them over in my hands, checking the size on the sole. They *were* brand new and in my size. Quite the coincidence, if you believed in coincidences.

'If they fit, you could try them out on the walk tomorrow, if you're up for it? We're doing one of the looped routes from Monicknew, up through Bawnrush. It's a lovely walk. Lots of uphill, though, I warn you.'

The truth was that the prospect exhausted me. Not just the hike, though the walk to the village had taken more out of me than I thought. It was the idea of having to talk to people; wear a mask of normality, pretend that everything was okay. Or worse, answer concerned questions. But I knew I needed company, that was something else I'd learned.

So I tried the boots on, and they fitted perfectly. I didn't for a second believe Maggie's story about ordering the wrong size; she was way too canny for that, and a considerably larger woman than me. But I thanked her and said I'd come.

'Good.' She beamed. 'Bring food and water; we'll be out all day. Now, how about some soup? Butternut squash?' She bent down to Finn with her hands on her thighs. 'Rasher?'

By the time she joined me at the table a few minutes later, Finn was flat out at my feet, though he managed to rouse himself for the bacon.

I'd been wondering if I should tell her what was on my mind. 'Can I ask you something?'

She rubbed Finn's head. 'Sure.'

I knew I could rationalise everything that had happened, that I probably *should*. An old house was bound to have strange noises and quirks. The woman at the tree could have been a trick of the light; the wardrobe door caused by uneven stone flags; waking up in another room nothing more than my own sleepwalking. But since I'd found the box, I wasn't sure I wanted to, and I thought Maggie would understand.

'I've seen someone. A woman. Standing by the hawthorn tree.'

Her eyes narrowed, but she said nothing, just kept playing with Finn's ears.

'I can't help thinking about Eliza. That library book I showed you? It says there were rumours that she gave birth twice, that one baby died.' My voice broke on the last few words and Maggie reached out for my hand.

'Pieter told me what the hawthorn tree could mean,' I continued. 'The one in my garden. Why they were planted on their own like that. I know it sounds crazy, but what if I saw Eliza visiting her baby's grave?'

I felt Maggie flinch.

'Am I losing my mind?' I asked with a tearful half-smile. I looked down at my hands, and saw that my cuticles were red and raw.

Maggie squeezed my hand but didn't confirm or deny it.

'But then, even if I imagined what I saw, even if Eliza wasn't visiting her baby in death, she still kept them close, burying them in the garden rather than the graveyard. She was a loving mother.' There was a lump in my throat.

Maggie nodded. 'I imagine she was.'

'So why then would she go off and leave her living child alone in her kitchen?' I cried. 'Just abandon her? I can't imagine doing that.' I felt the tears spill over my lashes. 'If I'd been given the chance.'

Maggie looked down and shook her head, curls falling over her face. And I wondered if she was crying too.

I called into the supermarket to grab some food before heading home, rolls for the walk the next day and, as an afterthought, a bottle of wine. I hadn't had a drink since I suspected I was pregnant, but I needed something to dull the edges again.

Finn stopped and started, sniffed and peed the whole way home, so progress was slow, allowing me time to think. I hadn't meant to pour all of that out to Maggie. She reacted how I'd have expected, that the loss of my pregnancy and waiting for news on Rory must be a strange and terrible time and it was completely understandable I would be thinking about such things. While she was kind, I couldn't help feeling that she didn't want to encourage me, so I'd decided not to tell her about the box I'd found.

But it didn't stop me thinking about it, wondering about the key and where I might find it, walking around the cottage in my head. The kitchen and bathroom were relatively modern additions, the bedroom had no cubbyholes, and the other room was tiny, which left only the living room: a neat square with a table and chairs and two armchairs in front of the fire.

Finn cocked his leg over a branch. A rural fire hydrant. And then it hit me. The fire! What if whoever owned the box had put the key in the fireplace? Or up the chimney.

I couldn't get home quickly enough. Once I'd fed Finn and put the groceries away, I stood in front of the fireplace examining it closely. It was so big I could probably stand *in* it; which meant there were bound to be ledges or holes inside where you could secrete a tiny key. Fire and smoke wouldn't damage a metal key; it might blacken but it would still work.

I grabbed the torch and stepped into the hearth. It felt pretty strange and I almost choked from the soot. But I used the beam to search the flue, trying and failing not to rub my clothes against the internal walls. I was just deciding it was a fool's errand, and that I was the fool, when I found it. Bingo! A tiny black key slid into a gap between two bricks. I couldn't take it out with my fingers; they were too thick. But as I crouched to step out of the fireplace, I felt my own key ring in my pocket and remembered that it had a miniature Swiss army knife on it – a present from Olivia from that school tour to Geneva. Stepping back in again, I used the tiny nail file to poke out the key, and it fell to the ground with a clatter.

When I emerged for the second time, I coughed, wiped my eyes, dropped the key onto the table and headed into the bedroom, where I peeled off my grimy clothes. Catching sight of myself in the pitted old glass of the dressing table mirror, I laughed – I looked like a chimney sweep from a Dickens adaptation – then cried out when I spotted a figure behind me. I turned quickly, and realised it was a shirt on a hanger swinging from the wardrobe door.

When I got out of the shower, I dressed and shoved the sooty clothes into the washing machine, then set about trying to open the box. The key fitted perfectly, and I turned it, heart thumping with excitement. Opening the lid, I found a leather-bound book inside, which I lifted out and carefully opened the cover. It seemed to be an appointment or accounts book; creamy white pages filled with columns of spidery writing in scratchy blue-black ink. On the flyleaf were the words I'd hoped for – *Miss Eliza Dunne, Parish of Rath, 1890*.

With a strange reverence, I turned the pages, reading names and initials, running my finger down the columns of tiny dates and figures. I felt as if I were talking to the dead just as Eliza had done. Payments included a chicken and potatoes. Tobacco. So it wasn't as simple as people finding money for her services, I thought. They paid her in kind, with things that she needed for herself and her child. And Maggie had been right. Eliza's clients were all women.

I ran my hands over the cover. No one knew what had happened to Eliza Dunne; her disappearance remained a mystery. But her descendants were still around, including Maggie herself. I knew how it felt to crave information about someone close to you. Surely, despite what Maggie said, she would want to know what had happened to Eliza? Perhaps the house was trying to give me that information, calling out for old wrongs to be righted.

That night, I picked up the library book that I'd left on my bedside table. Having discovered Eliza's book and seen her handwriting, I found I wanted more, craving her company. I took another look at her photograph before starting to read, picking up where I'd left off.

> It was the women of the area who went to Eliza. Most people come to spiritualism through the death of someone they love. Who wouldn't want to have certainty that life doesn't just end? To know that those who are gone are still watching over us? But what these women heard gave them strength,

the strength to speak their minds, to stand up to their men, believing that the advice Eliza gave them came from beyond the grave. People trusted what they were told by those who had passed over.

Eliza claimed that once she contacted someone, they would leave their essence behind, making it more likely that they would return. So the living returned to her too, to continue their conversations with their dead. Was Eliza taking advantage of vulnerable people, or was she providing solace and comfort to those who needed it?

'Spirit, are you there?' she would ask, and the spirits would tap, one for yes, two for no, one for 'a', two for 'b'.

I stopped reading. There it was again. The tapping that Olivia had mentioned. Was that what I'd been hearing? More than once, it was that very noise, a tapping, that had drawn me into the little room. Could it be an 'essence' left behind, as Eliza herself would have said?

I shivered, pulling my duvet more tightly around my shoulders, and read on.

Rumour had it that Eliza didn't like men, though it seems she gave birth at least twice. A woman who stood apart, who ploughed her own furrow, whose refusal to conform made her an object of derision, her sway over women would have made her a target for the local men. She must have known that she was risking their ire, but it is thought that she also enjoyed planting doubt, sowing the seeds of discontent. Eliza Dunne was a woman with influence.

Reaching the end of the piece, I put down the book and fell into an uneasy sleep.

CHAPTER THIRTY-THREE

After a disturbed night, I awoke so light-headed with exhaustion that I was tempted not to go on the walk. But I knew that I needed people around me, so I dressed for the outdoors.

After breakfast, and while Finn was eating his, I opened the wooden box again and took out the book. I'd been kept awake for much of the night by the notion that there was something in it that Eliza wanted me to see. I knew how crazy that sounded. Equally crazy was the notion that the house had gifted it to me, but now I wondered if it was Eliza herself. Maybe she was the one propelling me on?

I opened the cover, and saw again the columns and figures, the sums of money, the apples, the meat. Why would Eliza need to hide this, secrete it away where no one would find it? I understood why she would keep a record of what people paid her. But why conceal it? I remembered what Olivia had said about people's interest in spiritualism in Ireland remaining underground, needing to be hidden because of the Catholic Church. But there was no indication that this was the service Eliza was providing. No *proof*. She could have been doing anything in return for these payments. Sewing, washing, cures, anything.

I turned the pages slowly. The writing came to an end halfway through, the remaining pages blank. The final entry was on 29 December 1890 – the payment of one shilling from a Mary Tiernan, who seemed to be a regular visitor.

Disappointed, I turned to the last page. What I hadn't noticed was that there was writing there too, in the same scratchy ink pen. But this time it was upside down. I turned the book over and saw that it continued for a number of pages, as if Eliza had started writing from both ends. I wondered if they had been different years.

But when I started to read, I discovered that this section was different. There were no numbers or payments. Instead, there was information about people, personal information. Not just women. Men too. And while there were dates included here also, these were dates in the past, well before 1890.

> *Mary Mannion, died 1878. Priests' housekeeper. Child? Died of consumption.*
>
> *Francis Tobin, father of Susan, overly fond of whiskey and using his fists. Died in a ditch, summer of 1888.*

Were these snippets that Eliza had heard about people or things they'd told her themselves? At first I thought they must be secrets, things of which people were ashamed, that they wanted hidden. And I wondered if Eliza was blackmailing them. But somehow that didn't fit. I had nothing on which to ground my opinion, but I felt sure that Eliza Dunne was a good person, that she wanted to help others.

And anyway, this information all appeared to be about people who were long dead in 1890 when she made the entries. All had dates of death. What would be the point of blackmailing dead people? They had outrun their shame by dying. There had been times when I'd wanted to do that, to outrun my shame. That was much easier before the internet. Today your shame could outlive you.

But reading on, it hit me that not everything she wrote down would have been a secret or shameful. Some of it must have been common knowledge, at least while the people were alive.

> *Mary Tiernan, mother died of influenza at 77.*
>
> *James Tiernan, cooper, brother of Mary, father of Bridget Kennedy. Died at 48. Falling sickness. Birthmark in armpit.*
>
> *Mollie Coakley – a twin. Male twin died at birth. Never baptised.*

These were apparently insignificant details about people, seemingly written at different times. Pieces of information added here and there, presumably when Eliza came upon them. But why would she keep note of all this? The surnames were the same as those in the columns at the front of the book. Were these the dead relatives of the people who consulted her?

I thought about that line from the book – *People trusted what they were told by those who had passed over* – and an idea began to percolate. I remembered the scene I'd half written just before Rory was found. What if Eliza's story was more complicated than I thought? What if Eliza herself was more complicated?

I went to get my laptop, opened the scene and continued to write.

> Eliza gazed at the wall, a distant look in her eyes. 'Your father is here. He ~~wishes~~ wants to speak to you. He says you must leave Edward. That you must keep yourself safe.'

Bridget's eyes widened. It was what she had hoped for. But not quite what she had expected. She had expected more of a show. 'Does he not tap?'

'Your father's voice I can hear. Some I cannot.'

She seemed content with this. 'How do you know it is him?'

Eliza thought quickly. 'He had the falling sickness.'

But Bridget shook her head. That was well known. She was no fool.

And then Eliza remembered something that Mary Tiernan, Bridget's aunt, had said.

'He wonders if the child in your belly will be a boy, if his grandchild will have the same mark as he did. The heart-shaped birthmark under his arm.'

Bridget stared at her wide-eyed. For a moment she was speechless. She exhaled and touched her stomach, overcome by emotion, her poor cut lips unable to produce a sound. Eliza thought she was so frightened of her husband that she could not see it, could not identify the signs, even of something she craved. It was also her first time. Perhaps she did not bleed regularly.

'Is it true?'

It was early, but Eliza was sure; she could see the slight thickening at the waist, the fuller breasts. She'd been through it twice herself.

'It is your father who has told me,' she lied. 'He knows these things.'

Bridget left eggs. Eliza had no need of them – her own hens laid so many that she sold them in the village. But Bridget would only accept advice she paid for, and Eliza hoped it would give her courage.

I reread what I'd written, and was quite pleased with it. Then I caught the time at the bottom of the screen. Dammit. I was late. I pulled on my new boots and a jacket, grabbed the bread rolls I'd filled the night before and a bottle of water and shoved them in the backpack.

Weirdly, Finn didn't seem to want to leave the cottage this morning. In a complete reversal of how he'd been when we moved in, he hesitated in the doorway, a doubtful expression on his face. I tugged on his lead to get him to come, but he kept looking behind him as if waiting for someone to follow.

When Maggie pulled up at the main road, there was someone in the car with her. Pieter. He offered me the front seat, but I opted to sit in the back with Finn, who settled with his head resting on my knee, gratifying since he usually only did that with Rory.

'It's a nice day for it,' Maggie said, pulling away with the usual growl. 'Bright and cold. Perfect for a walk.'

Pieter turned in his seat to speak in his slightly awkward syntax. 'I keep meaning to ask. You don't drive or you just don't have a car?'

'I don't drive.'

'I could teach you if you like,' he smiled.

'Oh no, I *can* drive,' I said, flushing with embarrassment. 'I just lost my nerve.'

The truth was that I'd loved driving from the first time I got behind the wheel, even signing up for a course in car maintenance at school with the boys. It was the reason I'd been so excited when I passed my test just after my exams, desperate to drive every chance I got.

Other than the incident that landed me in St John of God's in my twenties, I hadn't driven since the accident. Until last year, when Rory persuaded me to drive his car into town. He'd said it would be good for me to face my fears. At first, I'd thought I was fine, happy that he had pushed me. I made it as far as the quays before my nerve failed. A panic attack at a set of traffic lights resulted in another motorist calling an ambulance; I remembered crouching down outside the car unable to breathe, flashing blue lights, paramedics. Rory took the bus into town to drive me home, after which the thought of being in charge of something that could kill terrified me.

'What happened?' Pieter asked, adding quickly, 'You don't have to say if you don't want to.'

I shook my head, shrugging it off. 'It was silly. City traffic. I'm sure I'll get over it in time.'

'I can still take you out sometime if you like,' he said kindly. 'Maybe you'll be able to drive here on the quieter roads.'

As he spoke, a Toyota with a souped-up engine and a giant exhaust overtook us, roaring past in a cloud of noxious fumes.

'Just maybe not this one,' Maggie said wryly over the din as I gripped Finn's collar.

We turned off the main road and headed up into the mountains, driving through a tunnel of trees before emerging at the entrance to a large car park on a steep rise. I was glad to see the waiting group was small. Jim and Cathy gave me sympathetic looks when we got out of the car, and I wondered if Maggie had told them what had happened. But no one mentioned my trip to hospital or the discovery of Rory's car, and I was grateful for that.

We set off, walking a short distance down the main road before cutting off to the left into dense forestry and down towards the river valley. Inhaling the cold woody air, I felt I could breathe properly for the first time in a week.

'The Glen river,' Maggie said, playing the tour guide, I presumed, for my benefit. The route meandered left up the mountain, but to the right was a fine old stone bridge, which she also pointed out, this time with a smile. 'The Glen bridge.'

All eyes were drawn to it, including mine. It was impressive, built in the style of a Roman arch, like an aqueduct or a railway bridge. It must have been ten metres high, and I gazed upwards as the water rushed through below.

And then suddenly my breath caught. The others were chatting, but their voices faded away to nothing as I had a flashback so real it was as if I was reliving it: that breathless terror, my hammering heart as the car sped out of control. A deafening crash, and then nothing. The bridge was identical to the one I'd driven into with my parents.

Somehow I managed to continue walking. But if I thought the others hadn't noticed, I was wrong. Cathy reached out to help me over a muddy trench and Jim apologised for spooking me about the cottage on the last walk.

I tried to brave it out. Nothing to see here. 'As a matter of fact, I did a little research after that. I'm reading about Eliza Dunne at the moment.'

Jim raised his eyebrows. 'The witch?'

I flinched. 'I thought she was a medium.'

'Same thing back then.' He raised his palms in a gesture of surrender when Cathy gave him a dig in the ribs. 'I'm not suggesting that's what she was,' he added quickly. 'I'm saying that people were superstitious. They didn't trust anyone who was different.'

'Particularly a woman,' his wife added darkly.

'Particularly a woman,' he conceded. 'They said that she left her child and ran off with some man, or because of the drink; that she always had a bottle of whiskey on her. The truth was that she was probably driven away because people were afraid of her. I'd say she was made to leave.'

I stepped over a bramble that snaked out across the path, this time ignoring the arm offered by Jim. 'I thought people consulted her?'

'In secret. They certainly wouldn't have talked about it. The Church disapproved.' He grinned. 'No change there. Anything they can't control, they don't like.'

This tallied with what Olivia had said.

'And I don't think her sort went to church. That was part of the problem.' He lowered his voice. 'Although her daughter, Gretta, is buried in the old graveyard down your lane. The child that was left behind? She was brought up by Harkin's ancestors, so she'd have been baptised.'

I remembered, suddenly, Cathy telling me that Jim claimed to have seen a woman in that graveyard, and I wondered if he would mention it. Before he had a chance, Maggie called me over, a bit abruptly, I thought.

'What did I say to you about not talking to other people about the cottage?' she hissed.

I was stung, startled by her sharp tone. She'd been so gentle with me since the miscarriage. It was true that I'd forgotten what she'd said, but Jim and Cathy didn't seem to mind talking about it. It was Maggie who did. Her attitude was confusing to me – it just didn't make sense.

Before I could reply, Cathy shouted suddenly, pointing to the sky. 'Are they raptors?'

We looked up in time to see a number of large birds soaring

and gliding majestically above us. Using the air currents to stay aloft.

'I'm pretty sure they're ravens,' Pieter responded, hand shielding his eyes.

Maggie confirmed it, and we watched as a they performed breathtaking tumbles and loops. A conversation ensued about how agile they were, how they hitched a ride on warm air to conserve energy, Maggie sharing her knowledge. I didn't participate. My cheeks remained hot with embarrassment, like a child who'd been told off in public.

While the others were distracted, Pieter whispered to me, 'Don't worry about it. I'll call and see you tomorrow.'

CHAPTER THIRTY-FOUR

It was a bright day for ~~October~~ November. Eliza tended her garden while Gretta played with the cat, throwing a discarded skein of wool along the grass and scattering the hens. She plucked large fruits that had failed to ripen from the fig trees, leaving the little pea-sized ones for next year, smiling as she imagined how tall Gretta would be by then. Then she went to tend her herb garden; it was time to take cuttings of rosemary, lemon verbena and thyme.

On her way there, she reached her hand out to touch the hawthorn tree, feeling a wave of sadness for the little boy who had lived only minutes. A brief happy time that ended too quickly when his father died before he was even born. It was then that Eliza knew for certain that she didn't have the gift, seventh daughter or not. If she had, he would have contacted her.

Her boy had been conceived in love. Unlike Gretta. Not that you could tell, thankfully. She heard her little girl chuckle as the cat tangled itself in knots. Eliza tried not to think of the fear and violence of that night. Tried only to remember that it had brought her daughter.

A twig broke and she spun around quickly. A visitor during the day was unusual. A man stood silhouetted in the winter gloom with the sun behind him. For a second she feared it might be Edward Kennedy. She had seen Bridget with him in town, listless and afraid, scurrying away on his arm. Her courage having clearly failed her so far.

Then she thought it might Gretta's father, although he had left Eliza alone since she was born, afraid of a likeness being seen. Too much of a risk, despite her being easy pickings. Despite their meeting almost every day on the lane.

But no, it was the priest, Brophy, looking for all the world like a raven in his black garb.

'To what do I owe this honour, Father?' Eliza's voice dripped with sarcasm as she rubbed her hands on her apron.

'You are one of my flock, are you not?' His face was pink with the exertion of walking up the lane, but his tone was still pious.

'Am I?' She smiled.

'Although you do not attend Mass, despite the chapel being so nearby.'

'I have other things to do.' She gestured towards the little basket of cuttings and fruit on the grass. 'As you see.'

'I know the things you are doing.' The priest's eyes narrowed into slits, his mask of politeness slipping.

'And what is that, Father?'

'You know that it is believed you have the ability to see spirits, and you encourage that falsehood.'

'I cannot help what people believe.'

He pointed a beringed finger at her face. 'You are a fraud. You do the work of the devil.'

Eliza laughed in contempt. 'If that is so, then both of us are charlatans. You with your smells and bells and me with my tapping and my voices.'

The priest spluttered. 'Then you do not deny it.'

'Only if you admit that we are cut from the same cloth, you and I.' She found she was enjoying taunting him.

A pulse beat in his neck just above his collar and she could see he was struggling to keep his temper. 'What have you been saying to Bridget Kennedy? Telling her to leave her husband. Convincing her that her dead father is speaking to her.'

Eliza kept her voice steady. Brophy did not frighten her, but she hoped for Bridget's sake that he had not spoken to Edward. 'You believe in the afterlife, do you not?' she said. 'In heaven and hell. The difference between us is that I don't judge.'

The priest sneered. 'Maybe it would serve you better if you did. Just because you are a woman of loose virtue, it does not give you the right to encourage others to follow the same dark path.'

Eliza did not like the way he looked at Gretta when he said that.

As if sensing weakness, he smiled, his voice low and dangerous. 'If you do not stop what you are doing, I will tell Edward Kennedy that you intend breaking up his family, as you have failed to do elsewhere.'

Eliza knew this threat was real. Though the priest had no truck with Edward's fairy talk, he would support him because of his sex. She knew it would be damaging for Kennedy if he were not man enough to keep his wife. That men were dangerous when they were afraid. That they needed the advantages of society, while women had to be strong enough to survive with all the odds stacked against them.

It was why Eliza had elected to fake her gift. So that she could help women, give them courage, their lives so often dictated by decisions made without their consent. And she would continue to do so whatever the priest said.

Determined not to show fear, she picked up her basket. 'I must get on. There are beans and cabbages to plant and I need to cut the stems of the raspberries and blackberries. God's gifts.'

The priest stood aside, seemingly satisfied. 'I've said what I came to say.'

Though she knew she should resist, that her pride would be her downfall, Eliza couldn't let him have the last word.

She shot the priest a narrow look, put down her basket, then rooted in the pocket of her apron, producing two hand-rolled cigarettes. She winked at him gamely. 'Would you like a smoke, Father? I use a mix of mugwort and mint. More fragrant than the incense you use in the chapel.'

The priest's eyes widened. 'Witch! Sinner!'

Once he was reduced to name-calling, Eliza knew she had bested him.

She laughed as she watched him leave, but knew she must take his threats seriously. She went back into the cottage and carefully put away her book of secrets, lifting her skirts to climb onto the table and hide it in the cubbyhole above the fireplace.

Eliza did not believe in an afterlife; the notion that the soul would survive the death of the body seemed unnecessarily cruel to her. But she could not have anyone know that, or she would be exposed. Her power to help women diminished.

Monday morning was cold, with frost on the grass. Finn hopped about impishly in the garden, enjoying the icy crunch underfoot, while I sipped my coffee at the back door, ready for my first day back at work in over a month.

My legs ached from the walk the day before, but I was far more stung by Maggie's scolding. It reminded me that I was a blow-in here, despite my attempts to convince myself otherwise, although I wouldn't have thought that Maggie would be the one doing the reminding. Despite what she'd said, I'd written another scene first thing, sitting up in bed with the laptop on my knee. I'd had too many people telling me what to think and advising that my reasoning was askew to allow her to stop me.

Back inside, I fed Finn and then logged on to work. My job was dull and tricky, the absolute worst of combinations, but it meant I had to concentrate, which after everything was a bit of a relief. I worked in the living room with Maggie's electric heater beside me while Finn slept in his bed or under the table at my feet.

At twelve o'clock, I rubbed my neck, tight from poring over figures, scrolling quickly through the list of instructions for the afternoon before logging off for lunch. I'd almost reached the end when a name stopped me in my tracks. Rory O'Riordan.

A pins-and-needles sensation worked its way up my neck and into my face. There in front of me were instructions to sue Rory, *my Rory*, for mortgage arrears on the apartment. Our home. The firm I worked for wouldn't have made the connection, wouldn't have known there was a conflict, since the instructions were sent automatically. And they were short, just the bare details: numbers, dates, address. But one thing was clear – Rory hadn't been paying the mortgage on the apartment for some time. The outstanding figure was significant.

I swallowed hard and sat back in my chair, trying to work it through. Our finances were separate. I earned less than Rory, but supplemented it with the small amount I had left from my inheritance – most had gone on my education. We had a joint account out of which bills were paid, or so I'd thought. I'd paid my contribution to the mortgage until I left, after which I assumed the rent would cover it, not knowing it was already in arrears. Severe enough arrears for Rory to be threatened with foreclosure. The instructions were dated before I'd moved out, so no rent had yet been paid at that point.

Was this why Rory had done what he did? Leased the apartment, then driven his car off a pier? He had swagger, so finding himself in debt would be a huge blow. Maybe he couldn't live with it. My eyes stung with tears. Why didn't he tell me?

Hands shaking, I rang the person I thought most likely to know. Sam.

He answered straight away, his voice hesitant, probably thinking I had news of the DNA results. 'Hi, Allie.' There were traffic noises in the background.

I launched straight in. 'Did you know Rory had money problems?'

The long pause was answer enough.

'Why didn't you tell me?' I heard my voice rise, a touch of hysteria in it. 'I asked you what you knew. Was that what you really rowed about? Did he ask you for money?'

'Not quite...'

'Were you lying when you said you were afraid that he'd had an accident? Did you think he might have killed himself?' One question followed the next, tumbling over each other in a torrent of emotion.

Sam's voice was quiet. 'Okay, yes, I knew he was in debt. I'm sorry. I should have told you, but I knew Rory wouldn't want me to. You know he submitted documentary ideas on his own, and a lot of them were being turned down...'

I remembered hearing Rory on the phone, his voice rising in frustration as his famous charm failed to land. Cursing the gender quotas. Cursing the stations that refused to do what they were supposed to. Making 'reality shite' or 'crap TV about home improvement'. He'd hated his role in *The Naked Lens*, although it was short-lived and gained him more attention than anything else he did; but of course he hated that too. But I'd assumed it was just Rory, expressing himself loudly as usual. Things always worked out for him in the end.

'But he had his work with you, didn't he?' I said now. 'That was just extra stuff he was doing on his own.'

The line went silent.

'Sam? Didn't he?'

'We'd stopped working together. This latest doc was to be our last.'

My stomach fell. Something else he hadn't told me. That would have been huge for Rory, breaking up with his work wife. Why hadn't I taken his concerns more seriously? Maybe he'd have told me what was going on. Shared his troubles. 'Why?' I asked.

'We felt differently about things. Some partnerships have a limited life span, Allie, that's all.' Sam breathed out heavily. 'Anyway, he was trying to get himself out of trouble and he came up with some fairly hare-brained schemes, which I couldn't go along with. That's what we rowed about.'

'What kind of schemes?'

'It doesn't matter,' he said quickly. 'It wasn't as if he went ahead with them. But we had a fight and he drove off in a temper. As I said, I was afraid that he'd crashed because he was angry and upset—'

I cut across him. 'So you don't think he killed himself because he was in debt?'

'No.' He sounded certain about that. 'No, I don't. I think it was an accident. He could be reckless in how he drove. We all knew that.'

Rory driving without headlights on a dark country road. Me screaming in terror.

There was a click, and I wondered if Sam had hung up. 'Sam? Are you still there?'

'Yes?'

The noise must have come from the kitchen, I decided. An anxious thrum sounded, which was probably the fridge, and then a car pulled up outside.

CHAPTER THIRTY-FIVE

I went take to look, peering out through a window that needed a good clean. It was Pieter. I could see his van. 'I've got to go,' I said.

'Allie ...' Sam protested, but I hung up and went to open the door.

Pieter saw my stricken face immediately, and his own softened in response. Uncharacteristically, he reached out his arms and pulled me in, giving me a hug. It was the first time we'd touched. I collapsed into him, inhaling wood and paint from his thick sweater, his strong and comforting presence a refuge from the swirling chaos around me. I wanted to stay there for ever, to burrow away from the world. But finally I pulled back, feeling embarrassed.

If he felt the same, he didn't show it. He stroked my upper arms to calm me and led me inside, where he sat me down at the table, pushing aside my still open laptop. 'Tell me? What is it? What's happened?'

I squared my shoulders, took a deep breath and told him. My work was confidential, so I really shouldn't have, but I desperately needed to speak to someone. Maybe Olivia was right about that.

'And you didn't know?'

I shook my head. 'It seems there's a lot I didn't know about Rory.'

Pieter nodded, but didn't ask what I meant. Instead, he went into the kitchen to make tea and brought a steaming mug to the table. 'The Irish cure,' he said with a shy smile.

'Thanks,' I said weakly as I took a sip.

'How did you meet?' He leaned forward, hands clasped in front of him, elbows resting on his knees. 'You and Rory?'

Classic distraction technique. It worked, though.

'In a nightclub. I was a bit of a party girl at one stage. Hard to believe now, I know.'

A half-smile. 'I don't know about that.'

'I'm not sure how much fun it was, to be honest. I used it as a coping mechanism. I was diagnosed with depression and anxiety after college, so I drank and did other things to mask it.' I looked down at my hands. 'I have no idea why I'm telling you this. I'm sorry.'

'Don't be. I was the same.'

I looked up at him, surprised.

He laughed. 'Not a party girl. Diagnosed with anxiety.' He made inverted commas with his fingers. 'Generalised anxiety disorder.'

My eyes widened. This fit outdoor man? A success at everything he did?

'It's a long time ago now, but I know how it feels to not be in control,' he said. 'Is that what happened with the driving?'

I shrugged. 'I think it was part of it.' I didn't want to mention the accident. How could I tell this man that I'd killed my own parents? 'I think Rory liked the party-girl me. I sometimes wonder if everything after that wasn't a disappointment.'

Pieter didn't respond. I was grateful that he didn't go for platitudes, shower me with fake compliments. He waited for me to drink a little more of my tea, then said, 'Do you want to go for a walk? Maybe just down the lane? Our friend looks as if he needs a bit of fresh air.'

He was right. Finn was getting edgy, gazing at us with ill-concealed intent.

Once outside, I began to feel calmer, ready to talk about something else. A tractor sounded in the distance.

'Do you remember yesterday when Maggie was annoyed with me for talking about the cottage?' I asked.

The tractor appeared and we hugged the hedge as it passed. Harkin acknowledged Pieter, I was surprised to see, giving him a nod. All men together?

'I think Maggie is a little sensitive,' Pieter said when he'd stepped back out again. 'It's her ancestors we're talking about, after all.'

'So you know about her connection with the cottage?' I asked, and he nodded.

Harkin disappeared around the bend in the lane, heading in that very direction, and I remembered that it was his family who had taken in Eliza's daughter, Gretta.

'Maggie is a good person, but she can get herself into trouble,' Pieter said. 'There are people who give her a wide berth. Am I using that expression correctly?'

'Really?' Until yesterday I wouldn't have been able to imagine that. But now I thought about the eternally empty café.

'She told me once that there was a lot of hurt in her family. That it was hard to shake that off. She was sent away to school, you know? Unusual in Ireland, I understand, but apparently she was a troubled kid. She was very unhappy there. I think she might even have been expelled.'

I nodded. I wouldn't ever have the nerve to ask Maggie this directly, and I hoped Pieter wouldn't pass it on. 'The woman who used to live in my cottage, Eliza? The librarian in Portlaoise said that Maggie was cut from the same cloth as her. Do you know what he meant by that?'

Before Pieter could reply, there was a shout. Or more accurately, the ear-splitting roar of someone in pain or fear. We ran towards it, in the direction of my cottage.

The tractor was parked about ten metres from my front door, completely blocking the lane as was Harkin's habit. At least I assumed it was the tractor. You couldn't see it, lost in a shroud of wheeling and diving birds. Harkin was on the steps of his cab, looking as if he was trying to climb back in, but the ravens wouldn't let him. They flew straight into his face, attacking him. He struck out, arms flailing, shouting expletives. They scattered briefly, then rose and came for him again, wings fluttering and beaks jabbing. A small raven dived at him, skimming the top of his head, and I caught sight of a white mark on the bird's shoulder. My little friend playing his part.

Pieter and I stood there helpless. There seemed to be nothing we could do but watch and listen to the whirring of wings and feathers. Harkin covered his head with his hands and finally managed to make it into the cab, slamming the door behind him. It was only then that I saw he had a shotgun. He certainly hadn't been given a chance to fire it. Eventually the birds withdrew, taking off in a black cloud.

Harkin was shaking his fist, still shouting, his aggression clearly directed at me. He opened the cab door. 'This is all your fault. It's only since you came that they're like this.'

I was indignant. How could it possibly be my fault? 'What do you mean?'

'You're feeding them. They're vicious birds. They steal seed, you know. They peck lambs' eyes out – they're not fucking pets.'

I felt a dart of panic. How could he have known that I was

feeding them? Had he been at the cottage? Had he left the dead raven in my living room? And what was he doing here now, parked outside my door? The gates to his fields were nowhere near here. Was that why the birds had attacked him? Was it possible – and surely I was losing my mind to even think this – that the birds were protecting me?

Pieter's voice was calm and authoritative. 'Please go.'

Harkin emitted one more curse, threw his hands up into the air in frustration, slammed the cab door and drove off in a roar of exhaust fumes.

'What on earth just happened?' I asked, staring at the departing tractor.

Pieter shook his head in disbelief. 'Come on, let's go inside.'

Finn, who had been surprisingly quiet during the commotion, happily accepted a treat in the kitchen.

'It's not true, you know,' Pieter said, standing at the back door. 'Ravens feed on crops but they hoover up pests in the process. And pecking out lambs' eyes? Most they do that with are dead already and almost none are likely to live.'

'I'm not sure I want to think about that,' I said wryly. 'Although I did see them threaten Harkin once before. They don't seem to like him.'

Pieter nodded. 'Corvids, that includes ravens and crows, learn from one another. They pass knowledge down the generations. They did an experiment once where a man wearing a mask trapped birds. After that, anyone who wore the same mask was attacked, more birds each day, proving that the story spread.' He crossed his arms. 'I'd say Harkin shot at the ravens at some stage and the birds remembered.'

I told him about the dead raven in the cottage and he frowned, looking around him as if searching for an access point. 'Do you think he got in here? Broke in to your cottage?'

'I don't know. I've had birds get trapped in here before. I wondered if maybe they were coming down the chimney. I guess that could have happened.'

'Maybe,' he said. 'Harkin's surly and a bit rude, but I can't imagine him doing that.' He paused. 'I heard that his son died in an accident when he was a teenager. Apparently he's never got over it.'

It should have made me feel sorry for him, but he'd been so unpleasant since I'd arrived, it was difficult. We stood at the back door for a while watching the ravens. They'd returned to their peaceful state, a distinct sort of *cronk* call exchanged as if they were conversing; I imagined a debrief.

'You know their calls vary regionally?' Pieter said.

'Really? Like an accent?'

He nodded. 'New birds joining a flock will mimic the more powerful members. And ravens are great mimics – they can imitate flushing toilets and car engines.'

I laughed. It felt good. I looked at Pieter's face, his kind smile, the electric-blue eyes. As if sensing my gaze, he turned. There was laughter in his eyes too. They locked on mine. All I could hear was my own breathing as I took a step towards him, amazed at my own brazenness. Close enough now to see tiny golden flecks in the blue. I put my hand on his chest. He leaned in and kissed me; the lightest of light touches, barely brushing my lips with his, leaving my head spinning.

He smiled when he pulled away, and then it faded. 'Should you tell the guards?'

'About what?' I replied, stupidly.

'About Rory's debt.'

I flushed. 'Of course.'

He touched my flaming cheek with his hand. 'I'll leave you to it.'

CHAPTER THIRTY-SIX

Suzanne

Suzanne listened in silence as she scribbled a note. She'd given her mobile number to Allie Garvey but hadn't really expected her to use it. Now she was glad she had. It showed that the woman trusted her, calling her mobile rather than the station. The fact that Suzanne was in the station and sitting at her desk when she rang was by the by.

She wrote the words *Mortgage in arrears!!* on her notepad. So Rory O'Riordan had money problems, did he? It made sense. It would explain why he'd done his disappearing trick, why he hadn't accessed his bank account and ultimately why he'd turned up dead. The oldest story in the book. Or one of them. Debt and suicide. She wondered fleetingly if he'd had gambling problems too. Suzanne had an uncle who'd virtually destroyed his family and business before joining Gamblers Anonymous. Wondered too if he'd borrowed money from the wrong people, something her uncle had also done. Giving him good reason to hide beneath the radar for a while.

Allie was still speaking. 'It must be why he rented out the apartment. I wish he'd told me. Why didn't he tell me?'

'Pride?' Suzanne said. 'Maybe he didn't want you to worry. Thought he could sort it out before you discovered it.' She paused.

'But thank you for letting us know.'

'I just don't know how he got himself into so much debt. He hadn't paid the mortgage for months. Not a cent of it.'

'I guess it's not hard these days to find yourself in trouble. We'll see what we can find out.'

Suzanne watched Dave approach from across the room, his eyebrows raised when he saw she was on her mobile. She mouthed the words 'Allie Garvey' at him and his eyes widened. He handed her a sheet of paper, pointing aggressively at it as if to say, *Read it now.*

She looked down. It was a printout with a handwritten note scrawled across the top. Dave's expression was smug, which unnerved her because it was so unusual. Dave didn't normally do the work required to look smug. What had he found out?

She switched the handset to her other ear. Allie was now telling her about the row Rory had had with his work colleague – Suzanne already knew about this from Sam, but she wasn't going to let on to Allie – saying that he knew Rory was in debt but thought he'd had an accident rather than taking his own life. That Allie herself wasn't sure. That Rory had kept so many things from her that she didn't know what to think any more. She even mentioned the affair for the first time. Suzanne had raised it with her in the past, and while not denying it, she'd changed the subject at the first opportunity, clearly not wishing to talk about it. But now the floodgates had opened.

Suzanne tried to keep listening, reluctant to cut the woman off when she was finally talking. Although she had a feeling that Allie might have had a drink, and it was the alcohol that was loosening her tongue. While she wasn't quite slurring, there was a blurring around the edges of her pronunciation that wasn't normally there.

What Suzanne really wanted to do was read what Dave had

handed her. She ran her fingers tantalisingly over the sheet like a piece of chocolate cake she wasn't allowed to have, while he loomed over her expectantly. He pointed again, this time jabbing at the printed words at the top of the page. She looked. *Shit.* It was the DNA results. Later, and also earlier, than expected.

Unable to resist now, she blocked out Allie's voice and scanned the contents, just about managing to take them in. She stared, her head starting to swim. Seriously? After everything that Allie had just said? When things were finally starting to make sense?

But that wasn't all of it. There was something else – the handwritten addition at the top, in Dave's messy scrawl. He'd actually done a bit of work before handing the results to her. Work he could do while sitting on his arse at his desk, but still. She was surprised. But not as surprised as she was by what he'd found out. *Jesus.*

Allie was still speaking, but Suzanne couldn't tell her about this straight away. She needed to absorb it, work out what it meant, filter it for public consumption.

She cut across her. 'I'm so sorry, Allie. Something's just come up. Do you mind if I ring you back?'

She put down the phone and looked up at Dave's self-satisfied face. 'What the hell?'

CHAPTER THIRTY-SEVEN

Allie

I was striding down the lane again with Finn when my phone rang. I couldn't just wait for Garda Phelan to call back, sitting in the cottage staring at the four walls. I needed to be moving. Plus, if I stayed there, I knew I'd only have another glass of wine, and that was certainly a bad idea. Especially now that it was clear why she'd hung up so abruptly.

I tried to make sense of what she was telling me. My lungs were tight, almost completely empty of air, when I asked her to repeat what she'd just said.

'It's not him. It's not Rory.' She sounded calm, as if she'd rehearsed this returned call. 'The DNA results confirm it.'

'Are you sure?' I tried to swallow. 'But you found his wallet.' My voice came out as nothing more than a rasp.

'I know. And the car is his, no question. But the body isn't. His brother gave us a DNA sample. No match.'

'So who is it?' My mind ran through possibilities and came up blank. Who else *could* it be? I stopped walking in the hope that it might help me think and speak, both of which were proving a challenge. Finn looked up at me, confused.

'That's the thing. We found a match elsewhere. We have an ID.'

Although I'd asked the question, this suddenly seemed irrelevant. What was important was that it wasn't Rory. What did that mean? I wished Pieter was with me to help figure this out, then immediately felt a rush of shame. I'd kissed him. I'd kissed another man, when Rory was still out there somewhere.

'His name is Mark Thompson. He has a criminal record for stealing cars, so his DNA is on our database. I'm so sorry. We should have had this earlier, but there's a backlog in the lab.' She sighed. 'There's always a backlog in the lab. And with the discovery of Rory's wallet, as you said, well, it wasn't considered urgent. It was assumed the body was him.'

Who the hell was Mark Thompson?

As if reading my mind, she said, 'I don't suppose you know a Mark Thompson? Or might Rory have known him? You haven't heard his name mentioned?'

I shook my head though she couldn't see me. 'No.' My mind raced ahead. 'So he stole Rory's car? Is that what you think?'

'It certainly looks like it. Seems the only explanation. We assume the wallet was in the car when he took it.'

I lowered myself to my hunkers, suddenly unable to stand, running my hand through my hair as I tried to take all of this in. 'So where is Rory? And why didn't he report the car stolen? Why hasn't he been in touch?' Back to the same questions I'd been asking myself since he disappeared.

'That's what we have to find out. It is pretty strange,' she admitted. 'This guy didn't have a history of violence, so we don't think he did anything to Rory, but of course we can't be sure of that.'

I pictured Rory lying hurt somewhere, retrieving that dog-eared mental image from weeks back, the one I'd torn up when Rory was found. When I'd *thought* he had been found.

'The post-mortem detected traces of heroin and alcohol in

Thompson's body, so it's likely his death was an accident, driving Rory's car off the pier. He was a bit of a black sheep, chaotic life, estranged from his family. No one reported him missing, so we weren't looking for him.'

I let out a deep breath as this new reality became clear. Surely I should be pleased that the body in the car wasn't Rory's? So why didn't it feel like a cause for celebration? The truth was that I didn't know how to feel or what to think.

'Look,' Suzanne said quickly, as if reading my mind, 'I know this isn't satisfactory. But all I can say is that we'll keep looking. This isn't over.'

'Okay,' I whispered.

'Have you someone there with you?'

I looked down at Finn, who was gazing up at me with his liquid brown eyes. 'I'm fine.'

'Okay. I'll be in touch. Soon. I promise. The good news is that this is now a crime, so we should get the resources we didn't have before.' She paused. 'I'm so sorry, Allie.'

She hung up, leaving me feeling more alone than I'd ever felt in my life. I looked around me, at the silent fields, the skeletal trees, the clouds so low I felt as if I could touch them. For a minute everything seemed still. There was a strange absence of light, the bleak winter landscape drained of all colour.

Then it hit me that I hadn't been paying attention to where I was walking, and I spun around trying to get my bearings. Where was I?

When my phone rang again, it was Pieter. This time I didn't answer.

Somehow I made it to the end of the day. I found my way back to the cottage easily enough, but that night I hardly slept. When I finally did, I searched for Rory in my dreams, just like in the days after he went missing, a desperate anguished quest where I raced along busy roads, weaving in and out of traffic, convinced I'd seen his car. Catching sight of him through shop windows, pushing my way inside only to find he'd disappeared. An elusive Scarlet Pimpernel, taunting me.

The next day I worked as best I could, though I knew I was losing focus. I did nothing with the instructions to sue Rory, just put them to one side. I didn't call anyone. I presumed the guards would let Rory's family know, but they didn't call me either. I knew that somehow they'd find a way to blame me for what had happened, and maybe they were right. I had moved on before I even knew for certain that the body was Rory's. What kind of person did that?

Pieter rang once more and texted a few times, but when I didn't reply, he respected my wishes and left me alone. I couldn't bring myself to speak to him. The guilt was overwhelming.

For two days I didn't leave the house other than to walk Finn. I began to see Rory everywhere, just as I had in Dublin. He followed me like a shadow, in the cottage and on the lane. I felt as if I would never sleep again. Other than Finn, the ravens were my only comfort. During the day I fed and talked to them, especially my little friend. At night I heard them jostling for space on the roof – shuffling, fluttering, a persistent beating of wings. Ever present. Minding me.

On Thursday morning, Olivia rang. I'd been ignoring her calls, but unlike Pieter, my sister was not a respecter of other people's boundaries, and she didn't give up. On her fifth call and fourth text I had no choice but to pick up.

'Why aren't you answering your phone?' she demanded.

'Because I don't want to speak to anyone.'

I went to the back door and opened it to toss scraps for the ravens. The little one dived, catching a hunk of bread in mid-air.

'I've seen it online, you know. I know the body in the car wasn't Rory.'

'Yes,' I said, dully. 'It's some car thief.'

She blew out a breath. 'You're kidding. The article didn't say who it was. So this guy stole his car and crashed it off a pier?'

'I suppose so.'

'I presume they're continuing to look for Rory?'

'Yes. I think so.'

I watched the birds swoop down. I felt myself drift, experiencing that dots-in-front-of-the-eyes sensation you get before you're about to pass out. I swayed and stumbled, knocking over a mug with a loud clatter. Had I been drinking something more than coffee? The sound of breaking crockery reverberated through the kitchen.

'Allie? Are you okay?'

'Fine. I just knocked over a mug. I'll call you back.' I had no intention of calling her back.

'Allie, don't go. Hang on a minute. Come and stay with us. Please. Just for a few nights.'

'I'm fine. And anyway, I have work.'

'You could work from here. We have Wi-Fi, you know.'

'I know, but—'

'The weekend, then. The boys would love to see Finn.' Olivia's trump card.

'No.'

She drove down to collect me that night. My big little sister.

CHAPTER THIRTY-EIGHT

Suzanne

Suzanne took a luxurious sip of her Guinness and placed the pint back down on the beer mat. Frank always insisted on Grogan's when he returned to the city, claiming the pub was the only thing he missed about Dublin. There were six of them out tonight, all from their garda college class in Templemore; a pretty good turn-out, but then Frank had always been popular. And despite that way-too-early pre-Christmas crush, they'd managed to nab a large table; not the prime spot by the stained-glass picture reserved for regulars, but the next best one, in the corner opposite.

Suzanne knew she was boring the pants off the rest of them with her talk about the Rory O'Riordan case – most had turned away to talk about non-work things – but Frank was still interested. Being just as tenacious about his own cases, he understood why one like this would bug her.

He sipped his whiskey and Coke. 'I was just as taken aback as you were that it wasn't him.'

Suzanne clicked her teeth. 'I don't know; I knew there was more to it somehow. Had a feeling about it from the first time we called round to see the girlfriend at their flat.'

'Copper's instinct?' Frank teased.

She rolled her eyes. 'Not sure I believe that exists. But Jesus, why didn't he report his car stolen? Is he lying dead somewhere? Did this guy Thompson *kill* him?' She rubbed her face in frustration.

'You think he did?' Frank reached for the open bag of dry-roasted peanuts on the table and popped a couple into his mouth.

'Seems really unlikely. Thompson had no previous for anything violent so it would be completely out of character for him. Unless he did it accidentally in the course of stealing the car. But then why haven't we found a body?'

Frank frowned. 'It's a bit weird all right. There was nothing much to be learned from the car. And the post-mortem on Thompson showed cause of death as drowning. If he hadn't been drunk and high when he died, he might have been able to save himself.'

She nodded. 'Thompson was a Dublin addict. Lord knows what he was doing in Mayo.'

'People do go to Mayo, you know,' Frank grinned. 'Even Dublin people. And not just for love, either.' His husband was from Foxford in County Mayo; they'd had a brilliant wedding there two years ago. Suzanne could still recall the epic hangover.

'All right. I know,' she said with a laugh. 'But we can't find any connections he had there. We're trying to look at his last movements. Talk to his friends and family. Figure out where exactly he stole the car and how. How and where he came across Rory O'Riordan.'

Frank took another nut. 'Any progress on that?'

'I spoke to the director who was working with O'Riordan in Galway. Sam...' She sucked air in through her teeth, then shook her head. 'Can't remember his surname. I asked him if he knew Thompson...' Her gaze drifted to the wall, coming to rest on a painting of a greyhound that reminded her of Allie's dog, Finn.

'And?' Frank prompted.

'And... I don't know. He said he didn't, but there was something about his reaction that made me wonder if he was telling the truth.'

'Why would he lie?'

She sighed. 'God knows. Why does anyone lie?'

Someone was standing up to get another round. Suzanne shook her head – she still had half a pint left, had been talking too much – but Frank nodded a yes.

'I should be able to get a ping on O'Riordan's mobile phone now, and Thompson's if he had one. That might tell us something.'

'What about financial stuff?' Frank nodded at the guy who'd just gone to the bar. 'Séamus is in the fraud squad now. He might have some ideas. You said this O'Riordan bloke was in serious debt.'

Suzanne didn't really think that was a route worth following. 'Thompson was a junkie. He probably just stole the car on impulse and then drove it off the pier. And O'Riordan's done nothing money-wise since he went missing. No activity on his bank account whatsoever. That might be explained by the stolen wallet. But if he is still alive, he'd need money. So why didn't he report his car and wallet missing? And if he's dead, why can't we find him?'

'Maybe he doesn't want to be found.' Frank drained his whiskey and placed the glass back down with a satisfying tap. 'What if his car got stolen and he thought "great, that's me off" and grabbed his chance. It's surprisingly easy. Thousands of people do it every year. He was a good-looking guy.'

Suzanne rolled her eyes wearily. 'You sound like Dave.' Dave had returned to his original theory, more convinced than ever now they'd discovered that Rory had money problems.

'Thanks a bunch.' Frank was about as far removed from

Dave as you could get. Physically fit, gay, conscientious. All the opposites.

'No, you're right. He was attractive,' Suzanne conceded. 'But he was also a good deal older than his girlfriend, partner, whatever you want to call her. A lot older. Something bothers me about their relationship that I can't put my finger on.'

'Okay.'

'And,' she paused to take a sip of her beer, 'she was involved in a car accident when she was a teenager in which her parents were killed. She was the one driving.'

'Ouch.' Frank winced.

'Exactly. Not surprisingly, she blamed herself, though it appears it wasn't her fault. It was an accident. Just one of those things. But she made herself ill with guilt. In fact, she had a stint in St John of God's a few years later because of it. Her sister told me.'

'Right,' Frank said slowly. 'Probably PTSD. And you think this is relevant how?'

Suzanne shook her head irritably. 'I don't know. It's just another knot in this damn case. But two major car accidents in her life? Both life-changing. Can it be just a coincidence?'

'She wasn't there for the second one, though.' Frank said. 'Even her boyfriend wasn't there for the second one.'

'I know.' Suzanne shook her head. 'I hate to agree with Dave, but there is something a little off about her. She's in Dublin staying with her sister at the moment and I'm going to go and see her.' Distractedly she picked up her pint again. 'I don't know whether to be worried for her or frightened of her.'

Frank grinned. 'That's my feeling when it comes to most women. Especially you.'

CHAPTER THIRTY-NINE

Allie

Waiting at the zebra crossing, observing my own breath cloud and dissipate, I realised that the hand holding Finn's leash was cold and that I should have worn gloves. Why was the traffic so heavy? I wondered. I was tired of the relentless noise, exhausts pumping fumes into the icy air. Where on earth was everyone going at nine o'clock on a Sunday morning?

My gaze moved to a gang of teenagers at a bus stop, coming to rest on one young couple in their midst: a girl of about fourteen in beige leggings and a bra top, the boy with his arms wrapped around her, hands squeezing her buttocks like he was checking tomatoes for ripeness. And then I remembered, this was the main route to Dundrum Shopping Centre. *Shopping for shite*, as Rory used to say, the eternal hobby of Dubliners, especially in the run-up to Christmas.

The lights turned red, the green man appeared and we crossed the road, Finn prancing along in a highly agitated state, his mood exacerbated by the throb of seemingly constant roadworks.

A voice called my name and I jumped. My own nerve endings were pretty raw too. I was always uneasy walking around here, afraid I would run into someone from my childhood, or worse, my school. Standing on the other side of the road was a man who was familiar but who I couldn't place; black beanie, heavy coat, Doc Marten boots, dressed more sensibly than some for the chilly December morning.

My instinct was to wave and walk on, but he clearly wanted to speak to me, so I reluctantly went over.

'Allie. I haven't seen you since...' He looked uncomfortable, the way you do when you meet somebody recently bereaved, when you haven't sent a card or been to the funeral, or basically shown that you care in any way and now have to fake it. Who was he? 'I've been meaning to call you but I didn't know whether you'd want... I mean, obviously the guards rang me when...'

And then I had it. Vince. The cameraman who'd been with Sam and Rory on the island.

'It's fine, and thanks,' I said. 'Nice to see you again.'

Nice to see you again. Jesus, what was wrong with me?

'How are you doing?'

But that was enough for me. I fled, couldn't get away from the man quickly enough. Relieved that he appeared to feel the same way. He was already crossing the road as I hurried off in the other direction.

I'd been in Olivia's house for three nights, being cooked for and minded, nursed as if I was an invalid. I knew I should be grateful, but the truth was that I was going slowly out of my mind. I felt as if I was being constantly watched in case I did something stupid. That's what happens when you have a breakdown; for the rest of your life people are nervous around you, treating you like some kind of skittish fawn who might startle with any sudden movement. At least I had the excuse of needing to walk Finn, which allowed me to escape every few hours.

Olivia's home, or 'our house' as she still insisted on calling it, was the house in which we'd grown up. After the accident in which our parents had died, our aunt and uncle had moved in to care for us. At the first opportunity, I'd moved out. I hadn't been back other than to visit my sister and nephews. But Olivia never left, taking over the mortgage and eventually moving her husband in and bringing up her own family there. She remained close to our aunt and uncle, who now lived in France, visiting them regularly and reporting back.

Olivia loved this house in the suburbs, with its neat garden and neat neighbours. I hated it. It was too full of memories for me, and they weren't happy ones. I'd read somewhere about it being possible for siblings raised in the same household with the same parents to have completely different upbringings, and it always felt that way for me. I'd assumed it was my fault, that I'd failed to be what they wanted, despite my best efforts. Olivia seemed to care less about their approval, and that gave her more freedom. But the worst memory of all was that terrible New Year's Eve. I remembered vividly being driven back in a garda car that freezing, awful night when everything changed. When I changed. This was not a house in which I wanted to be.

Olivia had renovated and redecorated, but that meant that not only did I hate the house but I felt out of place there too, just as she seemed out of place in the cottage. I was too unpolished for her beige carpets, her velvet sofa and armchairs, the kitchen with the black and white tiles and marble-topped island. God knows how she managed to keep it all so clean with two four-year-old boys, but a playroom and a cleaner probably helped.

I'd wanted to leave pretty much as soon as I'd arrived. But my sister had countered every reason I gave with an argument I couldn't match. I said I needed to work, but I'd made the mistake of bringing my laptop and they had high-speed broadband. I said Finn needed the space to run, and she pointed out how long he'd spent in an apartment. Plus, what a great garden they had and how close they were to the sea. How much Finn loved running on the sand. Olivia wore you down. I was trapped.

'There's someone to see you,' she said, standing in the doorway of her sitting room shortly after I came back from walking Finn.

Her hushed tone reminded me uncomfortably of a matron I used to know. And *someone*? As if I wouldn't know who the someone was. Olivia was there when I took the call from Garda Phelan. We were both expecting her.

Suzanne was back in uniform; it gave me quite a shudder to see a guard in the house again. I knew they'd had a chat in the kitchen first, she and Olivia. I'd stood behind the door to listen, hearing only snatches of their conversation. *How is she? Having a bad day today. Don't keep her long, be careful not to tire her out.* Nursing-home speak. Then they'd lowered their voices completely and there was a bit that I couldn't hear.

Suzanne took a seat in an armchair and drew out her notebook, while Olivia tactfully withdrew. 'I just want to ask you some questions, Allie, if that's okay?'

I stiffened, and sat up a little straighter. 'Questions?' This wasn't what I'd been anticipating. I'd expected more of a pastoral visit.

'Just about your relationship with Rory, that kind of thing, background stuff.'

'Okay,' I said slowly. She'd asked me this before. Had they found out something? Something else?

'So,' she prompted, 'how *were* things with Rory?'

'Good. They were good.' I paused. 'Sorry, why are you asking me this again?'

She looked apologetic. 'I'm afraid we're now dealing with a crime. Even though it may well have been an accident, we have to fully investigate Mr Thompson's death, and Rory's ...' she searched for the right word, 'absence is part of that.'

I noted the change of language. *Absence* seemed more accountable than either *disappearance* or *missing*. As if it was now somehow Rory's fault.

'So, things were good? Despite his keeping secrets. His debts, the affair?'

'Well, yes, but I knew about the affair. He told me, and as you said, he probably didn't want to worry me about the debts.'

I didn't feel like mentioning the woman at the airport and I hoped that Olivia hadn't either. Hoped that wasn't the exchange in the kitchen that I hadn't been able to hear.

Garda Phelan nodded as if accepting what I said. She made a note, and when she spoke again, her tone was gentler. A change of gear. 'We know what happened to your parents, Allie. We know that things haven't been easy for you.'

Bloody Olivia, I thought as I looked down, examining my nails.

'Your sister says that Rory could be …' Suzanne hesitated, 'controlling.'

I shook my head in disgust. So that was what they'd been whispering about. 'Well, she's wrong. My sister didn't like Rory. She was jealous of him.'

'Why was that?'

I shook my head. 'It doesn't matter.'

'Rory's brother, Andrew, mentioned that the two of you had arguments.' Suzanne looked down as if checking her notes, but I knew it was an act. I suspected that this was what she'd been leading up to all along, her whole reason for the visit. 'He said there were occasions when you drank heavily, when you lashed out, that you have a temper.'

I dipped my head, my cheeks warm. Hoped Olivia couldn't hear. She'd only confirm it, having seen my behaviour in Galway.

My phone buzzed with a text and I looked over at it sitting on the coffee table, distracted. I saw Maggie's name flash up. Why would Maggie be texting me on a Sunday? Surely she'd be out walking.

Suzanne paused, as if waiting for me to read it. I wanted to, but I had a feeling I'd have to show it to her if I did, so I resisted.

'Every couple has rows,' I said, sullenly.

She appeared to consider this for a moment. 'Okay, well if there's anything else you can tell us, let me know.' Her voice softened again. 'We have to ask these questions, Allie. Any little bit of information might help us find out what happened to Rory, and what happened to this man Thompson.'

'Do you think he's still alive?' I swallowed. 'Rory, I mean.'

'Honestly? We don't know. If he is, he's done a very impressive disappearing trick. He still hasn't accessed his bank accounts, so Lord knows what he's living on. His family are distraught.'

I nodded.

'As a matter of fact, we may go ahead with *Crime Files* now.'

Unease crept across my scalp.

She sat forward, her gaze meeting mine. 'This time we'd really like you to be involved, Allie.'

'On television?' My eyes widened in fright.

'Yes. It would be a proper appeal. They're often very successful.'

I shook my head vehemently. 'I can't.' I began playing with my sleeve, tugging at a loose thread in my cuff. 'I can't bear cameras. I'd freeze.'

This was true. For a long time, I'd avoided even having my photograph taken. After the accident, I thought people could tell just by looking at me that I'd killed my own mum and dad. Photographs of me were usually taken when I'd had too much to drink or was completely unaware of them.

My throat constricted in panic. Was Suzanne trying to trick me? Did she think I had something to do with what had happened to Rory, and that was why she wanted me on TV? Had his family suggested it? They'd been happy enough to go ahead without me the last time, so why include me now? I pressed my hand to my forehead, grabbing the glass of water that Olivia had left.

Suzanne tilted her head in sympathy, but her eyes were inscrutable. 'Just think about it, will you?'

I nodded, and eventually she stood up to leave. 'I'll see myself out.'

When I heard the front door close, I opened Maggie's text, reaching for the phone like a drowning man. There was a picture that she said was the view from the Stoney Man on the Ridge of Capard, a sweeping panoramic view of the mountains and forest, which she must have taken on their walk. She'd captioned it: *Wish you were here.*

It made my decision for me. I was too exposed here. It was too easy for people to get to me; too easy to just run into someone on the street, like Vince. And in order to take part in that TV programme, I'd need to be in Dublin. They couldn't make me do it if I wasn't physically here. Could they?

I made my way into the kitchen, where Olivia was stirring something on the cooker, Finn watching her with interest. She'd insisted on his bed staying in here, since it was the only room in the house without a beige carpet.

'I'm going back,' I announced. 'To the cottage.'

Her eyes widened in alarm. 'When?'

'Tomorrow morning.'

'Why? Did that guard say something? I thought she seemed nice...'

I shook my head. 'No, it's just work.'

Olivia looked relieved. 'Allie, we've had this conversation. You can work here. You have the spare room. The house is quiet during the day, isn't it?'

'I work better in my own space.' Repetition for emphasis. 'On my own.'

She sighed, and gave a tight nod. 'Okay.' Finally registering that keeping me here against my will was actually kidnapping.

I turned to leave, and then stopped. 'Why did you talk to that guard about me? About me and Rory?'

She put down the ladle. 'She asked me. She asked about your relationship and I told her. I said that I thought he was a little dominant. That he was a lot older than you and that you tended to do what he wanted. That he made the decisions. That's all.'

'She thinks I killed him.'

Olivia let out a burst of nervous laughter. 'Ah, come on. Why would she think that?'

'I don't know. Because of his family. Because of what happened to our parents.' I shrugged. 'Maybe she thinks I have form.'

'It was an accident and you were a teenager, Allie. There's no way she thinks that. You're overreacting. Look, stay this week at least. Then, if you feel like it, go back for a while and come and spend Christmas with us. It's only a few weeks away.' She squeezed my hand. 'At least think about it.'

The easiest way to handle Olivia was to let her think she'd won. So I said yes. I helped with dinner. I played with the twins. And then I used my laptop to book myself a bus ticket to Rath first thing the following morning. The cottage was calling me back. I felt the pull of it.

CHAPTER FORTY

A squally wind whipped up Rath's main street, catching me in a sudden gust when Finn and I stepped off the bus.

Pieter was coming out of Maggie's café, and I felt my stomach flip when I saw him. I had feelings for him. Real ones. I'd missed him while I was in Dublin. But that was even more of a reason to pull back if the guards thought I'd done something to Rory.

Pieter's face betrayed his hurt that I'd not been in touch, that I'd ignored his calls and texts, but he still managed a half-smile. 'How are you doing?' he asked, nodding at my bag as he bent down to pat Finn. 'Have you been away?'

'Just to visit my sister.' I paused. He clearly hadn't seen what Olivia had online, but I was surprised Facebook fan Cathy hadn't mentioned it. 'The guards got back to me last week – the body in the car wasn't Rory's.'

'Ah.' He nodded slowly, comprehending everything. 'I don't know what to say.'

'Neither do I.' Or feel, I thought.

He didn't ask me anything else, no details, not even who the body was. He just met my eyes with a kind gaze. 'I'm here whenever you need me. As a friend. And I'll still do the garden, if you want me to. There's a lot more to do.'

'Thanks.' I felt a lump in my throat, unable to look at him any longer. I remembered that kiss with something close to grief.

He nodded towards the café. 'Maggie will be pleased to see you. She's been wondering where you were. I know she called around to your cottage at the end of the week.'

'I should have let her know, but it all happened very quickly.'

'You were missed on the walk yesterday. There were only a few of us. Jim and Cathy are in the Maldives.' He smiled. 'Their regular pre-Christmas tan top-up.'

I nodded. 'She sent me a picture.' Added, 'Maggie, I mean, not Cathy.'

Reluctantly I let him go, watching him open the door of his van and swing himself into the driver's seat. He beeped the horn as he drove away, cheerful as always.

Maggie greeted me with a surprised smile from behind the counter. 'Hey, stranger. Where have you been?'

'In Dublin, visiting my sister.' As if it had been a choice. I felt suddenly very weak-willed. I'd barely resisted Olivia when she insisted that I come to stay, and I'd snuck out of her house this morning after she'd gone to work. It was as if the strength I'd gained from working on the house and living alone had leached out of me along with the pregnancy.

'Oh, good.' Maggie's expression grew serious. 'I thought maybe you'd gone to . . .'

'To bury Rory?' I shook my head. 'It wasn't him. The body they found in the car wasn't his. His car was stolen. It was the man who stole it who . . .'

She clapped her hands to her cheeks. 'Oh Lord. You poor thing.' She flushed. 'I mean, I'm sure you're glad it's not Rory, but . . .'

'No. I know what you mean.' I braved a smile. 'So, what have I missed here?'

She gave me a rueful look. 'I'm closing the café.'

'Oh no, that's awful.'

She looked around her at the empty room and shrugged. 'No point in flogging a dead horse any longer. I've just been putting off making the decision.'

'What'll you do?'

'Oh, I'll find something. I'm resourceful.' She paused. 'I'm thinking of having a dinner party. Here in the café. I'm dying to cook for people, and I reckon we could all do with a bit of cheering up. I haven't done it in ages, other than scones and sandwiches and soup. Would you be up for it? I'll understand if you're not.'

'No, I am. Thanks, Maggie.'

She beamed. 'Ah, great. A sort of early Christmas party and a bit of a goodbye to this place.' The smile fell away. 'I won't reopen in the new year.'

'I'm sorry,' I said, meaning it. The café had become an important place for me, had been since the day after I arrived.

'Thanks. Are you having something to eat? Coffee?' she asked.

I shook my head. 'I want to get back to the cottage.'

She looked at my bag and then at Finn, and said, 'How about I close up and give you a lift?'

'You can't do that.'

'Of course I can. I own the place.' A wistful smile. 'For the moment, at least.'

'There's no need,' I protested. 'I have to get some groceries first anyway.'

She came around the counter, leaned down to pat Finn's head and waved her hand at me. 'You go and do that then. Leave himself with me and we'll go when you get back.'

Gratefully I headed off to the little supermarket. I had my

usual friendly exchange with the shopkeeper, although this time he couldn't complain about Finn, and bought two bottles of wine now that I wasn't going to have to carry them home.

Ten minutes later, we turned into my lane in Maggie's rattly old car. A confetti of leaves danced around the house, and the ravens made a welcoming racket as I climbed out of the passenger seat and grabbed my bag.

Maggie refused my half-hearted invitation to come in, and I was glad. I wanted the cottage to myself. I was well aware of how much of a change that was: from a fear of being alone to a desire for solitude, to be alone with my thoughts. But this wasn't bravery. I wanted to hide away, not to have to deal with any of the attention that came with Rory's absence. I realised that Raven Cottage had become my refuge, a place for me to be at peace. As much as I could be, at any rate.

I'd had more than one reason for leaving Olivia's house, not least of which was that I'd lied to her about my work. On Friday, an email had come in from my boss demanding that I ring him. I'd felt a wave of panic. Whatever else was going on, I couldn't afford to lose my job. But when I made the call – at the end of the garden, where Olivia couldn't hear me – he was kind, kinder than he might have been in the circumstances. I'd been making mistakes, issuing proceedings for the wrong figures, adding the names of the wrong parties. Basic errors with tricky consequences that someone else would have to fix.

He took the opportunity to force me to take some extra leave. Compassionate leave, they called it, as if Rory had died. He suggested I wait till after Christmas to come back. It left me feeling as if I was taking something I wasn't entitled to, but if I was screwing up all over the place, which apparently I was, then I wasn't much use to him. I'd still be paid for the next few weeks anyway. But I couldn't spend those weeks sitting in Olivia's house pretending to work. The irony that Rory had been lying to me about something similar wasn't lost on me.

After I waved goodbye to Maggie, I turned towards the house. The ravens were waiting for me just like when I moved in, settled in rows on the eaves and the wire. But that day they'd been silent. Today they seemed agitated, and I wondered why. I searched for my little friend, but there were too many for me to spot him.

I turned the key and stepped inside. The house was chilly. Over a week with no one living here had made a big difference. I dropped my bag and my foot nudged something on the mat, giving me an unpleasant flashback to the dead raven, but when I looked down, it was post. I picked up a small white envelope, confused to see that there was no name and address and no stamp. It must have been hand-delivered.

I was about to open it when Finn whined and padded to the back door. He hadn't had a pee stop since Dublin, so it wasn't unreasonable. I put down the envelope and let him into the garden.

Standing for a few seconds on the back step, I watched him sniff about in the grass and under the hedge. The sky was hard and leaden, and the trees looked as if they'd been stripped with a razor. It was as if winter had arrived while I'd been in Dublin, snuck in when my back was turned. The hawthorn looked particularly bare, stark and exposed in the middle of the lawn. My guardian, I thought suddenly, and was surprised at how that seemed to fit.

It felt right to be back here at Raven Cottage. But what was I going to do with a few weeks more off work? I'd finished the painting I wanted to do and didn't have the motivation to do anything else to the cottage for the moment. Time stretched ahead, empty and dark. Like a country road at night where you can't see further than the next bend, further than the headlights allow. Or not at all, if you're in a car with Rory O'Riordan and he's up to his old tricks.

Where the hell was he? I stared into the distance as I wrapped my arms around myself, shivering against the cold wind. Was he dead? Should I be mourning him or nursing hope?

And then I remembered the envelope. I went back inside, put the kettle on to make tea and turned on the heater before picking it up again.

I slid open the seal and took out what was inside. It felt like a photograph, one of those old Polaroid photographs with a white frame. I hadn't seen one in ages, but I knew they'd become popular again. I turned it over, gasping for breath when I saw the image.

CHAPTER FORTY-ONE

I stared at the photograph in disbelief. Framed by the back door of Raven Cottage, *my cottage*, Pieter was kissing me. Or I was kissing Pieter. Either way I was facing the camera, so it was my features in shot. My betrayal clear. I'd let the picture fall from my hands onto the table as if it were red hot, but I couldn't tear my eyes from it. There was a grainy quality about the image, certainly not the pixel-sharp clarity of a digital photograph, but it was unmistakable nonetheless.

I realised I was shaking. Fear coursing through my veins as it dawned on me that the person who had held that camera couldn't have been very far away – there was no zoom facility on a Polaroid. And while I may have been distracted – clearly I was distracted, the evidence there for all to see – how had I not known I was being photographed? That I was being *watched*, presumably from my own garden? I felt exposed and raw, as if someone had peeled off an outer layer of skin.

Who had taken it? And why? Why had they posted it through my door? Was it a message of some kind? A warning? A *threat*? Could it have been Harkin, my neighbour? He was the only one I could think of who held a grudge against me. Although God knows why. Had he been angry enough after mine and Pieter's run-in with him to follow us back to the house and spy on us from the garden? Somehow, it didn't fit. I tried to picture Harkin sneaking around with a Polaroid camera and couldn't. He was upfront and bullish, direct in his aggression.

Whoever it was, I was terrified. The idea of someone watching me without my knowing, taking my photograph without my consent, filled me with a sick, giddy panic that made me want to throw up.

I picked the thing up again and held onto it for a long time. Staring at my face until it blurred, hands trembling as I pinched the edges of the photograph, remembering that guard holding the picture of myself and Rory in the apartment. A photograph taken while I was off my head on coke. Here I'd been stone-cold sober while kissing someone else. No excuse. Fresh fear flooded through me. Could it have been Rory? Why would he do that? Leave me and then photograph me with someone else? What on earth would he have to gain?

I don't know how long I stood there, but my hands and feet had grown cold when my phone rang on the table. I didn't recognise the number when I picked it up, but I answered anyway, fighting for control, eventually managing a hello.

'Allison?' The caller was hesitant, concerned. I must have sounded as shaken as I felt.

I struggled to recognise the voice, although I knew I should; my mind sluggish, thought processes not working properly. Grateful when he introduced himself as O'Neill, the solicitor.

'So, I've spoken to the vendors, like you asked,' he said. 'That American couple. They'll hire someone to clear out the stuff they left behind.'

'Okay.' With an effort, I recalled speaking to him about the shed. 'Thank you.'

He cleared his throat, sounding almost as uncomfortable

as I did. 'But they've asked you not to contact them again after that. They've said they don't want anything more to do with the cottage.'

Good, I thought. The cottage was mine. They hadn't loved it like I did. They'd abandoned it, leaving their rubbish behind. Suddenly I didn't like the thought of someone else in Raven Cottage. Some stranger with a van tramping all over the place. I wanted to be left in peace.

'Actually,' I said, 'tell them to forget about it. It's fine. I'll do it myself.'

O'Neill sounded doubtful. 'Are you sure? They really should have cleared out the place properly before closing. It's pretty standard.'

'I'm sure,' I said. 'Thanks for your help.'

I hung up before he could respond. There were a couple of missed calls, calls that had come in while I'd been speaking to O'Neill. Two from Olivia. She must have noticed my absence. My flit. One from Aoife, too. I imagined she was checking how I was. I hadn't spoken to her since I'd texted Sam to tell him the body wasn't Rory's. Something Olivia suggested I do while I was in Dublin.

I rubbed my face, feeling harassed. I counted to ten, breathed out heavily, then turned off my phone. I placed it on the table, face-down on top of the Polaroid photograph, blocking out the image. I didn't want to see or speak to anyone. All I wanted was to be left alone in my cottage. To hunker down and hibernate. To hide from view.

That night marked a return to my sleepwalking. I drank wine to help me sleep. It worked for the early part of the night, but I awoke again about three a.m. to find myself in the little room for the first time since Pieter had put a new lock on the door. I'd taken to keeping it locked at night, but I must have forgotten, probably because of the wine. My head ached as I slowly came to, feeling disorientated, my surroundings gradually coming into focus.

I got out of the chair, opened the door and left the room, pulling it closed behind me, ready to return to my bed. As I walked away, crossing the living room, I imagined I heard singing, like a lament, an old Irish song I felt sure I remembered from school. The sound grew fainter, then barely audible, then it disappeared completely.

Strangely, this time Finn hadn't noticed my absence. He lifted his head briefly and went back to sleep. I didn't find it quite so easy. I lay there in the dark, eyes blinking back the shadows. And then I heard the tapping. Too regular to be the birds; it was like a dripping tap or drumbeat, and it was coming from the little room, summoning me back.

This time I refused to investigate. Instead, I reached for the bedside light and switched it on. Remembering the names I'd found in Eliza's book of secrets, I picked up my laptop and started to write. Hammering out a daytime scene to drive away my fear.

> Eliza hurried down the village street, ~~delicately~~ balancing Gretta on her hip, swinging a basket of eggs from her arm. She came into town once a week, which was plenty. November had been a busy time for her. Samhain. The festival of the dead. People wanted to consult their dead when the connection was strong, the barrier between the living and the departed at its thinnest. The arrival of winter symbolising death and darkness. Not to speak of Christmas looming and all that entailed, the dangers produced by male drinking, male violence, male profligacy.

She was on her way to Sadie Fitzpatrick's grocery shop to sell her eggs, an errand she tolerated easily. Sadie was kind; she treated Eliza the same as she did everyone else, which was not something that could be said for all.

See that stout woman turning quickly away to duck into the chapel? Mollie Coakley had been drinking Eliza's tea and eating her bread and jam only two nights before, having asked Eliza to elicit her dead mother's advice as to whom her daughter should marry. A litany of names had been presented. One tap for yes, two for no.

And there was Sam Carty, driving his horse and cart, with his ruddy drinker's face and his limp. His wife now knew that he was forcing himself on their daughter and planned to douse him with boiling water tonight as soon as he passed out from too much porter. And Mary Tiernan herself, hurrying to speak to the coalman. She'd returned on Tuesday with a rash on her ankle she was convinced was the type of measles that could kill her. Until her dead aunt, who had the gift of the cure, told her otherwise and put her mind at rest. For another while at least.

Eliza hadn't heard from Bridget Kennedy since her visit. She worried for the young woman. Had she told Edward of her pregnancy? Or Mary Tiernan, her aunt. Mary hadn't mentioned it. It was a disadvantage of Eliza's trade that she could not enquire, that she must wait for others to come to her.

The faces that turned away or those that stared at her unashamedly – all knew that Eliza was dangerous, that any connection to her was not to be spoken of in public. That she was a keeper of secrets. Which made the walk down the main street of her own village a lonely one. She knew that the gift she claimed made her desired and feared in equal measure.

The only face Eliza could not bring herself to look at, tucking Gretta into her bosom when she saw him coming out of the haberdasher's with his wife, was that of Thomas Harkin. Whenever he cast his eyes over her little girl, it frightened her. But he never did it in the presence of his wife. Women saw things.

Eliza pushed open the door of Sadie Fitzpatrick's shop to the sound of the little bell and retreated inside.

CHAPTER FORTY-TWO

Suzanne

Suzanne rubbed her eyes as she read through her emails. She was tired. Apart from Saturday, she'd been working for ten days straight. Tony was not happy. He was making loud noises about a skiing trip over Christmas.

The call to see Allie Garvey had achieved very little, she thought; after that brief deviation during her phone call about Rory's debt, Allie had retreated firmly back into her shell. Her sister, on the other hand, was more than willing to talk, ushering Suzanne into the kitchen for a quick chat. Olivia certainly saw Allie as a victim, which, despite Suzanne's own concerns for her, had to be considered a little odd since it was Rory and not Allie who was missing, and a second man was dead.

Although it was clear that Allie was damaged; her visible flinch when Suzanne brought up her parents was painful to watch. Her responses were erratic; one minute her behaviour was just as you'd expect, the next it was way off. It was as if she was trying too hard, Suzanne thought; almost mimicking what she assumed was a typical response, until the mask slipped. One thing was for sure, Allie would not be co-operating with *Crime Files*. The alarm on her face when Suzanne had asked was even worse than when she'd brought up the parents' deaths.

She took a deep slug of her coffee as she stared at her computer screen. She hadn't had time for a run this morning, so this caffeine was badly needed. But Rory O'Riordan was now a victim of crime, and she had to take advantage of that change in classification.

An email popped up. It was from Séamus, Frank's friend, and it was about Mark Thompson, the man who had died in Rory O'Riordan's car.

Thompson was not a surprising culprit, having had multiple previous convictions for car theft, but a battered old Nissan was a damn strange choice of car to steal. They'd talked to his known associates, where was he last seen, what he'd been doing, and there had been nothing unusual. Then, at Frank's suggestion and Suzanne's request, Séamus had delved into his finances. Suzanne assumed these would be fairly simple, cash-based at the very least.

She read the email. Séamus had turned up something *very* unexpected. She must have gasped aloud, because Dave, suddenly looming up behind her chewing on yet another egg sandwich, said, 'Wha?'

She blew out a breath. 'Mark Thompson was a junkie. He never worked. Was in and out of prison since the children's court when he was fourteen, and he had a fucking cryptocurrency account?'

'Huh?' She heard Dave stop chewing. 'A what?'

Suzanne was glad she wasn't facing him; she could only imagine the view she'd have of his open mouth with its half-masticated contents.

'Cryptocurrency. It's a digital currency. To use it you need a cryptocurrency wallet.'

She was aware that she was sounding very knowledgeable about this, but she was actually reading some explanatory stuff that Séamus had just sent her. He'd titled it 'An idiot's guide to cryptocurrency'. Fair enough.

'How does a guy like that even get one of those, let alone need it?' she mused.

Although she now knew the answer to the first part of that question. The idiot's guide said that all you needed was a bank account. Séamus had also explained that there were now crypto ATMs from which you could withdraw cash. Thompson had opened a bank account and set up a cryptocurrency wallet. Séamus was still trying to work through it, but it seemed that quite a lot of cash had been withdrawn, leaving not very much. But they'd found no cash on Thompson. And there hadn't been any cash in Rory O'Riordan's wallet either.

'Did someone set it up for him?' Dave asked.

'God knows.' Suzanne shook her head. She still wasn't sure she understood it all, but one thing was for sure – this was a thread she wanted to pull, and see what unravelled.

CHAPTER FORTY-THREE

Allie

As usual, I printed out a hard copy to go through what I'd written, editing with a pen, crossing out words and sentences I didn't like. I wasn't sure where the idea that Harkin's ancestor was the father of Eliza's little girl had come from; I knew I was pushing the boundaries of what I'd discovered, but it seemed to fit. And it was so much easier to lose myself in Eliza's imagined world than face what was going on in mine. The Polaroid photograph lay in a drawer beneath layers of clothes, hidden only from myself, a completely pointless exercise since I thought about it all the time. It seemed to pulse as if electrified, reminding me that I had been watched.

The following night, I remembered to lock the small room, barricading myself into my own bedroom by dragging the heavy armchair from the living room and wedging it against the door. But when I finally slept, I dreamed of the covers being jerked off my bed, exposing my feet to the freezing air while I lay there unable to move. I woke again with a pounding head, moonlight spilling in through a gap in my curtains with what seemed like malevolent intent. Was it sleep paralysis again? Night terrors? I wasn't sure. All I knew was that I was afraid. It felt as if the cottage and I were in conflict for the first time.

Every night after that was disturbed, leaving me with the sense that the house wanted me in that little room and was aggrieved I was resisting. If I refused to go in there, it wouldn't let me sleep. But why was the cottage I loved sending me into the one room that made me unhappy?

The days were a blur. My brain felt wired. Memories returned unbidden. Of when my parents died. Of my last night with Rory. My mind seemed to confuse the two – there were times when I thought I was eighteen again and it was my parents I had just lost, not Rory. That I had crashed the car with Rory in it. Reality and imagination jumbled. Memories nudged at my consciousness, and when I tried to grab hold of them, they slithered from my grasp, slipping below the surface like a seal, leaving a sense of dread settling in the pit of my stomach.

I ate little but drank my two bottles of wine. Then I remembered a litre of Black Bush that I'd taken from the apartment, so I started to work my way through that. I kept odd hours, sleeping late. I dreamed of Rory. Of finding him, of not finding him. While I'd been waiting on the identification of the body in the car, I had something concrete to hold onto. News was due. Now I had nothing. I realised with horror that I might never find out what had happened to him. I was falling into an abyss with nothing to grab onto, no foothold to claim.

I don't think I had ever felt so exhausted. My shoulders ached. I was tired in my bones. By the afternoon I wanted to go to bed, but I knew I wouldn't sleep, afraid of the dreams and the night terrors. With no work to get up for, the days and nights melted into each other. I was lost. Barely functioning, with only Finn and the ravens for company.

And then one morning I saw a pale face at the window, looking in at me. Hollow-eyed and grey-faced. I flinched until I realised it was my own. I laughed with relief, my breath misting the glass.

The sound of my voice was surprising in the silent house, a balm to my frayed nerves. I hadn't spoken to anyone other than Finn for days.

And in that moment, I knew that I had no need to fear this house. It had been a mistake to lock the little room, to barricade myself into my bedroom at night. What I needed to do was surrender. If the cottage wanted me in that room, it must be trying to tell me something, to seek something from me. I would stop being afraid of it, I decided. I would allow myself to wake up in there.

I went out into the garden, caring little that my feet were bare, that my pyjamas provided scant protection from the winter cold. I walked across the frosty grass, spotting a little bank of pale pink flowers in the shade of the hedge, pretty in the early morning. I knew from Maggie that they were winter heliotrope. I picked a cluster of them and brought them inside, inhaling their vanilla scent. I found a mug in the cupboard above the sink, filled it with water and arranged the flowers with some of their heart-shaped leaves. Then I took them into the little room and left them on the windowsill. I felt a slight lifting of the atmosphere and convinced myself that the room welcomed my decision.

That night, I left the door unlocked and my bedroom door unbarricaded. At three a.m., I woke up in the little room just as I had expected to. It was in shadow, but I could see the flowers I'd left there, silhouetted against the dim winter light. I felt a presence. A benign presence, a feminine one. Don't ask me how I knew that, but it made me feel less afraid. I imagined the faintest hint of movement, and then I heard a voice whispering to me. Eliza telling me her story.

At first I couldn't make out what was being said. When the voice came again, there were goosebumps on my skin. A coldness spread through me, even though there was no draught and the air felt thick. But still I wasn't afraid.

'I died,' she said. 'They killed me.'

Her decision was made, Bridget Kennedy said. She would go after Christmas and before the new year.

Eliza ~~had been~~ was surprised but relieved to see the young woman at her door, the full moon lighting her way along the lane. She hadn't seen or heard anything about her in weeks.

Bridget drew in a breath, the light of the fire flickering on her pale face. This time she did not ask to speak to her dead father. She only wished to speak to Eliza. So they stayed in the warmth. Eliza would not take payment for tonight. What Bridget needed was a friend, and one did not charge for friendship.

'I'll speak to my aunt Mary and go stay with her. I have decided that I will tell her everything.' Bridget looked down. A weak smile. 'Even that I have heard my father's voice. She will think I am mad, but she will not go against her brother's wishes.'

Eliza did not say that Bridget's aunt was a regular visitor to this very hearth. That was for Mary to tell. She was just thankful that the young woman had found the courage she needed.

'I'm glad you are resolved.'

In truth, Bridget did not look resolved. She looked frightened, skin so pale as to be almost translucent, her mouth quivering as she spoke. As well she might. Eliza knew it would be dangerous for Bridget Kennedy to leave her husband, but she couldn't imagine how things could get any worse for her. She'd been burned on her stomach with the poker the night before, which had hardened her resolve.

'I think Edward has guessed.' Bridget put her hand on her belly. 'I have denied it, I've said I am just getting fat, that I know I cannot be with child since I am still bleeding.' She looked down. 'I know he will never let me go if I am carrying his baby.'

Eliza nodded.

'He will be drinking at Christmas.' Bridget closed her eyes, her jaw set in determination. 'I will get a chance some night when I know he is out for the evening.'

Eliza saw her to the door. As she watched the young woman depart with her guttering candle, hopeful that she would find some solace for herself and her baby, she contemplated her own fate. Another encounter with the priest had shaken her.

'You're being watched by God,' he had said, his wrath colouring his face as if he were wearing rouge. 'It's not your place to be telling these women what to do.'

Eliza had stuck firm to her lie. 'It's not me telling them, it's those who have passed on.'

'Stop what you are doing or there will be consequences for you,' he ordered her. 'It's not natural and it's not right.'

She wondered if she herself would also have to leave. Leave the cottage that she loved. It was not something she wanted to do. She felt a duty to these women, did not want to abandon them. Pregnancies made women vulnerable. Their men made them weak. But she could give them strength.

CHAPTER FORTY-FOUR

Strands of hair fell around me, raining onto the bathroom floor like leaves. I'd cut my own hair once before, although that was just trimming my fringe after a shower. It hadn't been a success. I hadn't wanted to go the hairdresser's with all that faff, the chat about holidays and nights out, tin foil, gowns and magazines. But Rory had laughed at the crooked edge I'd left.

It was harder cutting when the hair was dry. The black kitchen scissors were blunter than I'd have liked, but they did the job. I snipped my ponytail off first, then decided to go shorter, driven on by some imaginary force, vigorously chopping at the sides and the fringe until I was completely shorn. When I was finished, I studied myself in the mirror, satisfied. I looked just like Eliza in that picture.

When I think about that time now, I wonder if I was losing my mind, confusing myself and Eliza. I was hearing her voice, writing about her, retreating from my world into hers. There were times when I felt as if Allie Garvey was no longer real. When I no longer wanted her to be real. I preferred to be a facsimile of someone else. Someone I admired.

It's not even as if I believed in ghosts. But for some reason I believed in Eliza Dunne; I believed she was present in the cottage in some way, and I trusted her. I felt less alone at the thought that she was watching over me. It was comforting, that sense of someone else being there when things were at their worst. When I lost the baby, the hawthorn tree with the possibility of Eliza's own baby being buried beneath it made me feel as if I wasn't the only woman to whom this had happened. This gnarled old tree in my garden that I could touch, that I could walk around whenever I wanted to, seemed to ground me somehow.

It sounds odd, but I felt as if I knew Eliza as soon as I moved into the cottage, as if we existed side by side, she in the past and me in the present like some kind of weird housemates. Before I even knew who she was, I felt her presence, or thought I did. I knew her name before I was told it. The fact that Eliza was Maggie's ancestor made her feel even closer.

And at least I could be sure that it wasn't Eliza who was taking sneaky pictures of me. They didn't have Polaroid cameras in 1890. I knew because I googled it. People had box cameras back then. The flexible roll of film was invented in the 1880s, and the final decade of the nineteenth century was the beginning of consumer photography, when ordinary people started to partake. Although I assumed that Eliza's photograph, the one in the library book, had been taken by a professional, and I wondered why.

Maybe I was more susceptible after many nights of lousy and broken sleep. But when I wrote about her, I felt as if I was speaking to her, and she to me. She was telling me her story. And I wanted to listen.

The following morning, a car pulled up outside the cottage. I closed my laptop. Beside it was the library book. I'd taken to keeping it open at the picture of Eliza while I wrote, as if she were keeping me company. I covered both with a tea towel that I'd left hanging on the chair.

The knock on the door was hesitant, but I went to answer it. It was Pieter. He smiled, but his expression was concerned, his eyes widening into something close to shock when he saw me. I knew I hadn't showered in a few days, but did I really look that bad? And then I remembered my hair. Maybe I did look a little strange.

'I don't need to come in,' he said. 'I just thought I'd see if anything needs to be done in the garden. There are some storms forecast and I wanted to check . . .' He trailed off as if losing his train of thought, then cleared his throat. 'I wouldn't want anything to fall on the house.'

He seemed unsure of himself and I wondered why. Tentative, as if he was afraid his call wouldn't be welcome.

I opened the door wide. 'Of course, come in.'

He stepped so gingerly into the living room it was as if he was afraid of hurting the house. I realised suddenly that the Polaroid of us kissing was sitting in plain sight on the table. It had come out with a jumper I'd taken from the drawer and I'd forgotten to put it back. I moved quickly to slip it beneath my laptop and covered it again with the tea towel.

Pieter gave me an odd look, then glanced down as if he was ashamed of looking. 'Are you okay?' he asked. 'We haven't seen you for a while.'

I studied his kind face, those startling blue eyes. There was such tenderness in them that I thought about showing him the picture, but I knew it would reopen something I shouldn't. Every time I looked at him, it hurt. Conflicted didn't even touch the sides. So I just nodded, intending to say that I was fine but discovering that I couldn't speak, grateful for the distraction when Finn appeared from the kitchen.

Pieter stooped to scratch his ears. 'Shall we have a look at the garden?'

We made our way outside, and he had a wander about while I trailed after him, Finn trailing after me. There was an icy wind and I regretted not grabbing a jacket.

'If there's a bad storm, one of those spruce trees at the end of the garden might fall,' he said, looking up at them. 'It won't hit the house, it's too far away, so shouldn't do any damage. But just be careful. Give the garden a wide berth if it's very windy – a flying branch could really hurt you. Or Finn.'

'What about the hawthorn?' It was looking a little stooped but stubbornly held firm no matter what the weather.

He smiled. 'Oh, they're hardy trees. It might bend and sway but it won't break.'

I gave a half-smile, hugging myself against the cold, the chilled air sneaking through the holes in my jumper.

'You're freezing. Can I give you my jacket?'

I shook my head. 'I'm fine.' He looked down again and there was silence between us for a few minutes. So much unsaid.

Eventually he asked, 'Are you going to Maggie's party?'

I had forgotten all about the party. I wasn't even sure when it was, how much time had passed since I'd seen her.

'It's on Friday, the day after tomorrow,' he added as if reading my mind. 'She asked me to remind you. I think she's been trying to message you.'

I flushed. So today was Wednesday. I'd been back at the cottage for more than a week. It hit me that my phone had been off for all this time. What if there had been news of Rory? I felt a rising panic. How would that look? Surely they'd have come for me if anything had happened. Wouldn't they?

'Everyone's been asking after you. You missed the walk again on Sunday and you're not answering your phone.' He finally met my gaze. 'I understand if you want to be left alone, but people would be glad to see you.'

I glanced at the back door of my cottage. I felt a sudden compulsion to go back inside, to return to my laptop, to Eliza. I'd had an idea about the photograph.

I needed Pieter to go. So I nodded, and said, 'Yes. Of course I'll come.'

Eliza had made a mistake. A man had come looking for her, an Englishman with one of those box cameras. Her fame had spread without her knowing, and he wanted to take her photograph for a paper on spiritualism. She should not have allowed it, she knew that now. But her pride had got the better of her. The village was too small; it was all around Rath like measles.

Mary Tiernan worked in Kehoe's pub and she heard things. It was said that Eliza Dunne was no longer herself, that when that photograph was taken, she had been spirited away by the fairies and replaced with one of their own; that she was a changeling.

Eliza knew how dangerous a rumour like that could be; the winter before, a woman who had been seen with another man was burned in the fire, her face and arms permanently scarred. She knew that a woman who didn't obey the rules of society could not be allowed to get away with it. And that while men were circulating this story, women were staying quiet, in fear of their own secrets being exposed.

Eliza knew that she was in danger. She was not afraid for

herself but for her child; if something happened to her then Gretta would be left alone.

She would leave, she decided. But not yet. She could not go without knowing that Bridget Kennedy at least was safe.

CHAPTER FORTY-FIVE

I'd been keen when Maggie asked me originally, and while less so when reminded by Pieter, I fully intended going to the dinner. But when Friday evening came around, I didn't want to leave the cottage.

By eight o'clock I'd made no move to get ready, though it would take me at least twenty minutes to walk to the village. Pieter must have expected something of the sort, because at ten past I heard his van pull up outside the cottage. He claimed that he didn't like the idea of my walking in the dark along the main road, that the forecast wasn't great and it was too dangerous with a torch and a dog. I resisted, saying that I would be fine and that I would be along later, but he said that since Finn was invited too, I couldn't deprive him of the excellent leftovers. So I pulled on a clean top over my jeans, and we set off.

Parking outside Maggie's café in the village, I saw that she had decorated it for Christmas; a tree with twinkling lights glimmered through the window, while branches of mistletoe and holly with white and red berries were arranged along the sills.

I climbed out of Pieter's passenger seat feeling strange and achy, the way you do after you've had flu and not been out of the house for a while. Though it was dark, everything seemed a little glaring, my eyes struggling to adjust to life outside the cottage. Pieter looked as if he wanted to take my hand, but he refrained, giving me an encouraging smile as if I was an invalid taking my first steps. He let Finn out of the back of the van and we made our way to the door.

It was opened by Cathy, wearing a sparkly silver dress, a goblet of something red and steaming in her hand. 'Welcome to the wake!' she said expansively, and I could see immediately that the glass wasn't her first.

We stepped inside. The café was low-lit with fairy lights and candles, and a couple of the tables had been pushed together to make one large one. I could see that Maggie had gone to a lot of trouble, and I felt bad that I'd considered not coming, though I was conscious now of my unwashed cropped hair and my scuffed jeans. The place felt cosy and warm, in stark contrast to the cottage, which I was ashamed to say I'd also let go in the past couple of weeks.

Pieter handed over two bottles of wine, a red and a white, claiming they were from both of us, and I flushed, having forgotten to bring anything. I'd long since drunk the bottles I'd bought the last time I was in town, and the aromas emanating from the kitchen reminded me that I'd been surviving on tins I'd brought from the apartment weeks before.

There was no sign of Maggie. I assumed she was cooking. The only other person in the room was Jim, who was sitting at the head of the table, raising his glass to us in a toast.

He stood up. 'I'm under strict instructions to offer mulled wine. Mystic Maggie's special recipe. God knows what she puts in it, she won't tell us mere mortals, but it's bloody potent.'

'So I see.' Pieter grinned. 'Allie?'

I nodded, and Jim went behind the counter to a large steaming saucepan, emerging a few seconds later with two glass cups filled to the brim.

I took a sip; it was hot, spicy and strong, and I imagined there was some kind of spirit in it. I took a second drink and felt the warmth spread throughout my body, flowing through my veins, easing my muscles and stretching my limbs, soothing everything. Ridiculously, I felt like I wanted to cry.

A voice sounded from the kitchen and Maggie appeared with a tray of little pastries, stepping over Finn, who had flopped down in his usual draught-excluder pose, to plonk them onto the table.

'Ah, Allie.' She gave me a broad smile. 'I was afraid you wouldn't come. I've already had two last-minute cancellations. It's just the five of us now.'

I saw now that the table had been set for eight, and I wondered who the others had been.

'Come. Sit.' She waved at us all, and we clustered around one end of the large table.

Maggie had cooked a full Christmas dinner, turkey, ham and all the trimmings. Even a nut roast. Jim, who I discovered had a heavy pouring hand, took charge of the wine and Pieter helped with the delivery of the food to the table. Only Cathy and I stayed in our seats throughout.

I continued to feel a little peculiar, as if I wasn't really there. I tried to join in, to answer questions when I was asked, even offer the odd comment, but the whole thing felt like a film set, where everything was a little unreal and I was there to observe rather than participate. Despite the wine, and a certain looseness creeping in the more people drank – there was no water on the table, just a jug of something alcoholic; the remains of the mulled wine, I assumed – the conversation seemed stilted, though we were all at ease with one another when we walked.

'I have nine horses at the moment,' Cathy was saying. 'I mean, what's wrong with me? I spend my life absolutely covered in dust, running from one end of the arena to the other.'

I found myself drifting, and her voice faded into the background. The room seemed to shimmer like an asphalt road on a hot day. How much had I had to drink?

'Well?' Cathy's voice came back into focus, and I realised she was speaking to me.

'Sorry?'

'I said, are you going to give riding a go, like I suggested? I think it would be good for you, get you out and about in the fresh air...'

I was about to respond when I realised that the conversation had moved on without me. My reactions weren't fast enough.

Now Jim was teasing Pieter, slagging off the Belgians. 'They leave the office at five on the dot, go home, eat something healthy, and then go out to do something worthy on bikes, in groups. And some of them don't wear any underwear, which is very off-putting if you're behind them.'

'I think that might be the Dutch.' Pieter smiled. 'We Belgians like our beer.' He'd continued to be attentive to me, checking on me and passing me food. 'More roast potatoes?'

I shook my head, still feeling as if I was lagging a few seconds behind everyone else, when the conversation turned to memorable meals.

'Luxor,' Pieter said immediately when he was asked. 'Egypt. I was there for a week a couple of years ago and I ate almost every day in this little place that looked like a building site. Falafel, hummus, fava beans with garlic.' His eyes glazed over at the memory. 'Never had anything as good before or since. Even picked up some takeaway to eat on the plane home. A hell of a lot better than an Aer Lingus sandwich.'

'I bet you were popular with the other passengers,' Jim said. 'Speaking of sandwiches, my mother gave me corned beef ones in my school lunch box every day for six years. Still can't eat the stuff.' He made a face.

Maggie smiled, helping herself to some Brussels sprouts. 'You think that was bad. I was a boarder. We had hamburgers for tea one night. No buns, just the frozen patties. None of us ate them because they were so bloody awful, and they were served up to us again the next day for lunch. The exact same burgers! With the bites taken out of them.'

Everyone laughed, including me. But that story rang a bell that made me uneasy. I was sure I'd heard it before. But where? An anxious ticking started up in the corner of my mind as my brain picked over it.

'Right,' Cathy said, scrunching up her napkin and dumping it on her plate. 'I'm going out for a cigarette.'

I stood up, suddenly desperate for some fresh air. 'I'll come with you.'

Ignoring the surprised looks, I followed her out through the front door of the café and onto the street, shivering in the cold but glad of the break from the fug of food and wine. I must have drunk more than I thought.

'Everything all right?' she asked. Her eyes narrowed. 'Do you really want a cigarette?'

I nodded, and she took one out of her pack and lit it for me. A gusty wind was building and she had difficulty in keeping the lighter from flickering out, but she succeeded eventually.

I inhaled smoke deeply into my lungs, thinking about Eliza and her hand-rolled cigarettes, then immediately got that slightly stoned sensation you get when you haven't smoked for a while. It occurred to me that maybe this wasn't such a good idea, but I was feeling reckless.

'So did you watch *Crime Files*?' Cathy asked, crossing her arms against the chill and blowing a cloud of smoke into the night air.

And there it was. The reason everything was so odd this evening, why they were all a little twitchy around me. It was something of a relief. The *Crime Files* segment with Rory's disappearance must have been on during the week and they'd all seen it. If I hadn't been keeping my phone off, I was sure Olivia would have let me know, even if Rory's family didn't.

I shook my head. 'I don't have a television.'

'You don't need a television. You can watch it online.' I wondered if Cathy had been warned not to mention this and was grabbing her chance now that she had me on her own. 'You have a laptop, surely, or an iPad? You could still watch it on the player.' She peered at me suspiciously. 'Did they not ask you to be on it yourself?'

I shook my head and took another drag of my cigarette. The light-headedness was fading, my mind becoming clearer in the sharp wind. I'd started to think about Eliza again, feeling a pressing need to get back to her. Maybe Pieter would drive me home.

'Do you think a house can retain the memory of what happened in it?' I asked, wanting to steer the subject away from Rory.

Cathy gave a nervous laugh. 'That's more Jim's area than mine.' She shivered and put out her cigarette, grinding it into the footpath with her high heel. 'Let's go back inside. It's Baltic out here.'

Jim was teasing Maggie about something but stopped as soon as we reappeared, struggling to his feet and clapping his hands together. 'Right, I'm off to the jacks.'

Pieter shot me a concerned look, but I smiled reassuringly at him and sat down. I'd ask him to drive me home when we finished dessert.

Seconds later, not long enough for him to do what he'd intended, Jim stumbled back into the café grinning drunkenly, holding something aloft. 'Look what I found. We could have some fun with this!'

I stared at it. The large boxy object seemed to glow like a warning; cold, sick dread flooding through me when I saw that it was a Polaroid camera. And with sudden blinding clarity, I knew where I'd heard that hamburger story before.

Blood roaring in my ears, I grabbed Finn's leash and my coat and ran out.

CHAPTER FORTY-SIX

I ran until I was out of range of the lights of the village, badly out of breath after so much food and wine, Finn trotting along beside me. Pieter came after us in his van as I knew he would; he was right, the walk home along the main road didn't feel particularly safe, especially without a torch, and I'd left mine behind at the cottage when he drove me in. As soon as his headlights appeared, I ducked into a ditch, hiding myself and Finn behind a gate into a field until he passed by us for a second time on his way back to the village. I didn't want to speak to him. I didn't want to speak to anybody.

The whole evening had taken on a nightmarish quality in my head; I had the mortifying and possibly paranoid sense that everyone had been laughing at me, the people I'd considered friends. Maybe Rory was right about my tendency to trust the wrong people. Pieter seemed different, but what did I know? I wasn't sure what was real and what wasn't any more.

But I did know one thing. I remembered where I'd heard that story about the hamburgers with the bites taken out of them. Rory had told it to me, I was sure of it. It was one of his boarding school stories. I racked my brain to remember what else he had told me about his school. But all I knew was that it was somewhere outside of Dublin; he'd joked about the city boy being sent away to school in the sticks.

I stiffened when I had a sudden memory of Cathy on the bus pointing out a hotel with a golf course and river that used to be a boarding school. Had Rory mentioned a river? I wasn't sure. And then, horribly, I had a crystal-clear memory of his joking that he hoped the food had improved or they were going to be in trouble on TripAdvisor. So his school *was* now a hotel. Did this mean that he and Maggie had been in school together? That Rory knew Maggie? If so, why hadn't she said anything?

And that Polaroid camera. My heart lurched again when I thought about Jim coming back into the café holding it in his hands. Was it Maggie who had taken the picture of Pieter and me? Why would she do that? Out of loyalty to Rory?

Maggie was supposed to be my friend. *Mine.*

When I was sure that Pieter wasn't coming back, I clambered out from the field with a very confused Finn. I had a stitch from running so we set off walking again, our way lit every so often by a partial moon, which kept disappearing behind heavy clouds. The wind was increasing and I had the sense that a storm was building; twigs and branches skittered about the road, gusts causing the trees to creak. Then the moon disappeared completely and I couldn't see my way, couldn't even see Finn. I was close to tears. In desperation I turned on my phone for the first time in over a week. Message after message flashed up, but I ignored them, finding the torch app with shaking fingers and turning it on.

I convinced myself that I was almost home when I reached the start of the lane. But then it began to rain and I hid beneath a tree to shelter, good timing as it turned out – headlights appeared again, and I was pretty sure it was Pieter, so I ducked behind the trunk until he drove back the other way. Maybe he'd called at the cottage and got no answer.

By the time I finally got there, a savage wind was battering the hedgerows and trees, whipping into an angry gale. I'd left a light on in the living room, and I was glad. We rushed inside, myself and Finn, and closed the door against the world. Finn went immediately to the kitchen, as had become his habit; it was where I kept his food and water bowls. I grabbed a towel, rubbed him down and gave him some dried food. Listening to the wind building outside, rattling the windows, less sturdy here in the extension.

My phone buzzed with a text, making me jump, and I took it from my coat pocket. It was Pieter. *I'm worried about you – I drove after you but couldn't find you. There's a storm coming.* To keep him at bay, I responded. *I'm fine, I'm home. Speak to you tomorrow.* He replied, *Okay, well lock all your windows and doors and stay inside.*

While Finn ate, I went into the living room and slumped down into one of the armchairs, trying to make sense of what had happened. Had my new friendships all been in my head? Was there no one I could trust?

Finn nuzzled me and I rubbed his damp head. 'You're right, Finn boy. I have you.' With an effort I stood up. 'We should go to bed and put this night behind us.'

I drank a glass of water and brushed my teeth, listening to the sorrowful groans of the house as the storm continued to rage outside. The light in the bathroom flashed on and off, buzzing like an angry fly. Before climbing into bed, I gathered candles, torch and matches and placed them on the chair beside me, within reach, taking a last glance at Finn's anxious face before I turned out the light.

Darkness enveloped me and I tried to sleep but couldn't. The roof creaked as the wind rushed and moaned over the slates. There was too much noise, but I knew it was my own disturbed mind that was causing me to toss and turn. Blood pulsed in my ears while my mind raced, replaying over and over again the events of the evening.

There was the crack of cymbals, followed within seconds by a circle of bluish-white light. Thunder and lightning. A proper electric storm. Finn whimpered in his bed; he was terrified of thunder. I remembered him shivering in terror in the apartment. I turned on the light to comfort him. It flickered, threw brown shadows against the wall and went out. My heart sank, knowing it wasn't the bulb. The electricity had gone.

Within seconds, my phone buzzed and I reached for it. Pieter texting me again. *The electricity has gone here. The whole village is out. Are you okay?*

I'm fine, I responded. *Goodnight.*

I sensed him wanting to check that I had candles or a torch but resisting, my firm goodnight cutting him off. There had been nothing from Maggie since I'd left the party. Was that odd? Was she annoyed I'd left so abruptly? Or had she given up any pretence of being my friend? I was surprised by how much that hurt.

I jumped suddenly at a scratching and banging noise outside the window, something light and frantic repeatedly hitting the glass. Was it a flying branch? Or could it be my little raven friend? I hadn't seen him for a while, but he always came back. I assumed the birds would find shelter, but maybe he'd got lost.

I got up to investigate. My head ached and my limbs felt heavy as Finn got up too, body quivering with fear but still wanting to come. I switched on the torch and lit a candle, which I left in the bedroom propped up in a mug, taking the torch with me into the living room. A blast of soot came down the chimney, giving me a fright. The room was half alive with shadows, rain splattering the windows. Was that what I'd heard? The rain? My eyes adjusted as a white patch of light spread across the floor. Was it the lightning again? Or did I smell burning? Cigarette smoke?

Somehow I was sure that I was not alone in the darkness. I stayed very still, suddenly hoping it was Eliza. I found I was trembling, tears running down my face, whether from hope or fear I couldn't tell. All I could hear was my own breathing, and the wind. Where was Finn? I couldn't feel him. He'd been here a second ago.

And then the torch flickered and died. I tried to turn it on again, and in my panic, I tripped, arms flailing. Seconds later, I was on the floor. I'd fallen over the rug. As I tried to regulate my breathing, Finn reappeared, and I heaved a sigh of relief. I lay there exhausted, feeling that I could happily sleep right where I was.

Tap-tap-tap. A knock on the door nearly caused my heart to stop. *Tap-tap-tap.* I froze and listened. The latch was jiggled and the knock came again. Someone was trying to get in. Who could it be? Pieter? Maggie? My mind swirled. Finn was frozen rigid.

I pulled myself to my feet and went to the door. Was this my brain playing tricks, the product of my own disturbed mind? The door refused to give, the wind blowing against it. With a huge effort, I wrenched it open.

A man stood on the threshold, wet through, his hair plastered against his skull. Silhouetted against the blue-white as another crack of lightning flashed behind him. He had a beard. I didn't know any men with beards. But then he smiled.

I'd have known that smile anywhere.

PART III

CHAPTER FORTY-SEVEN

Allie

I ran straight into his embrace, clasping my arms around his neck as if I never wanted to let him go. Finn's excitement was even sweeter to see, leaping up on him, paws on his shoulders, before barrelling around the living room doing zoomies, then crouching into his submissive stance, which always broke my heart.

'Where have you been? What happened to you? Are you hurt?' I asked, as soon as I could get a word in. He didn't look hurt. Apart from the beard and slightly longer hair, he looked like his old self, although we only had torchlight.

Rory held my hands in his, smiling. 'One question at a time. Can we at least sit down? Maybe I could have something hot to drink? It's pretty rough out there.'

'You didn't walk, did you?' My gaze slid to the cottage windows, outside which the storm was still raging.

He laughed. 'Of course not. Tea?' he prompted.

'The electricity's gone.'

'Water, then? Help me here, Allie.'

'Sorry.' I fetched us two glasses and we sat at the table, the torch sitting upright between us like a candle in a romantic restaurant. Finn lay curled up on the rug with one eye on his master, afraid to close them both in case he left again.

Rory took a sip of his water, grimacing at first and then downing half the glass. 'Okay, that's better.'

'Tell me,' I said eagerly.

He leaned back and crossed his arms. 'I lost my memory after my car was stolen. The bastard who took it hit me over the head and dumped me on the side of the road. I must have passed out.'

'Did no one stop?' Tears blurred my eyes as I pictured him lying hurt with no one coming to his rescue. The image that had tortured me for weeks after he disappeared was true.

Rory shook his head. 'It was dark. A quiet road. I'm still not even sure where it was. When I came to, I couldn't remember who I was or what I was doing there. But I found a large wad of cash in an envelope in my pocket, which I realised afterwards was money to pay contributors to the documentary. At the time I thought I was just lucky that the car thief hadn't got it.'

Had Rory not made the payments because he'd stormed off on Sam after their row? I wondered. Sam hadn't mentioned that money to me, though he must have been aware it was missing. A kindness, saving me from yet another revelation?

'What did you do?' I asked. 'How badly hurt were you?'

'I had a pretty sore head.' He smiled. 'But I hitched. I haven't done that since I was in school, but a car came along eventually. I found a B&B, where I stayed a couple of nights before making my way to the North.'

My eyes widened. 'The North? Why the North? Why didn't you go for help, the guards or a hospital?'

He shrugged. 'I have absolutely no idea. Clearly I wasn't thinking straight. I didn't know what to do or where to go, so I ended up getting a lift to a small village on the Antrim coast, where I managed to rent a tiny cottage cheap out of season. I stayed there, days turning into weeks, until my memory gradually came back. And here I am.'

'All this time?' I asked, incredulously. 'That's where you were all this time? In a village in the North of Ireland?' I had so many questions that I couldn't decide which to ask first.

But Rory rubbed his eyes. 'Listen, babe, I'm exhausted. Can we do the rest in the morning? I can barely stand up.'

I felt a twitch of disappointment, but he did look tired, and I guessed he wasn't going anywhere. I'd have plenty of time to ask him whatever else I wanted to know.

But there was one obvious omission in what he'd told me.

'What did you do to earn money? The guards said your bank account hadn't been touched.'

He yawned. 'I did some labouring on a building site. The owner of the cottage set it up. He felt sorry for me, I think.'

I dipped my head. 'Right.' I didn't want to raise the subject of his debts the first night back. That would have to come later.

'Probably thought I was on the run,' he laughed. 'I turned up with a gash on my head and a wad of cash in my pocket.'

I woke late, with Rory squashed alongside me in my narrow bed, arm thrown heavily across me. I could tell immediately that the storm was over. The wind had stopped, allowing the ravens to make their usual racket in the roof, and the electricity was back too, my bedside lamp throwing out a dim lemony glow.

I tried to reach out to switch it off, but couldn't. I was trapped. Breathing was also a bit of a challenge with Rory's forearm right on my ribcage like a fallen tree, not to speak of his newly acquired beard scratching my cheek, but I couldn't exactly complain. This was what I had craved. Rory's return. Healthy, alive. I should be over the moon. I *was* over the moon, I told myself.

But as I looked at his sleeping features, the new facial hair giving him a rakish appearance he didn't have before, I still had so many questions. I'd have stayed up and talked all night, but he promised to tell me anything else I wanted to know this morning, and snuggling up together had seemed like a gift I couldn't turn down after everything that had happened.

He shifted in his sleep, limiting my space even further, my knee rammed painfully against the wall. So I lifted his arm and put it along his side, then sat up and climbed over him to get out of bed. He didn't stir. Although an early riser, when he was asleep Rory slept the sleep of the dead. Nothing could wake him.

I pulled on a dressing gown and slippers, surprised when Finn got up with me, trotting after me into the kitchen. I closed the bedroom door with a quiet click, let the dog out into the garden, then put the kettle on. While it was boiling, I grabbed the bag of nuts I kept under the sink and went outside to scatter some on the windowsill of the shed. The ravens flocked around me and I was glad to see my little friend amongst them. Had it been Rory or the little raven banging on the window the night before?

The air had that strange scent that comes the morning after a storm. There were pools of rainwater in the grass, and I smiled watching Finn prance about like a four-legged ballet dancer. I was glad to see that Pieter had been right about the hawthorn – it was undamaged, although twigs and branches of all sorts were strewn across the garden, which had taken quite a battering. I felt unsteady and disorientated too, as if someone had moved the furniture around just when I'd become used to where everything now was.

Rory's back. I kept repeating the words in my head, as if doing so would make them seem more real. The new world that I had built for myself had been dismantled and the old one had come back in to replace it. I wasn't sure how I felt about that.

I knew that my discomfort was partly because I had things to tell Rory too, and I didn't know how he would respond. About the baby. Pieter. The kiss. I felt sick when I realised that the Polaroid photograph was in a drawer in the room Rory was sleeping in right now.

Just as the thought crossed my mind, my phone buzzed on the kitchen counter, where it was charging. I went inside, made myself a coffee and took the phone back outside to check it. It was a text from Pieter. *Are you okay? Not been blown away?*

I smiled. Maybe I had been right to trust him, at least.

'So, who's making you look so happy?' Rory appeared in the doorway, that old familiar smirk on his face. 'I know it's not me because I'm here, phoneless.' He raised his arms and made jazz hands.

Guiltily I shoved the phone back into the pocket of my dressing gown. 'Just someone from the village checking on me after the storm.'

'Maggie?' he said.

I looked up, surprised. 'Do you know Maggie?'

He nodded. 'Of course. I told you that. I was in school with her, in boarding school. I said it would be nice to know someone down here.' He frowned. 'Don't you remember?'

I had no memory of this, although it explained the hamburger story. Could I really have forgotten? But why hadn't Maggie mentioned it? All she'd said was that she'd met Rory while he was down here filming. As if that had been the first time.

Rory grinned. 'You never really listen, do you? A demon with a ouija board was our Maggie. I'm surprised she didn't get you into it.'

Something about his expression made me want to look away. 'Do you want a coffee?' I asked. 'The kettle's boiled.'

'Great.' He turned and I followed him back into the kitchen.

'What on earth have you been eating?' Rory asked incredulously as he shut the door of the fridge in disgust. 'You have literally no food.'

'I was going to . . .' I trailed off, embarrassed.

But he'd already cut across me, picking up the mug of coffee I'd at least managed to make him with the dregs of the milk, still just about in date. 'It's no problem. I'll go into the village this morning and pick up a few things.'

I wasn't sure why this felt so off to me – Rory casually driving into Rath to do some grocery shopping as if we lived here together – but it did.

'Do you have a car?' I asked stupidly, picturing that poor man dead at the end of the pier in Rory's old Nissan.

He laughed. 'You asked me that last night. How do you think I got here? I hired one.'

Had I asked him that? 'Shouldn't you call the guards?' I said. 'Or your family? Let them know you're okay?'

He leaned back against the sink. The little raven with the white marking landed on the sill outside, keeping watch on us through the window.

'I rang Andrew yesterday on my way here. He said he'd contact the guards and let them know. I'll call them myself today.' He took a sip of his coffee and made a face. Maybe that milk wasn't so fresh after all.

'You contacted your family first?'

He threw the coffee into the sink then plonked the mug on the draining board, unwashed. 'I had to tell my mother. You understand that, don't you?'

I felt that old insecurity creeping in again. That not-quite-good-enough feeling that used to eat away at me.

'You know how you said your memory came back gradually?' I said, with the uneasy sense that I was picking at a scab that wasn't yet ready to come away. Rory's stony expression confirmed it, but I pushed on. 'So why didn't you do anything about it until yesterday?'

He held my gaze and I tried to remove any hint of accusation from my voice. 'You must have known you would be missed somewhere, even if you couldn't remember who you were. Why didn't you contact the guards? Or the Northern Irish police after you'd recovered from your head injury. Why didn't you get some help?'

Guilt flitted across his face, immediately followed by defensiveness. He looked down at his feet, which I noticed were bare. How was he not freezing? How was Rory so immune to everything?

He gave a tight nod. 'Okay, I admit, maybe I took a bit longer on my own than I needed to. Maybe I needed some headspace, some time out. You're not easy to live with, you know.' He crossed his arms. 'I knew people might be looking for me, of course I did, but no one recognised me in the North.'

'You grew a beard,' I said. 'Of course no one recognised you.'

His face flushed in annoyance. 'And *you* cut all your hair off,' he retorted. 'Seriously, did you do that while you were drunk?'

I said nothing. He hadn't mentioned my hair last night, though he must have noticed it.

'I don't know if you remember that last argument we had, Allie, the night I left. When you told that me that I couldn't leave you for three nights, that you wouldn't be able to cope. When you drank a whole bottle of wine and most of a second.'

Now I was the one who blushed.

'You don't, do you? No wonder you don't remember my telling you about Maggie.' He rubbed his palm along his beard. 'Jesus, Allie, there's a limit to how much someone can ...' He shook his head, eyes glistening. 'The truth is, I think I had some kind of breakdown.'

He left the words hanging, the implication being that I wasn't the only one who was allowed to have a breakdown. That in his case, I was the one who had driven him to it. I was responsible.

Without warning, that familiar dread, that terror of being abandoned came flooding back. All I wanted was his forgiveness, for everything to be okay.

I stepped towards him and folded myself into his arms, making myself small against his chest. 'I'm sorry.'

'It's okay,' he whispered into my hair. 'I'm back now. And we're fine. No need to rake over everything.'

I breathed in his familiar scent and let the tears come. Grateful.

When he pulled away from me, he said, 'So how are things here? Have you settled in to our cottage?'

Our cottage. Before I could reply, my phone, back charging on the counter, lit up with another message from Pieter.

Rory raised his eyebrows. 'That guy a friend, is he?'

I felt a flicker of unease. 'He's been helping me a bit with the garden and the house.'

He went to the back door and looked out. 'He's done a decent job. I remember what it was like before.' He turned back to me. 'But I'm here now. I've been gone for too long; I know that and I'm sorry. We'll have a great Christmas, I promise.'

Finn appeared at the door, expecting breakfast. He rolled over on his back and Rory went down on his hunkers to rub his tummy. 'This was what we wanted, Allie. Moving here. The good life.'

'I know.'

A shadow crossed his face briefly and was gone. 'I'll be honest with you. I've had a few money worries. TV doesn't pay as much as you think. But labouring pays well. And with the rent on the flat, we're on the pig's back. Aren't we, Finn?'

And just like that, he did exactly what he'd done after he left me for Clara. He left me with nothing to say, because he'd said it all. But I supposed he was right. This *was* what I'd wanted. And Finn was happy to see him. I just needed to burn that Polaroid picture.

CHAPTER FORTY-EIGHT

Suzanne

Who'd have thought that Dave would take such a shine to Koffee + Kale? They hadn't been to the chipper in weeks, and they were actually eating *in* this time, the pair of them sitting at one of the booths that looked out onto the road. Even the undertaker's alongside no longer seemed to bother him.

Unfathomable though it might seem, Suzanne had the feeling that Dave had acquired a girlfriend. He'd lost a few pounds, and while not exactly less slobbish, he seemed not to take quite the same pleasure in it.

'Okay, so I admit I was wrong. She didn't do him in,' he was saying in response to Suzanne's relating the story of Rory O'Riordan's reappearance.

'That's good of you,' she said sarcastically.

'I still think I was right about him doing a runner, though,' he muttered, spooning porridge into his mouth. He hadn't even ordered eggs. 'He must have changed his mind. Faraway fields not as green as he thought. Sometimes worth your while sticking at something.'

Suzanne raised her eyebrows. She was right. He *did* have a girlfriend. Where on earth had he met her? She knew he'd been keeping an eye on the little boy whose dad had locked his mother in the bathroom overnight. Was it possible his new girlfriend was the mother? Lord, she hoped not – that was not going to end well.

'Well, they're back together now,' she said, sipping her tea thoughtfully. 'All cosy in their little country cottage.'

Suzanne had been taken completely by surprise with this latest development; Rory O'Riordan turning up on his girlfriend's doorstep as if nothing had happened. According to his brother, who had been the one to let them know, he'd lost his memory. The sergeant said they had no choice but to believe him, but Suzanne wasn't convinced. Did that really happen in real life? People getting a bump on the head and forgetting who they were? Was Rory O'Riordan playing games with them? Or was Dave right? Did he run off with another woman and change his mind again? He had form.

'Maybe it was the *Crime Files* piece,' she said. 'It was broadcast only last week. Seems a bit of a coincidence that the man himself turns up only days later.'

'True.' Dave finished his porridge with relish and gazed at the bowl as if he was tempted to lick it. 'Although he was in the North, wasn't he? Do they get *Crime Files* there?'

'Hmm. Probably not. But what about all the social media posts before that? Facebook doesn't have borders.' Suzanne shrugged. 'Maybe it shows that if you really don't want to be found, you can still get away with it. He's got a beard now, apparently, so he looks very different.'

Not that Rory was admitting to not wanting to be found, she thought. Oh no, he'd had amnesia after a bump on the head, like Matt Damon in *The Bourne Identity*. The star of his own movie.

She took a sip of her tea and made a face. It was cold and stewed. She joined the queue at the counter to order another, along with an espresso for Dave. Espresso!

There were garda protocols for when a missing person

returned; the case couldn't be concluded until the person himself had been interviewed. So Rory O'Riordan had been told he needed to come to Dublin, and said he was more than willing to do that. The man hadn't committed a crime. He was a victim of one. The investigation into Thompson's death was winding up too. Despite his unusual financial set-up, nothing in the post-mortem had indicated foul play.

But Suzanne was troubled. The money issue still bugged her. She was going to raise it with Dave, but when she got back to the table, he had taken out his phone and was texting rapidly.

She mulled over it herself as she sipped her hot tea. Thompson must have been involved in something dodgy if he had a cryptocurrency account, but it wasn't as if he could be prosecuted, so they weren't pursuing it. Officially. It hadn't stopped her from having a nosy about, though. Along with the large sums withdrawn using ATMs, a number of significant payments had come *into* the account from a company called KNI. Suzanne hadn't been able to find any evidence of the company's existence, and she very much wanted to know why it was paying a drug addict such large sums. What service could he possibly have been providing in exchange?

She'd asked Séamus to help her, on the QT, and he'd hinted at the dark web. The dark web wasn't something that cropped up very often in day-to-day policing, but Suzanne knew it was that part of the internet consisting of hidden sites that weren't indexed by conventional search engines. She knew that you could get any illegal service you wanted there, that there were people who were desperate enough to do anything for easy cash, that you could hire a hitman as easily as buying a pack of cigarettes. Was Thompson one of those people?

Dave was saying something to her, having finished whatever he was doing on his phone. She asked him to repeat it.

'I said, I forgot to tell you that Paddy said that a guy called Vince Gage called for you.'

Suzanne frowned. 'Who?' The name was familiar but she couldn't place it.

'He says he's the cameraman who was working with Rory O'Riordan in Galway. He spoke to you way back when he first went missing.' Dave grinned. 'Maybe he hasn't heard that O'Riordan has slunk home with his tail between his legs.'

CHAPTER FORTY-NINE

Allie

Rory sped off in his hired BMW – so very different from that battered old Nissan I was used to seeing him drive – promising to get cracking on the garden as soon as he picked us up some nice food. I warned him about Harkin's tendency to abandon his tractor, thereby completely blocking the lane, but he didn't pay me much attention.

As soon as he was gone, I went to fetch the Polaroid photograph with the intention of burning it in the kitchen sink, feeling like a villain on some bad cop show. I was relieved to find it in the bedroom drawer where I'd left it, hidden away between the pages of the library book, and was about to head back into the kitchen when I caught sight of Rory's bag lying on the floor. The zip was partly open, revealing the corner of a laptop that had been stuffed inside.

I lifted it out and held it in my hands. It was brand new. Rory was right, labouring must have paid well. I assumed his old one had gone the way of the car, although I hadn't heard it specifically mentioned. I was tempted to turn it on. It hit me that despite trying to convince myself otherwise, I still harboured some doubts about everything he had told me. Those hands that had been tickling Finn's stomach looked just as soft and white as they ever had, certainly not the hands of someone who'd spent the past few weeks lifting concrete blocks on a building site. And that hire car? How had Rory rented a BMW with no ID and no credit card?

But I hated thinking like this, beads of suspicion already forming when he'd been back only one night. What kind of future did we have if I didn't trust him?

I sat on the bed with the closed laptop on my knee, in two minds. Rory's password had always been DOCUMENTARY, all upper-case letters, and I suspected he wouldn't have changed it. He was a creature of habit. I tapped the cover impatiently. No, I decided. I should trust him. Maybe he'd worn gloves on that building site; perhaps the man in whose cottage he'd been staying had loaned him a credit card. I put the laptop back where I'd found it and zipped up the bag, along with my suspicions.

I burned the photograph in the sink as I had intended, then immediately took Finn for a walk, removing myself from temptation. Remembering to leave the back door open for Rory in case he returned before we did. He didn't have a key.

We were gone for longer than I'd planned. It was a bright December day, the sky a cold, hard blue. But the air was fresh and I needed to clear my head. We made our way to the end of the lane, then turned in the opposite direction to the village, walking along the main road and turning up one of the side roads we hadn't yet explored. It was slow progress, Finn taking his time sniffing all the new scents.

By the time we got back, the BMW was parked again outside the cottage. I paused on the gravel, realising that the house felt completely different with Rory here. Less mine. I felt strangely proprietorial about it, resentful of his presence but trying not to be. What was wrong with me? I'd craved his return all these weeks, had missed him desperately.

The front door was closed, so rather than use my key, I went around the side to the garden. I was heading for the back door, Finn trotting eagerly alongside me, when something caught my eye. The hawthorn tree. Last night's wind had stripped the trees in the garden bare, but the hawthorn was listing as if it was injured. It hadn't been that way this morning, I was sure of it.

I felt something tighten in my chest as I walked towards it. The trunk had a chunk taken out of it, exposing raw white innards where the tree had been cut. It looked injured, almost maimed, as if someone had tried to chop it down. Branches had been hacked at too. Whoever it was had even begun to remove the stones at its base, rolling a couple of them away. I felt violated, as if I was the one who had been hacked at, and I pressed my fingers to my eyelids, unable to look. Rory. It must have been Rory. I didn't even know we had an axe.

The image of Eliza visiting this tree late at night loomed in my mind. Her baby was buried here. I was convinced of it. Which meant that a grave had been desecrated.

Finn sniffed about at the upturned soil and I dragged him away; the thought of him digging up a bone made me sick.

A voice called from the doorway. Rory was standing there holding a mug and munching on a KitKat, looking pleased with himself. 'Do you see? I've started already. Told you I'd throw myself into it. That has to go, doesn't it, that ugly old thing?'

I found I couldn't speak. I had no proof there were baby's bones here, but I felt it. Felt the hurt as if it was my own child. My lack of response must have registered with Rory, and finally he realised that something was wrong. 'Hey, what's up?'

He put the mug and chocolate down on the doorstep and came over to me, pulling me into his arms and clasping me tight. Then he held me away from him at arm's length and looked at me, examining my face.

I had to tell him about the baby. Our baby. If I didn't, someone else might. Maggie, for instance. Stuttering in between sobs, I managed to get the words out. Without mentioning Eliza, I told him what the hawthorn was supposed to symbolise, the local sensitivities around it and why it meant so much to me now because of what had happened. His face grew solemn and I felt that familiar guilt that I had let him down, that I hadn't managed to hold onto our baby.

But was he sad that I was no longer pregnant? I couldn't tell. Rory had always been circumspect about having children, and while he claimed he was sorry that we had lost the last pregnancy, he'd had no desire to try again. Maybe since he hadn't been here during this miscarriage it was hard for him to feel the same grief that I did. He hadn't actually known I was pregnant so didn't feel the loss in the same way. A bit like his leaving me for Clara and not telling me, I supposed.

But he responded in the right way, pulling me back into his arms, telling me how sorry he was, comforting me by saying that he was sure the hawthorn would recover. He hadn't been making a very good job of it anyway, was pretty sure the tree had been winning the battle. He was trying to make me smile, but how he could be sure of that was beyond me. The way he'd been tackling it, hacking haphazardly at the branches and trunk, made it clear he knew nothing about trees. But then Rory had never been plagued by self-doubt.

He brought me inside, made me some tea and gave me a KitKat. 'I do have some good news,' he said brightly. 'We've been invited to go on a walk tomorrow.'

Maggie, I assumed, although I didn't ask.

At three a.m., I was wide awake, Rory sleeping soundly beside me, so I snuck out of bed and took his laptop with me into the living toom. I turned it on and tried his password. DOCUMENTARY.

No luck. I tried his date of birth. No luck either. *Shit.* Only two more goes before it locked me out. I heard a creak and froze. Was it coming from the bedroom? Had he heard me get up?

I held my breath, heart hammering in my chest, and after a few seconds blissful silence returned. This was way too risky, I decided. I closed the laptop, tiptoed back into the bedroom and slipped it back into the bag.

The next morning Rory was up early. Normal service resumed, he said, shooting me that grand old smile of his as he attached Finn's leash to take him out. The walk wasn't till noon and the dog would need to get out before then.

'I'll replace those stones under your tree when I get back,' he promised.

I should have been pleased, but all I wanted was for him to go. I'd come up with more password possibilities during the night and was desperate to try them out.

I hadn't been able to sleep when I got back into bed, mind still racing. Finding myself squashed against the wall again at five a.m., I'd come to a decision. The doubts I'd been having the day before had only increased, beads of disquiet turning into big, ugly baubles of worry. There was something about Rory's jollying-me-along approach that just didn't ring true. I was certain there was something he didn't want me to see, something I wouldn't have noticed in the past because I believed everything he said, trusting that part of him he chose to put on display. I needed to get a look at that laptop.

He and Finn went out through the back door and I saw him pass the window of the living room as they set off. I was about to dart into the bedroom when my phone rang. Olivia. I'd rung her the day before to tell her that Rory was back. I knew she was repressing much of what she wanted to say and would let it all out now if I told her that Rory wasn't here. But I needed to work this out on my own. I let the call go to voicemail. I didn't know how long I had. Probably half an hour at the most.

I fetched the laptop into the living room, from where I could see Rory approach. It asked for a password. So I typed in DOC. RORY. No. Then DOC and the year. Bingo, it worked.

I went straight into Rory's Gmail. I don't know what I was expecting to see. An email from Clara, perhaps? Was that where he had been all this time? Had the woman on the island been Clara, or the woman Olivia had seen him with at the airport?

Eyes darting towards the window, nerves jangling, I scrolled through his inbox. I had no idea what I would say if he caught me doing this. It was a complete betrayal of trust, something he would never do to me. There were no emails from Clara, but a number of strange messages from a company called KNI. Each one seemed to have a link of some sort. I'd never heard of KNI. Should I open them? I hesitated. What if they contained a virus and I messed up Rory's laptop? I'd be busted.

I opened the most recent email and clicked on the link. It was a video. I pressed the arrow for it to start. The recording flickered a little and I clicked into full-screen mode. At first the screen was filled with static; *The Blair Witch Project* came to mind, a film that had terrified me. Then it showed a room, oddly lit, almost bleached. It was that eerie, glowing, night vision that you get in wildlife documentaries when they're filming a fox or some other nocturnal creature. Then the image froze for a few seconds and I saw a fireplace, armchairs, a rug. A dog bed.

Suddenly I couldn't breathe. I knew that room intimately. I was standing in it.

CHAPTER FIFTY

Suzanne

Suzanne got the impression that Vince Gage didn't like Rory O'Riordan very much. She'd finally got hold of the cameraman after a day and night of trying to return his call; he'd been away filming and out of coverage. When he answered, he sounded a little sheepish, as if he regretted making the call in the first place – he hadn't heard about Rory's return when he'd rung, so what he had to say now was probably irrelevant, he insisted.

But Suzanne wasn't going to let him get away with that. 'Tell me anyway,' she said. 'It might not be.'

It turned out that Rory O'Riordan had worked with Mark Thompson on a documentary about drug addiction a number of years before. He'd actually won an award for it, Vince said. An IFTA, an Irish Film and Television Award. The director, Sam, hadn't worked on that one, but Vince had. So when he saw the mention on *Crime Files* of Rory's car having been found with Thompson's body in it, the name had rung a bell. He'd checked some of his old rushes, and there he was – one of the contributors whose story they had followed. They'd only used his first name. Not a success story, unfortunately. Probably someone who would continue to be at risk from his addiction.

It seemed an odd coincidence to Vince, particularly the fact that the prior link between the two men hadn't been mentioned on *Crime Files*, so he'd thought he'd better tell someone.

Suzanne finally felt that things were beginning to make sense. She was so bloody close; she could smell it. Rory O'Riordan *knew* Mark Thompson. But what was really going on between them? She considered all the information she'd gathered to date, and wondered if it was worth having another look at everything in the light of this new development.

She started by bringing up the cryptocurrency account statement and the post-mortem results, placing them alongside one other onscreen. She scanned down through each one, and stopped dead. There it was. She hadn't made the connection before because it was the discovery of the car that had stuck in her head, but now they had an estimated date of death for Thompson. A number of ATM withdrawals had been made from the cryptocurrency account *after* Thompson's death, and from locations in the North. *Shit.* Was it possible they had been made by Rory O'Riordan? That the large payments into Thompson's account were meant for O'Riordan. That the two men had an arrangement of some sort, allowing O'Riordan to evade detection and his debts.

Suzanne suspected that Rory had not expected Thompson to crash his car, to be found dead and identified and for the cryptocurrency account to come to light as a consequence. For the payments into it to be traced. Perhaps that was why he came back. Maybe he thought it too risky to access the money any longer once Thompson had been identified.

But what were the payments for? That was the big question. What had Mark Thompson or Rory O'Riordan being doing in return for that money?

Suzanne was turning this over in her mind when an email popped up from Frank's mate Séamus. She opened it eagerly.

Séamus had been trying to uncover who KNI were – the company making large payments into Mark Thompson's cryptocurrency account. And it looked as if he'd succeeded.

She read through what he had sent. KNI were a streaming service, posting highly dodgy content onto the dark web, fuelling what appeared to be principally male fantasies. A shiver ran down her spine as he explained, almost apologetically, as if feeling responsible for his entire gender, that there was a market for watching frightened women, men who were turned on by it and prepared to pay for access to a hidden site. Mostly men who had lost control of their own lives, or their partners, he said. Pathetic men.

He'd attached a photograph that Suzanne was almost afraid to open, afraid it would contain violence or porn, or worse. Instead, the image was almost arthouse; a woman stared out through a tiny window, her features blurred, tear-stained and frightened.

Suzanne must have let out a sob, loud enough for Dave to come striding over. 'What's wrong?'

She was so bloody angry, she couldn't speak. But she had it. Finally, she had it.

'Jesus, Sue?' Dave was beginning to sound anxious.

She turned in her seat and showed him the picture. 'The bastard's been fucking filming her.'

CHAPTER FIFTY-ONE

Allie

I was falling through air. The world around me receded, and all that existed was the image before me on the screen. It was so clearly the cottage. Raven Cottage. *My* cottage.

A strange coldness seeped through me as I opened one of the other emails from KNI and clicked on the link. This one showed the bedroom. I rewound, played, rewound, froze the screen. There was Finn asleep in his bed. And me, also asleep. It was night-time. I pressed play, and saw myself climb out of bed as if in a trance and leave the room. After a few seconds, Finn followed me. Was this one of the nights I'd woken up in the little room?

Feeling as if I could hardly breathe, I opened another link. The bathroom. With mounting horror, I watched myself step out of the shower and reach for a towel. I wanted to scream at myself to wrap it around me, to cover myself up, but instead I slowly towelled myself dry, then dropped the towel and pinched a lump of loose, goose-pimpled flesh on my stomach. For what seemed like hours I stood in front of the mirror, twisting this way and that, examining my naked body with ill-concealed disgust. Then I picked up a pair of scissors and began hacking at my hair.

Another clip showed me hunched over in the kitchen like an animal, eating straight from a tin, something of which I had absolutely no memory. I looked deranged, almost feral. Whimpering in shame, I heard my own sobbing as if it were coming from someone else.

Though I didn't want to keep watching, I couldn't seem to stop. I was a rubbernecker at the scene of an accident, gaping horrified and open-mouthed, fascinated and appalled. I couldn't tear my eyes away from the screen, compulsively clicking on more and more links.

And then just as suddenly, I stopped. I didn't have time for this. I needed to think, to work out what I was seeing. Figure out who the hell was filming me, and why. Rory knew about these recordings, that was clear; the emails had been sent to him. They were short clips, with timings at the bottom of the screen on each one, showing dates and minutes and seconds.

I forced myself to read one of the emails, but I couldn't work it out. The words blurred in front of my eyes. They didn't seem to make sense. *The success of the channel ... the erotic essence of fear. Poignancy of despair ... the sensual sadness of a woman alone.* Disturbing, creepy words that made me want to take a shower.

And then it hit me. *The channel.* This was footage that had been live-streamed. People had been watching it via a website or an app. Watching *me*. In the living room, in the bedroom, the kitchen, the bathroom. Twenty-four hours a day if they wanted to. Eyes everywhere. For weeks. I was a shop that was permanently open.

I shuddered, felt my cheeks burn, bile rising in my throat. I ran to the bathroom to throw up, and when I finally stopped retching, my eyes darted around me. Was I being filmed even now? Where were the cameras? How come I hadn't seen them?

I rinsed out my mouth and wiped my face and eyes, mind reeling back to everything that had happened since I moved here. My loneliness. The miscarriage and my subsequent grief.

Sleepwalking. Waking up in the small room, barricading myself into my bedroom. Drinking wine, drinking whiskey. When I'd thought I was losing my mind. With a sickening realisation, it hit me that Rory had known about the miscarriage. He'd pretended he didn't. But when I was sobbing in his arms, telling him, he already knew. The knowledge pierced me with a pain that was deeper than anything I'd felt already, and I began to cry.

When I went back into the living room, my phone was ringing. Olivia again, I assumed. What the hell would I say? I'd barely be able to speak if I picked up the phone. But it was Suzanne, Garda Phelan. I couldn't bring myself to speak to her either, so I didn't answer it.

Instead I returned to the screen, so distracted that I didn't notice Rory's return until he arrived through the back door with Finn, whistling his happy Sunday whistle. I heard him give the dog a treat, and then he called out for me, wondering where I was. I didn't reply.

He stopped dead in the doorway when he saw me with his laptop. 'What are you doing?'

'I think that's a question I should be asking you, don't you?' My voice was cold as ice, now that I'd rubbed my tears away.

He came around my shoulder and peered at the screen, pretending he didn't know what I was watching. Brazening it out.

'Don't watch that,' he said, reaching for the power button on the keyboard.

I pushed his hand away roughly. 'Don't watch myself, you mean? Is this what you meant by labouring? A good honest day's work. Spying on women?'

He sat down heavily on the other chair. He didn't look particularly upset, more world-weary. I'd expected him to panic, his face to drain of colour when he knew he'd been found out. Instead he just seemed mildly irritated. 'I have cameras.'

'Where?' I spun around as if expecting to see huge, long-lensed contraptions like the ones he sometimes kept hold of for Vince or Sam, clogging up the hallway in our apartment.

'They're all over the house. They're tiny.' He waved his hand. 'They don't even need Wi-Fi; they have their own connectivity. But it's okay. It's done, they're not recording any more. The live feed is over.'

My throat constricted. *Live feed.* I was right. He sounded almost proud. 'Is that because *you're* here now and you don't want to be seen?' I fought for control. 'Because it might be, what? A fucking invasion of your privacy?'

He had the grace to look sheepish. But not enough. 'People have no interest in seeing me.'

'You mean men. Men have no interest in seeing you,' I said bitterly.

He rubbed his hand up and down his face. 'It was just for a short time.'

'I've been here for *weeks*.'

He shrugged. 'It went well. They wanted to extend it, so I agreed. Anyway, it's over,' he said again. 'We've made lots of money. They actually owe us for a few days. I had a bit of an issue with the payment method.' He shook his head dismissively. 'Anyway, our problems are solved. Don't make a fuss, Allie. You always have to make such a big deal out of everything.'

'Us? *Our* problems?' I said incredulously. Did he still think he could persuade me to do anything he wanted? 'I don't have money problems.'

'Well, you would have if I didn't pay most of the bills.' He smiled superciliously. 'Two thirds of the mortgage.'

'That apartment is *yours*. And I still paid my share. You were the one who didn't. And this is your way of making money?

Allowing people to watch me sleep? Eat. Not eat? Lose a baby?' I bit back rage. 'How sick do you have to be to want to see that?'

Rory's smile faded and he leaned forward. He clasped his hands, elbows resting on his knees, giving the impression of a doctor talking to a particularly difficult patient.

'It's the haunted house story, Allie. Everyone loves that. And this one was real. Some very strange things happened, you know. You didn't see it all. I'll show you some of the footage if you like. I think it's pretty good.'

I was in danger of throwing up again. 'You utter bastard.'

His expression darkened. 'I had no choice. You don't know how difficult things got for me work-wise, because you never asked. You always assumed I'd sort everything out, and you could just curl up into your little ball.' He shook his head in disgust. 'When I think about what fun you were when I first met you. Dancing in that club, you looked so confident, so cool. What a mess you turned into.'

'You mean when I was off my head on coke? Desperately unhappy and trying my best to mask it?'

Rory rolled his eyes. 'You're always unhappy, Allie. You were just more fun back then.'

Tears pricked my eyes and I blinked them away. 'Was this what you and Sam rowed about?'

'Sam doesn't get it.'

'Did he know you were going to do this?'

Rory shook his head.

'Has Clara got something to do with it? Olivia saw you with someone at the airport, and there was a woman on the island that Sam didn't know. Was that Clara?'

For the first time, Rory looked uncomfortable. 'Clara works for RTÉ. She has quite a bit of power in there. When our relationship ended, I lost work. The woman on the island and at the airport was helping me set things up. She came to meet me. She's part of this German company called KNI that—'

I cut across him. 'Films women without their knowing? Thank God for the sisterhood,' I said bitterly. And then I remembered something. 'I saw her outside the park near the apartment. What was she doing there?'

'She wanted to have a look at you. I told her you'd be out walking Finn early in the morning. She said you were just what they wanted – "gorgeous but fragile".' He smiled, as if I'd take it as a compliment.

'So I was *auditioning* without my knowledge. What the hell is wrong with you?' And then my legal brain clicked into gear. 'Surely there's a release I needed to sign for them to stream this? A consent of some sort.'

He looked away, and I knew. This wasn't legal. They didn't care about consent. In fact, consent would probably spoil things for the creepy bastards who wanted to watch a woman alone and afraid. The thrill must come from her not knowing that she was being watched. I felt flayed, as if my skin had been peeled back.

'What is it?' I cried. 'Fear *porn*?'

'It's nothing like that,' he said defensively. 'It's not porn. Writers put their characters under pressure to see what happens; they create an impossible situation and watch them get out of it. That's all I did. That's it. It's a story.'

I could hardly believe what he was saying. Did he think that what he'd done had some kind of integrity? Some creative value?

'It's not a *story*. And I'm not a character. I'm your girlfriend. This was real. Everything that happened to me was real.' My head was spinning now as I waved furiously at the laptop. 'These are not people who want a *story*. This is for men who want to watch real women in fear. Isn't it?'

He didn't respond. I stood up, and he grabbed me, clasping my arm tightly. 'Where are you going?'

It was a show of strength, but he was panicking, I could tell. A bubble of spit had collected in the corner of his mouth. I looked at his face now, the features I knew so well – his eyes, cheekbones, the angle of his jaw – and tried to find the man I loved.

'I've just had a missed call from the guard who was investigating your disappearance,' I said coldly. 'I'm going to ring her. I've got another crime to report.'

'You owe me,' he said, his expression suddenly hard. 'You don't know what it's like to live with someone like you for all these years.'

'I know that I drank too much,' I said regretfully. 'I know I lashed out. I'm sorry about that. But this—'

He laughed, a harsh, sneering kind of laugh that I'd never heard before. 'That might actually have been interesting. But no, you just fell asleep after you'd guzzled your bucket of wine. It was fun seeing your self-loathing the next day, but even that got boring after a while.'

I was speechless. There was a void there, a darkness I didn't recognise.

'I've done you a favour, you know, making you move here, forcing you to confront your own cowardice.' His tone softened into something silky. 'You were really brave sometimes. I saw you doing the decorating, burying that crow.'

'Raven,' I said. 'So you're trying to claim *credit*?'

'Of course,' he said brightly. 'You'd never have done it on your own. It's like throwing someone who can't swim into a river.'

Now he was trying to charm me. Rory's superpower, the one that had always worked for him in the past. But it was too late. And something else had just occurred to me, something that made what he'd done worse, not better.

It wouldn't make for good viewing, my coping. Not for the type of people who were watching me, anyway. I recalled the raven getting trapped in the house, the dead bird on the mat, the number of times I was woken in the middle of the night. The immersion producing boiling-hot water when I hadn't turned it on.

'Did you plant things to make me more scared?' I demanded. 'Because I wasn't frightened enough for you? For your *paying customers*.' I spat out the last two words.

He looked down, giving me my answer.

'But you were in the North,' I said. 'Hours away from here. Did someone do it for you?' And then I knew. Of course.

'Maggie owed me a favour,' he said. 'Back when we were teenagers ... It was that ouija board she had. One of the other kids got obsessed with it and killed himself. Cousin of hers or something. I kept her involvement to myself.'

But I'd stopped listening. All I wanted was to get out of here, away from him. I'd seen something in his face that frightened me even more than what he had done, and I couldn't understand why I had never seen it before.

I'd thought I loved him, but I'd just depended on him, allowing him to control me because he created that dependency. I was the actor in a supporting role who was nothing without the star. But all the time I'd thought I couldn't live without him, he was using me. He'd always said he wanted to mind me, and he had, or so I'd thought. He responded with such care when I was frightened or anxious, protecting me. But then he often provoked that fear, making me do things that scared me. Was he one of those men who was turned on by fear? Did he secretly like me weak, despite what he said? Had I blinded myself to what was in front of me all along?

I tried to leave, and he grabbed me again. This time Finn

appeared. I was astonished when he turned on Rory, barking and growling at him. It seemed to bring Rory to his senses.

He pushed me away. 'Oh, do what you want. But remember, I know how little you like attention. I don't think you'd want this all over the papers.' He fired one last parting shot before he made for the door. 'You're lucky to have me, Allie. No one else would put up with your fucking *passivity*.'

He stormed out through the door and climbed into his car. I ran after him just in time to see the birds that had been on the roof and the telephone wire, shuffling, tapping, wings brushing against each other, rise up in unison.

Rory started the engine with an aggressive roar and set off at speed. The birds followed him, lifting as one, riding the wind. I imagined them coming at him from the air, aiming for the windscreen, a black cloud in front of the car. I urged them on.

He rounded the bend and disappeared from view. Almost immediately, I heard an almighty crash. I ran, heart thumping, skidding to a stop when I saw Harkin's tractor parked in the middle of the lane, completely blocking it. The cab was empty. He must be down in the fields somewhere, having abandoned it as usual.

The BMW had crashed headlong into it, bonnet accordioned, smoke billowing from the engine. I peered through the window. Rory's head was lolling onto the steering wheel. He was unconscious. Finn came barrelling towards me and I held him in my arms.

Rory lifted his head. Blood trickled down his face and his eyes opened. They looked glazed. He tried to speak, and I saw him mouth two words. 'Get help.' Then he was gone again. No *please*. No *I'm sorry*. And I saw that he had no fear of me. He was confident that I would not report what he had done. He was probably right.

But I also knew that he was dying. I'd been here before. I knew what a traumatic head injury looked like. The idiot hadn't been wearing a seat belt.

I thought about what he had done, leaving me twice, allowing men to be entertained by my fear. And then I thought about the cottage. How it was my home now, mine and Finn's. And Eliza's, of course.

I opened the driver's door and felt for a pulse. It was there, but weak. I'd have to wait for a bit. But I was good at waiting. Rory had made sure of that.

So, I was passive, was I? Maybe that was true too. A passive person would be in no rush to ring anyone. No rush at all. As the birds flocked around me, I walked back to admire Raven Cottage. It really was very pretty, standing there steadfast and solid.

I wondered if I should paint it in the spring.

EPILOGUE

I didn't go on the walk. That would have been pushing it. I decided I'd go on New Year's Day instead. Pieter said they were intending to do the Clear Lake, a route I'd missed when I was in Dublin staying with Olivia. Rory would be buried by then.

I did call 999 eventually. After a while, Harkin arrived to reclaim his tractor, which left me with little choice. Rory had lost consciousness permanently by then and I chose not to tell anyone that he'd ever regained it. Then Garda Suzanne Phelan appeared in a squad car, almost at the same time as the ambulance; she'd been on her way when she'd called. She told me what she'd discovered. I knew most of it already by then, of course, or had figured it out. As I said, people thought I was stupid. I could even tell what she was thinking: *Another car accident in that woman's life. A third one...*

But this one had nothing to do with me. This was one for which I could thank the ravens. I'd warned Rory about Harkin's tractor, but then he always knew what was best.

It turned out that Maggie had taken the Polaroid photograph of Pieter and me, but she claimed it was an attempt to warn me that I was being watched. Rory had been blackmailing her. He'd filmed her at school with a ouija board. Harkin's son, the one

Pieter had mentioned to me, had become a little obsessed, finally losing his life in the river. I guess that was why Maggie and Harkin didn't speak. It may have been why she didn't want to speak about Eliza's gift. Why she suppressed her own.

She swore she didn't kill that raven, that she'd found him on the road and left him on the mat, knowing it would satisfy Rory but suspecting I would treat the bird with respect. She'd felt horribly guilty about everything. The boots, the food and all her other kindnesses were an attempt to assuage that guilt.

It wasn't enough for me to forgive her. But I didn't need Maggie any more. I had Eliza.

I remained convinced by my own version of Eliza's story. That the information in the accounts book had been gathered to give the voices of the dead authenticity. I imagined a dead grandmother saying, 'Don't marry that man. Your grandfather was a drunk too. I should have got out way earlier.' It was all about persuading people to believe you.

I imagined Eliza gave women courage but was a threat to their men. Always a dangerous position for a woman to be in. She gave *me* courage; I'm convinced of that. Every few days, now, I put fresh flowers in her room.

New year, new start. Just like that other New Year's Day when I was eighteen. Like I said, I'd been here before.

> In the end Eliza didn't have to leave her cottage. Of this she was glad. She was allowed to stay with one of her babies, at least, although Harkin stole Gretta.
>
> She'd been packing up her things to leave on New Year's Eve when she heard the tapping. A knocking at the door that she didn't answer, followed by angry male voices, and the

sound of breaking glass. Her breath coming in gasps, she found herself pushed roughly into the little room, shoved from behind, and the door slammed. Edward Kennedy, Tom Harkin, and the cowardly priest turning a blind eye. All those weak men who couldn't bear losing control. She could only hope that Gretta had slept through it all.

She hadn't stood a chance, was furious with herself that she'd left it too late to leave. They killed her easily and buried her under the hawthorn tree, knowing that no one would touch it, that no one would ever find her there. You could say they did her a favour. Now she would never have to leave Raven Cottage. She sometimes even visited Gretta in the graveyard.

But then that fool had tried to dig her up. Men just can't leave anything alone, can they? She couldn't let that happen. Her birds couldn't let that happen. Not after all this time.

ACKNOWLEDGEMENTS

There Came a-Tapping is my first standalone novel. Or at least, the first to be published. It would have remained in a drawer with the others without some very important people. Huge thanks go to my brilliant pal Henrietta McKervey who gamely ploughs through my terrible early drafts and tells me what I don't want to hear; to the irrepressible Catherine Ryan Howard who pretty much wrote my synopsis this time around (synopses are really hard); to the lovely Ber Burns, who although a painter rather than a writer, is also a reader, and gives me suggestions and reassurance when I need it most; and to the inimitable Neil Hegarty who provides coffee and cake and sage advice.

After six Inishowen mysteries, this is my first book not set in Donegal. I grew up in Ballyfin, Co. Laois, at the foot of the Slieve Bloom mountains and have wanted to set a book there for some time. My mother is part of the wonderful Slieve Bloom Walking Club (not the one in the book!). I've joined them on several walks and hope to again. As usual I've used a mix of real and fictitious locations. Rath is fictitious, but Portlaoise isn't. Portlaoise Library was the first library I joined (I'm told at the age of three!).

A number of books were invaluable to me in writing this one. Much of what I know about ravens came from the wonderful *In* the Company of Crows and Ravens by John Marzluff and Tony Angell. *The Burning of Bridget Cleary* by Angela Bourke gave me a sense of what life was like in rural Ireland at the time when Eliza was alive. My title comes from Edgar Allen Poe's *The Raven*. And, of course, I read Daphne du Maurier's wonderful story *The Birds*.

With research, it's important to ask the right people. This time I relied on both of my parents' expertise; my mother for her knowledge of botany and my father for historical research. Thank you also to talented documentary maker and friend Martin Danneels. And, seven books later, my old pal Mick still doesn't avoid my calls to meet for a coffee!

Any errors are my own or for the purposes of fiction.

We are privileged in Ireland to have a wonderful Arts Council from whom I received a bursary to write this book. Solitude came at the Tyrone Guthrie Centre at Annaghmakerrig, and the tiny but perfectly formed writers' cottage at Roundwood House in the Slieve Blooms.

Thank you to Little, Brown UK and Krystyna Green. Editor Tara Loder made the book *so* much better, as did brilliant copy-editor Jane Selley. An email from managing editor Amanda Keats, who has been there for all my books, means I'm in safe (and kind) hands.

My agent David Headley is a force of nature, bestower of champagne, hugs and other wise offerings and I feel incredibly lucky to have found my way back to him (long story). I am also privileged to have Emily Hayward-Whitlock in my corner for TV and film.

Hachette Ireland – especially Elaine Egan, Siobhan Tierney and Breda Purdue – has been highly supportive of my books, as have booksellers, librarians, bloggers, readers and my family.

And lastly, but most of all, thank you to Geoff. He is an early reader, but this time he allowed me to use him as a starting point for a character. I won't say which, in case you're reading the acknowledgments first, but suffice to say that Geoff, in almost every way, is the polar opposite of the character in the book (other than the relationship he has with our lurcher Liath, who was the inspiration for Finn!). Which is why I love him.

UNLOCK THE LATEST CRIME AND THRILLERS

Sign up to our newsletter for criminally good recommendations, exclusives and competitions.

www.thecrimevault.com

@TheCrimeVault